OXFORD WORLD'S CLASSICS

ÉMILE ZOLA

Money

Translated with an Introduction and Notes by
VALERIE MINOGUE

OXFORD
UNIVERSITY PRESS

OXFORD
UNIVERSITY PRESS

Great Clarendon Street, Oxford OX2 6DP
United Kingdom

Oxford University Press is a department of the University of Oxford.
It furthers the University's objective of excellence in research, scholarship,
and education by publishing worldwide. Oxford is a registered trade mark of
Oxford University Press in the UK and in certain other countries

Published in the United States of America by Oxford University Press
198 Madison Avenue, New York, NY 10016, United States of America

British Library Cataloguing in Publication Data
Data available

Library of Congress Control Number: 2013942702

ISBN 978–0–19–960837–9

Printed in Great Britain by
Clays Ltd, St Ives plc

CONTENTS

INTRODUCTION

Readers who do not wish to learn details of the plot may prefer to read the Introduction as an Afterword.

It was in 1868, at the age of twenty-eight, that Émile Zola hit on the idea of a series of novels based on one family, *Les Rougon-Macquart, Histoire naturelle et sociale d'une famille sous le Second Empire* ('Natural and Social History of a Family under the Second Empire'), in which he would trace the influence of heredity on the various members of a family in their social and political setting. Zola was already the author of two volumes of short stories, several novels, poetry, and a good deal of journalism when he embarked on what was to become a total of twenty novels, of which *Money (L'Argent)* is the eighteenth.

Setting out to do for the Second Empire what Balzac had done for an earlier age in *La Comédie humaine*, Zola intended to give as complete a view as possible of French society from the *coup d'état* of 1851 to the collapse of the Second Empire in 1870—a time he called 'a strange period of human folly and shame'.[1] He had denounced the corruption and excesses of the imperial regime in articles for republican newspapers; in his novels he would do so on a grander scale. The series would constitute a *natural* history, in so far as it took account of genetic and physiological features, and a *social* history in its coverage of all classes of French society. Louis-Napoleon's *coup d'état* in December 1851, which founded the Second Empire, also founded the fortunes of the Rougon-Macquart family, as Zola relates in the first novel of the series, *The Fortune of the Rougons* (1871).

As a realist and self-styled 'naturalist', Zola intended to present the unvarnished truth of life in the Second Empire. 'Naturalism' followed on from the realist traditions of Balzac and Flaubert, but with a new emphasis on science. Zola's account of his fictional family would be supported by study of contemporary scientific discoveries and theories. His earlier novel, *Thérèse Raquin*, was strongly influenced by the determinist theories of Hippolyte Taine, stressing heredity, environment, and historical context as major factors in the

---

[1] In the preface to the first novel of the series, *The Fortune of the Rougons*.

shaping of human destiny. Further studies—including Darwin's theories of evolution, Letourneau's *Physiologie des passions* (1868), Prosper Lucas's work on heredity (*Traité philosophique et physiologique de l'hérédité naturelle*, 1847)—were added to the scientific basis for Zola's work. When he read the physiologist Claude Bernard's work on Experimental Medicine (*Introduction à l'étude de la médécine expérimentale*, 1865), he was so impressed by its innovative vigour that he adopted its ideas to make a new theory of the novel, which he outlined in *The Experimental Novel*. This theory was greeted with some ridicule in so far as he appeared to be attempting to endow the novel with scientific authority, but Zola made it clear that he was well aware that a novel is not a laboratory, and that the 'results' of situations created by the writer's imagination were not at all the same thing as the results of laboratory tests. However, if the writer takes due account of available scientific data in setting up his 'experiments', that is, in his creation of characters and situations, then his 'results' should be at least plausible outcomes. Like the scientist who examines his material, however ugly, in order to analyse and heal, so the novelist would observe and accurately represent social ills in the hope that they might be remedied.

Zola's scientific and physiological studies provided him with a foundation and a discipline for his imaginative vision, but despite all his stress on the scientific approach, Zola's poetic imagination would obstinately make what he called 'the leap to the stars from the springboard of exact observation'. That 'exactitude' is itself open to question, for even in the act of observation his eye is inherently transformative, as is clear even in the preparatory notes for his novels, where metaphor and analogy constantly slide in to make each detail expressive rather than merely noted.

Throughout the Rougon-Macquart series Zola portrays the interaction of hereditary traits with external forces, creating a drama in which heredity plays an important role but does not work in straight lines, as is evident, for instance, in the shared heredity but very different characters of the three brothers Eugène, the government minister, Aristide ('Saccard'), the extravagant banker of *Money*, and Pascal, the doctor of the final volume, *Dr Pascal* (1893). Members of the family resist, or succumb to, the pressures of their environment, and that environment is the social, political, and economic reality of life in the Second Empire.

Historical Background

The history of the Second Empire can be briefly told. Following the abdication of King Louis-Philippe in 1848 a republic was declared; the workers demanded that the right to work should be guaranteed, and national workshops were created to help the large numbers of unemployed. The spirit of revolutionary reform, however, proved short-lived. Elections in April 1848 returned a mainly reactionary government, whose actions, which included discontinuing the national workshops and restricting the suffrage, provoked widespread protests which were brutally suppressed, with hundreds of thousands killed, arrested, imprisoned, or deported. In November a new constitution was established which provided for the election of a president with a fixed four-year term of office. In December, Louis-Napoleon, then aged forty, was elected President of the Second Republic by a huge majority (5.4 million votes), thanks largely to his being Napoleon I's nephew. To avoid losing his presidency in 1852 at the end of his four-year term, Louis-Napoleon dissolved the Assembly with a *coup d'état* on 2 December 1851. Presenting himself as a liberal and a defender of the people, he restored universal (male) suffrage and promised a plebiscite to accept or reject his seizure of power. Protests broke out but were suppressed, once more with widespread killings, imprisonment, and deportation. Leaders of the insurgents, Victor Hugo among them, were forced to flee. In the plebiscite that followed, the people gave Louis-Napoleon its overwhelming approval. One year later, on the same date of 2 December, which was also the anniversary of the coronation of his uncle Napoleon Bonaparte, he was crowned Emperor as Napoleon III,[2] ruler of the Second Empire.

When Zola started to plan the Rougon-Macquart series in 1868 it was possible to imagine that the Second Empire would last some considerable time. It seemed solid enough despite various contemporaneous upheavals, such as the Italian Wars of Independence and Bismarck's aggressive moves toward the unification of Germany. But in 1870 Napoleon III was goaded by Prussia over the issue of the Spanish Succession, for which Prussia was proposing a Habsburg prince. Napoleon, facing growing troubles on the home front and not wanting to see France sandwiched between Prussia and a Prussian-dominated

---

[2] 'Napoleon II never governed, the First Empire being replaced by the Bourbon Restoration in 1814.

Spain, declared war, a war that ended in the humiliating defeat at
Sedan, when Napoleon III and his entire army were captured.

A Third Republic was then declared. It continued the war for
some months, but after a long siege Paris fell to the better-organized
and better-equipped Prussian forces. The Second Empire, meant to
endure for at least a goodly number of Rougon-Macquart novels, had
come to an abrupt end. The Franco-Prussian War and the civil war
of the Commune that followed are the subject of the novel that comes
after *Money*, *La Débâcle* (1892). This early end of the Empire caused
some problems for Zola, who had to squeeze a great number of lives
and events into its unexpectedly short time-frame.

The Context of 1890, the Banking World, and Anti-Semitism

By the time Zola came to write *Money* in 1890 France had undergone
a period of great industrialization and expansion. Railways were
springing up everywhere, the press was growing in importance every
day, and investment banks were thriving. New ideas were abroad:
Karl Marx's *Das Kapital* had been published in 1867, and Marxist
ideas had taken root. All these developments are reflected in the plot
of *Money*. The Republic had suffered a series of government scandals, and there was a great deal of social unrest. The Suez Canal, the
subject of much animated discussion and speculation (in both senses)
in the first chapter of the novel, had been opened by the Empress in
1869. In 1890 it was the Panama Canal that was occupying people's
minds. The Panama Canal Company, in spite of huge contributions
from French investors, went into administration in February 1889,
and one of the biggest financial scandals of the nineteenth century
was just breaking. Hundreds of thousands of investors were ruined,
and the government was accused of bribery and corruption. Jewish
involvement in the bribery inflamed the already widespread French
anti-Semitism, and Drumont's *La France Juive* (1886), a two-volume,
1,200-page, violently anti-Semitic work, enjoyed a huge commercial
success. The new flare-up of anti-Semitism in the 1880s was much
the same as the anti-Semitism of the previous era, when there had
been deep resentment of the powerful Jewish bankers, particularly of
Baron James Mayer de Rothschild, whose role in the banking world is
the model for that of Saccard's great rival, the Jewish financier
Gundermann.

There had been so many disasters in financial institutions that Zola had no lack of models for Saccard's 'Universal Bank'. One was Mirès's innovative bank, the 'Caisse centrale des chemins de fer' ('Central Bank of Railways'), founded in 1850, which collapsed in 1861; then in 1852 the brothers Émile and Isaac Péreire founded the 'Crédit Mobilier', a bank expressly intended, like Saccard's Universal, to foster large enterprises. It played an important part in the economic surge of the period up to 1857, when a financial panic affected the Bourse, the London Stock Exchange, and even Wall Street. The shares of the Crédit Mobilier had risen with amazing rapidity, but the bank crashed disastrously in 1870. A third—and the principal—model for the Universal was the Union Générale of Paul Eugène Bontoux. Founded in 1878, it lay well outside the time-frame of *Money*, which covers the period from May 1864 to the spring of 1868, but Zola decided to overlook the anachronism since the Bontoux crash was similar to that of the Crédit Mobilier which had happened under the Second Empire. Indeed, history repeated itself sufficiently for Zola to push many features of the Third Republic back into the Second Empire without too grossly offending *vraisemblance*. Bontoux's bank, strongly supported by Catholics and monarchists, grew extremely rapidly; it financed and built Serbia's first railway, bought up insurance companies, and financed schemes in North Africa and Egypt, all the while speculating on the stock market and providing impressive dividends for shareholders. However, prices began to fall in 1880–1 and the bank set about buying its own shares, as Saccard would do, to try to avert disaster; but in January 1882 the Union Générale suspended payments and crashed, the fate that lies in store for Saccard's Universal.

The failure of Bontoux's Catholic bank further inflamed resentment of the Jewish banks, especially when Bontoux, with little justification, blamed an 'Israelite Syndicate' for bringing down his Union Générale. Zola, who closely followed the fortunes of Bontoux's bank and the accounts of his trial, and who had read Bontoux's history of the Union Générale,[3] also preserved his anti-Semitism, passing it on to Saccard in the guise of a quasi-hereditary feature: 'Ah, the Jews! Saccard had that ancient racial resentment of the Jews that is found especially in the south of France' (p. 78). That resentment is often

[3] *L'Union générale, sa vie, sa mort, son programme* (1888).

expressed in extreme and stereotyped terms of hatred of 'unclean Jewry' (p. 15). There is a great deal of ugly and angry defamation of Jews in the novel, an unpleasant but accurate reflection of the feelings of the time. Zola did not disguise it, though he was very far from agreeing with it. In his articles, such as 'Pour les Juifs',[4] and most strikingly in his defence of Dreyfus, Zola shows his abhorrence of such attitudes. In his open letter 'J'accuse', published in *L'Aurore* on 21 February 1898, he succeeded in reopening the case of the Jewish officer wrongly accused and convicted of treason and espionage. Zola's intervention in the Dreyfus case led to his being himself threatened with imprisonment, which he avoided by fleeing to temporary exile in England. The very outrageousness of Saccard's anti-Semitism underlines its stupidity. Its unreasonableness is further demonstrated by the fact that Saccard cannot help admiring, as well as envying, the Jewish banker Gundermann, the king of the Bourse. And if the behaviour of the Jewish Busch earns derogatory epithets, the same cannot be said for his equally Jewish brother, the Marxist philosopher Sigismond. The unbalanced anti-Semitism of Saccard is also tellingly opposed by the balanced and reasonable views of Madame Caroline, his mistress, who finds Saccard's views astonishing: 'For me, the Jews are just men like any others' (p. 358).

Money

'It's very difficult to write a novel about money. It's cold, icy, lacking in interest . . .', Zola remarked in an interview in April 1890. Money, greed, and ambition are the driving forces in the novel, and Zola was determined to avoid what he felt had become a conventional diatribe against money and speculation. He would not speak ill of money, he wrote in his preparatory notes, but would 'praise and exalt its generous and fecund power, its expansive force'. He embarked on a particularly onerous period of research, studying books and documents,[5] as well as interrogating suitably qualified persons, such as Eugène Fasquelle (an associate and son-in-law of Zola's publisher, Charpentier), who had spent some years working in brokerage. Few novels had been as

---

[4] In the journal *Le Figaro* (1896), collected in *Nouvelle campagne* (1897), 203–14.
[5] These included: Mirecourt's *La Bourse, ses abus et ses mystères* (1858), Ernest Feydeau's *Mémoires d'un coulissier* (1873), Proudhon's *Manuel du spéculateur à la Bourse* (1854, 1857), and Henri Cozic's *La Bourse mise à la portée de tous* (1885).

much trouble to prepare; Zola meticulously annotated the papers of the Bontoux trial, as well as those of Mirès and the Péreires, and studied every detail of the layout of the Bourse, visiting it almost every day for a month.

Zola's subject was clearly topical. Banking scandals were not confined to France, and in England the fraudulent speculations of the notorious swindler John Sadleir lay behind Dickens's creation of the unscrupulous banker Mr Merdle in *Little Dorrit* (1857). Eighteen years later, in 1875, just a few years outside the time-frame of *Money*, Anthony Trollope created the grand-scale swindler Melmotte, a man of mysterious foreign origins, in *The Way We Live Now*. Melmotte's ambitious schemes at times seem to echo those of Saccard, wrapping the pursuit of profit in a mantle of philanthropy: 'he would be able to open up new worlds, to afford relief to the oppressed nationalities of the over-populated old countries.'[6] But his schemes are only words and air, and unlike Saccard he leaves nothing of value behind him, finally ending his life with a dose of prussic acid, whereas Saccard goes on to further ventures. It is striking that one of the arguments offered in defence of Melmotte's risky activities—'You have to destroy a thousand living creatures every time you drink a glass of water, but you do not think of that when you are athirst . . .'[7]—is very like Saccard's dismissal of worry about the damage his risky activities may cause: 'As if life bothered about such matters! With every step we take, we destroy thousands of existences' (p. 357).

In France, a number of novels on the Bourse and on banking had already been written. Among them was *La Comtesse Shylock* (1885) by G. d'Orcet, which stressed the dominance of Jews in the banking world. Count Shylock, as Henri Mitterand points out,[8] has much in common with Gundermann, being based on the same figure: James de Rothschild. The novel also includes a Baroness Brandorff, addicted to playing the market like Zola's Baroness Sandorff, as well as an idealist dreamer not dissimilar to Sigismond Busch. It is reasonable to assume that Zola read *La Comtesse Shylock*, but he takes a wider overview of the banking crash, showing the way the financial world interlocks with the politics and the economy of the time, and introducing the clash between capitalism and socialism. Above all, Zola makes

[6] Anthony Trollope, *The Way We Live Now*, ch. 44 (World's Classics edition, 1982).
[7] Ibid., ch. 30.
[8] In the Pléiade edition of *Les Rougon-Macquart*, vol. 5, p. 1242.

of the subject an epic allegory, dominated by the riveting figure of Saccard.

Saccard

Whether the novel is seen primarily as a socio-political study, a financial document, or a penetrating and poetic reflection on a society on the brink of disaster, the figure of Saccard clearly dominates it. Villain or hero, he is a peculiarly fascinating creation, one who seems indeed to have fascinated his creator. Zola does not usually allow a character to return as frequently as Saccard in the annals of the Rougon-Macquart family.[9] In *The Fortune of the Rougons* (*La Fortune des Rougon*) Aristide Rougon is an opportunistic republican journalist, who swiftly becomes Bonapartist when success beckons on that side. He changes his name to Saccard in *The Kill* (*La Curée*), commenting: 'there's money in that name', and makes a great fortune in property speculation in the wake of Haussmann's reconstruction of Paris. The Saccard of *Money* is a more complex and ambiguous figure than the Saccard of *The Kill*, showing moments of compassion and remorse in the midst of his ruthlessness.

A great dynamic force, he is physically only a small figure, frequently seen stretching upward to gain height—an apt metaphor for the impatient ambition evident from the moment he enters the novel. He sees himself as a Napoleon of finance, aiming to achieve with money what Napoleon failed to achieve with the sword. He is also, as his son Maxime remarks, 'the poet of the million'. Money is his sword, his delight, his obsession. Even for philanthropic purposes, with no motive of personal gain, as in his dealings with Princess d'Orviedo, he is captivated by the sheer joy of manipulating large sums of money. Fired by ambitious schemes of grandeur, Saccard turns money into magic; it is the royalty of gold, it is a magic wand, conjuring the magic that runs right through the novel in the tinkling of fairy gold, the barrels of treasure straight out of the *Arabian Nights*, the enchanted cash desks, the magic wand of money and science working together. Saccard dreams of rivers, even oceans, of gold, the dance of millions, which will create grand, colossal things.

In his meeting with the Hamelins, brother and sister, Saccard's

[9] He is briefly mentioned in *The Belly of Paris* (*Le Ventre de Paris*), has a very minor role in *La Joie de vivre*, and is briefly recalled in *Dr Pascal*.

exuberant imagination takes wing, as he imagines the wonders to be performed, and makes the dreams of the Hamelins his own:

'Look,' cried Saccard, 'this Carmel Gorge in this drawing of yours, where there's nothing but stones and mastic trees, you'll see, once the silver mine gets going, first a village will spring up, then a town... . . . And on these depopulated plains, these deserted passes, where our railway lines will run, a veritable resurrection, yes! The fields will cease to lie fallow, roads and canals will appear, new cities will rise from the ground and life will at last return... Yes! Money will perform these miracles.' (p. 65)

It is Saccard's energy that produces what he later calls 'the pickaxe of progress', his Universal Bank, to sponsor these vast enterprises and at the same time satisfy what seems at times an almost physical, fetishistic need to see 'heaps of gold' and 'hear their music'. His recklessness manifests itself as soon as the Universal is launched, and illegality follows illegality. He aims to wrest control of the Bourse away from Gundermann, and will use every available means to that end. With Jantrou, he makes use of the growing power of the Press; the newspaper he purchases supports the bank with advertising and also provides potential leverage on the government by supporting or attacking the minister Rougon's policies in its pages. After its first triumph over the leaking of the peace treaty after Sadowa, the Universal goes from strength to strength, with Saccard increasing the bank's capital and using 'frontmen' to buy the bank's own shares. The share-prices rocket ever upward, and even Gundermann, relying on the force of logic to bring the bank down, is almost on the point of giving up against this seemingly unstoppable success. It is the treachery of Baroness Sandorff that tips the scales and leads to the destruction of the Universal, and it is Saccard's sexual appetite that has made that possible. In defeat Saccard stands resolutely beside his habitual pillar in the Bourse, not deigning to sit down until the moment of weakness when he thinks of 'the enormous mass of humble folk, wretched little investors who would be crushed to pieces under the wreckage of the Universal' (p. 308). Then he allows himself at last to sit, revealing a Saccard capable of real compassion—as he had indeed shown earlier in his dealings with the charitable Work Foundation.

Zola amply signposts Saccard's energy, creativity, and sexuality: the scene of Saccard caught *in flagrante* with Sandorff is surprisingly explicit, and his lustfulness is further demonstrated in his frequent visits to 'actresses' like Germaine Coeur, and his extravagant but unsuccessful bidding for the favours of pretty little Madame Conin. At times Saccard becomes positively phallic, as in his triumph at countering Gundermann's first attack on the Universal, when he is described as having really swollen and grown bigger. He succeeds in buying a night with Madame de Jeumont for a grotesquely huge sum, and parades her vaingloriously at the ball where, however, Bismarck watches them go by with an ironic smile. The smile is amply justified if Saccard here represents the dissolute society of the Empire, or even Napoleon III himself, who at Sedan would be crushed by the Prussians, accompanied by King Wilhelm I and Otto von Bismarck. Saccard becomes a metaphor for energy, sexual vitality, creativity, at times seeming the embodiment of money itself, creative and destructive, capable of much good and much evil. In his audacity, Saccard is indeed a Napoleon of finance, and like Napoleon he has his 'Austerlitz'. But he also meets his Waterloo when he is left on the trading-floor, waiting in vain for the promised troops from Daigremont, just as Napoleon at Waterloo awaited in vain the troops of Grouchy.

The fortunes of Saccard parallel the fortunes of the Empire, both reaching a peak with the Universal Exhibition of 1867, the 'Exposition Universelle', the extravagant world fair held in Paris under the auspices of Napoleon III, where forty-two nations were represented. The Empire is making a great display, and so is Saccard's 'Universal', with its new, extravagantly palatial premises. If the Universal Bank is built on sand and lies, as Madame Caroline remarks, so, Zola suggests, is the Empire itself, as it promotes itself with false glamour. On the day when the Emperor in person awards the prizes to the exhibitors, the event is described as a huge fairy-tale lie. The Emperor presents himself as 'master of Europe, speaking with calmness and strength and promising peace' (p. 234) on the very day that news had come of the execution of Maximilian.[10] Saccard's glittering bank, with its coffers full of gold, is also a huge fairy-tale lie; this is fairy gold that will not stand the light of day. When the Exhibition is over, Paris is left still giddy and intoxicated with Second Empire extravagance, not realizing that Krupp's splendid cannon, greatly admired in the Exhibition, would quite soon be pounding the city. At the end of the novel Saccard is bankrupt and so is the Empire, leaving France open to

[10] Archduke Maximilian of Austria, sent to be emperor of a (conquered) Mexico.

invasion and defeat: the Bourse, now deserted, is seen against a fiery sky that prefigures the fires that would rage through Paris in the violent days of the Commune: 'Twilight was falling, and the winter sky, laden with mist, had created behind the monument of the Bourse a cloud of dark and reddish smoke as if from a fire, as if made from the flames and dust of a city stormed' (p. 336).

Madame Caroline

It is a central paradox of the novel that Madame Caroline, seen by Zola as a sort of 'chorus' for his drama, the voice of morality and legality, should fall in love with Saccard, the financial pirate. Having fallen into his arms almost inadvertently after an emotional shock, Madame Caroline berates herself for her weakness, but Saccard's dynamism and energy again win her over. She shares his dreams of what 'the all-powerful magic wand of science and speculation' (p. 64) might achieve, and caught up by his enthusiasm she even finds him handsome and charming, though Madame Caroline is not endowed by Zola with anything like Saccard's sexuality or passion. He stresses above all her prudence and her frustrated maternal instincts, a frustration she shares with Princess d'Orviedo. It is largely on the basis of a quasi-maternal affection that she becomes Saccard's mistress, but when she learns of his affair with Baroness Sandorff she discovers, with a shock, that she really loves him. Her feeling for Saccard is one of the rare examples of genuine love in the novel: the other is the touching love of the Jordan couple, blessed as it is by their expected child.

Throughout the novel Madame Caroline provides a moral commentary on the character and conduct of Saccard as she tries to restrain his reckless illegalities, countering his excesses with her moderation and good sense. But he will not be restrained, and in the end, after promising so much, Saccard brings ruin, misery, and even death to his victims. Madame Caroline, the moral compass of the novel, condemns and curses the man she loved and almost sinks into despair. Her brother, however, persuades her to go and see the imprisoned Saccard. In their last interview Madame Caroline finally tells Saccard what has become of Victor, the illegitimate son he now regrets never having seen, and for the first time she sees him in tears. Unlike Hamelin, Saccard is not peacefully resigned. He demands—with some justification, given the weaknesses of the case against him and the vengeful involvement of Delcambre, the Public Prosecutor—to know why he and Hamelin are singled out for punishment. What about the directors who made huge amounts of money? And the auditors? Why are they all able to get away with it? If there were any justice, he argues, they and the heads of the major banks of Paris would be sharing his fate—questions and views that may strike a chord in contemporary Europe. Saccard's belief in himself is still unshaken, and Madame Caroline marvels at his irresponsible assurance. Yet, as she feels once more his astonishing strength and vitality she finds her anger dissolving, and there is a moment of subdued tenderness between them before they finally part.

In the final chapter Zola takes Madame Caroline all over Paris, linking up with almost all the main characters, starting with Princess d'Orviedo from whom she learns of the rape of Alice de Beauvilliers by the fifteen-year-old Victor at the Work Foundation—that institution built to help and educate the poor. Seeing again its lavish splendour, she asks herself what was the point of it all if it couldn't even turn one wretched boy into an honest citizen? Victor is now roaming at large, with no one to try to deliver him from his viciousness. The Beauvilliers have lost everything, with Alice raped, the son of the family dead, and what little money they had left lost in the collapse of Saccard's bank. Madame Caroline witnesses the atrocious scene in which Busch manages to deprive the Countess of the last bits of her family jewellery, and yet when Sigismond dies she is able, with characteristic tolerance and kindness, to feel sympathy and pity even for Busch in his agony at his brother's death.

Looking for help from Saccard's other son, Maxime, Madame Caroline finds him just about to set off to Naples for the winter. Reflecting once more on the huge difference between Saccard's two sons, Madame Caroline wonders if it is poverty that has made Victor a voracious wolf, and wealth that has made Maxime an elegant, idle dandy? When she finds the little girls in the Work Foundation saying prayers for Saccard, she is at first outraged, but then reminds herself that he had indeed been kind to them, and to many others at the Work Foundation, as well as to people like the Jordans, whom he befriended and helped. Perhaps she could forgive herself for having loved him. Looking back once more on her 'fall', and her guilty love for a man she could not esteem, she feels able to ease her shame, recognizing that a man may do much harm, yet also have much good in him. Madame Caroline now learns that Saccard has gone to the Netherlands, where he is already working on drainage schemes, reclaiming land from the sea. Hamelin is revisiting the places that feature in the maps and pictures that Madame Caroline now takes down from the walls, before going to join him. Saccard had promised so much, failed so badly, done so much damage, and yet some of those promised miracles have indeed happened. Hamelin, writing from the Carmel Gorge, tells her:

a whole population had grown up there... The village, at first of five hundred inhabitants, clustering round the workings of the mine, was at present a city of several thousand souls, a whole civilization, with roads, factories, and schools, creating life in this dead and savage place... And wasn't this the awakening of a world, with an expanded and happier humanity? (p. 371)

It is the realization of at least part of what Saccard had so enthusiastically prophesied, and money, filthy as it might be, had accomplished it. Money might be a dung-heap, but it was also the compost in which the future would grow. Saccard had argued that love itself can sometimes be sordid, and money, similarly, may be filthy but fruitful.

The novel is a mighty allegory, but not in terms of simple one-to-one correspondences: each figure is multiple, a nexus of meanings and contradictions. Madame Caroline herself, with all her good sense, does not entirely preserve her integrity; she is, after all, imperfect, but, as she herself suggests early on in the novel, her case is, 'in microcosm, the case of all humanity' (p. 62).

In the telegraphic style of his preparatory notes, Zola wrote: 'I should like, in this novel, not to conclude on disgust with life (pessimism). Life, just as it is, but accepted, in spite of everything, for love of itself, in its strength.' This was what he wanted to emerge from the whole Rougon-Macquart series. He had put much of himself into Madame Caroline, with her indestructible love of life and stubborn joy in being alive, and it is left to her at the end to bring all the paradoxes together, underlining the coexistence of good and evil in an imperfect but always interesting world.

Economics and Politics

Money reflects a sophisticated view of the economy, and it also shows economic concerns as deeply embedded in the social milieu, affecting both public and private life at every level. The people involved in speculation with the Universal Bank cover a huge social range—from pensioners with small savings to country priests, relatively well-off bourgeois, and aristocrats, both penurious and wealthy. Politics too plays an integral part. It is not by accident that the first chapter of the novel introduces references to political events that will affect the lives of the characters, and indeed the life of France and its people. Three of the political issues raised in the conversation in Champeaux's restaurant recur throughout the book: Mexico, Rome, and the foreign policy of Prussia. All three exemplify the weaknesses—some might say follies—of the foreign policy pursued under Napoleon III. In Mexico, the attempt to gain a foothold in the country through French military intervention, while the United States was preoccupied with the Civil War, failed dismally after only three years, ending with the execution of Maximilian, the emperor Napoleon III had chosen for Mexico. In the matter of Rome and the Italian Wars of Independence, Napoleon III's intervention to defend the Pope was driven as much by domestic politics and the need to keep the Catholics on side as by foreign-policy considerations. Italy was being created, with French support, out of a patchwork of small states, some controlled by Austria and some by the Pope. The decision to prevent the Papal States, including Rome, from being absorbed into Italy, with the use of 2,000 troops in 1867, as well as being expensive and ultimately ineffective, alienated those who supported the liberal cause of Italian nationalism while leaving the Catholics thoroughly dissatisfied.

Moser's references to the matter of the Duchies, wrested from Denmark by Prussia and Austria, not only serve to tie the novel into actual events of the period but also draw attention again to the inadequacies of the regime's foreign policy. When Moser remarks that 'when big fish start eating the little fish you can't tell where it will all end...' (p. 6), the reader is reminded of the end that lies in store. Bismarck was already steadily creating the German Confederation while France did nothing: 'In a few short years Bismarck had overturned the European balance of power and France, under the incompetent and vainglorious guidance of Napoleon III, found herself facing a politically unified and increasingly aggressive Germany.'[11]

Politics and the financial world are closely interlinked. Saccard

[11] Jeremy Jennings, *Revolution and the Republic: A History of Political Thought in France since the Eighteenth Century* (Oxford: Oxford University Press, 2011), 229.

views with envy the enormous power of the banker Gundermann, 'for whom ministers were no more than clerks, and who held whole states in his sovereign fiefdom' (p. 181). Eugène Rougon himself, powerful as he may be, cannot afford to offend Gundermann. Saccard's first great financial coup, after the defeat of Austria at the battle of Sadowa, is the result of political action. A change of fortunes in the Austro-Prussian War creates a sharp fall in share-prices, and Deputy Huret leaks information about a peace treaty, allowing Saccard to make a killing on the market. Rougon's juggling between liberals and Catholics seems to parody Napoleon III's efforts to pacify first one group then another, with dismal results. By dint of a mild anachronism, Zola brings in a reference to the formation of the Marxist-inspired First International (brought forward from its actual foundation in September 1864 to May in the novel), thus introducing the conflict of capitalism and socialism as represented by Saccard and Sigismond. In the view of William Gallois, Zola here undertakes 'a morality tale which describes how imperialism developed in France', and shows 'how elements of the modern world fitted together, how capitalism was an imperial culture, and how that culture operated'.[12] Gallois points to the way that Zola shows imperial ambition often expressed in terms of philanthropy and further cloaked by a mantle of religion, as is the case with the ambitions of Saccard's Universal Bank.

Contrasts, Oppositions, Repetitions

The novel is structured by means of contrasts, contrasts both between and within the characters. Saccard, the ruthless brigand, also shows compassion and kindness; the rapacious Busch is also the tender and loving carer of his brother. Gundermann, the king of the Bourse, the rock of logic on which Saccard's ship will founder, is also the frail, indulgent grandfather. Gundermann's logic and patience are set against Saccard's passion and impatience; and as a hoarder, accumulating wealth, Gundermann is opposed to Saccard, the spendthrift capitalist who spends for his personal pleasure but also for the furtherance of great and useful ventures. Because of his German origins Gundermann is also seen as Prussia, pitted against Saccard's France. The capitalist Saccard, with his passion for money, is set in conflict

[12] Gallois, in *Zola: The History of Capitalism* (Berne: Peter Lang, 2000), 119.

with Sigismond, the socialist philosopher who wants to ban money altogether. And money itself partakes of the general ambiguity: filthy and evil on the one hand, and potentially good as the agent of progress on the other.

Some scenes recur with contrasting variations, that underline the volatility of things. Delcambre's discovery of Baroness Sandorff with Saccard is doubled by Saccard's discovery of Sandorff in the arms of Sabatani. The first view of the beautiful Mazaud family in their beautiful apartment is savagely transformed when Madame Caroline comes upon Mazaud's body dripping blood on to the rich carpet while his wife utters unearthly screams of grief. Those screams will later be echoed in the screams of Busch, cradling the dead body of his brother. Madame Caroline remembers hearing such screams before, so that in quasi-Proustian fashion Madame Mazaud's cries are intermingled with those of Busch. People and events in this novel are complex, ambiguous, resistant to stable definition.

Nothing seems really solid: decay, corruption, and death are all around. The worm is indeed in the fruit, as suggested in the first chapter—the worm of greed, excess, and deceit. Zola shows the old landed aristocracy, in the persons of the impoverished Countess de Beauvilliers and her daughter, cruelly brought low and humiliated, while the 'aristocratic' Marquis de Bohain, with no probity and no substance, continues to thrive, with his little head atop his very large frame. Speculation is rife, as greed takes over one person after another. Not only Baroness Sandorff, but also the Maugendres, Dejoie, even little Flory, all fall prey to the gambling bug. Even the Hamelins are tainted, having accepted some of the profits of Saccard's speculation.

The social inequalities of the regime are vigorously highlighted in Madame Caroline's visit to the Cité de Naples. The dark and hideous makeshift hovels, the mud and the stinking open sewers, create a scene like something out of a horror movie. It reaches its climax when, through Madame Caroline's eyes, we see the filthy mattress on the ground where 'Mother' Eulalie lies, with her ulcerated legs, then Victor, with his stupefying resemblance to Saccard, suddenly revealed by the light from the open door. To underline the gap between destitution and luxury, Madame Caroline goes straight from the Cité de Naples to the sweet-scented apartment of Maxime. Such contrasts and oppositions question the very bases of this society. The contrast between the lives of Saccard's two sons could hardly be more stark, and Madame Caroline again reflects on the role of money: was it penury that gave rise to such degradation on one side, and was it money that led to such luxury and elegance on the other? 'Could money then mean education, health, and intelligence?' (p. 350), she wonders. But Maxime, in his idleness and self-centred, callous indifference to others, seems as corrupted by wealth as his half-brother by destitution.

Capitalism and Socialism

In the diametrically opposed views of Saccard and Sigismond we see the confrontation of capitalism and socialism, highlighted by Sigismond's three appearances, in the first chapter, the ninth, and the last. Sigismond is not really much of a Marxist—Zola had not studied Marx, but based Sigismond's ideas on what he had read of socialism,[13] and Sigismond's theories are presented as visions and dreams, rather than solid constructions. In the first chapter, Sigismond explains to an uneasy Saccard his notion of a world with no money, no business deals, and no Stock Exchange, and Saccard, looking down from the high window, sees the Bourse not only shrunk by distance, but also threatened: what if this dreamer were right? . . . Sigismond sees money as a corrupting evil, standing in the way of progress, an evil to be banished. Saccard, on the other hand, sees it as the very tool of progress. In their later interview Sigismond is much changed by his illness, grown thin and pale, 'with the eyes of a child, eyes drowning in dreams' (p. 261). Saccard finds him reading his 'Bible', the work of Karl Marx, which, in Sigismond's view, demonstrates the inevitable destruction of the capitalist system. In a world without money, 'work vouchers' would be the only currency, a notion that horrifies Saccard: 'Destroy money? But money is life itself! There would be nothing left. Nothing!' (p. 263). Saccard's capitalist economy is, according to Sigismond, unconsciously but inevitably working towards the great 'Collectivist' takeover, and the idyllic future he has mapped out and planned in detail in his papers. But it is indeed a paper future, and even Sigismond's papers will be destroyed.[14]

Before the novel quite ends Zola brings Sigismond back on stage

[13] Zola drew largely on Schaeffle, *La Quintessence du socialisme* (1886), and Georges Renard, 'Le Socialisme actuel en France', *La Revue socialiste* (1887–8).

[14] But the ideas of those papers are perhaps partly realized in *Toil* (1901), the second of Zola's *Four Gospels*.

once more, to explain, this time to Madame Caroline, the ideas that will carry mankind to universal peace and happiness. Zola positions this last appearance of the now-dying Sigismond alongside Madame Caroline's encounter with La Méchain, accompanied as ever by her huge black bag, bulging now with dead Universal shares. Earlier described as a predatory bird, feeding on the corpses of the battlefield, La Méchain is like an attendant Fury who has waited and watched and finally gathered up her prey.

In Sigismond's ideal city everything would be owned by the community. There would be no more prejudice against manual labour: everybody would work, 'a work at once personal, obligatory, and free' (p. 365). Sigismond's idealistic socialism contrasts sharply with Saccard's capitalist, even imperialist, notion of conquering the Middle East through finance and industrialization. Both men, in their different ways, are visionaries, and just as Saccard in his prison cell still radiates hope and vitality, so the dying Sigismond still sees in the distance the 'happy city, triumphant city, toward which mankind has been marching for so many centuries' (p. 367).

Modernity and Modernism

Money has an intrinsically cinematic quality, with its lively and varied visual scenes—excited clamouring in the Bourse, richly furnished interiors and salons, the streets of Paris with their bustling crowds and horse-drawn traffic, the horrific filth of the Cité de Naples—and Zola's narrative operates in a quite cinematic manner, with multiple changes of angle and perspective, moving through panning panoramas, close-ups, 'flashbacks', and expansions, changing the lighting and making expressionist transformations. Zola even manages his huge cast of characters like a film-director, giving each new character some special feature or recognizable 'tag'—Massias the jobber, always running; La Méchain with her sinister, bulging bag; Flory with his enveloping beard; Madame Conin with her pretty curls. This cinematic style, along with the topicality of the subject in the late 1920s, no doubt encouraged Marcel L'Herbier in 1928 to make his silent film of the novel, updating it from the 1860s to his own times; it is now regarded as a classic.

Zola shows the sort of writerly self-consciousness generally associated with the twentieth-century novel in its reflexivity, that is, the reflection of the work within the work. Repeatedly foregrounding the act of writing, Zola points obliquely to his own authorial activity, and in so doing subverts the Naturalist stance.

In the financial operations of Saccard the accountancy term 'jeux d'écritures' is used over and over. Translated as 'juggling the books' or 'false accountancy', it is literally 'games (or play) of writing', and there is a great deal of 'writing play' in this novel—everyone is writing and creating. The villainous Busch accumulates and classifies his papers with their histories of debt and deceit, then works to create something profitable out of them, while in the next room Sigismond is writing the work that outlines a new future for mankind. It is Hamelin's letters to his anxious sister that keep her on track, with their accounts of the great changes taking place abroad. Jantrou too is a writer, creating the persuasive fictions, the 'little novels' of his brochures, the advertisements that sell the Universal Bank to a gullible public. Saccard, writing a speech for Hamelin, is well pleased with the turn of phrase by which 'the ancient poetry of the Holy Land' colours the presentation of the Carmel Silver Mines. Even in his prison cell Saccard, surrounded by files, is writing up his account of events.

It is from the drawings, plans, maps, and watercolours tacked on the wall of the Hamelins' workroom that great new schemes arise, brought to life by Saccard's imagination and eloquence, just as it is from Zola's notes and tellingly named *ébauches* ('sketches') that the novel arises, brought to life by Zola's imagination and eloquence. And it is those maps and sketches and watercolours that Madame Caroline takes down and rolls up in the final chapter, as if enacting the closure of the narrative. In a further instance of reflexivity, Jordan, the honest, hard-working writer, forced by poverty into journalism but whose novel at last succeeds, is a pale reflection of the young Zola himself. In his earlier work *The Masterpiece* (*L'Oeuvre*, 1886), Zola had introduced the writer Sandoz, who declares that he will create a series of novels based on one family. And in the last novel of the series, Dr Pascal, like Zola, gathers together the whole history of the Rougon-Macquart family; Pascal's notes are destroyed, but Zola's happily survive, embodied in the Rougon-Macquart novels.

TRANSLATOR'S NOTE

THIS translation is based on the text of the novel in volume 5 of Henri Mitterand's excellent Bibliothèque de la Pléiade edition of *Les Rougon-Macquart* (Paris: Fasquelle et Gallimard, 1967), which offers, as well as a scrupulously annotated text, a critical study, and detailed information on Zola's sources and preparation for the novel and the reception of the novel by critics of the time. Other editions were also consulted.

The first English translation available in England was made by Ernest Alfred Vizetelly in 1894—*Money* [*l'Argent*] by Émile Zola (London: Chatto & Windus, 1894). Some earlier translations had appeared in America, where Zola's novels were translated piecemeal from serial episodes in the newspapers, before the novels appeared in volume form. Most of these have sunk without trace. Vizetelly mentions one as being 'of merit'—*Money* by Émile Zola, translated from the French by Benj. R. Tucker (Boston, Mass.: Benj. R Tucker Publishers, 1891). Benjamin R. Tucker was the editor and publisher of *Liberty*, a fortnightly organ of 'Anarchistic Socialism, the Pioneer of Anarchy in America'.

Vizetelly's version is extensively expurgated, with whole episodes omitted, and new passages invented to fill consequent gaps in the narrative. Tucker also suffers from censorship, and comments angrily on an omission he had to make:

In consequence of a disgraceful law... I am forced to omit from this picture a short but vigorous stroke of the word-painter's brush, hoping that the time is not far distant when a saner spirit, and healthier morality... will inspire Americans with a resolve to submit no longer to the enforced emasculation of the greatest works of the greatest authors of this time and of times past.

'Disgraceful law' does not, however, constrain Tucker nearly as thoroughly as Victorian 'morality' does Vizetelly, who has to omit, among other things, Saccard's bidding for the favours of Madame Conin and the rape of Alice de Beauvilliers. Vizetelly also comments on the regrettable omissions: 'Nobody can regret these changes more than I do myself, but before reviewers proceed to censure me... If they desire to have verbatim translations of M. Zola's works, let them help to establish literary freedom.' Vizetelly deserves considerable gratitude for bringing a version of Zola to English readers, in the face of censorship difficulties which had sent his father to prison. However, it is regrettable that subsequent editions have all been versions of that same translation, despite its defects and heavy bowdlerization. Vizetelly commented that publication was very timely in 1894, in view of what he called 'the rottenness of our financial world . . . and the inefficiency of our company laws'. It seems no less timely today for much the same reasons.

It has been a privilege to create the first new English translation of *Money* since the nineteenth century, a translation that can now cover the whole text. I have tried to keep the rhythm and emphases of Zola's writing, and to make the novel read easily for contemporary readers, while keeping the flavour of its own period. Above all, I have tried to keep the verve, the energy, and the poetic dimension of Zola's writing.

I should like here to thank those who, in different ways, have greatly helped me in this task, above all Nicholas Minogue, for untiring reading and helpful comment; Brian Nelson for advice and support; and Judith Luna for her unfailing (though sorely tried!) patience, support, and good humour.

SELECT BIBLIOGRAPHY

L'Argent was serialized in the newspaper *Gil Blas* from 30 November 1890 to 4 March 1891 and in *La Vie populaire* from 22 March 1891 to 30 August, 1891. It was published in volume form by Charpentier in March 1891. Paperback editions, with excellent critical introductions and notes, exist in the following collections: 'Folio classique', ed. Henri Mitterand, preface by André Wurmser (Paris, 1980); 'Classiques de Poche', ed. Philippe Hamon et Marie-France Azéma (Paris, 1998); GF Flammarion, ed. with introduction by Christophe Reffait, with illustrations, detailed notes, and financial lexicon (Paris, Éditions Flammarion, 2009). There is a very useful monograph on *L'Argent* by Colette Becker in the 'Connaissance d'une Oeuvre' series (Paris: Bréal, 2009). The invaluable *Dictionnaire d'Émile Zola* by Colette Becker, Gina Gourdin-Servenière, and Véronique Lavielle (Paris: Robert Laffont, 1993) offers exhaustive and alphabetically indexed information on Zola's life, work, and fictional characters. In *Cahiers naturalistes*, no. 86 (2012), 285–94, 'Zola et la Crise' by Christophe Reffait analyses the treatment of the Bourse in *L'Argent*, and outlines Zola's understanding of the periodicity of economic crises.

Biographies of Zola in English

Brown, Frederick, *Zola: A Life* (London: Macmillan, 1996); with discussion of *Money* in chapter 23.
Grant, Elliott M., *Émile Zola* (New York: Twayne Publishers, 1966).
Hemmings, F. W. J., *The Life and Times of Émile Zola* (London: Elek Books, 1977; also paperback, London: Bloomsbury Reader, 2013).
Schom, Alan, *Émile Zola: A Bourgeois Rebel* (London: Queen Anne Press, 1987).
Vizetelly, Ernest Alfred, *Émile Zola, Novelist and Reformer: An Account of his Life and Work* (London and New York: John Lane, The Bodley Head, 1904; repr. Cambridge, Mass.: Harvard University Press).
Walker, Philip, *Zola* (London: Routledge & Kegan Paul, 1985).

Studies of Zola and Naturalism in English

Baguley, David, *Naturalist Fiction: The Entropic Vision* (Cambridge: Cambridge University Press, 1990).
——(ed.) *Critical Essays on Émile Zola* (Boston: G. K. Hall & Co., 1986).
Berg, William J., and Martin, Laurey K., *Émile Zola Revisited* (New York: Twayne, 1992).
Bloom, Harold (ed.), *Émile Zola* (Philadelphia: Chelsea House, 2004).

Gallois, William, *Zola: The History of Capitalism* (Oxford, etc.: Peter Lang, 2000).

Griffiths, Kate, *Émile Zola and the Artistry of Adaptation* (London: Legenda, Modern Humanities Research Association and Maney Publishing, 2009).

Harrow, Susan, *Zola, the Body Modern: Pressures and Prospects of Representation* (London: Legenda, Modern Humanities Research Association and Maney Publishing, 2010).

Hemmings, F. W. J., *Émile Zola*, 2nd edn. (Oxford: Clarendon Press, 1966).

——(ed.), *The Age of Realism*, 'Pelican Guides to European Literature' (Brighton: Harvester and New Jersey: Humanities Press, 1978).

King, Graham, *Garden of Zola: Émile Zola and his Novels for English Readers* (London: Barrie & Jenkins, 1978).

Lethbridge, Robert, and Keefe, Terry (eds.), *Zola and the Craft of Fiction* (Leicester: Leicester University Press, 1990).

Levin, Harry, *The Gates of Horn: A Study of Five French Realists* (New York: Oxford University Press, 1963).

Mitterand, Henri, *Émile Zola: Fiction and Modernity*, trans. and ed. Monica Lebron and David Baguley (London: The Émile Zola Society, 2000).

Nelson, Brian, *Zola and the Bourgeoisie* (Basingstoke: Macmillan), includes 'L'Argent, Energy and Order', pp. 158–92.

——(ed.), *Naturalism in the European Novel: New Critical Perspectives* (New York and Oxford: Berg, 1992).

——(ed.), *The Cambridge Companion to Émile Zola* (Cambridge: Cambridge University Press, 2007).

Nelson, Roy Jay, *Causality and Narrative in French Fiction: From Zola to Robbe-Grillet* (Columbus, Ohio: Ohio State University Press, 1990); on Zola's Modernist aspects.

Pollard, Patrick (ed.), *Émile Zola Centenary Colloquium* (London: The Émile Zola Society, 1995).

Schor, Naomi, *Zola's Crowds* (Baltimore and London: The Johns Hopkins Press, 1978).

Thompson, Hannah (ed.), *New Approaches to Zola: Selected Papers from the 2002 Cambridge Centenary Colloquium* (London: The Émile Zola Society, 2003).

Wilson, Angus, *Émile Zola: An Introductory Study of his Novels* (London: Mercury Books, 1965).

Historical, Political, and Cultural Background

Baguley, David, *Napoleon III and His Regime: An Extravaganza* (Baton Rouge, La.: Louisiana State University Press, 2000).

Bell, David F., *Models of Power, Politics and Economics in Zola's 'Rougon-Macquart'* (Lincoln, Nebr.: University of Nebraska Press, 1988); includes a chapter on Saccard.

Brown, Frederick, *For the Soul of France: Culture Wars in the Age of Dreyfus* (New York: Anchor Books, 2010); includes chapter on crash of Bontoux's bank.

Friedrich, Otto, *Olympia: Paris in the Time of Manet* (London: Aurum Press, 1992).

Jennings, Jeremy, *Revolution and the Republic: A History of Political Thought in France since the Eighteenth Century* (Oxford: Oxford University Press, 2011).

Jones, Colin, *Paris: Biography of a City* (London: Penguin Books, 2004).

McAuliffe, Mary, *Dawn of the Belle Époque: The Paris of Monet, Zola, Bernhardt, Eiffel, Debussy, Clemenceau and their Friends* (Lanham, etc.: Rowman & Littlefield, 2011).

Ollivier, Émile, *The Liberal Empire of Napoleon III* (Oxford: Oxford University Press, 1963).

Thompson, Victoria E., *The Virtuous Marketplace: Women and Men, Money and Politics in Paris 1830–1870* (Baltimore, Md.: Johns Hopkins University Press, 2000).

Zeldin, Theodore, *France 1848–1945: Politics and Anger* (Oxford: Oxford University Press; repr. 1982).

Articles and Chapters of Special Interest

Cousins, Russell, 'The Serialization and Publication of *L'Argent*: The Genesis of a Literary Event in France and in England', *Bulletin of the Émile Zola Society*, 14 (Sept. 1996), 9–19.

Gallois, William, 'The Forgotten Legacy of Émile Zola', *Bulletin of the Émile Zola Society*, 18 (Sept. 1998), 7–12.

Harrow, Susan, 'Zola's Paris and the Spaces of Proto-modernism', *Bulletin of the Émile Zola Society*, 43–4 (Apr.–Oct. 2011), 40–51.

Mitterand, Henri, 'Zola, "ce rêveur définitif"', *Australian Journal of French Studies*, 38: 3, special issue: 'Zola: Modern Perspectives' (Sept.–Dec. 2001), 321–35 (repr. in Bloom (ed.), *Émile Zola*, above).

Filmography

A Danish film of *L'Argent* was made in 1913, and an Italian film in 1914.

Marcel L'Herbier: *L'Argent*, 1928.

Pierre Billon: *L'Argent*, 1936.

A television version in three parts was made in 1988 by Jacques Rouffio, from *L'Argent* adapted by Claude Brûlé.

Further Reading in Oxford World's Classics

Dickens, Charles, *Little Dorrit*, ed. Harvey Peter Sucksmith and Dennis Walder.

Trollope, Anthony, *The Way We Live Now*, ed. John Sutherland.

Zola, Émile, *L'Assommoir*, trans. Margaret Mauldon, ed. Robert Lethbridge.

—— *The Belly of Paris*, trans. Brian Nelson.

—— *La Bête humaine*, trans. Roger Pearson.

—— *The Fortune of the Rougons*, trans. Brian Nelson.

—— *Germinal*, trans. Peter Collier, ed. Robert Lethbridge.

—— *The Kill*, trans. Brian Nelson.

—— *The Ladies' Paradise*, trans. Brian Nelson.

—— *The Masterpiece*, trans. Thomas Walton, revised by Roger Pearson.

—— *Nana*, trans. Douglas Parmée.

—— *Pot Luck*, trans. Brian Nelson.

—— *Thérèse Raquin*, trans. Andrew Rothwell.

A CHRONOLOGY OF ÉMILE ZOLA

1840   (2 April) Born in Paris, the only child of Francesco Zola (b. 1795), an Italian engineer, and Émilie, née Aubert (b. 1819), the daughter of a glazier. The naturalist novelist was later proud that 'zolla' in Italian means 'clod of earth'.

1843   Family moves to Aix-en-Provence.

1847   (27 March) Death of father from pneumonia following a chill caught while supervising work on his scheme to supply Aix-en-Provence with drinking water.

1852–8   Boarder at the Collège Bourbon at Aix. Friendship with Baptistin Baille and Paul Cézanne. Zola, not Cézanne, wins the school prize for drawing.

1858   (February) Leaves Aix to settle in Paris with his mother (who had preceded him in December). Offered a place and bursary at the Lycée Saint-Louis. (November) Falls ill with 'brain fever' (typhoid) and convalescence is slow.

1859   Fails his *baccalauréat* twice.

1860   (Spring) Is found employment as a copy-clerk but abandons it after two months, preferring to eke out an existence as an impecunious writer in the Latin Quarter of Paris.

1861   Cézanne follows Zola to Paris, where he meets Camille Pissarro, fails the entrance examination to the École des Beaux-Arts, and returns to Aix in September.

1862   (February) Taken on by Hachette, the well-known publishing house, at first in the dispatch office and subsequently as head of the publicity department. (31 October) Naturalized as a French citizen. Cézanne returns to Paris and stays with Zola.

1863   (31 January) First literary article published. (1 May) Manet's *Déjeuner sur l'herbe* exhibited at the Salon des Refusés, which Zola visits with Cézanne.

1864   (October) *Tales for Ninon.*

1865   *Claude's Confession.* A *succès de scandale* thanks to its bedroom scenes. Meets future wife Alexandrine-Gabrielle Meley (b. 1839), the illegitimate daughter of teenage parents who soon separated, and whose mother died in September 1849.

1866   Resigns his position at Hachette (salary: 200 francs a month) and becomes a literary critic on the recently launched daily *L'Événement* (salary: 500 francs a month). Self-styled 'humble disciple' of Hippolyte Taine. Writes a series of provocative articles condemning the official Salon Selection Committee, expressing reservations about Courbet, and praising Manet and Monet. Begins to frequent the Café Guerbois in the Batignolles quarter of Paris, the meeting-place of the future Impressionists. Antoine Guillemet takes Zola to meet Manet. Summer months spent with Cézanne at Bennecourt on the Seine. (15 November) *L'Événement* suppressed by the authorities.

1867 (November) *Thérèse Raquin*.

1868 (April) Preface to second edition of *Thérèse Raquin*. (May) Manet's portrait of Zola exhibited at the Salon. (December) *Madeleine Férat*. Begins to plan for the Rougon-Macquart series of novels.

1868–70 Working as journalist for a number of different newspapers.

1870 (31 May) Marries Alexandrine in a registry office. (September) Moves temporarily to Marseilles because of the Franco-Prussian War.

1871 Political reporter for *La Cloche* (in Paris) and *Le Sémaphore de Marseille*. (March) Returns to Paris. (October) Publishes *The Fortune of the Rougons*, the first of the twenty novels making up the Rougon-Macquart series.

1872 *The Kill*.

1873 (April) *The Belly of Paris*.

1874 (May) *The Conquest of Plassans*. First independent Impressionist exhibition. (November) *Further Tales for Ninon*.

1875 Begins to contribute articles to the Russian newspaper *Vestnik Evropy* (*European Herald*). (April) *The Sin of Father Mouret*.

1876 (February) *His Excellency Eugène Rougon*. Second Impressionist exhibition.

1877 (February) *L'Assommoir*.

1878 Buys a house at Médan on the Seine, 40 kilometres west of Paris. (June) *A Page of Love*.

1880 (March) *Nana*. (May) *Les Soirées de Médan* (an anthology of short stories by Zola and some of his naturalist 'disciples', including Maupassant). (8 May) Death of Flaubert. (September) First of a series of articles for *Le Figaro*. (17 October) Death of his mother. (December) *The Experimental Novel*.

1882 (April) *Pot Luck* (*Pot-Bouille*). (3 September) Death of Turgenev.

1883   (13 February) Death of Wagner. (March) *The Ladies' Paradise* (*Au Bonheur des Dames*). (30 April) Death of Manet.

1884   (March) *La Joie de vivre*. Preface to catalogue of Manet exhibition.

1885   (March) *Germinal*. (12 May) Begins writing *The Masterpiece* (*L'Œuvre*). (22 May) Death of Victor Hugo. (23 December) First instalment of *The Masterpiece* appears in *Le Gil Blas*.

1886   (27 March) Final instalment of *The Masterpiece*, which is published in book form in April.

1887   (18 August) Denounced as an onanistic pornographer in the *Manifesto of the Five* in *Le Figaro*. (November) *Earth*.

1888   (October) *The Dream*. Jeanne Rozerot becomes his mistress.

1889   (20 September) Birth of Denise, daughter of Zola and Jeanne.

1890   (March) *The Beast in Man*.

1891   (March) *Money*. (April) Elected President of the Société des Gens de Lettres. (25 September) Birth of Jacques, son of Zola and Jeanne.

1892   (June) *La Débâcle*.

1893   (July) *Doctor Pascal*, the last of the Rougon–Macquart novels. Fêted on visit to London.

1894   (August) *Lourdes*, the first novel of the trilogy *Three Cities*. (22 December) Dreyfus found guilty by a court martial.

1896   (May) *Rome*.

1898   (13 January) 'J'accuse', his article in defence of Dreyfus, published in *L'Aurore*. (21 February) Found guilty of libelling the Minister of War and given the maximum sentence of one year's imprisonment and a fine of 3,000 francs. Appeal for retrial granted on a technicality. (March) *Paris*. (23 May) Retrial delayed. (18 July) Leaves for England instead of attending court.

1899   (4 June) Returns to France. (October) *Fecundity*, the first of his *Four Gospels*.

1901   (May) *Toil*, the second 'Gospel'.

1902   (29 September) Dies of fumes from his bedroom fire, the chimney having been capped either by accident or anti-Dreyfusard design. Wife survives. (5 October) Public funeral.

1903   (March) *Truth*, the third 'Gospel', published posthumously. *Justice* was to be the fourth.

1908   (4 June) Remains transferred to the Panthéon.

MONEY

CHAPTER I

THE clock on the Bourse* had just struck eleven when Saccard walked into Champeaux's,* into the white and gold dining-room, with its two tall windows looking out over the square. He cast his eye over the rows of little tables, where busy customers were huddled elbow to elbow, and he seemed surprised not to see the face he was looking for.

As a waiter went bustling by, loaded with dishes, he asked:

'Tell me, hasn't Monsieur Huret come in?'

'No sir, not yet.'

So Saccard made up his mind and sat down at a window-table that a customer was just leaving. He thought he was probably late, and while the tablecloth was being changed, he started to look outside, peering at the passers-by on the pavement. Even when the table had been relaid for him, he didn't order straight away, but waited a while, gazing out at the square, so pretty on this bright sunny day in early May.* At this time of day, when everybody was having lunch, it was almost deserted. Under the fresh green of the chestnut trees the benches were all empty, and along the railings where the carriages pull up, a line of cabs stretched from one end to the other, and the Bastille omnibus stopped at the kiosk on the corner of the garden without a single passenger getting on or off. The sun was beating down and the great monument of the Bourse was bathed in sunshine, with its colonnade, its two statues and its imposing flight of steps, at the top of which there was, as yet, just an army of chairs, drawn up in neat ranks.

But turning round, Saccard recognized Mazaud, the stockbroker,* at the table next to his. He held out his hand:

'Ah! it's you, Mazaud! Good-day!'

'Good-day,' Mazaud replied, with a perfunctory handshake.

Small, dark, and very lively, he was a good-looking man, who, at only thirty-two, had just inherited the business of one of his uncles. He seemed totally engrossed in the guest facing him across the table, a large gentleman with a florid, clean-shaven face, the celebrated Amadieu, revered by the Bourse ever since his famous coup on the Selsis Mines. When the Selsis shares had fallen to fifteen francs,* and only a madman would have been buying, he had put his entire fortune into them, two hundred thousand francs, quite haphazardly, with neither calculation nor flair, but only the pig-headedness of a lucky brute. Now that the discovery of real and substantial seams had raised the share-price to over a thousand francs, he had made about fifteen million francs, and his idiotic venture, for which he could have been locked up as a lunatic, now caused him to be regarded as one of the great financial masterminds. He was admired and, above all, consulted. Besides, he no longer did any buying, content now to sit enthroned upon his sole and legendary stroke of genius. Mazaud must be longing to acquire him as a client.

Saccard, having failed to get so much as a smile from Amadieu, greeted the table opposite where three speculators of his acquaintance were gathered, Pillerault, Moser, and Salmon.

'Good-day! Everything going well?'

'Yes, not bad... Good-day!'

He sensed a certain coldness, almost hostility, in these men too. Pillerault, however, very tall, thin, jerky in his movements, and with a razor-sharp nose in a bony face like that of a medieval knight, usually had the familiar air of a gambler who made a principle of recklessness, swearing that when he tried any serious thinking he just tumbled into disaster. He had the exuberant nature of a bull trader,* always expecting victory, whereas Moser, by contrast, short with a yellowish complexion, ravaged by a liver complaint, was always moaning, forever prey to fears of disaster. Salmon, a very handsome man, looking decidedly younger than his fifty years, and displaying a fine inky-black beard, was regarded as an extraordinarily clever fellow. He never spoke, he replied only with smiles. You couldn't tell what he was speculating in, or even if he was speculating at all, and his manner of listening made such an impression on Moser that after telling him something, disconcerted by his silence, he would often go dashing off to change an order.

Meeting with so much indifference, Saccard continued his tour of the room with fiery, challenging eyes. And the only person with whom he exchanged a nod was a tall young man sitting three tables away, the handsome Sabatani, a Levantine with a long, brown face, lit up by magnificent, dark eyes and marred only by a poor and rather disturbing mouth. The friendliness of this young man further exasperated Saccard: he was a defaulter from some foreign Stock Exchange, one of those mysterious fellows that women love. He had made an appearance on the market the previous autumn, and Saccard had already seen him acting as frontman in some banking disaster, but he was gradually winning the trust of both the trading-floor and the kerb market* by his studied correctness and untiring graciousness even towards the most disreputable.

A waiter was now standing over Saccard:

'What can I get for Monsieur?'

'Ah, yes... Whatever's going, a cutlet, some asparagus.'

Then he called the waiter back:

'You're quite sure Monsieur Huret didn't come in before me, and then leave?'

'Oh, absolutely sure.'

So that's how things now stood, since the disaster last October when he had once again been forced into liquidation and had to sell his mansion in the Parc Monceau* and rent an apartment. Now only people like Sabatani would greet him; his arrival in a restaurant where he had once ruled the roost no longer made every head turn and every hand stretch out towards him. He was a good loser and felt no resentment over that last scandalous and disastrous land-deal,* in which he had only just managed to save his skin, but a fever of revenge was awakening within him. The absence of Huret, who had solemnly promised to be there at eleven to let him know the result of the approach he'd undertaken to make on Saccard's behalf to his brother Rougon, now the powerful government minister,* made him furious above all with the latter. Huret, a docile member of Parliament,* a mere creature of the great man, was but an emissary. But Rougon, with all that power, could he really just abandon him? He had never been a good brother. It was quite understandable that he'd been angry over the disaster, and had broken with him to avoid being compromised himself; but after six months shouldn't he secretly have come to his aid? And would he now have the heart to refuse this last bit of support that he was having to seek through an intermediary, not daring to see him in person for fear of an explosion of rage? Rougon had only to say the word and he could set him back on his feet again, with the whole of great, cowardly Paris under his heel.

'What wine for Monsieur?' asked the wine-waiter.

'The house Bordeaux.'

Lost in thought, and not at all hungry, Saccard was letting his cutlet get cold, but he looked up when a shadow fell across the table.

It was Massias, a big, ruddy-faced chap, a jobber,* who when Saccard
first met him had been poor and needy; he was sliding around the
tables with his list of share-prices in his hand. Saccard felt sickened
to see him glide past without stopping, then go on to show the list to
Pillerault and Moser. Involved in their discussion, they paid no attention to him and scarcely glanced at the list. No, they had no orders for
him, perhaps some other time. Massias, not daring to approach the
celebrated Amadieu, who was bent over his lobster salad and talking
quietly to Mazaud, went back to Salmon, who took the list and studied
it at length before handing it back without a word. The dining-room
was getting busier as more jobbers came in, keeping the doors constantly swinging. Shouts were being exchanged across the room, and
business was growing more and more feverish as the hour advanced.
Saccard, with his eyes constantly returning to look outside, could see
the Place de la Bourse gradually filling up as carriages and pedestrians
flowed in; on the steps of the Bourse, now dazzlingly bright in the sun,
men were already appearing one by one, like so many black specks.

'I tell you again,' said Moser in his lugubrious voice, 'these March
by-elections are an extremely worrying sign... Indeed, it means the
whole of Paris gained for the Opposition.'*

Pillerault just shrugged. Carnot and Garnier-Pagès added to the
benches of the Left, what did it matter?

'It's like the Duchies question,'* Moser went on, 'it's really fraught
with complications... No, really, it's no laughing matter. I'm not
saying we had to go to war with Prussia to stop it getting fat at
Denmark's expense; but there were some possibilities for action...
Yes, indeed, when big fish start eating the little fish you can't tell
where it will all end*... And as for Mexico...'*

Pillerault, who was enjoying one of his days of total contentment,
interrupted him with a roar of laughter:

'Oh, no, my dear chap, don't bother us any more with your terrors
over Mexico; that will be the most glorious page in the history of the
reign...* Where the devil do you get the idea that the Empire is sick?
Didn't the three hundred million loan get covered more than fifteen
times over, back in January?* An overwhelming success!... Anyway,
let's talk again in '67, yes, in three years' time, when they'll be opening the Universal Exhibition the Emperor has just announced.'

'Things are really bad, I tell you,' Moser insisted in desperation.

'Oh, give it a rest, everything's fine.'

Salmon looked from one to the other, smiling with his air of pro-
fundity. And Saccard, who had been listening to them, began to con-
nect the difficulties of his own personal situation with the crisis the
Empire seemed to be heading for. He had been brought down once
again: and this Empire that had created him, was that too going to
tumble, suddenly crumbling from the highest down to the most
wretched of destinies? Ah, for twelve years now he had loved and
defended this regime, feeling himself living and growing, and swelling with sap, like a tree with its roots plunged deep in the nourishing
earth. But if his brother intended to uproot him, if he was to be
cut off from those who enjoyed the fruits of that rich soil, then let it
all be swept away in the final grand debacle that marks the end of
nights of festivity.

Now he was just waiting for his asparagus, quite detached from
this room with its ever-increasing bustle, lost in his memories. In a
big mirror on the opposite wall he had just seen his reflection, and it
had surprised him. Age didn't seem to have made any impression on
his slight figure; at fifty he looked no more than thirty-eight, still as
slim and lively as any young man. Indeed, with the years his dark and
hollowed marionette face, with its pointed nose and narrow, gleaming
eyes, seemed to have taken on the charm of this persistent youthfulness, so supple, so active, his hair still thick, with no trace of grey.
And inevitably he recalled his arrival in Paris, immediately after the
coup d'état,* that winter evening when he had found himself out on
the street, with empty pockets, ravenously hungry, and tormented by
all sorts of raging appetites. Oh! that first race through the streets
when, even before unpacking his trunk, he had had to launch himself
upon the city, in his worn-out boots and greasy overcoat, eager to
conquer it! Since that evening he had risen in the world many times, and
a river of millions of francs had flowed through his hands, but he had
never been able to make fortune his slave, like a personal possession,
at his disposal, alive, real, and kept under lock and key. His coffers
had always been full of lies and fictions, with mysterious holes that
seemed to drain away their gold. And now here he was back on the street
again, just as he started out long ago, just as young, just as hungry,
never satisfied, and still tortured by the same need for pleasures and
conquests. He had tasted everything without ever satisfying his appetite, never, he thought, having had the time and opportunity to bite
deeply enough into people and things. Now he felt quite wretched, a

good deal worse off than a mere beginner, who would have hope and illusion to sustain him. He was seized by a frenzied desire to start all over again, to conquer once more, to rise even higher than before and at last plant his foot firmly on the conquered city. No longer with the façade of mendacious wealth but the solid edifice of fortune, the true royalty of gold, reigning over well-filled bags of wealth.

Then the voice of Moser was heard once more, harsh and very sharp, drawing Saccard out of his reflections.

'The Mexico expedition is costing fourteen million a month, that's been proved by Thiers*... and you'd have to be blind not to see that the majority in the Chamber has been shaken. There are more than thirty now on the Left. The Emperor himself has seen that absolute power has become impossible, since he now presents himself as the champion of liberty.'*

Pillerault had ceased to respond, now just sneering contemptuously.

'Yes, I know, the market seems solid enough to you, and business is good. But wait for the end... You'll see there's been altogether too much demolition and rebuilding in Paris! These great public works have exhausted our savings. As for the powerful financial houses that seem so prosperous, just wait until one of them goes down and you'll see them all collapsing one after another... Not to mention the fact that the people are restive. This International Workingmen's Association* which has just been founded to improve conditions for the workers, that really frightens me. There's a protest movement, a revolutionary movement here in France, and it's growing stronger every day... I tell you, the worm is in the fruit. Everything is going to go bust.'

This provoked a roar of protest. That blasted Moser was decidedly liverish. But even while he spoke, Moser's eyes never left the table at which Mazaud and Amadieu, in spite of all the noise, were still talking quietly. Gradually the whole room began to be concerned about this very long, confidential chat. What could they have to say that needed all that whispering? Amadieu, no doubt, must be placing orders, preparing some financial coup. Over the last three days disturbing rumours had been circulating about the Suez project.* Moser narrowed his eyes, and he too lowered his voice to say:

'You know, the English want to stop all the work there. There could well be war.'

This time Pillerault was shaken by the very enormity of this piece of news. It was incredible, and immediately the word flew from table to table, acquiring the force of certainty: England had sent an ultimatum demanding the immediate cessation of work. That must obviously have been what Amadieu was talking to Mazaud about, giving him the order to sell all his Suez holdings. A buzz of panic arose in the air, among the rich smells and the increasing clatter of dishes. And at that moment what raised the excitement to a peak was the sudden entry of one of the stockbroker's clerks, little Flory, a lad with a gentle face almost swallowed whole by a thick brown beard. He rushed forward with a packet of order-cards in his hand, and handed them to his boss, whispering in his ear.

'Good,' was Mazaud's only answer, as he tucked the cards away in his order-book. Then, drawing out his watch:

'Nearly midday! Tell Berthier to wait for me. Be there yourself too, and go and pick up the telegrams.'

When Flory had gone, Mazaud resumed his conversation with Amadieu, took out some other cards from his pocket, and laid them on the table beside his plate; and every minute some departing customer would lean over as he went by and say something, which he promptly noted, between mouthfuls, on one of the pieces of paper. The false news from who knows where, arising out of nothing, was growing ever bigger, like a gathering storm-cloud.

'You're selling, aren't you?' Moser asked Salmon.

But the silent smile of the latter was so sharp with perspicacity that it left him anxious, worried now about this English ultimatum, not realizing that he had invented it himself.

'Personally, I'll buy whatever's on offer,' said Pillerault in conclusion, with the vainglorious temerity of a gambler with no system.

Saccard, his brow heated by the fever of speculation provoked by this noisy ending to lunch in the narrow dining-room, decided to eat his asparagus, irritated anew by Huret, whom he had now given up. For weeks now he, who was usually so quick to make decisions, had grown hesitant, troubled by uncertainties. He felt an imperative need for change, to start afresh, and his first idea had been of an entirely new life in the upper reaches of administration, or else in politics. Why shouldn't a position in the Legislative Assembly lead him on to the Council of Ministers, as it had his brother? What he didn't like about speculation was the constant instability, the huge sums lost as fast as they were gained: he had never been able to sleep on a real million, owing nothing to anyone. And now, as he took stock of things, he decided he was perhaps too passionate a person for this financial battle, which needed such a cool head. That must be why, after such an extraordinary life of both luxury and poverty, he had emerged empty-handed and burnt-out from those ten years of amazing land-deals in the new Paris, while others, less astute than he, had garnered colossal fortunes. Yes, perhaps he had been quite wrong about where his real talents lay; perhaps, with his energy and ardent convictions, he would triumph in one bound in the political fray. Everything would depend on his brother's response. If he pushed him away, threw him back into the abyss of speculation, well, it would be just too bad, for him and for others; he would take his chances on the big plan he hadn't mentioned to anyone, the enormous project he had dreamed of for weeks and which alarmed even himself, so vast was it and capable, if it succeeded or if it failed, of setting the world astir.

Pillerault raised his voice once more—

'Mazaud, is the Schlosser business settled?'

'Yes,' replied the broker, 'the notice will go up today... That's how it is... it's always unpleasant, but I'd had the most disturbing reports, and I was the first to make demand.* Now and again you just have to clear the ground.'

'I've been told', said Moser, 'that your colleagues, Jacoby and Delarocque, had some considerable sums invested.'

The broker made a vague gesture.

'Bah, there have to be some losses... That Schlosser must have been part of a group; and all he'll have to do is go off to Berlin or Vienna and start plundering the Stock Exchange there.'

Saccard's gaze had fallen upon Sabatani, of whose secret association with Schlosser he had happened to learn: the two men played the well-known game, one bidding up and the other bidding down for the same stock; the loser would simply share the profit of the other and disappear. But the young man was quietly paying the bill for the meal he had just eaten. Then, with the typical caressing grace of the Oriental mixed with Italian, he went over to shake hands with Mazaud, whose client he was. He leaned over, and placed an order that Mazaud wrote on a card.

'He's selling his Suez holdings,' murmured Moser.

Then, giving way to his need to know, sick with doubt as he was:

'So, what do you think about Suez?'

Silence fell on the hubbub of voices, and at the neighbouring tables every head turned round. The question summed up the increasing anxiety. But the back view of Amadieu, who had invited Mazaud to lunch simply to recommend one of his nephews to him, remained impenetrable, having indeed nothing to say. The stockbroker, on the other hand, increasingly astonished by the number of orders to sell he was getting, simply nodded, with his customary professional discretion.

'Suez is good!' declared Sabatani in his sing-song voice, making a detour to come over and very courteously shake Saccard's hand before he left.

The sensation of that handshake, so soft and supple, almost feminine, lingered for a moment with Saccard. In his uncertainty about the road he should take and how to rebuild his life, he decided they were all scoundrels, every man there. Ah, if he were forced to it, how he would hunt them down, how he'd fleece them all, the trembling Mosers, the boastful Pilleraults, the Salmons hollower than a drum, and people like Amadieu, seen as a genius on the strength of one success! The clatter of plates and glasses had resumed, voices were getting hoarse, the doors banged ever louder in the raging hurry to get to the market in case Suez should indeed be about to crash. Looking out of the window onto the middle of the square, lined by carriages and crammed with pedestrians, Saccard could see the sunlit steps of the Bourse, speckled now with the continual surge of human insects, men smartly dressed in black gradually filling the colonnade, while behind the railings a few women appeared, prowling around beneath the chestnut trees.

Suddenly, as he was about to start on the cheese he'd just ordered, a loud voice made him look up.

'I beg your pardon, my dear chap, I really was unable to get here any sooner.'

It was Huret at last, a Norman from Calvados with the thick, broad face of a wily peasant, but who affected to be a simple man. He immediately ordered something, whatever was available, the dish of the day, with a vegetable.

'Well...?' said Saccard curtly, trying to contain his annoyance.

But the other was in no hurry, looking at him with the air of a man both crafty and cautious. Then, starting to eat, he leaned towards him, lowering his voice:

'Well, I saw the great man... Yes, at his home, this morning... Oh, he was very kind, very well-disposed towards you...'

He paused, drank a large glass of wine, and popped a potato into his mouth.

'So…?'

'So, my dear chap, this is how it is… He's very willing to do all he can for you, he'll find you a very good position, but not in France… For instance, the governorship of one of our colonies, one of the better ones. You'd be the master there, a real little prince.'

Saccard had turned pale.

'Come now, you can't be serious, this is a joke!… Why not just deport me straight off!… Oh yes, he wants to be rid of me. He'd better be careful or I might end up seriously embarrassing him.'

Huret sat there with his mouth full, looking conciliatory.

'Come, come now, we only want what's best for you, just let us get on with it.'

'And allow myself to be wiped out, eh?… Well, just a little while back they were saying here that the Empire soon wouldn't have any more mistakes left to make. Yes, after the Italian war, and Mexico, and the attitude to Prussia. My word, it's the truth… You'll do so many stupid and crazy things that the whole of France will rise up to kick you out.'

With that the Deputy, faithful servant of his minister, turned pale and looked about him anxiously.

'Ah, please, allow me to say… I can't go along with you there… Rougon is an honest man, there is no danger of that, so long as he is there… No, don't say another word, you misjudge him, I must insist.'

Saccard interrupted him violently, controlling his voice between clenched teeth:

'So be it, go on loving him, carry on cooking up plans with him… Yes or no, will he give me his support in Paris?'

'In Paris, never!'

Without another word Saccard stood up and called the waiter over to pay the bill, while Huret, accustomed to his fits of rage, very calmly went on swallowing big mouthfuls of bread and let him go, for fear of a scene. But just then there was a great commotion in the room.

Gundermann had just come in, the banker-king, master of the Bourse and the world, a man of sixty, whose huge bald head, thick nose, and round, protruding eyes seemed to express immense obstinacy and weariness. He never went to the Bourse, even affecting not to send any official representative; nor did he ever eat in a public place.

Only once in a while he would happen, as on this day, to enter Champeaux's restaurant and sit at one of the tables, to order just a glass of Vichy water, on a plate. For the last twenty years he had suffered from a gastric complaint, and the only food he took was milk.

The restaurant staff were immediately in a flurry to bring the glass of water, and all the diners kept their heads down. Moser, looking quite overwhelmed, gazed at this man who knew all the secrets and made the market go up or down as he pleased, the way God controls the thunder. Pillerault, having faith only in the irresistible force of a billion francs, greeted him. It was half-past twelve, and Mazaud, swiftly abandoning Amadieu, came back and bowed to the banker, who occasionally did him the honour of placing an order. Many of the brokers who were just leaving stopped and stood around the god, paying court with their spines respectfully inclined, in the midst of the clutter of messy tables; and watched with veneration as he took the glass of water and raised it with trembling hands to his colourless lips.

Some time back, during the land speculation on the Monceau plain, Saccard had had some disagreements, and even quite a quarrel, with Gundermann. They were incapable of getting on, the one a gambler full of passion, the other cold, sober, and logical. So the former, already angry and exasperated by this triumphant entrance, was leaving when the other called out to him:

'Tell me, my dear friend, is it true? You're leaving the world of business... Upon my soul, you're doing the right thing. It's just as well...'

Saccard received this like the lash of a whip across his face. He drew up his slight frame and replied in a voice as sharp as steel:

'I am setting up a banking house with a capital of twenty-five million, and I expect to be calling on you soon.'

And he went out, leaving behind him the agitated hubbub of the room, where they were all jostling one another in their anxiety not to miss the opening of the Bourse. Oh! to be successful at last, and stamp on these people who were turning their backs on him, to engage in a struggle for power with this king of gold, and maybe one day bring him down! He hadn't really made up his mind about launching his grand plan, and he was still surprised at the declaration which his need to respond had drawn from him. But would he be able to try his luck elsewhere, now that his brother was abandoning him, now that men and even things seemed to be wounding him and throwing him back into the fight, like the bull that is led back, bleeding, into the ring?

For a moment he stood tremulously on the edge of the pavement. It was the busy time when all the life of Paris seems to pour into this central square between the Rue Montmartre and the Rue Richelieu, the two congested arteries carrying the crowds. From each of the four junctions at the four corners of the square flowed a constant, uninterrupted stream of vehicles, weaving their way along the road through the bustling mass of pedestrians. The two lines of cabs at the cab-stand along the railings kept breaking up and then re-forming; whilst on the Rue Vivienne the dealers' victorias* stretched out in a close-packed line, with the coachmen on top, reins in hand, ready to whip the horses forward at the first command. The steps and the peristyle of the Bourse were overrun with swarming black overcoats; and from the kerb market, already set up and at work beneath the clock, came the clamour of buying and selling, the tidal surge of speculation, rising above the noisy rumble of the city. Passers-by turned their heads, impelled by both desire and fear of what was going on there, in that mysterious world of financial dealings into which French brains but rarely penetrate, a world of ruin and bankruptcy and sudden inexplicable fortunes, in the midst of all that barbaric shouting and gesticulation. And Saccard, on the edge of the stream, deafened by the distant voices and elbowed by the jostling bustle of the crowd, was dreaming once more of the royalty of gold in this home of every feverish passion, with the Bourse at its centre, beating, from one o'clock until three, like an enormous heart.

But since his downfall he had not dared to go back into the Bourse, and even now a feeling of wounded vanity, the certainty of being greeted as a failure, still prevented him from climbing the steps. Like a lover driven from the boudoir of a mistress whom he desires all the more, even while telling himself he detests her, he kept coming back irresistibly, making a tour of the colonnade on various pretexts, crossing the garden as if taking a leisurely walk in the shade of the chestnut trees. In this sort of dusty square with neither grass nor flowers, on the benches among the urinals and the newspaper stands, swarmed a mixed crowd of shady speculators and bareheaded local women suckling their babies; here he affected a nonchalant saunter but kept looking up, watching, furiously imagining he was laying siege to the monument, surrounding it in an ever tighter circle, to re-enter it one day, in triumph.

He went over to the corner on the right, under the trees that face the Rue de la Banque, and immediately came upon the Little Bourse, trading in downgraded shares: the 'Wet Feet',* as these bric-à-brac dealers are ironically and contemptuously known, who trade in the shares of dead companies in the open air, out in the wind and, on rainy days, in the mud. Here was a tumultuous group of unclean Jewry, with fat shiny faces, and the desiccated profiles of predatory birds, an extraordinary gathering of typically Jewish noses, huddled together as if fighting fiercely over their prey with guttural cries, ready to devour each other. As he went by he noticed a big man standing a little to one side looking at a ruby in the sunlight, delicately lifting it up in the air with huge and dirty fingers.

'Ah, Busch!… Seeing you reminds me, I was intending to call on you.'

Busch, who had an office in the Rue Feydeau, on the corner of the Rue Vivienne, had on several occasions been very useful to Saccard in difficult circumstances. He was standing there in ecstasy, examining the purity of the gem, his broad, rather featureless face thrown back, his big grey eyes seeming dulled by the brightness of the light; one could see the white cravat he always wore, rolled into a string; while his secondhand overcoat, once superb, now extraordinarily shabby and stained, reached right up into his colourless hair, which straggled from his bare skull in rare, rebellious strands. His hat, yellowed by the sun and washed by the rain, was now of indeterminate age.

At last, he decided to come back down to earth.

'Ah, Monsieur Saccard, so you're taking a little walk round here…'

'Yes, it's about a letter in Russian, a letter from a Russian banker based in Constantinople. So I thought of your brother, to translate it for me.'

Busch, still unconsciously rolling the ruby tenderly in his right hand, extended his left hand, saying the translation would be sent that very evening. But Saccard explained that it was only a matter of ten lines.

'I'll come up, and your brother will read it for me straight away…'

He was now interrupted by the arrival of an enormous woman, Madame Méchain, well known to the regulars at the Bourse, one of those rabid and wretched speculators whose greasy hands are always poking into all sorts of dubious activities. Her moon face, red and puffy, with narrow blue eyes, an almost invisible little nose, and a small mouth from which emerged a child-like fluting voice, seemed to spill out from under her old mauve hat, tied on lopsidedly with red ribbons; and her enormous bosom and dropsical belly seemed to stretch to the limit her mud-bespattered poplin dress, once green, now turning yellow. She carried on her arm a huge old black-leather bag, as deep as a suitcase; this she was never without. That day the bag, full to bursting, was pulling her over to the right, like a bent tree.

'Ah, there you are,' said Busch, who must have been waiting for her.

'Yes, and I've received the Vendôme papers, I have them with me.'

'Good, let's go to my office; there's nothing to be done here today.'

Saccard's eye flickered over the huge leather bag. He knew that this was where downgraded stocks would inevitably end up, along with the shares of bankrupt companies in which the 'Wet Feet' go on trading: five-hundred-franc shares fought over for twenty sous, or even ten, in the vague hope of an unlikely recovery, or more practically as criminal merchandise, passed on at a profit to bankers needing to inflate their losses. In the murderous battles of the financial world La Méchain was the crow following the marching armies; no company and no bank could be founded without her appearing with her bag, sniffing the air, waiting for the corpses, even in the prosperous times of successful share-issues; for she well knew that failure was inevitable, that the day of massacre would come, the day when there would be dead bodies to devour and shares to pick up for nothing from the mud and blood. And as Saccard turned over in his head his grand banking project, he gave a slight shiver, feeling a premonition as he looked at that bag, that charnel-house of devalued stock, into which went all the dirty paper swept up from the Bourse.

As Busch was leading the old woman away, Saccard stopped him.

'Shall I go up then, can I be sure of finding your brother?'

The eyes of the Jew softened, expressing a worried surprise.

'My brother? But of course! Where else would he be?'

'Very well, I'll see you later!'

And Saccard, letting them go, resumed his slow walk by the trees, towards the Rue Notre-Dame-des-Victoires. This side of the square is one of the busiest, full of small businesses and minor workshops,

with their gilded signs blazing in the sun. Blinds flapped on the bal-
conies, and a whole family, up from the provinces, stood gaping
from the window of a hotel room. Without thinking, he had raised his
head and looked at these people, whose amazement made him smile,
comforting him with the thought that there would always be shareholders somewhere in the provinces. Behind him the clamour of the
Bourse, the roar of the distant flood-tide, was still there, nagging at
him, following him, as if threatening to swallow him up.

Just then another encounter made him pause.

'What's this, Jordan, you at the Bourse?' he shouted, shaking the
hand of a tall, dark young man with a small moustache and a resolute,
determined air.

The son of a Marseilles banker who had committed suicide a while
ago after some disastrous speculation, Jordan had been tramping
the streets of Paris for ten years, madly devoted to literature, and
struggling bravely against dire poverty. One of his cousins, who lived
in Plassans* and knew the Saccard family, had recommended him
to Saccard back when the latter was entertaining all of Paris at his
Parc Monceau mansion.

'Oh no, not at the Bourse, never!' the young man replied, with
a violent gesture, as if he were driving away the tragic memory of
his father.

Then, starting to smile again:

'You know of course that I got married... Yes, to a childhood
sweetheart. Our engagement was arranged when I was still rich, but
she insisted she still wanted the poor devil I've become.'

'Yes indeed, I received the announcement,' said Saccard. 'And do
you know, I was in touch with your father-in-law, Monsieur
Maugendre, some time ago, when he had his tarpaulin factory in La
Villette. He must have made a pretty penny out of that.'

They were having this conversation near a bench, and Jordan broke
off to introduce Saccard to a short, fat, military-looking gentleman
who was sitting there, and with whom he had been chatting when
Saccard came along.

'This is Captain Chave, an uncle of my wife's... Madame
Maugendre, my mother-in-law, is a Chave from Marseilles.'

The captain rose and Saccard shook his hand. He knew by sight
this apoplectic face, with a neck stiff from wearing the military collar,
one of those petty-cash speculators who could always be seen around

here from one o'clock until three. They played for tiny but almost certain winnings of fifteen to twenty francs, which had to be realized within one session of the Bourse.

Jordan had added, with a pleasant laugh, to explain his presence there:

'A ferocious speculator, my uncle, I just come along from time to time to shake his hand as I go by.'

'My word,' said the captain, 'I have to gamble; on the government pension I'd starve.'

Then Saccard, who took an interest in this young man on account of his robust attitude to life, asked him how things were going on the literary front. And Jordan, brightening up, told him that his needy family was now installed on the fifth floor in the Avenue de Clichy, for the Maugendres, distrustful of a poet and feeling they had done more than enough just by consenting to the marriage, had given them nothing, on the pretext that after their death, their daughter would have their whole fortune, untouched and fattened by savings. No, literature did not feed a man, but he had in mind an idea for a novel, which he didn't have time to write, so he had had to go into journalism where he dashed off anything he could get, from writing a column to doing the law reports or even little news items.

'Oh well,' said Saccard, 'if I get my grand plan going I shall perhaps have a job for you. So come and see me.'

After saying goodbye, he turned to go round the back of the Bourse. Here at last the distant clamour, the barking of the stock-market, was no more than a vague hum, lost in the roaring traffic of the square. On this side the steps were just as crowded with people, but the stockbrokers' offices, whose red curtains could be seen through the tall windows, insulated the colonnade from the din of the trading hall, and here various speculators, the rich and fastidious, were sitting comfortably in the shade, some alone and some in little groups, transforming the huge portico, open to the sky, into a sort of private club. The rear of the building was rather like the wrong side of a theatre, or the stage-door, with this seedy, relatively quiet street, the Rue Notre-Dame-des-Victoires, entirely occupied by wine-merchants, cafés, brasseries, and taverns swarming with a particular, strangely mixed set of customers. The shop-signs too clearly indi-cated the sort of noxious vegetation that had grown up on the edge of the huge cesspit nearby: disreputable insurance companies, crooked financial journals, company offices, banks, agencies, moneylenders, a whole range of small-time gambling-joints established in shops or on mezzanines the size of a pocket-handkerchief. Everywhere, on the pavements and in the middle of the road, men were prowling about, loitering as if in some dark alley.

Saccard had stopped just inside the railings and was looking up at the door leading to the stockbrokers' offices, with the piercing gaze of an army chief inspecting from every angle the place he intends to attack, when a tall fellow, coming out of a tavern, crossed the street and made him a very low bow.

'Ah, Monsieur Saccard, don't you have anything for me? I have now at last left the Crédit Mobilier* and I'm looking for a job.'

Jantrou was a former professor, come to Paris from Bordeaux after some shady affair. He had had to leave the university, had lost his place in the world, but was still a good-looking chap, with his ample black beard and his precocious baldness, well-read too, intelligent and amiable; he had started off at the Bourse when he was about twenty-eight, and had trailed around getting his hands dirty for ten years as a jobber, earning scarcely enough money to keep him in his vices. And today, completely bald and complaining like a whore whose wrinkles threaten her livelihood, he was still waiting for the opportunity that would launch him into success and fortune.

Seeing him so humble, Saccard remembered with some bitterness the greeting of Sabatani at Champeaux's: clearly all he had left now was the flawed and the failed. But he was not without esteem for this man's lively intelligence, and he well knew that desperate men make the bravest and most daring troops, having nothing to lose and everything to gain. So he made himself agreeable.

'A job,' he repeated. 'Well, that might be possible. Come and see me.'

'It's Rue Saint-Lazare now, isn't it?'

'Yes, Rue Saint-Lazare. In the morning.'

They chatted. Jantrou had plenty to say against the Bourse, insisting, with all the rancour of an unsuccessful scoundrel, that you had to be a scoundrel to succeed in it. That was all over now, he wanted to try something else, and he felt that, given his university background and his knowledge of the world, he would be able to find a good position in management. Saccard nodded approvingly. And as they were now outside the railings, walking along the pavement up to the Rue

Brongniart, the attention of both men was caught by a dark coupé,*
very well turned-out, which was standing in that street with the horse
facing the Rue Montmartre. They had noticed that while the back of
the coachman, perched on his high seat, was as still as if made of stone,
a woman's head on two occasions appeared at the carriage door then
quickly vanished. Suddenly the head leaned out and remained there,
casting a long, impatient look back towards the Bourse.

'Baroness Sandorff,' murmured Saccard.

It was a very strange, dark head, with black eyes burning beneath
bruised eyelids, a face of passion, with blood-red mouth, a face marred
only by an overlong nose. She seemed very pretty, and unusually
mature for her twenty-five years, with the look of a Bacchante,* dressed
by the great dress-designers of the age.

'Yes, the Baroness,' echoed Jantrou, 'I met her when she was a girl
living with her father, Count de Ladricourt. Oh! a crazy speculator
and a man of appalling brutality! I used to go to get his orders every
morning, and one day he came close to beating me. I shed no tears for
him when he died of apoplexy, ruined after a series of terrible losses
on the market... So the girl had to resign herself to marrying Baron
Sandorff, Counsellor at the Austrian Embassy, thirty-five years her
senior, whom she had quite driven mad with her fiery eyes.'

Saccard just said: 'I know.'

Once more the head of the Baroness had disappeared inside the
coupé. But almost immediately it reappeared, her face more ardent
and her neck straining to see over the square, in the distance.

'She plays the market, doesn't she?'

'Oh, like one demented! Every time there's a crisis you can see her
here, in her carriage, watching the market quotations, feverishly
taking notes in her notebook and placing orders... And look! It was
Massias she was waiting for, and here he comes to join her.'

Indeed, Massias was running as fast as his short legs would carry
him, his list of market-rates in his hand, and they saw him leaning
over the carriage door, he too now plunging his head inside, deep in
discussion with the Baroness. Then, as they were moving off a little
to avoid being caught spying, and the broker had started back, still
running, they called out to him. First he glanced sideways to make
sure he was hidden by the corner of the street; then he stopped,
breathless, his florid face all puffed up but still cheerful, and his big
blue eyes as limpid as a child's.

'Whatever is the matter with them!' he exclaimed. 'Now it's Suez collapsing. And they're talking of a war with England. A piece of news that is totally upsetting everyone, and no one knows where it came from... I ask you, war! Who can possibly have invented that? Unless it just invented itself... Honestly, a bolt from the blue!'

Jantrou gave a wink.

'The lady's still at it?'

'Oh! like a madwoman! I'm taking her orders over to Nathansohn.'

Saccard, who was listening, reflected aloud:

'Oh yes! indeed, I'd been told that Nathansohn had entered the kerb market.'

'A very nice young chap, Nathansohn,' said Jantrou, 'he deserves to be successful. We were together at the Crédit Mobilier... But he'll get on all right, since he's a Jew. His father is an Austrian, living in Besançon, a watchmaker I believe... You know, one day, there at the Crédit, seeing how it all worked, he got the idea. He decided it wasn't all that clever; all you needed was a room with a railed-off counter such as bank-cashiers have, so he opened a counter... And you, Massias, are you doing well?'

'Doing well? Oh, you've been through it, you're right to say you have to be a Jew; without that, no good trying to understand, one doesn't have the flair, it's just filthy luck... What a rotten job! But once in it, one stays in it. Besides, I still have good strong legs, so I keep hoping.'

And off he ran with a laugh. He was said to be the son of a disgraced magistrate from Lyons, who, after his father disappeared, decided not to go on with his law studies and ended up in the Bourse.

Saccard and Jantrou, walking slowly, came back towards the Rue Brongniart; there they again saw the coupé of the Baroness; but the windows were raised and the mysterious vehicle seemed quite empty, while the coachman seemed even more still than before, in his long wait that often lasted until the close of the market.

'She is devilishly exciting,' Saccard brusquely remarked, 'I can understand the old Baron.'

Jantrou gave an odd smile.

'Oh! The Baron had enough some time ago, I believe. And he's very miserly, they say... So do you know who she's taken up with, to pay her bills—since she never makes enough on the market?'

'No.'

'Delcambre.'

'Delcambre, the Public Prosecutor, that dry stick of a man, so jaundiced and stiff!... Oh, I'd really like to see those two together!'

At this the two men, highly amused and titillated, went their separate ways with a vigorous handshake, one reminding the other that he would take the liberty of calling on him shortly.

As soon as he was alone again Saccard was once more overtaken by the loud voice of the Bourse, breaking over his head with the insistence of a flood-tide on the turn. He had gone round the corner now, and was walking back towards the Rue Vivienne, along that side of the square which, lacking any cafés, looks rather severe. He carried on past the Chamber of Commerce, the post-office, and the large advertising agencies, getting more and more deafened and feverish as he came back in front of the main façade; and when he managed to cast a sideways glance over the portico he paused anew, as if not yet ready to complete the tour of the colonnade and end this sort of passionate siege in which he was enfolding it. Here, on this wider part of the pavement, life was in full swing, even bursting out: a flood of customers filled the cafés, the patisserie was permanently crowded; the window displays were bringing the crowds flocking, especially the goldsmith's, ablaze with large pieces of silverware. And at the four corners, the four intersections, the flow of cabs and pedestrians grew ever more intense, in an inextricable tangle, while the omnibus office added to the congestion and the jobbers' carriages stood in line, blocking the pavement from one end of the railings to the other. But Saccard's eyes were glued to the top of the steps, where the frock-coats followed one another in the sunshine. Then his gaze went back up towards the columns, into the compact mass, a swarming blackness brightened only by the pale patches of faces. Everyone was standing, the chairs were not visible, and the circle of the kerb market, sitting under the clock, could only be guessed at from a sort of bubbling, a frenzy of words and gestures that had set the air a-tremble. Over on the left the group of bankers engaged in arbitrage, foreign-currency operations, and English cheques* was quieter than the rest, though a queue of people kept passing through to get to the telegraph office. Even the side galleries were crammed with a crush of speculators; and between the columns, leaning against the metal handrails, some were showing their backs or bellies, seeming quite at ease, as if leaning on the velvet of a box at the theatre. The vibration and rumbling, like an engine getting up steam, grew ever louder, making the whole of the Bourse shake like the flickering of a flame. Suddenly he saw the jobber Massias racing down the steps and leaping into his carriage, whereupon the coachman immediately set the horse off at a gallop.

Then Saccard felt his fists clenching. Violently tearing himself away, he turned into the Rue Vivienne, crossing the road to reach the corner of the Rue Feydeau, where Busch lived. He had just remembered the Russian letter that he needed to get translated. But as he entered, he was greeted by a young man standing by the stationer's on the ground floor, and he recognized Gustave Sédille, the son of a silk manufacturer in the Rue des Jeûneurs; his father had placed him with Mazaud to study the workings of the world of finance. He smiled paternally at the tall, elegant lad, readily guessing what he was up to, waiting there. Conin's stationery shop had been supplying notebooks to the whole of the Bourse ever since little Madame Conin had begun helping her husband, big Monsieur Conin, who never came out from the back of the shop; he attended to the manufacturing, while she was forever coming and going, serving at the counter and running errands outside. She was plump and blonde and pink, a real little curly lamb with her pale, silky hair, very pleasant and affectionate and always in good spirits. She was fond of her husband, it was said, but this didn't stop her from a bit of dalliance when one of the broker customers took her fancy; but not for money, only for pleasure, and once only, in a friend's house nearby, or so it was said. In any case, the favoured ones must have been both discreet and grateful, for she was still adored and made a fuss of, with no ugly rumours about her. And the stationer's continued to prosper, it was a real little nest of happiness. As he passed by, Saccard saw Madame Conin smiling at Gustave through the window. Such a pretty little lamb! He felt a delicious sensation like a caress. Then he went up the stairs.

For twenty years now Busch had occupied a cramped lodging right at the top, on the fifth floor, just two bedrooms and a kitchen. Born in Nancy, of German parents, he had ended up here after leaving his home town, and had gradually widened his extraordinarily complicated business circle, without feeling the need for a larger office, leaving the room on the street side to his brother Sigismond and keeping for himself only the little room overlooking the interior yard, and there the heaps of paper, the files and packages of all sorts, were piled up to such an extent that there was only room for one single chair beside the desk. One of his main concerns was trading in collapsed stocks; he collected them together and acted as intermediary between the Little Bourse of the 'Wet Feet' and the bankrupts with holes to account for in their books; so he followed the market rates closely, occasionally buying directly, but mainly being supplied from stocks that were brought to him. Besides moneylending and a covert traffic in jewels and precious stones, he particularly occupied himself with buying up debts. That was what filled his office to bursting-point and sent him to the four corners of Paris, sniffing and watching, with inside contacts in every level of society. As soon as he learned of a bankruptcy he would rush along, prowling around the receiver, eventually buying up everything that offered no immediate profit to anyone. He kept an eye on solicitors' offices, waiting for the opening of difficult inheritance cases and attending the auctioning of hopeless debts. He also advertised, attracting impatient creditors who preferred to get a few sous at once rather than run the risk of taking their debtors to court. From these multiple sources came paper by the basketful, constantly adding to the heap of this ragpicker of debts—unpaid promissory notes, failed agreements, fruitless acknowledgements of liability, commitments unfulfilled. Then came the sorting, the picking through these seedy remains, and this required a special and very delicate flair. In this ocean of disappeared or insolvent debtors choices had to be made to avoid waste of effort. Busch maintained as a general principle that any debt, however seemingly hopeless, might prove to be of value, and he had a series of admirably classified files, with a corresponding index of names, which he read over from time to time to refresh his memory. But among the insolvents he naturally followed most closely those he felt might perhaps come into money one day; his investigations stripped people bare, delved into family secrets, took note of wealthy relatives, of any resources people had, and especially of any new employment which would allow him to sequester payments. Often he would allow a man to 'ripen' over several years, only to strangle him at his first success. As for debtors who had disappeared, they excited his passions even more, throwing him into a fever of search after search, scanning the business signboards and every name printed in the newspapers, seeking out addresses like a dog hunting game. Once he had his hands on them, the insolvent and the disappeared, he became ferocious, devouring them with all sorts of charges, bleeding them dry, getting a hundred francs for what had cost him ten sous, with brutal explanations of the risks involved in his operations, which meant he had to recoup from those he caught all that he claimed to lose on the ones who slipped through his fingers like smoke.

In this hunt for debtors La Méchain was one of the helpers he most liked to use, for though he had to have a little troupe of hunting-assistants working for him, he was always distrustful of that disreputable and hungry gang; La Méchain, on the other hand, had her own property, a sort of housing estate behind the Butte Montmartre called the Cité de Naples, a vast acreage covered with rickety sheds that she leased by the month: a place of appalling poverty, with starvelings living on top of each other in the filth, fighting over holes fit for pigs from which she would ruthlessly sweep them, along with their rubbish, the minute they ceased to pay. What was eating her up and swallowing the profits of her 'estate' was her unfortunate passion for speculation. She also had a taste for financial disasters, ruins and fires from which one can steal melted jewels. When Busch set her to seeking some information or unearthing a debtor, she threw herself into it for sheer pleasure, even using some of her own money. She described herself as a widow, but no one had ever met her husband. She came from who knows where, seemed always to have been fifty and hugely fat, with the reedy voice of a little girl.

On this occasion, as soon as La Méchain was seated on the only chair, the office was full, as if bunged up by the arrival of this last packet of flesh. Busch, imprisoned at his desk, seemed quite buried, with only his square head rising above the sea of files.

'Here,' she said, emptying her old bag of the enormous pile of papers with which it bulged, 'here's what Fayeux sent me from Vendôme... He bought everything for you in that Charpier bankruptcy you asked me to point out to him... One hundred and ten francs.'

Fayeux, whom she called her cousin, had just set up an office there as a collector of revenues.* His ostensible business was receiving the bonds of the small investors of the region; and as the agent for these bonds and money he speculated wildly.

'The provinces are not much use,' muttered Busch, 'but there are still some finds to be made.'

He sniffed at the papers, sorting them already with an expert hand, classifying them roughly at a first estimate, according to their smell. His flat face darkened, and showed disappointment.

'Hmm, not much here, nothing to get one's teeth into. Fortunately, this didn't cost much... Here are some promissory notes... More notes... If these fellows are young, and if they've come to Paris, we may perhaps catch up with them...'

But then, he gave a slight exclamation of surprise.

'Hold on. What's this?'

He had just seen, at the bottom of a sheet of stamped paper,* the signature of the Count de Beauvilliers, and there were only three lines on the page, written in a large, senile hand: 'I undertake to pay the sum of ten thousand francs to Mademoiselle Léonie Cron, upon her coming of age.'

'Count de Beauvilliers,' he repeated slowly, thinking aloud, 'oh yes, he had farms and an entire estate, near Vendôme... He died in a hunting accident, and left a wife and two children in straitened circumstances. I had some promissory notes of his some time ago, which they had some trouble paying... A buffoon, a good-for-nothing...'

Then suddenly he burst into a loud laugh, as he reconstructed the story.

'Ah! the old rogue! He must have got the girl into trouble... she was unwilling, but he must have persuaded her with this scrap of paper, which was of no legal value. Then he died... Let's see, it's dated 1854, just ten years ago. The girl must be of age by now! How did this statement of debt get into Charpier's hands?... A seed-merchant, this Charpier, and a short-term moneylender. The girl no doubt left him this as a deposit for a few écus; or perhaps he had undertaken to collect the debt...'

'But,' La Méchain broke in, 'that's really good, that, a real stroke of luck!'

Busch shrugged his shoulders disdainfully.

'Oh no, let me tell you, this isn't worth anything in law... If I present this to his heirs they can send me packing, because I'd have to prove that the money is actually owing... However, if we find the girl I hope I could persuade them to be generous and come to some agreement, to avoid an unpleasant scandal... You understand? Look for this Léonie Cron, write to Fayeux asking him to dig her out over there. Then we can have some fun.'

He had put the papers into two piles, which he promised himself he'd examine thoroughly once he was alone, and he stayed quite still, with his hands open, one on each pile.

After a silence, La Méchain said:

'I've looked into the Jordan notes... I really thought I'd found our man. He had a job somewhere, and now he's writing for the newspapers. But the newspaper offices are so unhelpful; they refuse to give out addresses. And anyway, I don't think he signs his articles with his real name.'

Without a word, Busch had stretched out his arm to take the Jordan file out of its alphabetical niche. There were six fifty-franc promissory notes, already five years old, and spread out over several months, a total of three hundred francs that the young man had signed to a tailor when he was hard up. Not paid when presented, the notes had accumulated huge charges, and the whole file was overflowing with papers of legal proceedings. At this time the debt had reached seven hundred and thirty francs and fifteen centimes.

'If the lad has any future,' murmured Busch, 'we'll catch him yet.'

Then, doubtless following an association of ideas, he cried out:

'Now tell me, what about the Sicardot affair? Are we giving up on it?'

La Méchain raised her fat arms heavenwards, in a mournful gesture. A shudder of despair shook her whole monstrous person.

'Oh! Dear Lord!' she moaned in her fluting voice, 'it'll be the death of me!'

The Sicardot affair was a quite novelettish story that she loved to tell. A cousin of hers, Rosalie Chavaille, a daughter born late in life to one of her father's sisters, had, one evening when she was sixteen, been taken on a staircase in a house on the Rue de la Harpe, where she and her mother occupied a small lodging on the sixth floor. The worst of it was that the gentleman, a married man who had come with his wife, barely a week before, to a room sub-let by a lady on the second floor, had proved so amorous that poor Rosalie, pushed back too eagerly against the edge of one of the steps, had suffered a dislocated shoulder. Thereupon came justifiable rage from her mother, almost leading to a frightful scene, in spite of the tears of the girl who admitted she had been quite willing, that it was just an accident, and she would be too miserable if the gentleman was sent to prison. At this the mother quietened down and contented herself with demanding from him the sum of six hundred francs, to be paid in twelve notes of hand, at fifty francs a month for a year, and there had been no ugly haggling; indeed the demand was even rather modest, since the daughter, just completing her apprenticeship as a dressmaker, now had no earnings, lying ill in bed, costing a lot, and getting such poor treatment that the muscles in her arm had shrunk, leaving her disabled. Before the end of the first month the gentleman had disappeared, leaving no address. And misfortunes continued, falling thick as hail: Rosalie gave birth to a boy, lost her mother, and fell into a life of wretchedness and dire poverty. Ending up at her cousin's Cité de Naples, she had trailed around the streets until she was twenty-six, sometimes selling lemons at Les Halles, and disappearing for weeks with various men, to return drunk and bruised black and blue. At last, just a year ago, she had had the good fortune to die, as a result of an even more thorough beating than usual. And La Méchain had been left looking after the baby, Victor; all that remained of this adventure were the twelve unpaid notes, signed Sicardot. Nothing more had ever been discovered about him: the gentleman's name was Sicardot.

Reaching out again, Busch took down the Sicardot file, a slim folder of grey paper. No costs had been added, all it contained were the twelve promissory notes.

'If Victor were at least a nice child,' lamented the old woman. 'But honestly, he's simply dreadful... Oh! It's hard getting that sort of inheritance, a kid who'll end up on the scaffold, and these bits of paper I'll never make anything out of!'

Busch kept his big, pale eyes stubbornly fixed on the notes. So many times he had studied them like this, always hoping to find a clue in some overlooked detail, the shape of the letters or the grain of the stamped paper. He maintained that this fine, pointed handwriting could not be quite unknown to him.

'It's curious,' he repeated once more, 'I've certainly seen "a"s and "o"s like these before, so elongated that they look like "i"s.'

Just then there was a knock at the door, and he asked La Méchain to reach out to open it, for the room opened directly on to the stairs. You had to go through this room to reach the other, the one on the street side. As for the kitchen, an airless cubby-hole, it was on the other side of the landing.

'Come in, Monsieur.'

And it was Saccard who came in. He was smiling, inwardly amused by the brass plate screwed on the door, bearing in bold black letters the word: 'Litigation.'

'Ah, yes, Monsieur Saccard, you've come about that translation... My brother is there, in the next room... Come in, come in.'

But La Méchain was absolutely blocking the way, and she was staring at the newcomer, looking more and more surprised. It took quite a lot of manoeuvring; he backed out into the staircase, then she went out, squeezing past him on the landing, so that he could go in and at last get to the next room, into which he disappeared. During all these complicated manoeuvres she never once took her eyes off him.

'Oh!' she gasped, as if overcome, 'this Monsieur Saccard, I had never seen much of him before... Victor is the spitting image of him.'

Busch, not understanding at once, was gazing at her. Then, with a sudden illumination, he let out a strangled oath.

'Hell-fire! That's it, I knew I'd seen that somewhere before.'

This time he stood up and ransacked the files, at last finding a letter Saccard had written to him the year before, asking for more time on behalf of some bankrupt lady. He hastily compared the writing on the notes to that on the letter: the 'a's and the 'o's were indeed the same, having with time become even more pointed; and the capital letters too were identical.

'It's him, it's him...', he kept saying. 'Only, after all, why Sicardot, why not Saccard?'

But a vague story was now stirring in his memory, he had been told of Saccard's past by a business agent called Larsonneau, now a millionaire: Saccard turning up in Paris on the morrow of the *coup d'état* to take advantage of the growing power of his brother Rougon, and at first wretched poverty in the dark streets of the old Latin Quarter, then a rapid rise to fortune thanks to a somewhat shady marriage, after he'd had the good luck to lose his first wife.* It was during these difficult beginnings that he had changed his name of Rougon to that of Saccard, simply altering the name of the first wife, who was called Sicardot.

'Yes, yes, Sicardot, I remember now,' Busch murmured. 'He had the gall to use his wife's name to sign the notes. The couple had no doubt used that name when they arrived in the Rue de la Harpe. The rotter must have been taking every precaution, ready to move out at the first sign of danger... Oh! he wasn't only after money, he was also into tumbling young girls on the stairs! That's stupid. That'll catch him out one of these days.'

'Hush, hush!' said La Méchain. 'We've got him, that just shows there is a God. I shall at last be rewarded for all I've done for that poor little Victor. I do love him after all, even if there's no way of civilizing him.'

She was beaming, her narrow eyes sparkling in the greasy fat of her face.

But Busch, after the sudden excitement of the long-sought solution that chance had suddenly brought him, had cooled down on reflection and was shaking his head. Even if Saccard was ruined just now, he was still worth fleecing. There were less profitable fathers in the world. Only this one wouldn't stand for any hassling, he could turn savage. And then what? He certainly didn't even know he had a son, he could deny everything, in spite of the extraordinary resemblance that so amazed La Méchain. Besides, he was a widower for the second time, a free man, not having to account for his past to anyone, so even if he were to accept the boy there would be no fear or threat to hold over him. As for getting out of his paternity only the six hundred francs of the promissory notes, that would really be too wretched; hardly worth being given such a miraculous stroke of luck. No, no, he needed to think, to let it mature, and find a way to gather the harvest when it was fully ripe.

'Let's not be hasty,' Busch concluded. 'Besides, he's right down now, let's give him time to get himself up again.'

And before dismissing La Méchain he finished going over with her some petty matters that she was dealing with, a young woman who had pawned her jewels for a lover; a son-in-law whose debt would be paid by his mother-in-law, who was his mistress, if they played their cards right; in short, the most delicate varieties of the so complex and difficult business of collecting bad debts.

Saccard, entering the adjoining room, stood dazzled for a moment by the bright light from the uncurtained, sunlit window. This room, with its light wallpaper patterned with little blue flowers, was bare: just a small iron bed in one corner, a pine table in the middle, and two straw-bottomed chairs. Along the left-hand wall some planks, hardly even planed, served as bookshelves, loaded with books, pamphlets, newspapers, papers of all sorts. But the light flooding from the sky on this top floor gave the bareness of the room a sort of youthful gaiety, like the sound of fresh and innocent laughter. And Busch's brother, Sigismond, a fellow of thirty-five, clean-shaven with long and sparse brown hair, was sitting at the table with his broad, domed brow held in his bony hand, so absorbed by the manuscript he was reading that he didn't even turn his head, not having heard the door opening.

He was an intelligent man, this Sigismond, educated in the German universities and speaking German, English, and Russian, as well as his native French. In 1849, in Cologne, he had met Karl Marx, and had become the most appreciated contributor to his *New Rhenish Gazette*,* and from that moment on his religion had been fixed, he embraced socialism with an ardent faith, giving himself body and soul to the idea of the coming social reforms which would assure the happiness of the poor and humble. Ever since his master, banished from Germany and forced, after the June Days,* to leave Paris, had settled in London, writing and trying to organize the Party, he, for his part, had been vegetating, lost in his dreams, so careless of his material existence that he would surely have died of hunger if his brother had not taken him in on the Rue Feydeau, near the Bourse, and given him the idea of using his knowledge of languages to set himself up as a translator. The elder brother adored his young sibling with a maternal passion, a ferocious wolf with debtors, capable of spilling a man's blood to steal ten sous, yet immediately moved to tears, full of the devoted and passionate tenderness of a woman, where this tall and absent-minded fellow was concerned, this boy who had never grown up. He had given him the good room overlooking the street, and tended him like a servant, running their strange household, sweeping, making the beds, getting the food delivered twice a day from a little restaurant nearby. He, so active, his head crammed with a thousand business matters, tolerated idleness in his brother, for the translation business, always hindered by his personal work, was not going well; he would even forbid him to work, worried by his nasty little cough; and in spite of his steely love of money, and the murderous greed which made the acquisition of money his sole reason for living, he would smile indulgently at the theories of this revolutionary and hand over his money, as one hands a toy to a child, knowing it may get broken.

Sigismond, for his part, had no idea what his brother did in the next room. He knew nothing of that dreadful trading in depreciated stock and buying up of debts, he lived on a higher plane, in a sovereign dream of justice. The idea of charity wounded him, made him terribly angry; charity was alms-giving, it was inequality consecrated by kindness; he accepted only justice, the rights of the individual reasserted and laid down as immutable principles in the new social order. So, like Karl Marx, with whom he was constantly in correspondence, he would spend his days studying this organization, modifying, ceaselessly improving on paper the society of tomorrow, covering page after page with figures, finding a base in science for the complicated framework of universal happiness.* He took away capital from some to share it out among others, and with one stroke of his pen he moved billions, rearranging the wealth of the world; and all in this bare room, with no other passion than his dream, with no need for any enjoyment, and of such frugality that his brother had to scold him to make him drink wine and eat meat. What he wanted was that each man's work, measured according to his strength, should be sufficient to satisfy his appetites: while he, for his own part, was killing himself with work and living on nothing. A real sage, impassioned about his studies, detached from material existence, very gentle and very pure. Ever since the previous autumn he had been coughing more and more, as the consumption spread through him, without his even deigning to notice and take care of himself.

But at a movement from Saccard, Sigismond at last looked up with his big, vague eyes, and expressed surprise, although he knew the visitor.

'I've come about a letter to translate.'

The young man was even more surprised, for he had been discouraging clients, the bankers, speculators, and currency dealers, all those Bourse people who receive, especially from England and Germany, a great deal of correspondence, circulars, and company statutes.

'Yes, a letter in Russian. Oh! only ten lines.'

At this Sigismond held out his hand, for Russian had remained his speciality; he alone, among the other translators of the neighbourhood who made their living on English and German, translated it fluently. The rarity of Russian documents in the Paris market explained his long periods of unemployment.

He read the letter aloud, in French. It was a favourable response, in three sentences, from a banker in Constantinople, a simple 'Yes' to a deal.

'Ah, thank you,' exclaimed Saccard, who seemed delighted.

And he asked Sigismond to write the few lines of the translation on the back of the letter. But Sigismond was seized by a terrible fit of coughing that he tried to smother in his handkerchief so as not to disturb his brother, who would come running as soon as he heard him coughing like that. When the spasm was over he got up and went to the window, throwing it wide open, suffocating, needing air. Saccard, who had followed him, glanced outside and gave a slight gasp.

'Oh, you can see the Bourse! My! How funny it looks from here.'

Indeed he had never before seen it from such a strange angle, a bird's-eye-view, with the four huge zinc slopes of the roof exposed in amazing detail, bristling with a forest of pipes. The points of the lightning-conductors stood up like giant lances, threatening the sky. And the great building itself was now no more than a cube of stone, striped by rows of columns, a dirty, grey cube, bare and ugly, with a ragged flag on top. But what astonished him most was the steps and the peristyle, dotted with black ants, a whole anthill in turmoil, rest-lessly moving, creating a huge disturbance that from up here seemed incomprehensible, and even pitiable.

'How small it all looks!' he continued. 'As if one could grab them all up in one handful!'

Then, being familiar with the ideas of his companion, he added with a laugh:

'When are you going to get rid of all that, with one swift kick?'

Sigismond shrugged.

'What's the point? You're already doing the demolishing yourselves.'

And bit by bit he grew animated, overflowing with the subject he was so full of. A proselytizing urge launched him, at the slightest excuse, into an exposition of his system.

'Yes indeed, you're working for us without realizing it... There you are, a few usurpers, dispossessing the masses, and once you are gorged we, in turn, will only have to dispossess you... Every kind of monopolizing, every centralization, leads to collectivism. You are giving us a practical lesson: in the same way that big estates swallow up small plots of land, big manufacturers devour cottage industry and large banks and big stores kill off all competition, growing fat on the ruin of small banks and little shops—they are all, in fact, slowly but surely moving towards the new social order... We are waiting for it all to break down, waiting for the current mode of production to end in the intolerable disorder of its final consequences. Then the bourgeois and the peasants themselves will help us.'

Intrigued, Saccard gazed at him with a vague disquiet, although he thought him quite mad.

'Well all right, tell me about it, what is this collectivism of yours?'

'Collectivism is the transformation of private capital, living by the strife of competition, into a unitary social capital, created by the work of all... Imagine a society in which the instruments of production are the property of all, in which everyone works according to his intelligence and strength and the products of this social co-operation are distributed to each and all, in proportion to their effort. Surely nothing could be simpler? Communal production in the factories, yards, and workshops of the nation; then an exchange, a payment in kind. If there is a surplus of production it's placed in public warehouses, from where it can be recovered to make good any shortages that may occur. It's a matter of striking a balance... And all this, like the stroke of an axe, fells the rotten tree. No more competition, no more private capital, so no more business of any kind, no commerce, no markets, no stock exchanges. The idea of profit no longer has any meaning. The sources of speculation, unearned incomes, simply are no more.'

'Oh! Oh!' Saccard interrupted, 'that would make a terrific change in the way of life of a lot of people! But what about those who live on private incomes now? Gundermann, for instance, would you take away his billion?'

'Not at all; we are not thieves. We would buy back his billion, his shares, his income bonds, with a set of vouchers divided into annuities. And just imagine that immense capital replaced in this way by a suffocating wealth of consumer vouchers: in less than a hundred years the descendants of that Gundermann of yours would be reduced to personal labour, like all the other citizens, for the annuities would eventually run out and they would not have been able to turn their forced savings, the excess of that crushing surplus of provisions, into capital, even if the right of inheritance were retained... I tell you, this sweeps away at a stroke not only individual businesses, companies of shareholders, and associations of private capital but all the indirect sources of income, all the credit systems, loans, rents, and tenant farming... There would no longer be any measure of value other than labour. Wages are of course abolished, for in the present capitalist system they are not equivalent to the actual product of labour, since they never represent anything more than what is strictly necessary for the worker's daily livelihood. And it must be admitted that it's the present system that is alone to blame, for even the most honest employer has to follow the harsh law of competition and exploit his workers if he wants to make a living. Our whole social system has to be destroyed... Oh! Gundermann choking under the weight of his vouchers! And Gundermann's heirs not managing to use it all up, forced to give to others and take up the pickaxe or the workman's tools, just like their comrades!'

And Sigismond burst out laughing, like a child in a playground, but still standing at the window with his eyes on the Bourse, where the black ant-hill of speculation still swarmed. Burning patches of red appeared on his cheeks; imagining the amusing ironies of the justice of the future was his one entertainment.

Saccard had grown more and more uneasy. What if this dreamer was right after all? What if he had correctly divined the future? He explained things in a way that seemed very clear and sensible.

'Bah!' he muttered to reassure himself. 'All this is not going to happen next year!'

'Of course not,' the young man went on, once more solemn and weary. 'We're in the time of transition, the time of agitation. Perhaps there will be some outbreaks of revolutionary violence, they are often inevitable. But the excesses and outbursts are temporary... Oh, I don't try to disguise the immediate difficulties. All that dreamed-of future seems impossible, it's hard to give people a reasonable idea of that future society, that society of fair labour whose way of life will be so different from ours. It's like another world on another planet... And it has to be admitted: reorganization isn't ready yet, we're still finding our way. I, who hardly sleep any more, spend my nights on it. For instance, we can certainly be told: "If things are as they are, it's because the logic of human activity has made them so." So what a task it is, to take the river back to its source and direct it into another valley!... Certainly, the present state of society has owed its prosperity over the centuries to the individualist principle, which through emulation and personal interest becomes an endlessly renewed source of fertile production. Will collectivism ever reach that level of fecundity, and how are we to activate the productive function of the worker once the idea of earnings has been destroyed? This, for me, is where the doubt and anguish lie, the weak ground on which we must fight if we want the victory of socialism to be won on it one day... But we will overcome, for we are justice itself. Look! You see that monument before you... Do you see it?'

'The Bourse?' Saccard answered. 'Lord, yes, I can see it!'

'Well, it would be stupid to blow it up, it would simply get rebuilt elsewhere. But I predict that it will blow itself up, once the state has taken it over and become, in consequence, the sole and universal bank of the nation. And who knows? It may then serve as a public warehouse for our excess of wealth, one of those granaries of abundance in which our grandchildren will find the luxuries for their feast-days.'

With an expansive gesture, Sigismond seemed to open up this future of general and widespread happiness. And he was so carried away that a new fit of coughing shook his frame as he returned to his table, with his elbows among the papers and holding his head in his hands to smother the hacking rattle of his throat. But this time it would not calm down. Suddenly the door opened and Busch, having sent away La Méchain, ran in looking distraught, as if he himself was suffering that abominable coughing. He at once leaned over and took his brother in his broad arms, as if rocking an unhappy child.

'Come on, my dear, what is making you choke like this? You know I want you to call a doctor. This is just not sensible... you must have been talking too much, for sure.'

And he cast a sidelong glance at Saccard, still standing in the middle of the room, decidedly disturbed by what he had just heard from the mouth of this tall fellow, so passionate and so ill, who from his window up here must be casting a spell over the Bourse with his notions of sweeping everything away and rebuilding.

'Thanks, I'll leave you now,' said the visitor, eager to be outside. Send me my letter, with the ten lines of translation... I'm expecting some more, so we'll settle the whole lot together.'

But, now the crisis was over, Busch kept him back a moment or two more.

'By the way, the lady who was here just now had met you before, oh! a long time ago.'

'Ah! Where was that?'

'Rue de la Harpe, in '52.'

Self-controlled as he was, Saccard nevertheless lost colour. A nervous tic twitched at his mouth. It wasn't that he remembered at that instant the girl he'd tumbled on the staircase: he hadn't known about her pregnancy, and did not know there was a child. But the memory of those first wretched years was always very disagreeable.

'Rue de la Harpe. Oh, I only stayed there about a week when I first arrived in Paris, while I looked for somewhere to live… Au revoir!'

'Au revoir!' Busch pointedly repeated, mistakenly seeing Saccard's embarrassment as an admission of guilt, and already thinking about how best to exploit this affair.

Down in the street again Saccard went back automatically towards the Place de la Bourse. He was quite shivery, he did not even look at little Madame Conin, whose pretty blonde face was smiling from the stationer's door. In the square the commotion had increased, the clamour of trading was beating down on pavements teeming with people with the unfettered violence of a high tide. It was the quarter-to-three shouting-match, the battle of the last calls, the frenzy to find out who would emerge with full pockets. And standing at the corner of the Rue de la Bourse, opposite the peristyle, he thought he saw, in the confused jostling under the columns, the bear-trader Moser and the bull trader Pillerault, both doing battle, and fancied he could hear, emerging from the main hall, the shrill voice of the broker Mazaud, occasionally smothered by great bursts from Nathansohn, who was sitting under the clock in the kerb market. But a carriage going by, on the edge of the gutter, almost splattered him. Massias leaped from it even before the coachman had reined in, and ran up the steps in one bound, breathlessly carrying some client's last order.

And Saccard, still standing motionless, gazing at the milling crowd up there, was mulling over his life, haunted by the memory of his beginnings reawakened by Busch's question. He recalled the Rue de la Harpe, then the Rue Saint-Jacques, to which he had dragged his down-at-heel conquering-hero boots when newly arrived in Paris and determined to master it; and fury once more seized hold of him at the thought that he had not yet conquered, that he was once again out on the streets, seeking his fortune, unsatisfied, and tormented by a hunger for gratification such as he had never before experienced so painfully. That madman Sigismond spoke truly: work cannot make a life, the wretched and the stupid labour only to make others grow fat. There was only speculation, speculation which, from one day to the next, could at a stroke give well-being, luxury, an expansive life, life whole and entire. If this old social world had to crumble away one day, wouldn't a man like him still manage to find the time and place to satisfy his desires before the collapse?

But a passer-by jostled him and didn't even turn round to apologize. He saw it was Gundermann, taking his little daily constitutional; he watched him go into a sweetshop from which this king of gold frequently bought a one-franc box of sweets for his granddaughters. And that jostling, at that moment, in the fever that had been mounting in him since he started his circling of the Bourse, was like a whiplash, the final decisive thrust. He had finished his siege of the square, he would attack. It was a vow of merciless struggle: he would not leave France, he would defy his brother, he would risk everything in a battle of terrible audacity, which would either lay Paris at his feet or throw him broken into the gutter.

Until the market closed Saccard stayed resolutely at his post of observation and menacing intent. He watched the peristyle emptying and the steps filling with the slow disbanding of all these excited, weary people. Around him the roadway and the pavements were still crowded with an uninterrupted flow of people, the eternal crowd, ready to be exploited, the shareholders of tomorrow, who could not go past this great lottery of speculation without turning their heads, impelled by desire and fear of what went on in there, the mystery of financial transactions, a mystery all the more attractive to French brains since so few of them ever penetrate it.

CHAPTER II

AFTER Saccard's last disastrous land-deal, when he had to leave his palace in the Parc Monceau, abandoning it to his creditors to avoid an even greater catastrophe, his first idea had been to take refuge with his son Maxime. Maxime, since the death of his wife, who now lay in a little cemetery in Lombardy,* had been living on his own in a mansion on the Avenue de l'Impératrice,* where he had organized his life with a careful and ferocious egoism; as a young man prematurely aged by vice, he was impeccably eating up the fortune of his dead wife, and firmly refused to take his father in, explaining, with an air of sweet reasonableness, that this was so that they could go on living in harmony.

After that Saccard thought of another refuge. He would rent a little house in Passy, a bourgeois retreat for retired businessmen, then he remembered that the ground floor and first floor of the Orviedo mansion on the Rue Saint-Lazare were still lying empty, their doors and windows shuttered. The Princess d'Orviedo had been living in three rooms on the second floor since the death of her husband, and she had not even had a sign put up at the carriage entrance, now overgrown with weeds. A low door at the other end of the front of the building led to the second floor by a servants' staircase. Saccard had frequently been in touch with the Princess over business matters, and had been astonished, on his visits to her, at her failure to try and make some profit out of her building. But she would just shake her head; she had her own ideas on money matters. However, when he suggested himself as a tenant she agreed at once, granting him, for a derisory rent of ten thousand francs, the use of the sumptuous ground floor and first floor, a princely accommodation worth at least double.

People had not forgotten the lavish splendour of the Prince. It was in the feverish excitement of his immense financial fortune, when he first came to Paris from Spain, arriving in a shower of millions, that he had bought this mansion and had it restored, pending the day when he could astonish people with the palace of marble and gold he had in mind. The building dated from the previous century, one of those *maisons de plaisance** built in the middle of vast gardens by philandering lords, but it had been partly demolished, then rebuilt in more severe proportions. Of its former park it had kept only a large courtyard surrounded by stables and outbuildings, all of which would surely be carried away by the planned Rue du Cardinal Fesch.* The prince had acquired it as part of the estate of a spinster lady of the Saint-Germain family: her property had once extended right up to the Rue des Trois Frères, the former continuation of the Rue Taitbout. Indeed, the mansion still had its entrance on the Rue Saint-Lazare, right beside a large building of the same era, the Folie-Beauvilliers as it was known, where the Beauvilliers still lived after a period of gradual ruin; and they still owned what was left of an admirable garden, with magnificent trees which were also doomed to disappear in the impending upheaval of the neighbourhood.

In the midst of his disaster Saccard had still dragged along with him a trail of servants, the debris of his over-numerous staff, a valet, a chef, and his wife who looked after the clothes, another woman who was still there for no obvious reason, a coachman and two grooms; and he filled up the stables and the outbuildings, putting in two horses and three carriages, and setting up a refectory for his staff on the ground floor. This man, with less than five hundred solid francs in his coffers, was living at the rate of two or three hundred thousand francs a year. He even managed, on his own, to occupy the vast apartments of the first floor, the three drawing-rooms and five bedrooms, not to mention the enormous dining-room with a table seating fifty. Here, at one time, there had been a door opening on to an internal staircase leading to the second floor, and another, smaller dining-room; and as the Princess had recently let that part of the second floor to an engineer, a Monsieur Hamelin, a bachelor who lived with his sister, she had simply had the door sealed off, fastened with two strong screws. She thus shared the old servants' stairs with this tenant, while Saccard had sole use of the grand staircase. He partly furnished a few rooms with what was left from the Parc Monceau, and left the others empty, but somehow managed to give some life to this long succession of dull bare walls, from which some determined hand seemed, after the death of the Prince, to have torn away even the slightest scraps of covering. And here Saccard was able to start once more his dream of a great fortune.

Princess d'Orviedo was at that time one of the oddities of Paris. Fifteen years ago she had resigned herself to marrying the Prince, whom she did not love, in obedience to the formal command of her mother, the Duchess de Combeville. At the time, this young woman of twenty was renowned for both beauty and good conduct, being deeply religious and a shade too serious, though she adored the social world. She knew nothing of the strange stories circulating about the Prince and the origins of his kingly fortune, estimated at three hundred millions, derived from a lifetime of fearsome robbery, carried out not as an armed man in some remote spot, like the noble adventurers of old, but as a well-dressed modern bandit in the bright sunshine of the Bourse, stealing from the pockets of poor credulous folk, bringing them ruin and death. For twenty years, back in Spain and here in France, the Prince had played the major role in all the great swindles that had become the stuff of legend. Although knowing nothing of the mire and blood in which he had amassed such millions, she had, from their very first meeting, felt a repugnance for him that even her religion had failed to overcome; and soon to that antipathy had been added a dull and growing resentment at having no child from this marriage, to which she had submitted out of obedience. Motherhood would have been enough for her, for she adored children, but she began to hate this man who, after destroying all hope of love, could not even satisfy her maternal longings. It was then that the Princess was seen to throw herself into unheard-of luxury, dazzling Paris with the brilliance of her parties, living in a style of such splendour that it was said to be the envy of the Tuileries.* Then suddenly, the day after the Prince died, struck down by apoplexy, the mansion in the Rue Saint-Lazare had fallen into absolute silence and total darkness. Not a light, not a sound; doors and windows remained closed; and it was rumoured that the Princess, after violently clearing the ground floor and the first floor, had withdrawn like a recluse to three small rooms on the second floor with old Sophie, a former maid of her mother's, who had brought her up. When she reappeared she was dressed in a simple black wool dress, with a lace scarf over her hair, still small and plump, with her narrow brow, her pretty, round face and pearly teeth between her pursed lips, but already with the yellowish complexion and the impassive, single-minded face of a long-cloistered nun. She had then just turned thirty, and ever since she had lived solely for huge charitable works.

Great was the surprise in Paris, and all sorts of extraordinary stories went around. The Princess had inherited the whole fortune, the famous three hundred million to which entire columns were devoted in the press. And the tale that finally got established was quite romantic. A man, a stranger dressed in black, so the story went, had suddenly appeared in the Princess's bedroom just as she was preparing for bed, without her ever fathoming by what secret door he had been able to get in; and what this man had told her no one in the world knew; but he must have revealed to her the abominable origins of the three hundred million, perhaps demanding that she swear to make reparation for so much iniquity if she wanted to avoid terrible catastrophes. Then the man had disappeared. Was it then, for the five years since her widowhood, a response to an order from the hereafter, or was it rather the straightforward revolt of her honesty once she had seen the records of her fortune? The truth was that she now lived only in an ardent fever of renunciation and reparation. In this woman who had never been a lover and had been unable to be a mother, all her repressed tenderness, and especially her thwarted love of children, blossomed into a real passion for the poor, the weak, the disinherited, the suffering, all those from whom she felt her millions had been stolen and whom she swore to repay royally, showering them with alms. Ever since, she had been possessed by one idea; obsession had hammered its way into her brain: she thought of herself now only as a banker with whom the poor had deposited the three hundred millions so that they could be put to the best use; she was just an accountant, a business agent living among lists of figures, surrounded by a population of solicitors, workmen and architects. Outside, she had set up a vast office with twenty or so employees. In her own quarters, in her three small rooms, she received only four or five intermediaries, her lieutenants; and she spent her days there at her desk, like the director of a great company, cloistered far from intruders, in an overflowing heap of papers. Her dream was to relieve every misery, from the child who suffers in being born, to the old man who cannot die without suffering. During these five years, scattering her gold in great handfuls, she had founded the Sainte-Marie Children's Hospital at La Villette, with white cradles for the littlest and blue beds for the older ones, a vast establishment full of light, already holding three hundred children; then the Saint-Joseph Orphanage at Saint-Mandé, where a hundred boys and a hundred girls were receiving the sort of education and instruction that bourgeois families would provide for their children; and in addition, a home for old people at Châtillon,* housing fifty men and fifty women, and a hospital of two hundred beds in one of the suburbs, the Saint-Marceau Hospital, which had only just been opened. But her favourite project, the one that just now engaged her whole heart, was the Work Foundation,* her own creation, an institution that was to replace the House of Correction. In the Work Foundation three hundred children, one hundred and fifty boys and one hundred and fifty girls, gathered up from the streets of Paris, from lives of debauchery and crime, were being given a new life through proper care and apprenticeship to a trade. These diverse foundations, her substantial donations, and her wild prodigality in giving to charity had consumed almost a hundred million in five years. A few more years of this and she would be ruined, without even having kept in reserve the small income needed for the bread and milk on which she now lived. When Sophie, her old servant, broke her usual silence to scold her sternly, warning her she would die destitute, she would just give a faint smile, the only smile that ever appeared now upon her colourless lips, a divine smile of hope.

It was in fact on the occasion of the setting up of the Work Foundation that Saccard first became acquainted with the Princess. He was one of the owners of the land she bought for this foundation, an ancient garden planted with fine trees, which lay at the edge of the Parc de Neuilly and ran alongside the Boulevard Bineau. He had charmed her by his brisk way of doing business, and she decided to see him again when faced by some difficulties with her contractors. For his part he had become interested in these works, which had captured his imagination, and he was delighted by the grandeur of the plan she had imposed on the architect: two monumental wings, one for the boys and the other for the girls, the two linked by a central building containing the chapel, communal area, administrative offices, and all the service departments; each wing had its own huge courtyard, its workshops and outbuildings of all sorts. But what most roused Saccard's passion, given his own taste for the grand and sumptuous, was the opulence of it all, this huge construction built with materials that would last for centuries, a lavish use of marble, a tiled kitchen large enough to roast an ox, immense dining-halls with rich oak panelling, dormitories flooded with light and brightly painted in light colours, a laundry, a bathroom, an infirmary, all done up with excessive refinements; and everywhere vast open areas, stairs and corridors, airy in summer and heated in winter; and the entire house bathed in sunshine, with a youthful gaiety, all the comforts of a huge fortune. When the architect, concerned about all this useless magnificence, tried to speak of the expense, the Princess would stop him with one word: she had enjoyed luxury and she wanted to give it to the poor so that they, they who create the luxury of the rich, could in their turn enjoy it. This dream was her obsession: to give joy to the wretched, to let them sleep in beds and sit at the table of the fortunate of this world; no longer receiving the charity of a crust of bread or a makeshift pallet, but an expansive life in palaces that would be their home, where they would have their revenge, and taste the pleasures of those who always triumph. But in all this wasteful spending, with enormous estimates on all sides, she was being abominably robbed; a swarm of contractors were living off her, not to mention losses due to poor supervision; the wealth of the poor was being squandered. It was Saccard who opened her eyes, begging her to let him put her accounts in order, and this was completely disinterested, for it was the sole pleasure of regulating this crazy dance of millions that so excited him. Never had Saccard shown such scrupulous honesty. In this colossal and complicated affair he was the most active, the most trustworthy of collaborators, giving his time and even his money, finding his reward simply in the joy of having such considerable sums passing through his hands. He was the one who was known at the Work Foundation, for the Princess never went there, any more than she ever visited any of her other foundations, staying hidden away in her three little rooms like some benevolent, invisible goddess; while he was adored and blessed, loaded with all the gratitude that she seemed not to want.

Ever since, Saccard had no doubt been nurturing a vague plan, and this, once he was installed as a tenant in the Orviedo mansion, took on the sharp clarity of a desire. Why shouldn't he devote himself entirely to administering the charitable works of the Princess? In this period of doubt and uncertainty, defeated in the world of speculation and not knowing what kind of fortune he could rebuild, this seemed to him like a new incarnation, a sudden soaring apotheosis: becoming the dispenser of this royal charity, channelling this flow of gold pouring over Paris. There were still two hundred millions left; what great new works could yet be created, what miracle city could be brought forth from the ground? Besides, he would be able to make those millions bear fruit, he could double, even triple them, would use them so well that he would create a whole world out of them. Then, with his usual

passion, it all grew bigger and bigger, and he now lived for the intoxicating idea of spreading those millions in endless charities, pouring
them out over a joyful France; and he grew sentimental, for he was
scrupulously honest and not a penny of it stuck to his fingers. In the
head of this visionary, it was a gigantic idyll, the idyll of an unreflect-
ing man free of any wish to redeem his former financial piracy. All the
more so in that this, after all, was his life-long dream, the conquest of
Paris. To be the king of charity, the god adored by the masses of the
poor, to become unique and popular, to make the world take notice of
him—this even went beyond his ambitions. What prodigies could he
not achieve if he were to employ in being good all his businessman's
talents, his cunning, his determination, his total lack of prejudice!
And he would have that irresistible power that wins battles—money,
coffers full of money, money that often does so much harm, but
would do so much good if all one's pleasure and pride lay in the act
of giving.

Then, in a further enlargement of his plan, Saccard even started to
wonder whether he might marry the Princess d'Orviedo. That would
stabilize their position and put an end to undesirable interpretations.
For a whole month he manoeuvred skilfully, presented superb plans,
and felt he had made himself indispensable; then one day, very
calmly, quite ingenuous once more, he made his suggestion and outlined his great plan. It was a genuine partnership he was offering, he
would become the liquidator of the money stolen by the Prince, and
he promised to return it, tenfold, to the poor. The Princess meanwhile, in her everlasting black dress with her lace scarf on her head,
listened attentively, with no trace of emotion on her yellowish face.
She was very struck by the advantages that might derive from such a
partnership, and quite indifferent to any other considerations it might
involve. She put off her reply to the next day, and in the end refused;
she had no doubt reflected that she would no longer be sole mistress
of her charities, and she meant to have sovereign and absolute power
to dispense them just as she wished, even foolishly. However, she
explained that she would be happy to keep him as her adviser, and
showed how precious his collaboration seemed to her by asking him
to continue to look after the Work Foundation, of which he was in
fact the real director.

For a whole week Saccard was extremely distressed, as at the loss
of a cherished idea; not that he felt himself sinking back into the abyss

of brigandage, but just as a sentimental song will bring tears to the eyes of even the most abject drunkard, the colossal idyll of the good to be done with millions and millions had really touched his old pirate's soul. Here he was, falling down again, and from a great height, as if dethroned. Through money he had always wanted not just to satisfy his appetites but to have all the magnificence of a princely life; and never had he achieved it, never reached high enough. He grew more and more angry as each new fall carried away yet another hope. So when his plans collapsed in the face of the Princess's calm and clear refusal, he found himself cast back into a furious longing for battle. To fight, to win in the hard battle of speculation, to devour others before they could devour you—this, after his thirst for splendour and enjoyment, this was the driving force, the sole cause of his passion for business. He was not a hoarder, his joy lay elsewhere, in the battle of the big numbers, fortunes deployed like battalions, the clash of opposing millions, the defeats and victories, this was what intoxicated him. And all at once his hatred for Gundermann rose again to the surface, along with his fevered need for revenge: to bring down Gundermann, that wild desire possessed him whenever he found himself brought low and defeated. Even if he recognized the childishness of such an enterprise, couldn't he at least damage him a little, make a place for himself, facing the man and forcing him to a sharing of power, like those monarchs of neighbouring countries of equal might who treat each other as cousins? It was then that he was again attracted by the Bourse, his head full of new business ventures, pulled in every direction by contradictory plans, in such a fever that he didn't know what to decide on until the day when one supreme, wildly extravagant idea detached itself from the rest and gradually took possession of him.

While living at the Orviedo mansion Saccard from time to time saw the sister of Hamelin, the engineer who lived in the little apartment on the second floor, a splendid figure of a woman, Madame Caroline as she was familiarly known. What had struck him above all at their first encounter was her superb white hair, a royal crown of white hair which created such a curious effect on the brow of this still young woman, barely more than thirty-six at most. It had gone completely white when she was only twenty-five. Her eyebrows, which had remained black and quite thick, kept their youthfulness, and gave a lively oddity to her ermine-framed face. She had never been pretty,

with too strong a chin and nose and a wide mouth with full lips that
seemed to express an exquisite kindness. But certainly that white fleece,
that fly-away whiteness of fine silky hair, softened her otherwise
slightly hard features and gave her the smiling charm of a grand-
mother, along with the freshness and strength as of a beautiful woman
in love. She was tall and solidly built, and she walked with naturalness
and nobility.

Every time he saw her, Saccard, who was shorter than she was,
followed her with his eyes with some interest, and secret envy of that
tall, broad-shouldered figure. And gradually, through the servants,
he got to know the whole history of the Hamelins. They were,
Caroline and Georges, the children of a Montpellier doctor, a notable
scholar and fervent Catholic who had died leaving nothing. When the
father passed away, the daughter was eighteen and the son nineteen;
and as the latter had just started at the École Polytechnique* his sister
followed him to Paris, where she found a post as a teacher. It was she
who slipped him the odd hundred-sou coin, and kept him in pocket-
money over the two years of his course. Later, when he graduated
with a rather poor degree, he had a hard time of it looking for work
and it was his sister, once more, who kept him going until he found a
job. These two children adored each other, and it was their dream to
stay together always. However, when an unexpected marriage presented itself, the grace and lively intelligence of the young woman
having conquered a millionaire brewer in the house where she was
working, Georges urged her to accept, advice he cruelly regretted
when, after a few years of marriage, Caroline had to demand a separ-
ation to avoid being killed by her husband, who drank, and chased
her with a knife during fits of imbecile jealousy. She was then twenty-
six and poor once more, since she had obstinately refused to ask for
any allowance from the man she was leaving. By then her brother,
after many attempts, had at last found a post that suited him; he was
going to leave for Egypt, with the Commission set up to make the
first studies for the Suez Canal, and he took his sister with him. She
bravely settled in Alexandria and started giving lessons again, while
he travelled around the country. In this way they remained in Egypt
until 1859 and witnessed the first strokes of the pickaxe on the beach
of Port Said:* a meagre crew of barely a hundred and fifty navvies,
lost amid the sands, with a handful of engineers in command. Then
Hamelin was sent to Syria to ensure the supply of provisions, and

remained there after a quarrel with his bosses. He sent for Caroline to come to Beirut, where she found further pupils while he launched himself into a huge project, under the aegis of a French company, laying out the route for a carriageable road from Beirut to Damascus, the first, indeed the only road through the gorges of the Lebanon range;* there they lived for three more years until the road was finished, while he made trips into the mountains and spent two months away in Constantinople, across the Taurus range,* while she would follow as soon as she could get away, embracing the plans of reawakening that her brother was making as he tramped around this ancient land slumbering beneath the ashes of dead civilizations. He had gathered together a whole portfolio overflowing with ideas and plans, and now felt an urgent need to return to France if he was going to put some flesh on his vast collection of undertakings, forming companies and finding capital. And after a stay of nine years in the East, they left, and curiosity led them to return through Egypt, where the work on the Suez Canal filled them with enthusiasm: in four years a town had sprung up in the sands of the beach of Port Said, an entire population was busily at work, the human ants had multiplied and were changing the face of the earth. But back in Paris some serious ill-fortune awaited Hamelin. For fifteen months he had been struggling with his projects, unable to communicate his confidence to anyone, being too modest and not much of a talker, and so ending up in this second floor of the Orviedo mansion, in a little five-room apartment rented for twelve hundred francs, even further from success than when he was roaming the mountains and plains of Asia. The savings of brother and sister were rapidly dwindling, and they were beginning to face real hardship.

It was this, in fact, that captured Saccard's attention, the increasing sadness of Madame Caroline, her lovely gaiety darkened by the discouragement she saw settling over her brother. It was she who seemed to be the man of the house. Physically Georges was very like her, but in a frailer version and with exceptional faculties for study; but he was absorbed in his books, and there was no getting him out of them. He had never wished to marry, feeling no need for that—just adoring his sister was enough for him. He probably had occasional mistresses, though nobody knew them. This former researcher of the École Polytechnique, with such vast ideas, such ardent zeal in everything he undertook, sometimes displayed such naivety that he might have been thought stupid. Brought up in the strictest Catholic faith, he had retained the religious beliefs of a child and practised his faith with great conviction, while his sister had revised her views through her immense reading and all the vast learning she had acquired while her brother was deep in his technical works. She spoke four languages and had read the economists and philosophers, quite carried away for a while by socialist and evolutionist theories; but she had steadied herself; and thanks especially to her travels and her long sojourns among distant civilizations, she had acquired great tolerance and a fine and balanced common sense. Although no longer a believer herself, she retained respect for her brother's faith. They had had the matter out between them, and after that never mentioned it again. In her simplicity and kindliness she was a woman of real intelligence; with an extraordinary zest for living, a joyfully brave spirit that withstood the cruelties of fate, she would sometimes say that the one grief she still felt keenly was that of never having had a child.

Saccard was able to do Hamelin a service, procuring a small job for him for some business partners who needed an engineer for a report on the profitability of a new machine. This carried him into the intimate world of the brother and sister; he often went up to spend an hour with them in their living-room, their one large room, which they had converted into a workroom. It was still utterly bare, furnished only with a long designer's table, another smaller table loaded with papers, and half-a-dozen chairs. Books were piled up on the mantelpiece. But on the walls an improvised decoration-scheme cheered up the emptiness with a series of maps and a set of bright watercolours, each piece of paper tacked up with four nails. It was his portfolio of projects that Hamelin had displayed there, the notes he had taken in Syria, the whole of his future fortune; and the watercolours were by Madame Caroline, views from back there, and typical figures and costumes, things she had observed and sketched while accompanying her brother, with her own very individual approach as a colourist and quite without pretentiousness. Two wide windows overlooking the garden of the Beauvilliers mansion threw a brilliant light over this proliferation of drawings, evoking a quite other life, the dream of an ancient society crumbling into dust, that the firm mathematical lines of the technical drawings seemed to be trying to set upright again, supported by the solid scaffolding of modern science. When he had made himself useful, with that eager energy that was part of his charm, Saccard would linger, especially captivated by the maps and watercolours, forever asking for more information about them. In his head the launching of a vast enterprise was already germinating.

One morning he found Madame Caroline alone, sitting at the little table she used as her desk. She was dreadfully sad, her hands lying idle among the papers.

'What can one do? Things are going really badly... not that I'm faint-hearted, but we are going to find ourselves lacking everything all at once; and what distresses me is the helplessness to which misfortune is reducing my brother, for he has courage and strength only for his work... I had thought of finding myself a position as a teacher again, just to be able at least to be some help. But I've looked around and found nothing... And I can't start working as a cleaner.'

Never had Saccard seen her so disconcerted, so cast down.

'Good heavens, no! It hasn't come to that!' he cried.

She shook her head, showing some bitterness towards life, life that she normally accepted so cheerfully, even when it was unkind. And as Hamelin came in just then, bringing news of his most recent setback, large, slow tears began to fall and she said no more, sitting with clenched fists at her table, her eyes staring into space.

'And to think', Hamelin muttered, 'that back there millions are waiting for us, if only someone would help me to make them.'

Saccard had planted himself in front of a drawing showing the plan of a house in the middle of vast warehouses.

'What is this?' he asked.

'Oh, I was just amusing myself,' the engineer explained. 'It's the plan for a house back there in Beirut for the director of the company I dreamed of, you know, the General United Steamboat Company.'

Warming to the subject, he gave some new details. During his stay in the East he had observed how poor the transport services were. The few companies involved, based in Marseilles, were ruining each other with competition, unable to provide adequate and comfortable vessels; one of his first ideas, which was the very basis of the whole of his ventures, was to syndicate these companies, form them into one huge company with a capital of millions, which would exploit the whole Mediterranean area, over which it would have sovereign control, setting up shipping lines to all the ports of Africa, Spain, Italy, Greece, Egypt, and Asia right up to the edge of the Black Sea.

The whole scheme showed him to be a very shrewd organizer and a great patriot: this was the East conquered and given to France, not to mention that he was also drawing closer to Syria, where his vast field of operations would unfold.

'Syndicates,' murmured Saccard, 'that's where the future seems to lie today... It is such a powerful form of association! Three or four small enterprises which on their own just vegetate gain an irresistible vitality and prosperity if they join forces... Yes, tomorrow belongs to huge amounts of capital and the centralized efforts of great masses. All industry and commerce will end up as one single, immense market, supplying everything.'

He had come to a stop once more, this time before a watercolour representing a wild area, an arid gorge, blocked by a gigantic pile of rocks covered with bushes.

'Oh, oh!' he went on. 'Now this is the uttermost end of the world. No risk of being jostled by passers-by in that place.'

'One of the Carmel gorges,' Hamelin said in reply, 'my sister painted that, while I was studying the area.'

Then he simply added:

'Between the cretaceous limestone and the porphyries that have pushed up the limestone, over the whole side of the mountain there is a considerable deposit of silver sulphite—oh yes, a silver mine, whose exploitation, according to my calculations, would guarantee enormous profits.'

'A silver mine,' Saccard repeated eagerly.

Madame Caroline, her eyes still focused far away in her sadness, had heard this, and it was as if a vision had been called up:

'Carmel, ah! What a desert, what days of solitude! It's full of myrtle and broom, and smells so good, the warm air is perfumed with their sweet scent. And eagles forever glide high overhead... But all that silver, sleeping in that tomb, alongside such poverty! One would like to see happy crowds of people, building-work going on, towns being born, and an entire people regenerated by work.'

'A road could easily be opened from Carmel to Saint-Jean-d'Acre,' Hamelin went on, 'and I believe iron would also be discovered, for there's a lot of it in the mountains of that area... I've also been studying a new method of extraction which would allow considerable savings to be made. Everything is ready, it's just a matter of finding the capital.'

'The Carmel Silver Mines Company,' murmured Saccard.

Money

But it was the engineer now who was looking up, going from one map to another, once more in the grip of this, his life's work, and feverishly thinking of the dazzling future slumbering there, paralysed by lack of money.

'And these are just the small things to start off with,' he continued. 'Look at this series of maps, this is the big project, an entire railway system* running across Asia Minor from one end to the other... The lack of convenient and rapid communications is the primary cause for the stagnation in which this country, with all its riches, is sunk. You wouldn't find a single carriageable highway there; every journey and all the transport has to be made by mule or camel... So just imagine what a revolution it would be if railway lines ran right up to the edges of the desert! Industry and commerce would be increased tenfold, civilization would triumph, Europe would at last open up the gates to the Orient... Oh, if it's of interest to you we can talk about it in detail. And you'll see! You'll see!'

In fact he couldn't help entering immediately into the details. It was mainly during his journey to Constantinople that he had studied the outline of his railway system. The main—the sole—difficulty was the crossing of the Taurus mountains; but he had gone around the different passes, and was sure there could be a direct and relatively inexpensive route. Besides, he wasn't thinking of creating the whole system at one stroke. After obtaining the whole concession from the Sultan* it would be sensible to start at first only with the main line from Brousse to Beirut, via Angora and Aleppo. Later there would be the branch from Smyrna to Angora, and one from Trebizond to Angora by way of Erzerum and Sivas.

'Later, and later still...' he went on.

But he stopped there and merely smiled, not daring to tell to what lengths he had dared to push his projects. It was his dream.

'Oh, the plains at the foot of the Taurus range,' Madame Caroline took up the theme in her slow voice, as if in a waking dream, 'what a delightful paradise! You scarcely have to scratch the surface of the soil and harvests appear in abundance. Fruit trees—peach, cherry, fig, and almond—breaking under the weight of fruit. And such fields of olive and mulberry trees, like great forests! And what a natural and easy existence it was in that light air, under a sky always blue.'

Saccard began to laugh, with that keen and hungry laugh he had when he scented fortune. And as Hamelin went on to speak of other projects, among them the creation of a bank in Constantinople* and the all-powerful contacts he had established there, especially with the Grand Vizier,* he gaily interrupted him.

'But it's a wonderland—very saleable!'

Then, resting his hands very familiarly upon the shoulders of Madame Caroline, who was still sitting down:

'Don't despair, Madame Caroline! I am fond of you both, you'll see, and I'll get something done with your brother, which will be good for all of us… Be patient. Just wait.'

In the month that followed, Saccard again found some little jobs for the engineer, and though he said no more about those grand schemes, he must have been thinking of them all the time, preoccupied and hesitant over the overwhelming scale of the ventures. But what tightened the growing link of intimacy between them was the way that Madame Caroline began to concern herself with the household of this man on his own, who was being eaten up by needless expense, and the more servants he had, the worse he was served. He, so clever everywhere else, admired for his firm and vigorous dealing with the havoc of grand-scale theft, just let everything go from bad to worse in his own household, careless of the fearful waste that tripled his costs; and the absence of a woman made itself cruelly felt even in the tiniest things. When Madame Caroline observed the pillaging that was going on, she first gave him some advice, then ended up taking it upon herself to help him to make some savings; so one day he suggested with a laugh that she should be his housekeeper—and why not? She had been looking for a teaching post, so she could accept a position which was quite honourable for her, and would give her some breathing-space. The offer, made as a joke, became serious. Wouldn't it, after all, be a way of keeping busy, and helping her brother out with the three hundred francs a month that Saccard would pay her? She accepted, and within a week, she had reformed the household, dismissing the chef and his wife, replacing them simply with a cook, who, along with the valet and the coachman, should be sufficient. She also kept only one horse and one carriage, took complete charge of everything, and examined the accounts so scrupulously that by the end of the first fortnight she had reduced the expenses by half. Saccard was delighted, and joked that he was now the one who was robbing her, and she should have demanded a percentage on all the savings she was making for him.

Their relationship now began to be very close. Saccard had had the idea of removing the screws fastening the communicating door between the two apartments so they could move easily from one dining-room to the other, using the internal staircase, and while her brother was shut in, working upstairs from morning till night, putting his files on the Orient in order, Madame Caroline, leaving her own house-work to the one maid they had kept, would go down at any time of the day to give orders as if she were at home. It had become a joy to Saccard to see the frequent appearances of this tall and beautiful woman walking through the rooms, so strong and proud, with that always unexpected gaiety of her white hair flying around her young face. She was very cheerful once more, she had recovered her former stalwart attitude to life now that she felt useful, and was busy all the time, always on her feet. Without any affectation of simplicity she now always wore a black dress, and in its pockets could be heard the clear jangling of her bunch of keys; and certainly it amused her that she, the scholar, the philosopher, should now be no more than a good domestic, acting as housekeeper to a prodigal whom she was begin-ning to love, the way one always loves naughty children. He, very attracted to her for a moment, and thinking that there were, after all, only fourteen years between them, had wondered what would happen if, one fine evening, he simply took her in his arms. Was it believable that for the ten years since she had had to flee from her husband, from whom she had received as many blows as caresses, she had lived like a soldier on campaign, without ever seeing a person of the oppo-site sex? Perhaps her travels had protected her. However, he knew that a friend of her brother's, a Monsieur Beaudoin, a businessman who had remained in Beirut but whose imminent return was expected, had been very much in love with her, so much so indeed that to marry her he had been prepared to wait for the death of her husband, who had just been locked up in an asylum, driven mad by alcoholism. Of course that marriage would only have regularized a very excusable, almost legitimate, situation. Therefore, since there had already been one, why shouldn't he be the second? But Saccard got no further than thinking about it, finding in her such a good comrade that the woman in her almost disappeared. When, seeing her go by with her admir-able figure, he asked himself the question: what would happen if he were to kiss her, he told himself that what would happen would be very ordinary, perhaps tiresome; and he would put the experiment off until some other time, shaking her hand vigorously, delighted at her cordiality.

Then suddenly Madame Caroline fell back into deep sadness. One morning she came down looking very depressed, very pale, and with swollen eyes; he could get nothing out of her; he gave up asking in the face of her obstinate insistence that there was nothing wrong, that she was just the same as always. It was only on the following day that he understood, when he found, in the upper apartment, a letter-card announcing the marriage of Monsieur Beaudoin to the very young and immensely rich daughter of an English consul. The blow must have been all the harder in that the news had arrived in this banal letter, with nothing to prepare her for it, not even a goodbye. Part of the very existence of this unhappy woman had crumbled away with the loss of that distant hope to which she had clung in times of disaster. And with one of fortune's own abominable cruelties, she had learned, just two days before, that her husband had died, so for forty-eight hours she had been able to believe in the imminent fulfilment of her dream. Her life was in pieces, and she was devastated. That very evening another shock awaited her: when she went in to see Saccard as usual, before going to bed, to discuss the orders for the next day, he spoke of her unhappiness so gently that she burst into sobs; then, in the throes of this emotion, in a sort of paralysis of her will, she found herself in his arms and gave herself to him, without any joy for either of them. When she came to herself she was not appalled, but her sadness was now infinitely greater. Why had she allowed this to happen? She did not love this man, and he surely didn't love her. It wasn't that he seemed to her to be unworthy of love through age or appearance; he certainly wasn't handsome, and he was already old, but he interested her, with his ever-changing features and the energy of the whole of his small dark figure; and not yet knowing him she wanted to think him helpful, a man of superior intelligence, capable of bringing her brother's great schemes to fruition and as averagely honest as any man. But what a stupid fall! She who was so sensible, she who had learned so much from hard experience and was so much the mistress of herself—that she should have succumbed like that, not knowing how or why, in a flood of tears, like some sentimental chit of a girl! The worst of it was that she felt him to be just as astonished as she was, and almost annoyed at this event. When he tried to comfort her, speaking of Monsieur Beaudoin as a former lover whose base treachery deserved only that she forget him, she had protested, swearing that nothing had ever happened between them. At first he had thought she was lying out of womanly pride; but she had repeated her statement with such force, and with eyes so beautiful, so clear and candid, that he ended up convinced of the truth of her story; she, keeping herself through rectitude and dignity for the day of her marriage, and the man, waiting patiently for two years, then growing weary and marrying another, faced by too tempting an offer of youth and wealth. And the odd thing was that this discovery, this conviction that should have delighted Saccard, filled him instead with a sort of embarrassment, so thoroughly did he grasp the stupid fatality of his good fortune. In any case, it did not happen again, for neither of them seemed to want it.

For a whole fortnight Madame Caroline remained dreadfully unhappy. The life-force, that drive that makes life both necessary and joyful, had left her. She attended to her multiple tasks, but as if she were not really there, not even allowing herself any illusions about the reasons for, or the interest of, anything. She was the human machine, going on working even in despair at the emptiness of everything. And in this shipwreck of her courage and gaiety she enjoyed only one distraction, and that was to spend her free hours with her brow pressed against the glass of one of the windows in the big workroom, her eyes fixed on the next-door garden of the Beauvilliers mansion, where, ever since she had first moved in, she had sensed distress, one of those cases of dire poverty, carefully concealed, so painful in the effort to keep up appearances. There too people were suffering, and her own grief seemed as if soaked in their tears; she was dying of melancholy, to the point of believing herself numb and dead, lost in the pain of others.

These Beauvilliers who, in addition to their vast estates in Touraine and Anjou, had once owned a magnificent mansion on the Rue de Grenelle, now in Paris had only this one-time *maison de plaisance*, built just outside the city at the beginning of the previous century but now shut in among the dark buildings of the Rue Saint-Lazare. The few fine trees in the garden now seemed to be at the bottom of a well, and moss was creeping over the cracked and crumbling steps down to the garden. It was as if a corner of nature had been put in prison, a soft and sad corner of mute despair, down where the sun only entered with a greenish light that provoked an icy shudder in the shoulders.

And in this damp and cellar-like peace, the first person Madame Caroline had seen, standing at the top of the broken steps, was the Countess de Beauvilliers, a tall, thin, white-haired woman of sixty, with a very noble air, as of an earlier age. With her long, straight nose, her thin lips, and her unusually long neck she had the look of some very ancient swan, of desolate gentleness. Then, behind her, almost at once, her daughter had appeared, Alice de Beauvilliers, twenty-five years old but of so impoverished a body that she could have been taken for a little girl, except for her already spoiled complexion and pinched features. She was her mother all over again, but puny and lacking her aristocratic nobility, with a calamitously long neck, and having only the pitiable charm of the end of a great line. The two women lived alone since the son, Ferdinand de Beauvilliers, had joined the Papal Zouaves after the Battle of Castelfidardo, which had been lost by Lamoricière.* Every day, if it wasn't raining, they would appear in this way, one behind the other, descending the flight of steps and walking around the narrow patch of grass in the middle without exchanging a word. The borders were simply ivy, flowers would not have grown there, or perhaps they would have been too expensive. This slow promenade, no doubt a simple constitutional, made by these two very pale women under the centuries-old trees, which had seen such grand festivities and were now suffocated by the bourgeois houses all around, took on a melancholy sadness as if it were a procession of mourning for old, dead things.

So, her interest aroused, Madame Caroline had been watching her neighbours with a tender sympathy, without any unpleasant curiosity, and gradually, looking out over the garden, she began to see into their life, the life they hid with such jealous care from the street. There was still a horse in the stable and a carriage in the outhouse, tended by an old servant who was valet, coachman, and concierge all in one. Similarly there was a cook who also acted as housemaid; but though the carriage still went out from the main entrance with the horse properly harnessed, carrying these ladies on their errands, and though the table still showed a certain luxury in the winter, for the fortnightly dinners for a few friends, through what lengthy fasting and with what sordid and constant economies had that mendacious appearance of wealth been bought! In a small shed, safe from all eyes, there was perpetual washing to reduce the laundress's bill, poor old garments worn out from soaping, mended thread by thread, and just four vegetables peeled for the evening meal, bread left on a board to go stale so they would eat less; all sorts of miserly practices, petty and touching; the old coachman sewing up the holes in Mademoiselle's boots, the cook using ink to cover up the ends of Madame's too shabby gloves. And the mother's dresses passed on to the daughter after ingenious alterations, and the hats that lasted for years, thanks to changes of flowers and ribbons. When no visitor was expected the reception-rooms on the ground floor were carefully locked up, along with the large rooms on the first floor; for in all this vast house the two women now occupied only one small room, which served as their dining-room and boudoir. When the window was half-open the Countess could be seen mending her linen, like a needy little bourgeois housewife, while the daughter, in between her piano-playing and watercolours, knitted stockings and mittens for her mother. One day when there was a big storm both women were seen going down to the garden to gather up the sand the ferocious rain was washing off the path.

By now Madame Caroline knew their history. The Countess de Beauvilliers had suffered a great deal because of her husband, a profligate about whom she had never complained. One evening he had been carried back to her in Vendôme dying, with a bullet-hole in his body. There was talk of a hunting accident, a shot fired by a jealous gamekeeper whose wife or daughter he must have seduced. And the worst of it was that there disappeared with him the once-colossal fortune of the Beauvilliers, based on huge areas of land and royal domains; the Revolution had already reduced it, and he and his father had finished it off. Of all those vast possessions only one farm remained, Les Aublets, a few leagues from Vendôme, bringing in about fifteen thousand francs a year, the sole source of income for the widow and her two children. The mansion on the Rue de Grenelle had been sold long since, and the one on the Rue Saint-Lazare, mortgaged to the hilt, ate up the greater part of the fifteen thousand francs from the farm, and was also in danger of being sold if the interest wasn't paid; there remained scarcely more than six or seven thousand francs for the maintenance of four people and the lifestyle of this noble family which refused to renounce its status. Eight years ago, when she had become a widow with a boy of twenty and a girl of seventeen, even as her house collapsed around her, the Countess had stiffened in her aristocratic pride, vowing she would live on bread and water rather than lower her standards. From that time on she had had but one thought—to maintain her status, marry her daughter to a man of equal rank, and make a soldier of her son. Ferdinand had at first caused her mortal anguish as a result of some youthful follies and debts that had had to be paid; but after being warned about their situation in a solemn interview he had never done that again, being a tender soul at heart but idle and useless, cut off from any kind of work and with no possible place in contemporary society. Now he was a soldier of the Pope he was still a cause of secret anxiety for her, for his health was poor and beneath his proud appearance he was delicate, his blood impoverished and thin, which made the Roman climate dangerous for him. As for the marriage of Alice, it was so slow in coming that the sad mother's eyes would fill with tears as she looked at her, seeing her already ageing, withering away in the long wait. For all her appearance of melancholy and insignificance Alice was not stupid, and she longed ardently for life, for a man who would love her, for happiness; but not wishing to sadden the household further she pretended she had renounced everything, joking about marriage and saying she had a vocation for spinsterhood; and at night she sobbed into her pillow, thinking she would die of the grief of being alone. The Countess, however, through her miserly miracles, had managed to save twenty thousand francs, which was Alice's entire dowry; she had also saved from the wreckage some jewellery, a bracelet, some rings, some earrings, which might be worth about ten thousand francs; a very meagre dowry, a package of wedding gifts of which she did not even dare to speak, hardly enough indeed to face the immediate expenses if the long-awaited husband should appear. And yet she would not give up hope, but went on struggling, not surrendering any of the privileges of her birth, always just as haughty and pretending to an appropriate fortune, incapable of going out on foot or cutting back one side-dish from an evening reception, but penny-pinching in her hidden life, condemning herself to weeks of plain potatoes with no butter, to add fifty francs to the eternally insufficient dowry for her daughter. It was a painful and puerile daily heroism, while with each day the house crumbled a little more about their heads.

So far Madame Caroline had not had the opportunity to speak to the Countess and her daughter. She had ended up knowing the most intimate details of their life, even the things they thought they had kept hidden from the whole world, yet they had done no more than exchange glances, but glances of the sort that leave behind a sudden sensation of close sympathy. It was the Princess d'Orviedo who was to bring them together. She had had the idea of creating, for her Work Foundation, a sort of supervisory committee composed of ten ladies who met twice a month, made careful inspections of the Foundation, and checked on all the services. As she had reserved for herself the choice of these ladies, among the first she had selected was Madame de Beauvilliers, one of her great friends in former times, though simply a neighbour now that she had withdrawn from the world. And as the supervisory committee had suddenly lost their secretary, Saccard, who was still in charge of the administration of the institution, had thought of recommending Madame Caroline as a model secretary whose like could not be found; in fact the job was quite demanding; there was a great deal of paperwork, and even some physical tasks that these ladies found rather repugnant; and from the start Madame Caroline had shown herself to be an admirable charity-worker, for her unsatisfied maternal longings and her desperate love of children fired her with an active tenderness for all these poor beings that they were trying to save from the gutters of Paris. So, at the most recent meeting of the committee she had met the Countess de Beauvilliers, who, however, only greeted her rather coldly to hide her secret embarrassment, feeling, no doubt, that here was one who knew of her dire poverty. Both now exchanged a greeting every time their eyes met and it would have been grossly rude to pretend not to know each other.

One day, in the big workroom, while Hamelin was making corrections to a map in accordance with some new calculations and Saccard was standing watching him work, Madame Caroline, at the window as usual, was gazing at the Countess and her daughter making their tour of the garden. That morning she could see they were wearing shoes that a rag-picker would not have gathered up from the road.

'Oh, those poor women!' she murmured. 'How terrible it must be, all that charade of wealth they feel they must perform.'

And she drew back, hiding behind the window-curtain for fear the mother might see her and suffer even more from being watched. For herself, she had become more tranquil during the three weeks in which she had lingered each morning at this window; the great pain of her abandonment was no longer so sharp; it seemed as if the sight of other people's disasters gave her more courage to accept her own, that disaster she had thought was the ruin of her whole life. To her surprise she found herself laughing again.

For just a moment more she followed the women in the mossy green of the garden, with the air of one deep in thought. Then, turning to Saccard, she quickly said:

'Just tell me why I can't be sad... No, it just doesn't last, it has never lasted, I can't be sad, no matter what happens to me... Is it egoism? Really, I don't think so. That would be too awful, and besides, no matter how cheerful I am, I still break my heart at the sight of the slightest suffering. Make sense of that if you can—I am cheerful, yet I'd weep over all the unhappy souls I see if I didn't restrain myself, knowing that the smallest bit of bread would do them much more good than my useless tears.'

As she said this she laughed with her splendidly robust laugh, that of a valiant soul who preferred action to garrulous expressions of pity.

'God knows, however,' she continued, 'if I haven't had cause enough to despair of everything. Oh, luck has not been over-favourable to me thus far... After my marriage, that hell I fell into, insulted and beaten, I thought the only thing left was to drown myself. But I didn't; and just a fortnight later I was throbbing with joyfulness and filled with immense hope, when I set off with my brother for the East... And when we came back to Paris, when we were without almost everything, I had some appalling nights, in which I could see us dying of hunger over our lovely plans. We didn't die, and I began once more to dream of amazing things, happy things that sometimes made me laugh even on my own... And recently, when I was dealt that blow I don't yet dare to speak of, it seemed as if my heart had been torn out; yes, I definitely felt that it had stopped beating; I thought it was all over, I thought I was finished, quite destroyed. And then, not at all! Life picks me up again, and today I'm laughing and tomorrow I shall have hope, I shall want to go on living, want to live forever... Isn't it extraordinary, to be unable to be sad for long!'

Saccard, who was now laughing himself, shrugged his shoulders.

'Bah! You're just like everybody else. That's how life is.'

'Do you think so?' she cried in astonishment. 'It seems to me that there are some people who are so sad, never cheerful, and who make life impossible for themselves, painting everything so black... Oh, it's not that I have illusions about the sweetness and beauty life offers.

It has been too harsh with me, I have seen it up close, everywhere and abundantly. It is execrable, when it isn't vile. But there you are! I love it. Why? I don't know. Everything around me can topple and collapse, but the next day there I am, still cheerful and confident among the ruins... I've often thought that my case is, in microcosm, the case of all humanity, living in the midst of terrible wretchedness, yes, but always cheered by the youthfulness of the next generation. After each one of these crises that knock me down there comes a sort of new youth, a springtime, whose promises of new life revive me and lift up my heart. All of that is so true that after some great sorrow, if I go out into the street in the sun, I immediately begin once more to love, to hope, and be happy. And age has no influence on me, I am naive enough to grow old without noticing... You see, I've read far too much for a woman, I don't know at all where I'm going, any more indeed than this great world does. Only, in spite of myself, it seems to me that I'm going, that we're all going, to something very nice and perfectly happy.'

She ended up making a joke of it, though very moved and trying to hide the emotion attached to her hopes; while her brother, who had looked up, was gazing at her with an adoration full of gratitude.

'Oh, you,' he cried, 'you're just made for catastrophes, you really embody the love of life!'

In these daily morning conversations an excitement had gradually become evident, and if Madame Caroline was getting back to that natural joyfulness that was part of her very health, this derived from the courage Saccard brought to them with his active fervour for great ventures. The matter was almost decided, they would exploit the famous portfolio. Under the outbursts of his shrill voice, everything came to life and became extravagant. First they would get their hands on the Mediterranean, they would conquer it with the General United Steamboat Company; and he listed the ports of all the countries along the coast where they would set up stations, mixing some faded classical memories into his enthusiasm as a speculator, celebrating this sea, the only sea the ancient world had known, this blue sea around which civilization had flourished, its waves lapping the ancient cities: Athens, Rome, Tyre, Alexandria, Carthage, Marseilles, the cities that created Europe. Then, once this vast path to the Orient had been secured, they would start over there in Syria with the little venture of the Carmel Silver Mines Company, just a few millions to pick up along the way, but an excellent launching-pad, for the idea of a silver mine, of silver found in the earth and collected by the shovel-ful, this was always powerfully attractive to the public, especially when you could attach to it a prestigious and resonant name like Carmel.* There were coal mines there too, coal lying close to the surface that would be worth its weight in gold when once the country was covered with factories; not to mention some other smaller ven-tures which would serve as interludes: the founding of banks, syndi-cates for the flourishing businesses, exploitation of the vast forests of Lebanon, whose giant trees were simply rotting on the spot for lack of roads. Then at last he came to the big one, the Oriental Railway Company, and at this point he began to talk wildly, for this railway system, cast like a net across Asia Minor from one end to the other, this, for him, was speculation, this was the life of money, taking hold of that old world in one fell swoop like a new prey, still intact, a prey of incalculable wealth, hidden under the ignorance and dirt of centur-ies. He could smell treasure, and seemed to whinny like a warhorse at the scent of battle.

Madame Caroline, with her solid common sense, normally very resistant to overheated imaginings, nevertheless allowed herself to be carried along by this enthusiasm, no longer able to see its excessive-ness with any clarity. In truth it appealed to that love she had for the Orient, her nostalgia for that admirable land where she had believed herself to be happy; and in a logical counter-effect it was she, with her colourful descriptions and her flood of detail, who, without meaning to, whipped up Saccard's fever more and more. When she talked about Beirut, where she had lived for three years, there was no stop-ping her: Beirut, at the foot of the Lebanon, on that tongue of land between stretches of red sand and piles of fallen rocks, Beirut with its houses built like an amphitheatre, set in vast gardens, a delightful paradise planted with orange trees, lemon trees, and palms. Then it was all the coastal towns—Antioch in the north, now bereft of its splendour, and in the south Saida, the Sidon of long ago, Saint-Jean-d'Acre, Jaffa, and Tyre, now Sour, whose story is the story of them all: Tyre, whose merchants were kings, whose sailors had sailed around Africa, and which now, its harbour choked with sand, is no more than a field of ruins and the dust of palaces, on which are scat-tered only some wretched fishermen's huts. She had accompanied her brother everywhere, she knew Aleppo, Angora, Bursa, Smyrna, and even Trebizond; she had lived for a month in Jerusalem, the city half asleep amid the trafficking round the holy places, then two months in Damascus, the queen of the Orient in the middle of its vast plain, the city of trade and industry, made by the caravans from Mecca and Baghdad into a centre full of milling crowds. And she also knew the valleys and mountains, the villages of the Maronites and the Druze, perched high over the plateaus or hidden in the depths of the gorges, and the cultivated fields and the barren ones. And from the smallest corners, from the silent deserts as well as the great cities, she had brought back the same admiration for inexhaustible, luxuriant nature and the same anger at the stupidity and wickedness of men. All those natural riches scorned or spoiled! She spoke of the taxes that crush trade and industry, the idiotic law that limits the amount of capital that can be put into agriculture; and the stagnation that leaves in the hands of the peasant today the plough that was in use before the time of Christ, and the ignorance in which millions of men still languish like idiot children, their development arrested. In former times the coast was too small, the towns almost ran into each other; now life has moved away to the West, and it is as if one were travelling through a vast abandoned cemetery. No schools, no roads, the worst of governments, justice for sale, execrable public servants, excessive taxation, ridiculous laws, laziness and fanaticism; not to mention the continual upheavals of civil wars, and massacres that wipe out entire villages. Then she would grow angry, asking how it could be permitted to spoil in this way the work of nature, a blessed land of exquisite charm, a land where every climate could be found, burning plains and temperate mountainsides and eternal snow on the high summits. And her love of life, her persistent hopefulness, made her passionate about the idea of the all-powerful magic wand of science and speculation that could strike this ancient slumbering land into life.

'Look,' cried Saccard, 'this Carmel Gorge in this drawing of yours, where there's nothing but stones and mastic trees, you'll see, once the silver mine gets going, first a village will spring up, then a town... And all those ports silted up with sand, we'll clean them out and protect them with strong jetties. Great ships will anchor where now even small boats do not dare to moor... And on these depopulated plains, these deserted passes, where our railway lines will run, you'll see a veritable resurrection, yes! The fields will cease to lie fallow, roads and canals will appear, new cities will rise from the ground and life will at last return, as it does to a sick body when new blood is made to circulate through the depleted veins... Yes! Money will perform these miracles.'

And in what his piercing voice described, Madame Caroline could really see that predicted civilization arising. Those dry technical drawings and those linear outlines came to life, full of people: it was the dream she had sometimes had of an Orient cleansed of its dirt, pulled out of its ignorance, enjoying the fertility of its soil, the charms of its sky, with all the refinements of science. She had already seen such a miracle in Port Said, which in so few years had pushed out on to a bare beach, first sheds to shelter the few workers at the start of the excavation, then the city of two thousand souls, and next the city of ten thousand souls, houses, huge warehouses, an immense jetty, life and well-being stubbornly created by the human ants. And that was what she could see rising up once more, the irresistible forward march, the social drive that rushes towards the greatest possible happiness, the urge to act, to move forward without knowing exactly where one is going, but to go more easily and in better conditions; and the globe turned upside down by the anthill rebuilding its home, and the continual work, new possibilities of enjoyment acquired, man's power multiplied tenfold, the earth belonging to him more and more each day. Money, backing up science, created progress.

Hamelin, who was listening with a smile, then made a wise remark.

'All this is the poetry of results, but we haven't yet even reached the prose of implementation.'

But it was only the excessiveness of his ideas that really excited Saccard, and it got worse on the day when, having started reading books on the Orient, he opened a history of the Egyptian expedition.* He was already haunted by the memory of the Crusades, that return of the West to its cradle in the East, that great movement which had brought the furthest parts of Europe back to the countries of their origin, which were still flourishing and where there was so much to learn. But the lofty figure of Napoleon struck him even more, setting off there to wage war, with a grandiose and mysterious aim. If he spoke of conquering Egypt and setting up a French establishment there, thus giving France the trade of the Levant, he was certainly not telling the whole story: and Saccard tried to read into what remained vague and enigmatic about the expedition some sort of colossally ambitious project, the reconstruction of a huge empire,

Napoleon crowned in Constantinople, emperor of the Orient and the Indies, realizing the dream of Alexander, greater than that of Caesar or Charlemagne. Didn't he say, in Saint-Helena, speaking of Sidney, the English general who had stopped him at the Battle of St-Jean-d'Acre:* 'That man made me miss my destiny.' And what the Crusades had attempted, what Napoleon had been unable to accomplish, it was that gigantic idea of conquest of the Orient that fired the imagination of Saccard, a carefully planned conquest, achieved by the twin forces of science and money. Since civilization had spread from East to West, why shouldn't it go back to the East, returning to the original garden of humanity, to that Eden of the Hindustan peninsula which lay asleep in the weariness of centuries? It would be a new period of youth, it would galvanize the Earthly Paradise, making it habitable once more with steam and electricity, putting Asia Minor back at the centre of that ancient world, as the point of intersection of the great natural paths that link the continents. It was now a matter of making not millions, but billions and billions.

From then on Hamelin and he had long discussions every morning. If their hopes were vast, the difficulties were numerous and enormous. The engineer, who indeed had been in Beirut in 1862 during the terrible butchery that the Druzes carried out on the Maronite Christians, an event in which France had had to intervene,* did not conceal the obstacles they would meet among these perpetually warring peoples, dependent on the whims of the local powers. But he did have powerful contacts in Constantinople, he had secured the support of the Grand Vizier Fuad Pasha,* a man of real merit, a declared partisan of reform; and he flattered himself he would be able to obtain all the necessary concessions from him. On the other hand, although he predicted the fatal bankruptcy of the Ottoman Empire, he saw a rather favourable circumstance in its frantic need for money, and the continual loans it took out year after year; a needy government, though it offers no personal guarantee, is very ready to make deals with particular enterprises if it sees the slightest benefit in so doing. And wasn't it a practical way of answering the everlasting and burdensome question of the Orient, to interest the Empire in great civilizing works and lead it towards progress, so that it would no longer be that monstrous barrier standing between Europe and Asia? What a fine, patriotic role would be played in all this by French companies!

Then one morning Hamelin calmly broached the secret programme to which he had occasionally alluded, the one he referred to, with a smile, as the crowning of the edifice.

'After this, once we are the masters, we shall remake the kingdom of Palestine and install the Pope there... At first it could be just Jerusalem, with Jaffa as the seaport. Then Syria will be declared independent and we shall add it on... You know, the time draws near when it will be impossible for the Papacy to remain in Rome, with all the revolting humiliations in store for it there. We must be prepared for that day!'

Saccard listened to him open-mouthed as he said these things quite simply, with his profound Catholic faith. He did not himself shrink from extravagant imaginings but would never have gone quite that far. This man of science, so apparently cold, absolutely amazed him.

'That's mad!' he cried. 'The Porte* won't give up Jerusalem.'

'Oh, why not?' Hamelin tranquilly continued. 'It is in such urgent need of money! Jerusalem is a bother, they'd be glad to get rid of it. They often don't know which side to take between the diverse faiths fighting for possession of the sanctuaries. Besides, the Pope would have real support in Syria from the Maronites, for, as you know, he has established a College in Rome for their priests... In short, I've really thought it out, I've seen how it would all work, and it will be the new era, the triumphant era of Catholicism. Some may say this is going too far, that the Pope would find himself isolated, cut off from European affairs. But what glory and authority he will have when he reigns over the sacred places, speaking in the name of Christ, from the Holy Land where Christ himself once spoke! That is where his patrimony lies, that must be his kingdom. And rest assured, we shall make it powerful and solid, that kingdom; we shall put it beyond the reach of political disturbance by basing its budget, guaranteed by the resources of the country, upon a vast bank in which Catholics the world over will fight to have shares.'

Saccard, who had begun to smile, already delighted if not entirely convinced by the hugeness of the project, could not help baptizing this bank, with a joyful cry of discovery:

'The Treasury of the Holy Sepulchre, eh? Superb! Just what we need!'

But he then met the sensible gaze of Madame Caroline, also smiling but sceptical, even slightly irritated; and he felt ashamed of his enthusiasm.

'No matter, my dear Hamelin, we had best keep secret that crowning of the edifice, as you call it. We'd be laughed at. And besides, our programme is already very heavily loaded, it's a good idea to reserve for the initiate the final consequences, the glorious end.'

'Undoubtedly, that has always been my intention,' said the engineer. That will be the mystery.'

And it was with that word, on that day, that the exploitation of the portfolio, the putting into operation of the whole enormous series of projects, was definitively decided. They would begin by creating a modest lending-house to launch the first deals; then, with success helping them along, they would gradually become masters of the market and conquer the world.

The next day, as Saccard had gone up to see the Princess d'Orviedo to get her orders on the subject of the Work Foundation, he remembered the dream he had briefly cherished of becoming the prince consort of this queen of charity, a mere distributor and administrator of the fortune of the poor. And he smiled, for all that now seemed to him rather silly. He was built to create life, not to treat the wounds that life has made. Now at last he was going to get back to his own work, in the thick of the battles of finance, in that race for happiness which has always been the very march of humanity through the centuries, always moving toward more joy and more light.

That same day he came upon Madame Caroline alone in the study. She was standing at one of the windows, held there by the appearance of the Countess de Beauvilliers and her daughter in the next-door garden at an unaccustomed hour. The two women were reading a letter with an air of great sadness, no doubt a letter from the son Ferdinand, whose position in Rome was probably far from brilliant.

'Look,' said Madame Caroline when she saw Saccard. 'Yet more trouble for those unfortunate women. Beggar-women in the street cause me less pain.'

'Bah!' he cried gaily, 'you must ask them to come and see me. We'll make them rich too, since we're going to make everybody's fortune!'

And in the fervour of his happiness he tried to kiss her on the lips. But she had moved her head away, suddenly grave and pale with some involuntary malaise.

'No, please don't.'

It was the first time he had tried to approach her again since she had abandoned herself to him in a moment when she had lost all self-awareness. Now that the serious business matters were arranged, he was able to think about his good fortune as a lover, and wanted to settle matters on this side of things too. Her sharp movement of withdrawal astonished him.

'Really? Would that truly displease you?'

'Yes, really. Very much so.'

She was calmer now, and she in turn was smiling.

'Besides, admit it, it doesn't matter that much to you either.'

'Oh, but I adore you.'

'No, don't say that, you're going to be so busy! Besides, I assure you that I'm ready to have a real friendship with you, if you are the man of action I take you to be and if you do all the great things you say you'll do... Anyway, friendship is better!'

He listened to her, still smiling but embarrassed and put out by her rejection all the same. She was refusing him, it was ridiculous to have possessed her only once and then by surprise. But it was only his vanity that suffered.

'So... Just friends?'

'Yes, I'll be your friend, and I'll help you... Friends, great friends!' She held out her face to him, and he, quite won over, deciding she was right, planted two big kisses upon each cheek.

CHAPTER III

THE letter from the Russian banker in Constantinople, that Sigismond had translated, was the favourable reply Saccard had been waiting for to get things started in Paris; and two days later, as soon as he woke up, Saccard had the sudden conviction that he must act that very day, that he must before nightfall have formed the syndicate he wanted to secure, in order to pre-place the fifty thousand shares at five hundred francs in his new company, to be launched with a capital of twenty-five million.

As he leapt out of bed he had at last found a name for his company, the name for which he had long been searching. The words 'Universal Bank' had suddenly flared up before him as if in letters of fire, in the darkness of his bedroom.

'Universal Bank,' he said over and over again as he got dressed. 'Universal Bank, it's simple, it's big, it includes everything, it covers the world... Yes, yes, excellent! The Universal Bank!'*

Until half-past nine he paced through the vast rooms, absorbed in his thoughts, not knowing where in Paris to begin the hunt for the millions he needed. It was still possible to find twenty-five million without going far afield; indeed, it was having too much choice that gave him pause, for he wanted to set about things methodically. He drank a cup of milk, and didn't get angry when the coachman came to tell him that the horse was sick, probably a chill, and it would be wiser to call in the vet.

'Fine, take care of it... I'll get a cab.'

But out on the pavement he was surprised at the bitter wind blowing, as if with a sudden return to winter in this month of May, so mild just the day before. Still, it wasn't raining, though large yellow clouds were looming on the horizon. So he didn't take a cab, deciding to walk to keep warm. He thought he'd first go on foot to drop in on Mazaud the stockbroker in the Rue de la Banque; it had occurred to him to sound out Mazaud about Daigremont, the well-known speculator, the lucky man in every syndicate. However, on the Rue Vivienne, from a sky now laden with livid clouds, such a downpour of rain and hail came bursting down that he took shelter under the carriage entrance of a house.

Saccard had been standing there for a minute, watching the rain falling, when over and above the rumble of the water the bright tinkling of gold coins made him prick up his ears. It seemed to be emerging from the very bowels of the earth, continuous, light and musical, like something out of a tale in the *Arabian Nights*. He turned his head and realized where he was, saw that he was standing in the doorway of a banker, Kolb, who dealt mostly in gold arbitrage, buying coinage in states where the value of gold was low then melting it down and selling the ingots to countries where the price of gold was high; so from morning to night, on smelting days, there rose from the basement the crystalline sound of gold coins being stirred, shovelled out of crates, and flung into the crucible. Passers-by on the pavement could hear it ringing in their ears from one year's end to the other. Saccard smiled with contentment at this music, which seemed like the subterranean voice of the neighbourhood of the Bourse. It struck him as a good omen.

The rain had stopped now, so he crossed the square and was at once at Mazaud's office. Unusually, the young stockbroker had made his private home on the first floor of the same building as his business offices, which occupied the whole of the second floor. He had simply taken over his uncle's apartment, when, after the latter's death, he made an agreement with his co-inheritors to buy out the business.

The clock was striking ten and Saccard went straight up to the offices, encountering Gustave Sédille at the door.

'Is Monsieur Mazaud in?'

'I don't know, Monsieur, I've just got here.'

The young man was smiling, he was always late, not taking seriously his unpaid, purely amateur post, but resigned to spending a year or two there just to please his father, the silk manufacturer in the Rue des Jeûneurs.

Saccard walked through the payments office, where the cashier and the securities clerk greeted him, then entered the office of the stockbroker's two managers, where he found only Berthier, the manager in charge of client dealings, the one who accompanied his employer to the Bourse.

'Is Monsieur Mazaud in?'

'Well, I think so, I just came from his office... Oh! No, he's not there now... He must be in the cash office.'

He pushed open a communicating door and cast his eye around a rather large room where five employees were working under the orders of the head clerk.

'No, that's odd… Take a look for yourself in accounts, there in the next room.'

Saccard walked into the accounts office. This was where the head of accounts, the linchpin of the practice, assisted by seven clerks, went through the notebook the stockbroker gave him each day after the close of the markets, then attributed to the clients the various transactions made on orders received, using for this purpose the cards which were kept to provide the names, for the notebook contains no names, just a brief indication of the purchase or sale of which shares, how many, at what price, and from which broker.

'Have you seen Monsieur Mazaud?' asked Saccard.

But no one even bothered to reply. As the head of accounts was out, three of the clerks were reading the newspaper, two others were gazing into space; but the arrival of Gustave Sédille had been of keen interest to young Flory, who in the morning made entries in the accounts and exchanged deals with other brokers, and in the afternoon went to the Bourse, where he was in charge of telegrams. Born in Saintes, of a registry-clerk father, he'd first worked as clerk for a banker in Bordeaux, then towards the end of the previous autumn ended up working for Mazaud in Paris, and had no prospects other than perhaps, in ten years, doubling his earnings there. Until now his conduct had been good, consistent and conscientious. However, ever since Gustave had joined the office a month ago he had been veering off course, led on by his new friend, who was very elegant and dashing, had plenty of money, and had introduced him to women. Beneath the beard which hid a good deal of his face Flory had a nose that suggested passion, a kindly mouth, and tender eyes; and he had now reached the stage of having little private parties, not too expensive, with Mademoiselle Chuchu, a performer at the Théâtre des Variétés,* a skinny grasshopper from the Paris streets, the runaway daughter of a Montmartre concierge; she was amusing, with her papier-mâché face and shining, beautiful, big brown eyes.

Gustave started telling Flory about his evening even before he took his coat off.

'Yes, my dear chap, I really thought Germaine would kick me out, because Jacoby turned up. But it was he that she managed to get rid of, goodness only knows how! So I stayed.'

They both spluttered with laughter. They were talking about Germaine Coeur, a superb woman of twenty-five, rather indolent and languid, with her ample bosom; she was kept on a monthly basis by the Jew Jacoby, a colleague of Mazaud's. She had always been with brokers, always on a monthly basis, which was convenient for very busy men with their heads stuffed with figures, who paid for love like everything else, never having time for any real passion. She had just one real worry in her little apartment on the Rue de la Michodière, and that was to avoid meetings between gentlemen who might know each other.

'But I say,' said Flory, 'I thought you were saving yourself for the pretty stationer?'

This allusion to Madame Conin, however, made Gustave grow serious. She was someone to be respected: she was an honest woman; and when she had proved willing, no man had ever been known to chat about it, such good friends did they remain. So, not wishing to answer, Gustave asked a question of his own.

'And Chuchu, did you take her to Mabille?'*

'Goodness no! Too expensive. We went home and had some tea.'

Standing behind the young men, Saccard had overheard these hastily whispered women's names. He smiled and spoke to Flory.

'Have you not seen Monsieur Mazaud?'

'Yes I have, Monsieur, he came to give me an order then went back down to his apartment... I believe his little boy is unwell, someone told him the doctor had arrived... You should ring downstairs, because he may well go straight out without coming back up.'

Saccard thanked him and hurried down to the floor below. Mazaud was one of the youngest stockbrokers around, blessed by fate, having had the stroke of luck of his uncle's death which had made him the holder of one of the biggest businesses in Paris at an age when most men are still learning their trade. Small in stature, he had pleasant features, with a small brown moustache and piercing black eyes; he seemed a very active person, with a very keen intelligence besides. On the trading-floor he was already well known for this mental and phys-ical vigour, so essential in his profession, and which, combined with great flair and remarkable intuition, would carry him to the highest rank; in addition he had a piercing voice, first-hand information from foreign exchanges, contacts with all the big bankers, and even, so it was said, a distant cousin at the Havas agency.* His wife, whom he'd married for love, had brought him a dowry of twelve hundred thousand francs; she was a charming young woman who had already borne him two children, a little girl of three and a boy of eighteen months.

Mazaud was indeed just showing out the doctor, who was reassuring him and laughing.

'Do come in,' he said to Saccard. 'It's true, when it comes to these little beings we immediately start worrying; the slightest little thing and we think they're at death's door.'

And he led him into the sitting-room, where his wife was still holding the baby on her lap and the little girl, pleased to see her mother looking happy, was reaching up to give her a kiss. They were blond, all three of them, fresh as daisies, and the young mother looked as delicate and guileless as the children. Mazaud placed a kiss on the top of her head.

'You see? We were being silly.'

'Oh! It doesn't matter, dearest, I'm so glad he's been able to reassure us!'

Saccard stopped and bowed in the face of all this happiness. The room, luxuriously furnished, smelled sweetly of a joyful family life which nothing had yet come to fracture: in the four years since his marriage Mazaud was hardly suspected of anything more than a passing curiosity in a singer from the Opéra-Comique.* He remained a faithful husband, and similarly, in spite of the ardour of youth, was reputed, so far, not to be speculating overmuch on his own account. And the sweet smell of good luck and unclouded bliss was really present, in the discreet calm of the carpets and hangings, and in the scent with which a large bouquet of roses, spilling out of a Chinese vase, was filling the whole room.

Madame Mazaud, who knew Saccard slightly, said to him gaily:

'Isn't it true, Monsieur, that to be always happy one simply has to want to be so?'

'I'm convinced of it, Madame,' he replied. 'And then, some people are so beautiful and so good that misfortune dare not touch them.'

She rose to her feet, radiant. She returned her husband's kiss and off she went, carrying the little boy and followed by the little girl, who had been clinging round her father's neck. The latter, trying to hide his feelings, turned to his visitor with a dash of Parisian humour:

'As you see, there's always something happening here.'

Then, briskly:

'You have something to say to me?... Let's go upstairs, shall we? We'll be more comfortable.'

Back upstairs Saccard recognized Sabatani, standing at the cash desk to collect his profits; and he was surprised at the warmth of the handshake the broker exchanged with his client. Then, as soon as he was sitting in Mazaud's office, he explained the reason for his visit, asking him about the formalities necessary for getting shares officially listed. Casually he told him about the business he was going to launch, the Universal Bank, with a capital of twenty-five million francs. Yes, a lending-bank, created primarily to sponsor some big enterprises to which he briefly referred. Mazaud listened calmly, and very kindly explained the necessary formalities. He was no fool, however, and did not think Saccard would have come all this way for so little. So when Saccard finally pronounced the name of Daigremont he smiled involuntarily. Of course, Daigremont had a colossal fortune behind him; some said he wasn't entirely trustworthy; but then, who was, in business and in love? Nobody! In any case, Mazaud had scruples about telling him the truth about Daigremont, after their big quarrel which had been the talk of the Bourse. Daigremont now gave most of his orders to Jacoby, a Jew from Bordeaux, a strapping chap of sixty with a broad, cheerful face and a famously bellowing voice, but he was growing stout and developing a pot-belly; a sort of rivalry had grown up between the two brokers, the young man favoured by good luck, and the old man having attained seniority as a former manager, whose sponsors had finally allowed him to buy his employer's business, a man of experience and extraordinary shrewdness, undermined, unfortunately, by his passion for speculation, so that he was always on the brink of disaster in spite of some considerable gains. Everything disappeared into settlements of debt. Germaine Coeur cost him only a few thousand-franc notes, and his wife was never seen.

'Anyway, in that Caracas affair,' Mazaud went on, giving way to resentment in spite of all his scruples, 'it's certain that Daigremont betrayed them and scooped the profits... He's a very dangerous man.'

Then, after a pause:

'But why don't you go to Gundermann?'

'Never!' cried Saccard, with real passion.

Just then Berthier, the manager, came in and whispered a few words in the broker's ear. It was Baroness Sandorff, who had come to settle her account and was raising all sorts of quibbles to try and get her bill reduced. Normally Mazaud would hurry out in person to greet the Baroness, but when she had lost he avoided her like the plague, knowing she would make too severe an assault on his gallantry. There are no worse clients than women, nor any more absolutely untrustworthy when it comes to paying.

'No, no, say I'm not in,' he replied with annoyance. 'And don't let her off a single centime, do you hear!'

And when Berthier had left, seeing from Saccard's smile that he had overheard:

'It's true, my dear chap, she's very nice of course, but you've no idea how rapacious she can be... Ah! these clients, how they would love us if only they always won! And the richer they are, the higher on the social scale, God forgive me! the less I trust them, the more I fear I won't be paid... Yes, there are days when, apart from the big companies, I'd rather do business only with provincials.'

The door had opened again, and a clerk handed him a file he had asked for that morning then went away.

'Well, well! That's good timing. Here we have a collector of revenues based in Vendôme, a certain Monsieur Fayeux... I tell you, you wouldn't believe the number of orders I receive from this correspondent. Admittedly, the orders are fairly insignificant, coming from the lower middle classes, small tradesmen and farmers. But there are so many of them... In fact, the best part, the very foundation of our companies is made up of the modest speculators, the great anonymous crowd that plays the market.'

By an association of ideas, Saccard remembered Sabatani at the cash office.

'So Sabatani is with you now?' he asked.

'Yes, for a year now, I think,' replied the broker with an air of amiable indifference. 'He's a nice lad, isn't he? He's made a modest start, he's very sensible and he'll get on.'

What he didn't say, what he no longer even remembered, was that Sabatani had made an original covering deposit of only two thousand francs. Hence his starting with only very moderate speculation. The Levantine was no doubt waiting, like so many others, for the paucity of his guarantee to be forgotten; and he was demonstrating prudence, raising the level of his orders only gradually, until the day when, toppling into a big settlement order, he would just disappear. How could one show any distrust towards a charming young man who has become a friend? How could one doubt his solvency when one saw him looking happy and apparently rich, with that elegance of dress that is indispensable to—indeed, almost the uniform of—larceny on the Stock Exchange.

'Very nice, very intelligent,' Saccard repeated, making a mental note to think of Sabatani when he needed to find a chap both discreet and unscrupulous. Then, getting to his feet and taking his leave:

'Well, goodbye now!... When our shares are ready I'll come and see you again, before I try to get them listed.'

And Mazaud, shaking his hand at the door of his office, said:

'You're wrong, you really should see Gundermann about your syndicate.'

'Never!' Saccard shouted once more, looking furious.

He was at last leaving when he recognized Moser and Pillerault at the cash desk: the former, looking very sad, was pocketing his fortnight's gains, seven or eight thousand-franc notes; while the latter, who had lost, was paying out ten-or-so thousand francs, shouting loudly and looking very aggressive and arrogant as if after a victory. It was nearly time for lunch and the opening of the Bourse, so the office was soon going to be almost empty; and as the door of the accounts room was half-open, laughter could be heard from within, as Gustave told Flory abut a boating expedition in which the helmswoman had fallen into the Seine and lost everything, down to her stockings.

Out in the street Saccard glanced at his watch. Eleven o'clock, what a lot of time wasted! No, he would not go and see Daigremont; and although he had been enraged by the very mention of Gundermann's name, he suddenly decided to call on him. Besides, hadn't he said he would be paying him a visit when he announced his grand project at Champeaux's, just to put a stop to that mocking laugh of his? He even gave himself the excuse that he didn't want to get anything out of it, merely wanted to face up to him and triumph over him, this man who affected to treat him like a little boy. And as a fresh downpour sent torrents of water beating down on the pavement, he jumped into a cab and called out the address, Rue de Provence, to the driver.

This was where Gundermann occupied a huge mansion, which was only just big enough for his very numerous family. He had five daughters and four sons, three of the daughters and three of the sons were married and had already given him fourteen grandchildren.

When they were all gathered together for the evening meal they were thirty-one at table, including his wife and himself. And apart from two of his sons-in-law who didn't live in the mansion, they all had their own apartments there, in the east and west wings, which opened on to the gardens, while the central block was entirely taken up by the vast offices of the bank. In less than a century a monstrous fortune of a billion francs had been born, had grown, and had overflowed into this family, through thrift and with the help of favourable events. It seemed like predestination, aided by keen intelligence, relentless work, and prudent, invincible effort, continually striving towards the same goal. All the rivers of gold now flowed into this sea; more and more millions disappeared into these millions, in a swallowing-up of public wealth into the depths of the ever-increasing wealth of one individual; and Gundermann was the real master, the all-powerful king, feared and obeyed by Paris and the world.

As Saccard climbed the wide stone staircase, its steps worn by the continual coming and going of crowds of people, more deeply worn already than the thresholds of ancient churches, he felt the surge of an inextinguishable hatred for this man. Ah, the Jews! Saccard had that ancient racial resentment of the Jews that is found especially in the south of France. It was a sort of revolt of his very flesh, a revulsion of his skin, which, at the idea of the slightest contact, filled him with uncontrollable disgust and violence beyond all reason. But the curious thing was that Saccard, this tremendous business tycoon, this financial thug with his far-from-clean hands, lost all self-awareness as soon as a Jew was involved, and he spoke of Jews with harshness and vengeful indignation as if he were a respectable man who lived by the sweat of his brow, innocent of any dealings in usury. He had a list of grievances against this race, this accursed race which has no homeland or prince of its own, but lives like a parasite on other nations, pretending to recognize their laws but in reality obeying only its own God of theft, blood, and wrath; and he would describe it as everywhere fulfilling the mission of ferocious conquest entrusted to it by this same God, establishing itself in every nation like a spider at the centre of its web, awaiting its prey, sucking everyone's blood, and growing fat on the life of others. Had anyone ever seen a Jew using his own two hands to earn a living? Are there any Jewish peasants, Jewish workers? No, work is dishonourable for them, their religion practically forbids it, it exalts only the exploitation of the labour of others! The scoundrels! Saccard's rage seemed all the greater for the fact that he admired them, envied their prodigious financial abilities, their innate understanding of numbers, their natural ease in the most complicated of calculations, that flair and that luck which mean success in everything they undertake. In this game of thieves, he would say, Christians are not up to it, they always go under in the end; but take a Jew who doesn't even know how to keep books, throw him into the troubled waters of some murky business, and he'll get out safely, carrying all the profits with him. It's a gift of the race, its reason for existing amid all the nationalities that come and go. And he would angrily prophesy the final conquest of every nation by the Jews, once they got their hands on the entire wealth of the globe, and that time was not far off, for they were every day allowed to extend their kingdom without any restraint, and already, in Paris, you could see a Gundermann reigning on a throne more solid and respected than that of the Emperor.

Upstairs, just as he was about to enter the vast antechamber, Saccard paused, seeing it full of jobbers and all sorts of petitioners, men and women, a whole tumultuous, seething crowd. The jobbers especially were fighting over who would get there first, with the unlikely hope of leaving with an order; for the great banker had his own brokers, but it was an honour and a recommendation just to be received, and each of them wanted to be able to boast of it. So the wait was never a long one, the two office-boys served only to organize the procession, the never-ending procession, a veritable gallop through the swinging doors. And in spite of the crowd, Saccard almost immediately went in, joining the flow.

Gundermann's office was an immense room, in which he occupied only a small corner at the far end near the most distant window. Sitting at a simple mahogany desk, he had his back to the light so his face was completely in shadow. Up at five o'clock, he was already at work while Paris still slept; and when, towards nine o'clock, the crush of greedy appetites began to rush past him at the gallop, his day was already done. In the middle of the office, at larger desks, two of his sons and one of his sons-in-law were helping him, rarely sitting down, moving about amid the comings and goings of a multitude of clerks. But this was the inner mechanism of the bank. The streets outside seemed to come in across the room, going only to him, the master, in his modest corner; and for hours on end, until lunchtime, with an impassive and gloomy air, he would receive people, often with a gesture, sometimes with a word if he wished to be particularly agreeable.

As soon as Gundermann caught sight of Saccard his face lit up with a faintly mocking smile.

'Ah! It's you, my good friend... Sit down for a moment, if you have something to say to me. I'll be with you shortly.'

He then affected to forget him. Saccard, however, was not impatient, fascinated by the procession of jobbers coming in hot on each other's heels, all entering with the same deep bow and drawing from their irreproachable frock-coats the same little card, their quotes, with the prices on the Bourse, which they presented to the banker with the same gesture of entreaty and respect. Ten went past, then twenty. Each time, the banker would take the card, glance at it, and hand it back; and the only thing to equal his patience was his utter indifference beneath this hail of offers.

But Massias appeared, with his cheerful, anxious air, like a deserving dogsbody. Sometimes he was received so poorly he could have wept. That day, no doubt, he had run short of humility, for he allowed himself to be unexpectedly insistent.

'Look, Monsieur, Mobiliers are very low... How many should I buy for you?'

Gundermann, not taking his quote, raised his glaucous eyes upon this young man who was being so familiar. Then, brusquely, he said:

'Tell me, my friend, do you think I enjoy receiving you?'

'My word, Monsieur,' Massias began, now quite pale, 'I enjoy even less coming here every morning for nothing, for the past three months.'

'Well then, don't come back.'

The jobber bowed and withdrew, after exchanging with Saccard the furious and desolate glance of a young man who had just realized that he would never make his fortune.

Saccard was indeed beginning to ask himself what interest Gundermann could possibly have in receiving all these people. He obviously had a special ability to cut himself off, he retreated into himself and went on thinking; besides, this must also be a discipline, his way of undertaking every morning a review of the market, in the course of which he could always find some profit to be made, however minimal. He very brutally deducted eighty francs from a dealer to whom he had given an order the previous day, and who was anyway robbing him. Then a dealer in curios arrived, with an enamelled gold box from the last century, an object that had been partially restored, and the banker immediately detected the fraud. Next were two ladies, one old, with a nose like the beak of a predatory bird, and one young, dark-haired and very beautiful, who wanted to show him a Louis-Quinze chest of drawers they had at home and which he refused outright to go and see. Then came a jeweller with some rubies, two inventors, a few Englishmen, some Germans and Italians, every language and every sex. And the procession of jobbers still continued in between the other visits, endlessly repeating the same gesture, the mechanical presentation of the quote; and as the opening hour of the Bourse drew near, the stream of clerks coming through grew ever larger, bringing dispatches and coming for signatures.

But the commotion reached new heights when a little boy of five or six burst into the office, riding on a stick and blowing a trumpet, and following him came two more children, two little girls, one aged three and the other eight; they besieged their grandfather's chair, tugged on his arms and hung around his neck, all of which he placidly allowed, kissing them back with that Jewish passion for the family, the long line of descendants which gives strength and must be defended.

All at once he seemed to remember Saccard.

'Ah! My good friend, please excuse me, as you see, I don't have a minute to myself... You're going to tell me about your business.'

And he was just beginning to listen when a clerk who had shown in a tall, blond gentleman came and whispered a name in his ear, and he stood up at once, though quite unhurriedly, and went to confer with the gentleman in front of another window while one of his sons carried on receiving the jobbers and dealers in his stead.

In spite of his suppressed irritation Saccard was beginning to feel a certain respect. He had recognized the blond gentleman, a representative of one of the Great Powers, full of arrogance at the Tuileries but here with head slightly bowed, smiling and seeking a favour. Top public-service officials, even ministers of the Emperor, would quite frequently be received like that, standing up, in this room which was as public as any square in the city and filled with the noise of children. And all this confirmed the universal sovereignty of this man, who had his own ambassadors in every court in the world, consuls in every province, agencies in every city, and vessels on every sea. He was no speculator, no master adventurer handling other people's millions and dreaming, like Saccard, of heroic battles in which he would be victorious and win some colossal booty thanks to the help of gold, that mercenary enlisted in his service; he was, as he would often good-humouredly say, a simple money-trader, but the cleverest and keenest there could be. But to establish his power he had to dominate the Bourse; so each settlement was a new battle in which victory was unfailingly his, thanks to the decisive power of his big battalions. Watching him, Saccard was for a moment overwhelmed by the thought that all the money that Gundermann was moving around was his own, and that he had, in his vaults, an inexhaustible merchandise, that he bought and sold like a wise and wily trader and absolute master, obeyed at a glance, and determined to hear, see, and do everything for himself. A billion of one's own, handled in this way, is an impregnable force.

'We shan't have a minute to ourselves, my friend,' Gundermann came back to say. 'Look, I'm going to have lunch now, come with me into the next room. Perhaps we'll get a bit of peace.'

It was the small dining-room of the mansion, the one used in the morning when the family was never present all at the same time. That day there were only nineteen at the table, of whom eight were children. The banker sat in the middle, with just a bowl of milk before him.

He sat for a moment with his eyes closed, drained with fatigue, his face very pale and drawn, for he had a malady of the liver and kidneys; then, when he had, with trembling hands, carried the bowl to his lips and drunk a mouthful, he sighed:

'Oh! I'm worn out today!'

'Why don't you rest?' asked Saccard.

Gundermann turned to him with an astonished expression, and simply answered:

'But I can't!'

And indeed, he wasn't even allowed to drink his milk in peace, for the reception of jobbers had resumed and now came galloping through the dining-room, while the men and women of the family, used to all this rushing about, laughed and tucked in to the cold meats and pastries, while the children, excited by a mouthful of undiluted wine, were making a deafening row.

And Saccard, still watching him, marvelled to see him swallow his milk in slow gulps, with such an effort that it seemed he would never reach the bottom of the bowl. He had been put on a diet of milk, he couldn't touch meat or cake anymore. So what good was a billion? Nor had he ever been tempted by women; for forty years he had remained strictly faithful to his wife, and now his good behaviour was compulsory, definitive and irrevocable. So why get up at five in the morning, do this abominable job, be crushed by this immense fatigue, and lead the life of a galley-slave, a life that no beggarman would accept, his memory stuffed with numbers and his skull bursting with a multitude of worries? Why add more useless gold to so much gold, when you can't even buy a pound of cherries to eat in the street or take some passing girl to a dance-hall by the river, or enjoy any of the things that can be bought, like idleness and freedom? And Saccard who, for all his terrible appetites, still recognized the disinterested love of money for the power it gives, felt seized by a kind of sacred terror at seeing this figure before him, not the classic miser hoarding his gold, but the blameless worker with no physical needs, an almost abstract figure in his ailing old age, obstinately continuing to build his tower of millions, with the sole dream of leaving it to his descendants so that they could make it even bigger, until it would dominate the earth.

At last Gundermann leaned over and allowed him quietly to explain his planned creation of the Universal Bank. However, Saccard was sparing of details and made just one allusion to the projects in Hamelin's portfolio, having sensed from his very first words that the banker wanted to get him to tell all, being resolved in advance to turn him away afterwards.

'Another bank, my dear friend, another bank!' Gundermann repeated in a mocking tone. 'But what I'd rather put my money into would be a machine, yes, a guillotine, to chop the heads off all these banks that are being set up... Hmm? Or a rake to clean out the Bourse. Hasn't your engineer got one of those among his papers?'

Then, affecting a paternal air, he said with tranquil cruelty:

'Come on, be sensible, you know what I told you... You're wrong to go back into business, I'm doing you a favour in refusing to launch your syndicate... You will inevitably go down, it's a mathematical certainty; you're too passionate and you have too much imagination; besides, things always go wrong when one is dealing with other people's money... Why doesn't your brother find you a nice position, hmm?

As a prefect or collector of revenues or—no, not a collector of revenues, that's too dangerous. Beware, my friend, beware!'

Trembling, Saccard had risen to his feet.

'So it's quite decided, you won't take any shares, you don't want to be with us?'

'With you? Absolutely never! You'll be eaten up within three years.'

There was a silence, pregnant with battle, and a sharp exchange of challenging looks.

'Goodbye then... I haven't had lunch yet and I'm hungry. We shall see which one of us gets eaten up.'

And Saccard left him surrounded by his tribe still noisily scoffing pastries, receiving the last tardy dealers, occasionally closing his eyes in weariness while he finished his bowl in little sips, his lips all white with milk.

Saccard flung himself into his cab, giving the address of the Rue Saint-Lazare. One o'clock was striking, the day was wasted, and he went home to have lunch, beside himself with rage. Oh, that dirty Jew! Now there, for sure, was one he would really have liked to crush with a single bite, the way a dog crunches a bone! But as for devouring him, he was too terrible and large a morsel. But then, who could tell? Even the greatest empires had collapsed, and the time always comes when even the powerful succumb. No, he shouldn't try to devour him but take a bite out of him, tear a few shreds off his billion; and then devour him, yes! Why not? And so destroy them all in the person of their undisputed king, these Jews who thought themselves the masters of the feast! And these reflections, this anger that he carried away from his meeting with Gundermann, filled Saccard with a furious zeal, a need for business, a need for immediate success: he would have liked to build his banking house with a wave of his hand and set it to work, to triumph, and crush the rival banks. Suddenly the memory of Daigremont came back to him, and with no pause for further thought, in one irresistible movement, he leaned forward and shouted to the coachman to drive to the Rue Rochefoucauld. If he wanted to see Daigremont he needed to make haste, he could always lunch later on, for he knew Daigremont went out at about one o'clock. Without any doubt this Christian was worth two Jews, he was viewed as an ogre who devoured new enterprises entrusted to his care. But at that moment Saccard would have dealt with Cartouche* himself for the sake of victory, even if it meant sharing the winnings. Later on they'd see, he would be the victor.

Meanwhile the cab, climbing with difficulty the steep slope of the street, came to a halt before the high monumental gate of one of the last grand mansions of this district, which had seen some very fine ones. The main body of buildings, at the far end of a vast, paved courtyard, had an air of royal grandeur; and the garden beyond, still lined with century-old trees, remained a real park, quite remote from the crowded streets. All of Paris knew this mansion for its splendid entertainments, and above all, its admirable collection of paintings which no grand-duke on his travels would fail to visit. Married to a woman renowned for her beauty, like his paintings, and who was brilliantly successful in society as a singer, the master of the house led the life of a prince, as proud of his racing stable as his gallery; he belonged to one of the grand clubs, was seen with the most expensive women, had a box at the Opéra, a chair at the Hôtel Drouot,* and a reserved seat in all the fashionable, disreputable places. And all of this expansive life, this luxury, blazing in an apotheosis of caprice and art, was entirely paid for by speculation, a constantly shifting fortune which seemed as infinite as the sea, but also ebbed and flowed like the sea, with differences of two or three hundred thousand francs at every fortnightly settlement.

When Saccard had climbed up the majestic front steps a valet announced him, and led him through three reception-rooms laden with marvels to a small smoking-room where Daigremont was just finishing a cigar before going out. Already forty-five, battling against stoutness, he was tall, very elegant with an immaculate hairstyle, and sported just a moustache and a goatee beard, like a true devotee of the Tuileries.* He showed great amiability and total self-confidence, certain of having the upper hand.

He hurried forward at once.

'Ah! My dear friend, what have you been doing with yourself? I was just thinking of you the other day... But aren't we now neighbours?'

However, he calmed down, abandoning the effusiveness he kept for the rank-and-file, when Saccard, deciding there was no need for excessive subtlety, came straight to the point of his visit. He spoke of his great project, and explained that before founding the Universal Bank with a capital of twenty-five million francs he was looking to form a syndicate of friends, bankers, and industrialists who would guarantee in advance the success of the share issue, by committing themselves to taking up four-fifths of the issue, in other words, at least forty thousand shares. Daigremont had become very serious, listening and watching him as if probing the depths of his brain, to see what effort, what activity useful to himself he might yet get out of this man whom he had seen so active, so full of marvellous qualities in his disorganized enthusiasm. At first he hesitated.

'No, no, I'm overloaded already, I don't want to take on anything new.'

Then, tempted all the same, he asked some questions, wanting to know what projects the new lending-house would sponsor, projects which his interlocutor was wise enough to outline only with the utmost restraint. And when he learned of the first project which would be launched, the consolidation of all the transport companies of the Mediterranean under the corporate name of the United General Steamboat Company, he seemed very struck by the idea and gave in all at once.

'Very well, I agree to join in. But on one condition... How do things stand with your brother, the Minister?'

Saccard, surprised, was frank enough to show his bitterness.

'With my brother... Oh! He takes care of his business and I take care of mine. He's rather short of fraternal feeling, my brother.'

'Ah well, too bad then,' Daigremont declared firmly, 'I will only be with you if your brother is in it too... You understand, I don't want you to be on bad terms.'

With an angry gesture of impatience, Saccard protested. What did they need Rougon for? Wasn't that just looking for chains to bind themselves hand and foot? But at the same time a voice of good sense, stronger than his irritation, was telling him that he had at least to ensure the neutrality of the great man. Meanwhile he went on refusing violently.

'No, no, he's always been too much of a swine to me. I will never take the first step.'

'Listen,' Daigremont went on, 'I'm expecting Huret at five o'clock about a little job he's doing for me... You go along to the Chamber of Deputies, take Huret aside and tell him your plans; he will talk to Rougon about it straight away and find out what he thinks, then we'll have the answer at five... So! Meet here at five?'

With lowered head, Saccard was thinking it over.

'Oh Lord! If that's what you want!'

'Yes, absolutely! Without Rougon, nothing; with Rougon, whatever you like.'

'Very well. I'll go.'

He was leaving, after a vigorous handshake, when the other called him back.

'Ah! Look here, if you feel that things are starting to come together, then on your way back, drop in on the Marquis de Bohain, and Sédille, let them know that I'm in, and ask them to join us... I want them to be in on it.'

At the door Saccard found his cab, which he had kept even though he only had to go to the end of the street to get home. He sent it away, reflecting that he could use his own carriage in the afternoon, and quickly went home to have lunch. They had given up waiting for him, so it was the cook herself who served him a slice of cold meat, which he devoured, all the while quarrelling with the coachman; for the latter, when summoned, had recounted the visit to the vet, the result of which was that the horse had to be allowed to rest for three or four days. With his mouth full, Saccard accused the coachman of not looking after the horse properly and threatened him with Madame Caroline, who would soon sort him out. In the end he shouted at him at least to go and find a cab. An utterly torrential downpour was once more sweeping across the street, and Saccard had to wait more than a quarter of an hour for the carriage, finally getting in under a deluge of water and flinging out the address:

'The Chamber of Deputies!'

His plan was to arrive before the session began, so as to catch Huret on the way in and have a quiet word with him. Unfortunately a heated debate was expected to take place that day, for a member of the Opposition was going to bring up the constantly recurring question of Mexico; and Rougon, no doubt, would be forced to reply.

As Saccard entered the long entrance hall he was lucky enough to chance upon the deputy. Huret took him into one of the little reception-rooms nearby; there they were alone, thanks to the great excitement going on in the corridors. The Opposition was becoming more and more of a threat, the wind of disaster was starting to blow, a wind that would grow stronger and blow everything down. So the preoccupied Huret didn't immediately understand and made Saccard explain twice over the mission he was being given. This only increased his alarm.

'Oh! My dear friend, what are you thinking of? Try to talk to Rougon just now? He'll send me packing for sure!'

Then concern for his own personal interests came to the fore. He only existed through the great man, to whom he owed his official candidature, his election, and his position as a general dogsbody, living on the crumbs of his master's favour. In this job for the past two years, thanks to bribes, and some prudent under-the-counter earnings, he had been enlarging his vast estates in Calvados, with the intention of retiring there and living like a lord after the downfall. His broad face, that of a wily peasant, had darkened, showing his confusion at this request for him to intervene without giving him time to work out whether this would be to his personal benefit or detriment.

'No, no! I cannot... I passed on your brother's wishes to you, I can't go back to him again. Good heavens! Have some consideration for me. He's hardly what you'd call gentle with people who bother him, and Lord! I have no desire to take the rap for you, and lose my standing with him.'

Then Saccard, getting the drift, now concentrated solely on convincing Huret of the millions to be gained in the launching of the Universal Bank. In broad strokes, with his ardent words transforming a business venture into a poetic tale, he outlined the magnificent operations and the certain and colossal success. Daigremont, full of enthusiasm, was putting himself at the head of the syndicate. Bohain and Sédille had already asked to be part of it. It was impossible that he, Huret, should not take part: these gentlemen were insisting he should be with them, on account of his high political position. They were even hoping that he would consent to be on the board of directors, since his name stood for order and probity.

At the promise of appointment to the board Huret looked him straight in the eye.

'All right then, what is it you want of me? What response do you want me to get from Rougon?'

'My word!' said Saccard. 'For myself, I would happily have done without my brother. But it's Daigremont who insists that I make my peace with him. Maybe he's right... So I think you should simply tell the terrible fellow about our business, and obtain, if not his help, then at least a promise that he won't be against us.'

Huret, with half-closed eyes, still could not decide.

'Look! If you bring back a kind word, just a kind word, do you understand? Then Daigremont will be satisfied and the three of us will get it all sewn up this evening.'

'Well then, I'll try,' the deputy declared roughly, affecting a peasant's bluntness. 'But just as well it's for you, because he's not an easy man, oh no, especially when he's being teased by the Left ... Five o'clock, then!'

'Five o'clock!'

Saccard stayed on for nearly an hour, very worried by the rumours going round about a struggle. He heard one of the great Opposition orators announce that he was going to speak. On hearing this he wanted for a moment to get back to Huret, to ask him if it wouldn't be wiser to put off the meeting with Rougon until the next day. Then, fatalistic and believing in chance, he trembled at the idea of everything being compromised if he altered what had been decided. Perhaps, in all the commotion, his brother would more easily let slip the word they hoped for. And to allow things to sort themselves out, he left, got back in his cab, and was already on the way back to the Pont de la Concorde when he remembered the wish that Daigremont had expressed.

'Driver, Rue de Babylone.'

The Rue de Babylone was where the Marquis de Bohain lived. He occupied the former outbuildings of a grand mansion, a building which had once housed the stable staff and which had been made into a very comfortable modern house. The furnishings were luxurious, with a fine air of chic aristocracy. His wife was never seen, being unwell, said the Marquis, and kept to her apartment by infirmity. However, the house and furniture were hers, and he merely lodged there in a furnished apartment, owning only his personal effects, in a trunk he could have carried away in a cab; they had been legally separated ever since he started living on speculation. There had been two catastrophes already, in which he had blankly refused to pay what he owed and the official receiver, having taken stock of the situation, had not even bothered to send him an official document. The slate was simply wiped clean. As long as he won, he pocketed the money. Then, when he lost, he didn't pay: everyone knew it and everyone was resigned to it. He had an illustrious name, he made an excellent ornament for boards of directors; so new companies, looking for golden mastheads, fought over him: he was never unemployed. At the

Bourse he had his own chair on the Rue Notre-Dame-des-Victoires side, the side of the rich speculators who pretended to take no interest in the petty rumours of the day. He was respected, and much-consulted. He had often had an influence on the market. In short, he was a real personage.

Saccard knew him well, but was nevertheless impressed by the extreme courtesy of the reception he received from this handsome old man of sixty, his very small head set on the body of a colossus, and his pale face, framed by a dark wig, looking extremely grand.

'Monsieur le Marquis, I've come to seek your help...'

He explained the reason for his visit, without at first going into details. Besides, from his very first words the Marquis stopped him.

'No, no, my time is all taken up, I already have ten proposals that I shall have to refuse.'

Then, when Saccard smiled and added: 'It was Daigremont who sent me, it was he who thought of you...', he at once cried:

'Ah! you have Daigremont in with you... Fine! Fine! If Daigremont is involved then so am I. You can count on me.'

And when the visitor tried to provide him with at least a bit of information to let him know what sort of business he was getting into, he silenced him with the amiable nonchalance of a great lord who doesn't go into such details and has a natural confidence in the honesty of people.

'Please, don't say another word... I do not wish to know. You need my name, I lend it to you, and I am very happy to do so, that's all... Just tell Daigremont to arrange things as he thinks best.'

As he got back in his cab Saccard, greatly cheered, laughed to himself.

'He'll be expensive, that fellow,' he thought, 'but he really is very charming.'

Then, aloud, he said:

'Driver, Rue des Jeûneurs.'

That was where Sédille had his warehouses and offices, which occupied the whole of the vast ground floor at the far end of a courtyard. After thirty years of work, Sédille, who came from Lyons, where he still had some workshops, had at last succeeded in making his silk business one of the best-known and most solid in Paris when, after some chance incident, a passion for speculation had manifested itself and spread right through him with the violent destructiveness of a fire. Two considerable wins, one after another, made him lose his head.

What was the point of giving thirty years of one's life to earning a paltry million, when one could pocket that much in one hour with a simple transaction on the Bourse? From that moment on he had gradually lost all interest in his business, which carried on under its own momentum; but he now lived entirely in the hope of some financial coup on the market; and since bad luck had come his way, and persisted, he had begun to swallow up in his gambling all the profits from his business. The worst of this fever is that one loses the taste for legitimate earnings, and ends up having no clear idea at all about money. And ruin inevitably lay ahead if the workshops in Lyons earned him two hundred thousand francs while he lost three hundred thousand on the stock-market.

Saccard found Sédille looking agitated and worried, for, as a speculator, he was neither stoical nor philosophical. He lived in a state of constant guilt, always hopeful, always disappointed, and sick with uncertainty, for he remained an honest man at heart. The settlement at the end of April had just proved disastrous for him. However, his plump face with thick blond sideburns took on some colour at Saccard's first words.

'Ah, my dear chap, if it's luck you're bringing me then you're very welcome!'

Then, however, he took fright.

'No, no! Don't tempt me. I'd do better to lock myself in with my lengths of silk, and not budge from my counter.'

To help him calm down, Saccard talked to him about his son Gustave, mentioning that he'd seen him that morning at Mazaud's. But this was yet another source of grief for the merchant, for he had dreamed of handing over his business to his son, who, however, despised trade; he was a creature made for joy and festivities, with the white teeth that the sons of parvenus have, teeth only good for crunching up ready-made fortunes. His father had placed him with Mazaud to see if he might get his teeth into financial matters.

'Ever since his poor mother died,' he murmured, 'he's given me little enough cause for satisfaction. Anyway, perhaps there, in that office, he may learn things that will be useful to me.'

'Well then!' said Saccard briskly, 'are you with us? Daigremont told me to come and tell you that he was in it.'

Sédille raised his trembling arms to the sky. And, in a voice marked by both desire and fear:

'But yes, of course I am! You know very well I can't do otherwise than join in! If I refused and your venture flourished, I'd be sick with regret... Tell Daigremont I'm in.'

Once back in the street, Saccard took out his watch and saw it was barely four o'clock. With plenty of time ahead of him, an impulse to walk for a while prompted him to let his cab go. He regretted this almost immediately, for he had not even reached the Boulevard when a new shower, a deluge of rain and hail, forced him to seek refuge in a doorway. What filthy weather for conquering Paris! After watching the rain falling for a quarter of an hour, impatience overcame him and he hailed an empty cab that was passing. It was a victoria, and try as he might to pull the leather apron over his legs, he arrived at the Rue La Rochefoucauld soaked through and a full half-hour early.

In the smoking-room where the valet left him, saying that Monsieur had not yet returned, Saccard walked around slowly, looking at the pictures. But a superb female voice, a contralto of deep and melancholy power, rose up from within the silence of the house, and he went over to the open window to listen: it was Madame at the piano, rehearsing a piece she would no doubt be singing that evening at some reception. Then, lulled by the music, he began to recall the extraordinary stories told about Daigremont: especially the tale of the Hadamantine company, that loan of fifty million francs in which he had kept back the entire stock, getting it sold and resold five times over using his own dealers, until he had created a market for it and established a price; then, when serious selling began, came the inevitable fall from three hundred to fifteen francs, and enormous profits were made out of a little group of simple souls who were all instantly ruined. Ah! He was good at it, quite terrible! The voice of Madame continued, sending forth a lament of despairing love, of tragic depth; meanwhile Saccard, getting back into the middle of the room, paused in front of a Meissonier,* which he guessed to be worth a hundred thousand francs.

But someone came in, and he was surprised to see that it was Huret.

'What! You're here already? It's not yet five... Is the session finished then?'

'Ah yes! Finished... they're still squabbling.'

And he explained that as the Opposition member was still talking, Rougon would certainly be unable to deliver his response until tomorrow. So when he realized this he had risked pestering the minister again, very hurriedly, during a brief pause in the session.

'And?' Saccard asked irritably, 'What did my illustrious brother say?'

Huret didn't answer straight away.

'Oh! He was in an absolutely foul mood... I must admit, I was counting on the state of exasperation he was in, hoping he'd simply send me packing... So I told him about your affair, and said you didn't want to undertake anything without his approval.'

'So?'

'So then he seized me by both arms, shook me, and yelled into my face: "Let him go and get himself hanged!" And then he left me standing there.'

Saccard, suddenly very pale, gave a forced laugh.

'That's good of him.'

'I'll say! Yes, it is good,' Huret carried on, in a tone of conviction. 'I wasn't expecting as much... With that, we can get on with things.'

And as he heard in the next room the footsteps of Daigremont returning home, he added quietly:

'Leave it to me.'

Of course, Huret was very keen to see the Universal Bank founded and to be in on it. He had no doubt already worked out what part he might play. So, as soon as he had shaken hands with Daigremont he took on a radiant expression and waved his arms in the air.

'Victory!' he cried. 'Victory!'

'Ah! Really. Tell me all about it.'

'My word! The great man was all that he was meant to be. He replied, "May my brother succeed!"'

At this Daigremont was utterly delighted, and thought the remark quite charming. 'May he succeed!' That said it all: if he's stupid enough to fail I'll abandon him, but so long as he succeeds I'll help him. Truly exquisite!

'And my dear Saccard, we shall succeed, have no fear... We shall do everything required to that end.'

Then, when the three men were sitting down to decide on the main points, Daigremont got up and closed the window; for Madame's voice, gradually getting louder, was tearing out such a sob of infinite despair that they could not hear each other speak. And even with the window shut, that banished lamentation still accompanied them while they settled on the creation of a lending-house, the Universal Bank, with a capital of twenty-five million francs divided into fifty thousand shares of five hundred francs each. It was further agreed that Daigremont, Huret, Sédille, the Marquis de Bohain and a few of their friends would form a syndicate which would in advance take up and share between them four-fifths of the stock, in other words forty thousand shares; in this way, the success of the share-issue was guaranteed, and later on, holding on to the securities and making them scarce on the market, they could make their value rise at will. But everything almost came adrift when Daigremont demanded a bonus of four hundred thousand francs spread across the forty thousand shares, that is, ten francs per share. Saccard protested, declaring that it was unreasonable to make the cow moo even before they milked her.* Things would be difficult enough at the beginning, so why complicate the situation further? He had to give in, however, faced with the attitude of Huret, who calmly said he found it quite natural and that was how it was always done.

They were going their separate ways, having agreed a meeting for the next day, a meeting at which the engineer Hamelin was to be present, when Daigremont suddenly struck his brow with an expression of despair.

'I was forgetting Kolb! Oh! he'd never forgive me, he must be in on this... Saccard, dear boy, would you be so kind as to go to him straight away? It's not yet six o'clock, you'd still find him at home... Yes, you yourself, and now, this evening, not tomorrow, because that will make a good impression on him and he can be useful to us.'

Saccard obediently set off once more, conscious that lucky days don't come around twice. But he had yet again dismissed his cab, hoping to return home only a few yards away; and as the rain seemed at last to be stopping he went on foot, happy to feel beneath his heels these Paris streets he was reconquering. In the Rue Montmartre a few drops of rain made him decide to go by way of the covered passages.* He went through the Passage Verdeau and the Passage Jouffroy, then, in the Passage des Panoramas, as he was taking a short-cut to the Rue Vivienne through a side arcade, he was surprised to see Gustave Sédille coming out of a dark alley and disappearing without turning round. Saccard too had stopped and was looking at the house, a discreet establishment of furnished rooms, when a small, blonde woman, wearing a veil, also came out, and he clearly recognized Madame

Conin, the pretty stationer's wife. So this was where she brought her one-day lovers when she had a fancy for love, while that great, jolly fellow of a husband of hers thought she was out chasing up bills! This secluded spot, right in the middle of the district, was very nicely chosen, and it was the merest chance that had revealed its secret. Saccard smiled, quite cheered up, envying Gustave: Germaine Coeur in the morning, Madame Conin in the afternoon, that young man was getting double helpings! And he looked twice more at the door so he could remember it, much tempted to be in on the act himself.

In the Rue Vivienne, just as he was going into Kolb's house, Saccard gave a start and again came to a halt. A light, crystalline music, coming up from the ground like the voice of the fairies of legend, wrapped itself around him, and he recognized the music of gold, the constant tinkling of this district of trade and speculation, the sound he had already heard that morning. The end of the day seemed to be linking up with the beginning. He basked in the caressing sound of that voice, as if it were confirming his good omens.

Kolb was in fact downstairs, in the smelting workshop; and as a friend of the family, Saccard went down to join him. In the bareness of the basement, eternally lit by large gas-flames, the two smelters were using spades to empty the zinc-lined chests, today full of Spanish coins which they were throwing into the crucible on the big, square furnace. The heat was fierce, one had to talk loudly to be heard amid the harmonica-like ringing, which resounded under the low vaulted ceiling. Newly forged ingots, slabs of gold with the vivid brilliance of new metal, were lined up along the table of the assayer, who fixed their values. And since that morning more than six million had gone through, giving the banker a profit of scarcely three or four hundred francs; for the arbitrage on gold, on the difference realized between two currency markets, is of the slightest, counted in thousandths, so very substantial quantities of molten metal are needed to yield any profit. Hence this tinkling of gold, this stream of gold from morning to night, from one year's end to the next, down in this cellar where gold arrived in minted coins and left in gold ingots, only to return as coins and leave again as ingots, indefinitely, with the sole object of leaving in the hands of the dealer a few particles of gold.

Kolb was a small, very dark man, whose nose, like an eagle's beak, emerging from a dense beard, gave away his Jewish origins, and as soon as he had understood what Saccard was offering, even through the rattling hail of gold, he accepted.

'Perfect!' he cried. 'Glad to be in on it, if Daigremont is in on it! And thank you for going to so much trouble!'

But they could scarcely hear each other, and both fell silent, standing there for a moment longer, blissfully dazed by that clear and furious ringing which made their flesh quiver, like too high a note on a violin, held for so long that it makes one shudder.

Outside, in spite of the return of good weather and a limpid May evening, Saccard, desperately tired, called another cab to take him home. A hard day, but well spent!

CHAPTER IV

SOME difficulties arose, the affair dragged on, and five months went by before anything could be finalized. September was already coming to an end, and Saccard was exasperated to see that, in spite of his zealous efforts, obstacles kept springing up and a whole series of minor matters had to be settled if they were going to create something serious and substantial. Such was his impatience that at one point he almost sent the whole syndicate packing, suddenly captivated and enchanted by the idea of doing the whole thing with the Princess d'Orviedo alone. She had the millions needed for the initial launching, why shouldn't she put them into this superb venture? They could always let in smaller clients for the later increases of capital he already had in mind. He was utterly sincere, convinced he would be bringing her an investment that would multiply her fortune, the fortune of the poor, ten times over, so she could give it away even more generously.

So one morning Saccard went up to see the Princess, and in his dual role as friend and business associate explained to her the intentions behind, and the mechanisms of, the bank he wanted to create. He told her everything, outlining the contents of Hamelin's portfolio, omitting not one of the Eastern enterprises. Giving in to that tendency of his to become intoxicated with his own enthusiasm, and even arriving at religious faith through his burning desire for success, he revealed the mad dream of the Papacy in Jerusalem, and spoke of the definitive triumph of Catholicism, the Pope reigning over the Holy Land and dominating the world, supported by a budget fit for a king, thanks to the creation of the Treasury of the Holy Sepulchre. The Princess, who was fervently devout, was hardly affected at all except by this ultimate project, the pinnacle of the whole structure, whose fabulous grandeur appealed to that unbalanced imagination of hers that made her throw away her millions on good works of colossal and useless opulence. In fact, the French Catholics had just been dismayed and angered by the agreement the Emperor had concluded with the King of Italy, by which he undertook, under certain guaranteed conditions, to withdraw the detachment of French troops now occupying Rome.* This surely meant a Rome surrendered to Italy, and they could already imagine the Pope being driven out, dependent on charity,

wandering from city to city with a beggar's staff; and what a prodigiously happy ending it would be for the Pope to find himself instead,
pontiff and king in Jerusalem, established there and supported by a
bank in which Christians the world over would consider it an honour
to hold shares! It was so splendid that the Princess declared it the
greatest idea of the century, worthy of inspiring passion in any well-
born religious person. She thought it was bound to be a thundering
success. Her esteem for Hamelin the engineer, whom she had been
treating with great consideration ever since discovering he was a
practising Catholic, grew even greater as a result. But she totally
refused to be part of the enterprise, intent on being true to the vow
she had made to give all her millions back to the poor, without ever
again earning a single cent, wanting all the money gained from speculation to be lost, to be drained away by poverty, like poisoned water
which had to disappear. The argument that the poor would profit
from the speculation failed to touch her, even irritated her. No! No!
That accursed spring would be dried up, that was her sole mission.

Disconcerted, all Saccard could do was take advantage of her sympathy to obtain her permission for something he had previously
requested in vain. He had had the idea—or rather, it was Madame
Caroline who had suggested it—of installing the Universal Bank, once
it was set up, in the mansion itself; he himself had rather grander
ideas, he would have liked a palace straight away. They would simply
make a glass roof for the courtyard to serve as the main hall, and con-
vert the whole of the ground floor, stables, and outbuildings into
offices; on the first floor he would give up his reception-room to serve
as boardroom, while his dining-room and six other rooms would provide more offices, and he would keep only a bedroom and bathroom
for himself, since he could mainly live on the upper floor with the
Hamelins, eating with them and spending his evenings there; so, with
little expenditure the bank would be installed, in a slightly cramped
but very respectable style. As owner of the building the Princess, with
her hatred of any kind of financial dealing, had at first refused: never
would such an abomination find shelter under her roof. Then, that
day, with religion involved in the affair, she was moved by the grandeur of the aim and gave her consent. It was a very big concession, for it
was with a shudder that she thought of allowing that infernal machine
of a lending-house, that house of stock-markets and interest-rates,
into her building, with all its machinery of death and ruin.

At last, a week after this abortive attempt, Saccard had the joy of seeing the project so long beset by obstacles suddenly come together in a few days. One morning Daigremont came to tell him that he had all the signatures and they could get things started. They then went over the proposed statutes one last time, and drew up the formal instrument of association. Nor was it a moment too soon for the Hamelins, whose life was beginning to get difficult again. For years Hamelin's one dream had been to work as consultant engineer for a big lending-house: he would undertake, as he put it, to bring the water to the mill. Little by little he had caught Saccard's fever, so he now burned with the same zeal and impatience. Madame Caroline, on the contrary, after being fired by enthusiasm at the idea of all the fine and useful things they were going to accomplish, seemed rather more cold and pensive now that they were getting into the troublesome and thorny details of its execution. Her sound common sense and upright nature could anticipate all sorts of dark and dirty pitfalls lying ahead; above all she trembled for her beloved brother, whom she sometimes laughingly called a 'big ninny' in spite of all his learning; not that she had the slightest doubt about the absolute honesty of their friend, who was so evidently devoted to making their fortune; but she had a strange sensation of the ground shifting beneath her feet, a fear of falling and being swallowed up if they so much as put a foot wrong.

That morning, when Daigremont had gone, a beaming Saccard came up to the workroom.

'At last it's done!' he cried.

Hamelin, quite amazed and with tears in his eyes, went to shake his hands, almost crushing them in his fervour. And since Madame Caroline had merely turned towards him, looking rather pale, Saccard added:

'Well then, what about you? Is that all you have to say? Doesn't it make you any happier than that?'

Then she gave a pleasant smile.

'But I assure you, of course I'm happy, very happy.'

When he had given her brother some details about the syndicate, now in its final form, she intervened in her quiet way:

'So that's allowed then, is it? For several people to get together and divide the shares of a bank between them, even before the shares have been issued?'

He made an emphatic gesture of affirmation.

'But of course it's allowed!... Do you think we'd be stupid enough to risk failure? Not to mention the fact that we need to have solid people, people who can influence the market if things are difficult at the beginning... That means four-fifths of our shares are in safe hands. Now we can go to the notary and sign the deed of association.'

She was bold enough to stand her ground.

'I thought the law required subscription of the whole of the share capital.'

This time, really surprised, he looked her straight in the eye.

'You've been reading the Code?'*

She blushed slightly, for he had guessed right: the evening before, giving in to her uneasiness, that vague fear with no precise cause, she had done some reading on company law. For a moment she was tempted to lie. Then, with a laugh, she admitted it:

'It's true, I read the Code yesterday. I came out of it doubting my own honesty and everyone else's, in the same way one emerges from medical books with every one of the ailments.'

But he was really annoyed, for the fact that she had tried to get information showed her to be distrustful and ready to keep watch over him with those woman's eyes of hers, so inquisitive and intelligent.

'Ah!' he continued, brushing aside such vain scruples with a wave of his hand, 'if you think we're going to comply with all the fiddling complications of the Code! We'd never get anywhere that way, we'd be shackled at every step, while others, all our competitors, would be striding ahead right past us! No, no, I'm certainly not going to wait until all the capital has been subscribed; anyway, I prefer to hold back some shares, and I shall find a man we can trust, a frontman in short, for whom I can open an account.'

'That's not allowed,' she declared simply but gravely with her splendid voice.

'You're right, it's not allowed, but every company does it.'

'Well they shouldn't, because it's wrong.'

Keeping his temper by an effort of will, Saccard thought it best to turn to Hamelin, who was listening with some embarrassment but keeping out of it.

'My dear friend, I hope you don't have any doubts about me... I'm an old campaigner with plenty of experience, you can place yourself in my hands for the financial side of things. Bring me good ideas and

I'll undertake to make them as profitable as we could wish, at the least possible risk. I believe a practical man can't say better than that.'

The engineer, with his invincible timidity and weakness, turned the matter into a joke to avoid making a direct reply:

'Oh, Caroline will keep you in order; she's a born schoolmistress.'

'And I'll be very happy to be in her classroom,' Saccard gallantly declared.

Even Madame Caroline had started to laugh again. And the conversation continued in a familiar, good-natured manner.

'The thing is, I'm very fond of my brother, and I'm very fond of you too, more so than you think, and it would really hurt me to see you getting involved in shady dealings, which in the end lead to nothing but disaster and sorrow... And look, while we're on the subject, I have a real terror of speculation and playing the stock-market. When you had me copy out the proposed statutes I was so pleased when I read Article 8, stating that the company was strictly forbidden to deal in futures. That meant, no speculation, didn't it? And then you disabused me, making fun of me, explaining that the article was simply cosmetic, a stylistic formula that all companies are honour-bound to include but not one of them observes... Do you know what I would like, if it were up to me? I would like it if, instead of these shares, these fifty thousand shares that you're launching, you only issued bonds. Oh, you see how knowledgeable I've become since reading the Code! I now know that one cannot speculate in bonds, and that a bondholder is simply a lender who earns a certain percentage on his loan without having any part of the profits, while a shareholder is an associate who runs the risk of profit and loss... Tell me, why can't we have bonds instead?—That would greatly reassure me and I'd be so happy!'

She jokingly exaggerated the tone of supplication in her request, to mask her real anxiety. And Saccard replied in the same vein, with a comic show of anger.

'Bonds, bonds! Never!... What the devil do you want with bonds, I ask you? That's just dead stuff... What you have to understand is that speculation, playing the market, is the central motor, the very heart of a vast affair such as ours. Yes! It brings new blood into the system, it takes small streams of it from all over the place then collects it together and sends it out in rivers, in all directions, creating an enormous circulation of money which is the very lifeblood of great enterprises. Without it major movements of capital, and the great civilizing works that result, are fundamentally impossible... It's the same for limited-liability companies—what an outcry there was against them! Weren't we told, over and over, that they were disreputable and dangerous? The truth is that without them we wouldn't have railways or any of the great new enterprises that have modernized the world; no single fortune would have been sufficient to carry them to success, just as no single individual, nor even any group of individuals, would have been willing to take the risks. Risk, that's the essential, that and the grandeur of the aim too. There has to be a vast project, a project big enough to capture the imagination; there has to be hope of substantial gain, of winning a jackpot that will give ten times the initial outlay, unless of course it gets swept away instead; that's what provokes passions, so life floods in, everyone brings his money, and the world can be reshaped. What evil do you see in that? The risks are taken voluntarily and spread over an infinite number of people, unevenly and in line with the size of each person's wealth and audacity. You can lose but you can also win, you hope for a lucky number but you have to be ready for an unlucky one, and mankind has no more stubborn nor more ardent dream than trying one's luck and winning everything through a whim of fortune, becoming a king, or a god!'

As he went on Saccard wasn't laughing any more, he was drawing himself up on his short legs, glowing with lyrical ardour and making gestures that flung his words to the four corners of the heavens.

'Look! What about us with our Universal Bank, shan't we be opening up the widest horizon, a real opening onto the ancient world of Asia, a limitless field for the pickaxe of progress and the dreams of fortune-hunters? Yes, there's never been a more colossal ambition, and I grant you, never have the conditions for success or failure been more obscure. But that is precisely why we tick all the right boxes, and why I'm convinced we'll create a real craze in the public as soon as we get known... Our Universal Bank, my word!—at first it will be a traditional establishment dealing in all kinds of banking business, credit and discounts, taking in funds in current accounts, making contracts, arranging or granting loans. But what I want above all is to make it a vehicle for launching your brother's great projects: that will be its true role, with its profits increasing and its power gradually dominating the market. It is being founded, in short, to provide support

for the financial and industrial companies we'll be setting up in foreign countries, whose shares we shall hold and which will thus owe
their lives to us and guarantee our supremacy... And in the face of
this dazzling vision of future conquests, you're asking me whether
it's permissible to form a syndicate and give its members a bonus that
can be written off against start-up costs; you're worrying about little
unavoidable irregularities, some unsubscribed shares that the company will need to keep, using a frontman as cover; in fact you're
declaring war on speculation, on speculation—great heavens!—the
very soul, the core, the inner flame of this gigantic mechanism I'm
trying to create! You need to realize that all this, so far, is nothing,
this paltry little capital of twenty-five million is just a bit of kindling
that we're throwing into the engine to get the fire going! I expect to
double it, quadruple it, quintuple it, as our operations expand! We
need a hail of gold, a dance of millions, if we want to achieve out there
the miracles predicted! But damn it! I can't guarantee there'll be no
breakages, you can't go stirring up the world without stepping on a
few toes along the way.'

She was watching him, and in her love of life and of everything
strong and active, she ended up finding him quite handsome, charming
in his verve and conviction. And so, without accepting his theories,
which offended her upright and lucid intelligence, she pretended to
have been won over.

'All right, let's say I'm only a woman and life's great battles frighten
me... Only please try to tread on as few toes as possible, and especially
not the toes of anyone I care about!'

Intoxicated by his burst of eloquence, and exulting over the vast
project he'd outlined, as if it were all done already, Saccard was now
quite benign.

'Have no fear! I may act the ogre but I'm just teasing... We're all
going to be very rich.'

Then they chatted quietly about the arrangements to be made, and
it was agreed that the very next day, after the official foundation of
the company, Hamelin would go to Marseilles and from there to the
Orient, to put their great plans into operation. However, there was
already gossip on the Paris market, rumours were bringing the name
of Saccard back from the murky depths into which it had briefly
sunk; at first the news was whispered, then spoken more loudly, and
then it rang out clearly, promising imminent success, so that once

again, as before in the Parc Monceau, Saccard's waiting-room was full of people every morning. He found Mazaud dropping by to shake his hand and discuss the day's news; he had visits from other brokers, including Jacoby, the Jew with the booming voice, and his brother-in-law Delarocque, a big red-haired man who caused his wife so much grief. The kerb market came to call too, in the person of Nathansohn, a small and lively fair-haired man, much favoured by fortune. As for Massias, resigned to his hard lot as an unlucky jobber, he was already turning up every day even though there weren't yet any orders to be had. The crowd kept on growing larger.

One morning Saccard found the waiting-room full though it was only nine o'clock. As he had not yet taken on any special staff he was being helped, very inadequately, by his valet, and most of the time took it upon himself to let people in. That day, as he was opening the door of his office, he saw Jantrou waiting to enter; but he had caught sight of Sabatani, whom he'd been trying to get hold of for two days.

'Forgive me, my friend,' he said, stopping the former professor so that he could let the Levantine in first.

Sabatani, with his disturbing, caressing smile and serpentine suppleness, left the talking to Saccard, and he, knowing his man, made his proposition very plainly:

'My dear fellow, I need you... We need a frontman. I'll open an account for you and make you the buyer of a certain number of our shares,* that you'll pay for simply with some juggling of the accounts... As you see, I'm getting straight to the point and treating you as a friend.'

The young man looked at him with his beautiful, velvety eyes, eyes of such softness in his long, dark face.

'The law, dear Sir, formally requires payment in cash... Oh! it's not for my sake that I mention this. You're treating me as a friend, which makes me very proud... I'll do whatever you want!'

Then Saccard, just to be agreeable, mentioned the high esteem in which Sabatani was held by Mazaud, who now even took his orders without any cover. Then he teased him about Germaine Coeur, with whom he had seen him the day before, and made a crude allusion to the rumours about his being prodigiously well endowed with something exceptionally gigantic, which set the girls in the world of the Bourse dreaming and tormented them with curiosity. Sabatani didn't deny it, but just laughed noncommittally on this unseemly subject: oh, yes! the ladies were very amusing, the way they chased after him, they all wanted to see for themselves.

'Ah! By the way,' Saccard broke in, 'we shall also need some signatures to regularize certain operations, transfers, for instance... May I send the packets of papers to you for signing?'

'But certainly, my dear sir. Whatever you want!'

He didn't even raise the matter of payment, knowing full well that such services are beyond price; and when Saccard added that he would be paid one franc per signature for his time, he simply nodded his agreement. Then, with that smile of his:

'I also hope, dear sir, that you won't refuse me your advice. After all, you'll be so well placed I shall come to you for information.'

'Absolutely,' concluded Saccard, catching his meaning. 'Goodbye, then... Take it easy now, and don't go giving in too much to the curiosity of the ladies.'

And with renewed amusement, Saccard saw him off through a side-door that allowed callers to be let out without having to go through the waiting-room.

Saccard then went to open the other door and call in Jantrou. He saw at a glance that the man was a wreck, at the end of his tether, the sleeves of his frock-coat frayed from sitting at café tables waiting for work. The Bourse continued to have no love for him yet he still seemed debonair, with his bushy beard, cynical and highly literate, occasionally uttering a flowery phrase that recalled his former career as an academic.

'I was just about to write to you,' said Saccard. 'We're drawing up a list of personnel, yours was one of the first names I put down, and I expect I'll be calling you to our share-issuing office.'

Jantrou stopped him with a wave of the hand.

'That's very kind of you, thanks... But I have a business proposition for you.'

He didn't immediately explain himself, but launched into general matters, asking what role newspapers would play in the launching of the Universal Bank. At the first words on this subject Saccard showed eager enthusiasm, declaring that he was in favour of the widest possible publicity and would devote all available money to that end. No newspaper was to be shunned, not even the most downmarket rag, for his motto was that any publicity was good publicity. His dream would be to have control of all the newspapers; but that would be too expensive.

'So, would you be thinking of organizing our advertising?... That might not be a bad idea at that. We can talk it over.'

'Yes, later on, if you like... But what would you say to your own newspaper, entirely yours, with me as editor? Every morning you'd have a page to yourself, with articles singing your praises, notes calling attention to you, references to you in pieces quite unrelated to the world of finance... in other words, a thorough campaign about everything and nothing, ceaselessly glorifying you—over the dead bodies of your rivals... Does that sound tempting?'

'I'll say! So long as it doesn't cost a fortune.'

'No, the cost would be quite reasonable.'

At last he gave the name of the paper, *L'Espérance*,* a publication founded two years before by a small group of prominent Catholics, the extremists of the party currently waging a fierce war against the Empire. They had enjoyed absolutely no success, and the paper's imminent disappearance was being announced every day. Saccard protested.

'But it has a print-run of less than two thousand!'

'That will be our job, to increase the circulation.'

'Anyway, it's impossible: that paper's been dragging my brother through the mud, and I can't fall out with my brother right at the start.'

Jantrou gave a gentle shrug.

'You don't have to fall out with anyone... You know as well as I do, when a bank owns a paper it's of little importance whether it supports or attacks the government: if it's pro-government the bank is sure to be part of every syndicate created by the Minister of Finance to promote the success of state and municipal loans; if it's for the Opposition the very same minister will have every kind of consideration for the bank it represents, wanting to disarm it and win it over, which usually translates into even more favours... So don't worry about what colour *L'Espérance* is. Just have a paper, it's a source of power.'*

Saccard was silent for a moment, already developing a plan with that lively intelligence of his which instantly allowed him to take over someone else's idea, explore its possibilities, and adapt it to his needs, making it completely his own: he would buy *L'Espérance*, get rid of any bitter polemics, and lay it at the feet of his brother, who would be forced to be grateful to him for that; but he would retain its Catholic colouration, keeping this as a threat, as a mechanism always ready to resume its terrible campaign in the name of the interests of religion. And if there was no cooperation he would brandish Rome and the risk of the great Jerusalem coup. That would be a very nice last card to play.

'Would we be free?' he asked brusquely.

'Absolutely free. They've had enough of it, the paper has fallen into the hands of a needy chap who will let us have it for ten or so thousand francs. We can do whatever we like with it.'

Saccard took a minute again to reflect.

'All right then, it's agreed! Arrange a meeting and bring me your man... You will be editor and I shall put all our publicity in your hands, and I want it to be exceptional, enormous—Oh! later of course, when we have the wherewithal to get the engine going properly.'

He stood up. Jantrou too rose to his feet, trying to hide his joy at finding the means to earn his crust under the bantering laugh of one who has lost his social standing and is weary of the mud of Paris.

'At last! I'll be back in my element, my beloved world of letters.'

'Don't take anyone on just yet,' Saccard went on as he escorted him out. 'And, while I think of it, make a note of a protégé of mine, Paul Jordan, a young man who, in my view, has a remarkable talent and will make an excellent literary journalist for you. I shall write to him telling him to come and see you.'

Jantrou was just going out through the side-door when he was struck by the happy arrangement of the two exits.

'My word, that's handy!' he said with his usual familiarity. 'People can just disappear... When lovely ladies come calling—like the one I greeted just now in the waiting-room, Baroness Sandorff...'

Saccard had no idea she was there; he shrugged to show his indifference, but Jantrou sniggered, refusing to believe in this lack of interest. The two men shook hands with some vigour.

When he was alone again Saccard instinctively went over to the mirror and ran a hand through his hair, where no hint of white was yet visible. All the same, he had not been lying, women had not been on his mind at all since he had been totally caught up again in business matters; and he was only indulging in that instinctive Gallic gallantry that means a man in France cannot find himself alone with a woman without fearing to be thought a fool if he doesn't make a conquest. As soon as he had let the Baroness in he made a great fuss of her.

'Madame, pray, do sit down...'

Never had he seen her looking so strangely alluring, with her red lips, her burning eyes with the bruised lids, deep-set beneath thick eyebrows. What could she want of him? And he was surprised, almost disappointed, when she explained the purpose of her visit.

'Ah Monsieur, I do apologize for disturbing you, and to so little purpose as far as you are concerned, but people of our social circle have to help each other out in these little matters... Until recently you had a chef, whom my husband is now about to engage. So I've come simply to ask for some information about him.'

So he allowed her to question him, answering in the most obliging way without ever taking his eyes off her, for he thought he could guess that this was just a pretext: she didn't care in the least about the chef, she had clearly come for something else. And indeed, she organized the conversation in such a way as to bring in the name of a mutual friend, the Marquis de Bohain, who had spoken to her about the Universal Bank. It was so difficult to place one's money, so hard to find really solid investments! At last he realized she would really like to buy some shares, with the ten per cent bonus for members of the syndicate, and he realized too, even more clearly, that if he opened an account for her she would not pay up.

'I have my own private fortune, my husband has nothing to do with it. It's a lot of bother but I quite enjoy it, I must admit... But when a woman is seen to be dealing in money matters, and especially a young woman, don't you think? People are surprised and tend to think ill of her... There are days when I find myself in dire difficulties, having no friends at hand to advise me. Just a fortnight ago, for lack of information, I lost a considerable sum of money... Ah! Now that you are going to be so well placed for information, if you could be so kind, if you would be willing to...'

Beneath the woman of the world the gambler showed through, the desperate, obsessive speculator, this daughter of the Ladricourt family, one of whose ancestors had captured Antioch; this diplomat's wife, so highly respected by the foreign colony of Paris but whose passion sent her scurrying round the financial world seeking favours. Her lips were blood-red, her eyes burned even more intensely, her desire burst forth, bringing to the surface the passionate woman she seemed to be. And he was naive enough to think that she had come to offer herself to him, simply to be in on his grand project and from time to time get useful tips for the Bourse.

'But Madame, there's nothing I'd like better than to lay my experience at your feet!'

He drew his chair closer and took her hand. This at once brought her to her senses. Ah no, she had not come to such a pass, the time was still far off when she had to pay for information with a night in her bed. Her affair with the Public Prosecutor Delcambre was already a ghastly chore for her, such a dried-up and jaundiced man whom she had been forced to accept because of the miserliness of her husband. Her indifference to sensuality and the secret contempt she felt for men had suddenly shown up in the pallid weariness on this face, that so falsely betokened the woman of passion when her sole passion was for speculation. She rose to her feet in a rebellion that sprang from her birth and education and still caused her to lose some business opportunities.

'So, Monsieur, you're saying you were satisfied with your chef?'

Quite astonished, Saccard also stood up. What had she been expecting? That he would add her to his register and give her information for nothing? Women, decidedly, were not to be trusted, they went into deals with the most amazing bad faith. And although he did want this woman, he didn't persist but bowed with a smile that said: 'As you please, dear lady, when you're ready,' while aloud he said:

'Very satisfied, as I said. It was only a change in my domestic arrangements that led me to part with him.'

Baroness Sandorff hesitated, though barely a second—not that she regretted her revolt, but she doubtless felt how naive it was to have come to see a man like Saccard without being resigned to the consequences. That made her irritated with herself, for she thought of herself as a woman of sense. She finally responded with a simple nod to the respectful bow with which he bade her farewell; and he was just taking her to the little side-door when it was suddenly thrown open by a familiar hand. It was Maxime, who was having lunch with his father that morning and, as a member of the family, had come in by the side-entrance. He stood back and also bowed, allowing the Baroness to leave. Then, when she had gone, he gave a short laugh:

'So business is taking off, is it? Starting to collect your bonuses?'

Although he was still very young, he had the self-confidence of a man of experience who wouldn't waste his time uselessly for the sake of some risky pleasure. His father recognized this attitude of ironic superiority.

'In fact no, not collecting anything at all, and not because I couldn't, dear boy, for I'm as proud of still being a twenty-year-old as you seem to be of already being sixty.'

Maxime just laughed the more, his old, tinkling, girlish laugh, with that suggestive cooing sound he still had, even in the very proper style he had taken on as a settled young man, anxious to do no further damage to his life. He affected the utmost indulgence, provided there was no danger to anything of his.

'My word, you're quite right, just as long as it doesn't wear you out... As for me, you know, I already have rheumatism.'

Then he installed himself comfortably in an armchair and picked up a newspaper. 'Don't worry about me, you can go on receiving your callers, if I'm not in your way... I came early because I had to go and see my doctor and he wasn't there.'

At that moment the valet came in to say that the Countess de Beauvilliers was asking to be admitted. Somewhat surprised, although he had already met his noble neighbour, as he called her, at the Work Foundation, Saccard had her shown in at once; then, calling the valet back, told him to send everyone else away, for he was tired and very hungry.

When the Countess came in she didn't even notice Maxime, hidden behind the back of his armchair. And Saccard was yet more surprised when he saw that she had brought her daughter Alice with her. This gave an extra solemnity to her visit: the two women were so sad and pale, the mother tall, thin, white-haired, and looking as if she belonged to another era, and the daughter prematurely aged, with a long, even disastrously long, neck. He drew two chairs forward with bustling politeness, the better to show his deference.

'Madame, I am extremely honoured... If I could have the pleasure of serving you in some way...'

The Countess, who was a very shy woman beneath her haughty airs, eventually managed to explain the reason for her visit.

'Monsieur, it was after a conversation with my friend, the Princess d'Orviedo, that I had the idea of coming to see you... I confess that I hesitated at first, for at my age it is not easy to change one's ideas, and I've always been very much afraid of present-day things that I don't understand... However, I've talked to my daughter about it, and I believe that it is my duty to put aside my scruples and try to secure the happiness of my loved ones.'

And she went on, telling him that the Princess had told her about the Universal Bank, a lending-house like any other in the eyes of the profane but which, to the initiated, would have an unquestionable justification, an aim so meritorious and lofty that it would silence even the most timorous consciences. She did not mention the Pope nor Jerusalem: that was left unspoken, scarcely even whispered among the faithful, that was the secret that stirred the passions; but from every word she uttered, from every allusion and suggestion, a hope and a faith came through, giving a religious fire to her belief in the success of the new bank.

Saccard himself was astonished at her restrained emotion and the tremor in her voice. He had only ever spoken of Jerusalem in his more frenzied lyrical excesses, he didn't really believe in that crazy plan, sensing something ridiculous about it and always ready to abandon it with a laugh if it met with mockery. And the deeply felt action of this saintly woman, who brought her daughter with her, and the profound way in which she implied that she and all her kin and the whole of the French aristocracy would believe with all their hearts, struck him forcibly, giving substance to what had been a mere dream and infinitely extending its scope for development. So it was true then, this was a lever with which he could lift the whole world. With his capacity for swift assimilation he at once grasped the situation, he too now spoke in mysterious terms of that ultimate triumph he would be silently pursuing; and his words were full of fervour, for he had indeed just been touched by faith, faith in the excellence of the instrument that the present crisis of the Papacy had placed in his hands. He had a happy knack of becoming a believer whenever his plans required it.

'In short, Monsieur,' the Countess went on, 'I have decided to do something which I formerly found repugnant... It's true, the idea of putting money to work and placing it at interest had never entered my head: old-fashioned ways of looking at life, scruples which are becoming a little silly, I know; but what can you do? It's not easy to go against beliefs one drank in with one's mother's milk, and I always imagined that land alone, the large estate, would provide for people like us... Unfortunately, the large estate...'

She blushed slightly, for she was about to admit to the ruin she took such care to conceal.

'The large estate scarcely exists any more... We have had a lot of difficulties... All we have left is one farm.'

At this Saccard, to spare her any embarrassment, added passionately:

'But Madame, nobody lives off estates any more... The old land-based fortune is an antiquated form of wealth which no longer has any purpose. It represented the very stagnation of money, money whose value we have multiplied tenfold by throwing it into circulation, with paper money and with commercial and financial securities of all sorts. That's how the world will be renewed, for without money, liquid money, flowing and infiltrating everywhere, nothing was possible, not scientific inventions nor ultimate, universal peace... Landed wealth, oh dear! That went out with the stagecoach! You can starve with a million in land, but you can live on a quarter of that amount placed in sound investments at fifteen, twenty, even thirty per cent.'

Gently, in her infinitely sad way, the Countess shook her head.

'I hardly understand what you're saying and, as I've told you, I still belong to an era when such things were frightening, were seen as bad and forbidden... But I am not alone, I must above all think of my daughter. Over the past few years I've managed to put aside, oh, just a small sum...'

She was blushing again.

'Twenty thousand francs, lying in a drawer at home. Later on I might perhaps have regretted leaving them there, earning nothing; and since your project is a worthy one, as my friend has confided to me, and since you will be working towards what we all desire with our most ardent wishes, I am taking the risk... In short, I'd be grateful if you could set aside shares for me in your bank, for ten to twelve thousand francs. I have had my daughter come with me, for I won't hide from you that this money is hers.'

Up to that point Alice had not opened her mouth, staying in the background in spite of the lively intelligence of her eyes. She made a gesture of tender reproach.

'Mine, Mother? Is there anything of mine which isn't yours?'

'But your marriage, my child?'

'But you know I don't want to be married!'

She had spoken too quickly, and the pain of her solitude cried out in her reedy voice. Her mother hushed her with a look of distress; and they gazed at each other for a moment, unable to lie to each other in their daily sharing of what they had to suffer and conceal.

Saccard was very moved.

'Madame, if there were no shares left I would still find some for you. Oh yes, if necessary I'll take some out of my own... I am infinitely touched by your decision, and I am very honoured by the trust you are showing in me...'

And at that precise moment he really did believe he would make the fortune of these poor women, that he was bringing them a share in the shower of gold that was about to rain down on himself and all around him.

The ladies rose and began to take their leave. Only when she reached the door did the Countess allow herself to make a direct allusion to the great project that remained unspoken.

'I have received from my son Ferdinand in Rome a distressing letter about the sadness produced there by the announcement about the withdrawal of our troops.'

'Have patience!' Saccard declared with conviction. 'We are coming to the rescue.'

Deep bows were exchanged and he accompanied them out to the landing, this time going through the waiting-room, which he believed to be empty. But as he came back he saw, sitting on a bench, a tall, sharp-featured man of about fifty, dressed like a worker in his Sunday best, and with him a pretty girl of eighteen, slim and pale.

'What's this! What are you doing here?'

The girl rose first, and the man, intimidated by this brusque greeting, started to stammer out a confused explanation.

'I had given orders for everyone to be sent away! So why are you here? At least tell me your name.'

'Dejoie, Monsieur, and this is my daughter Nathalie...'

Then he got into a muddle again, so much so that Saccard, losing patience, was about to push him towards the door, when at last he gathered that it was Madame Caroline who had told him to come and wait, as she had known him a long time.

'Ah! Madame Caroline sent you. You should have said so straight away. Come in, and do hurry up because I'm really hungry.'

Once in his office he left Dejoie and Nathalie standing and did not himself sit down, so as to get rid of them more quickly. Maxime, who had risen from his armchair when the Countess left, did not this time withdraw discreetly but stayed, looking over the new arrivals with a curious eye. And Dejoie lengthily explained what he had come about.

'This is how it is, Monsieur... I got my discharge,* then I went as office-boy for Monsieur Durieu, Madame Caroline's husband, when he was still alive and had his brewery. Then I went to Monsieur Lamberthier, in the market-hall. Then I went to Monsieur Bisot, a banker you know well: he blew his brains out two months ago so now I haven't got a job... I should tell you, first of all, that I had got married. Yes, I married my wife Joséphine when I was at Monsieur Durieu's in fact, and she worked as cook for Monsieur's sister-in-law Madame Lévêque, a lady well known to Madame Caroline. And then, when I was at Monsieur Lamberthier's, Joséphine couldn't get a place there so she went to work for a doctor in Grenelle, a Monsieur Renaudin. Then she went to the Trois-Frères shop on the Rue Rambuteau where, as if it was fated, there was never a place for me...'

'In short,' Saccard interrupted him, 'you've come to me for a job, is that it?'

But Dejoie was intent on telling him the sad story of his life, the unhappy chance which had made him marry a cook without ever being able to find a job in the same household as hers. It was almost as if they'd never been properly married, never having their own bed-room, meeting each other at wine-shops and kissing behind kitchen doors. When their daughter Nathalie was born they had to leave her with a nurse until she was eight years old, until one day when her father, tired of being alone, had taken her back into his cramped bachelor's lodgings. So he had become the real mother of the little girl, bringing her up, taking her to school, and looking after her with the utmost care, his heart overflowing with ever greater adoration.

'Oh, I can happily say, Monsieur, that she has given me great satis-faction. She's educated, she's honest... And you can see for yourself, she has no equal for sweetness of nature.'

Indeed Saccard found her charming, this blonde flower of the Paris streets, with her frail grace and her large eyes beneath little curls of fair hair. She accepted her father's adoration, still well-behaved, having had no reason not to be, but with a fierce and tranquil egoism in the limpid brilliance of her eyes.

'So, Monsieur, she is now of an age to be married, and in fact a good suitor has just come forward, the son of our neighbour the cardboard manufacturer. But he's a lad who wants to go into business, and he's asking for six thousand francs. It's not too much, he could very well find a girl who'd bring him more... I must add that I lost my wife four years ago and she left us her savings, her little earnings as a cook, you see?... So I have four thousand francs; but that's not six thousand, and the young man is in a hurry, so is Nathalie...'

The girl, who was listening and smiling, with her clear gaze, so cold and so determined, gave a sharp nod of agreement.

'Of course... I'm fed up, I want to see an end of it one way or the other.'

Once more Saccard cut in. He had judged the man to be unimaginative but very capable, very good-hearted, and accustomed to military discipline. And it was enough that he'd come on the advice of Madame Caroline.

'That's fine, my friend... I am going to have a newspaper, and I'm taking you on as office-boy... leave me your address, and goodbye for now.'

However, Dejoie made no move to go. He went on, with some embarrassment:

'Monsieur is most kind, and I gratefully accept the post, for I must work when once I've got Nathalie settled... But I came about something else. Yes, I learned, through Madame Caroline and some others, that Monsieur is going to be involved in some grand ventures and will be able to make as much profit as he likes for his friends and acquaintances... So, if Monsieur would kindly concern himself with us, if Monsieur would be willing to let us have some shares...'

Saccard for the second time was moved, more even than he had been on the first occasion, when it was the Countess who had entrusted to him her daughter's dowry. This simple man, this petty capitalist with savings scraped together sou by sou, didn't he represent the trusting multitude of believers, the great multitude that creates abundant and substantial numbers of customers, the fanatical army that endows a bank with invincible strength? If this good man came running to him like this, ahead of any publicity, what would it be like when the counters were open? He smiled in tenderness at this first little shareholder, seeing him as an omen of great success.

'Agreed, my friend, you shall have your shares.'

Dejoie's face lit up as if he had been granted some unhoped-for favour.

'Monsieur is too kind... in six months then, with my four thousand

I can gain two thousand, can't I? And so make up the whole amount...
and since I have Monsieur's consent, I prefer to settle straight away.
I've brought the money.'

He felt in his pockets and pulled out an envelope which he offered
to Saccard, who stood stock still and silent, struck with delighted
admiration at this final touch. And the terrible pirate, who had
already creamed off so many fortunes, finally burst into a happy
laugh, honestly resolved to make him rich too, this man of faith.

'But my dear chap, that's not how it's done. Keep your money, I
shall put you on the register and you will pay in due course.'

This time he saw them out, after Dejoie had got Nathalie to thank
him, with a smile of satisfaction lighting up her beautiful, hard and
candid eyes.

When Maxime was finally alone with his father he said, with his
insolent and mocking air:

'So now you're providing dowries for young girls.'

'Why not?' Saccard answered gaily. 'Happiness for others is a good
investment.'

He was putting away some papers before leaving the office. Then
he suddenly said:

'What about you? Don't you want some shares?'

Maxime, who was ambling about, gave a start, wheeled round, and
faced him.

'Oh no, what an idea! Do you take me for a fool?'

Finding this reply lacking in respect and showing a deplorable
spirit, Saccard made an angry gesture and was on the point of shouting at him that it was a genuinely splendid deal, and that Maxime was
really too stupid if he thought that he was just another thief like so
many others. But, looking at him, he felt pity for his poor son, worn
out at twenty-five, set in his ways and even miserly, so aged by vice,
so anxious about his health, that he wouldn't risk any expense or self-
indulgence unless he had already carefully calculated the benefit.
And quite comforted, full of pride in the passionate temerity of his
fifty years, he began to laugh again and clapped him on the shoulder.

'Come on! Let's go and have lunch, my poor boy, and you just take
care of your rheumatics.'

It was two days later, on the fifth of October, that Saccard, accompanied by Hamelin and Daigremont, went to the chambers of Maître
Lelorrain, a notary on the Rue Sainte-Anne, and there the deed

constituting a public company in the name of the Universal Bank Company was executed, with a capital of twenty five millions, divided into fifty thousand shares of five hundred francs each, only a quarter of which had to be paid on allocation. The offices of the company were registered as the Hôtel d'Orviedo in the Rue Saint-Lazare. A copy of the statutes, drawn up in accordance with the deed, was deposited in the office of Maître Lelorrain. It was a day of bright autumn sunshine, and when these gentlemen left the notary's office they lit their cigars and slowly strolled back up the boulevard and the Rue de la Chaussée-d'Antin, glad to be alive and happy as schoolboys let out of school.

The inaugural general meeting did not take place until the following week, in the Rue Blanche, in the premises of a little dance-hall which had gone out of business and in which an industrialist was now trying to set up art exhibitions. The syndicate members had already placed the shares they had taken but weren't keeping for themselves; and one hundred and twenty-two shareholders came, representing nearly forty thousand shares, which should have given a total of two thousand votes since only holders of twenty or more shares had the right to attend and vote. However, since no single shareholder could cast more than ten votes no matter how many shares he held, the precise number of votes was sixteen hundred and forty-three.

Saccard insisted that Hamelin should chair the meeting. As for himself, he deliberately melted into the crowd. He had registered the engineer and himself for five hundred shares apiece, which he would pay for by juggling the accounts. All the syndicate members were there: Daigremont, Huret, Sédille, Kolb, and the Marquis de Bohain, each with the group of shareholders under their command. Sabatani, one of the largest shareholders, could also be seen, and Jantrou too, surrounded by several of the bank's senior clerks, appointed two days before. And all the decisions that had to be made had been so well foreseen and decided in advance that never was an inaugural meeting so beautifully calm, simple, and cooperative. A unanimous vote endorsed the declaration that the capital had been fully subscribed and that one hundred and twenty-five francs had been paid for each share. The company was then solemnly declared to be established. Next the board of directors was appointed: this was to comprise twenty members who, as well as their attendance fees, amounting to an annual total of fifty thousand francs, would receive in accordance with one of the articles in the statutes ten per cent of the profits. This was not to be sneezed at, and every syndicate member had demanded to be on the board; Daigremont, Huret, Sédille, Kolb, and the Marquis de Bohain, in addition to Hamelin, whom they wanted as president, all naturally went to the top of the list, along with fourteen other less important men chosen from the most obedient and ornamental of the shareholders. Finally Saccard, who until then had stayed in the background, made an appearance when the moment arrived for choosing a general manager, and Hamelin then proposed him. A murmur of sympathy greeted his name, and he too was a unanimous choice. It remained only to elect the two official auditors, responsible for presenting the meeting with a report on the balance sheet and for checking the accounts provided by the management, a function as delicate as it was useless, and for which Saccard had designated a certain Rousseau and Lavignière, the former being completely under the thumb of Lavignière, who was tall, fair-haired, very polite, always approving, and consumed with the desire eventually to get on to the board once his services had given satisfaction. With Rousseau and Lavignière appointed, the meeting was about to be closed when the president thought it necessary to mention the ten per cent bonus granted to the syndicate members, four hundred thousand francs in all, and at his suggestion the meeting charged this to the start-up costs. It was a mere trifle, some expense was inevitable; and letting the mass of small shareholders drift away like a flock of sheep, the big investors stayed on to the last, with smiling faces, still exchanging handshakes out on the pavement.

The very next day the directors met at the Hôtel d'Orviedo, in Saccard's former drawing-room, now converted into a boardroom. A vast table, covered in green velvet and surrounded by twenty chairs upholstered in the same material, took up the centre of the room; there was no other furniture save two large bookcases, whose glass doors were adorned on the inside with little silk curtains, also in green. The room was darkened by its deep-red hangings, and the three windows looked down on to the garden of the Hôtel Beauvilliers, from which came only a dusky light, like the peace of an old cloister, slumbering in the green shade of its trees. The general effect was both severe and noble, creating an impression of antique honesty.

The board was meeting to appoint its officers, and they were all there almost at once, on the stroke of four. The Marquis de Bohain, with his great height and small, pale, aristocratic head was the very essence of the old French nobility, while the affable Daigremont personified the wealthy class of the Empire in its ostentatious success. Sédille, looking less worried than usual, was chatting to Kolb about an unexpected movement that had just occurred on the Vienna market; and around them the other directors, the whole crowd, listened in, trying to pick up a tip, or else talked among themselves about their own business, being there only to make up the numbers and collect their share, on the days when there was something to be shared. Huret, as ever, arrived late and out of breath, having got away at the last minute from a parliamentary commission. He apologized and everyone took their seats around the table.

The Marquis de Bohain, as the most senior figure, had taken the presidential chair, which was higher and more gilded than the rest. As general manager, Saccard had placed himself opposite. And immediately, as soon as the Marquis announced that they were going to proceed to the appointment of the chairman, Hamelin rose to his feet to decline any candidature: he understood that several of the gentlemen had thought of proposing him, but he wished to point out that he was to leave for the Orient the very next day, and besides had no experience whatsoever of accountancy, banks, or stock-markets, and finally that he could not accept the weight of responsibility involved. Saccard listened with great surprise, for only the day before it had all been agreed, and he guessed it was Madame Caroline who had influenced her brother, since he knew they had had a long conversation together that morning. So, not wanting to have anyone else as chairman, some independent person who might get in his way, Saccard decided to intervene, explaining that the office was purely honorific, that the chairman had only to be present at the general meetings, to support the proposals of the board and deliver the customary speeches. Besides, they were going to elect a vice-chairman who would do all the signing. And for the rest, the merely technical part dealing with accountancy, the Bourse, and the myriad little details of a large bank, wouldn't it be himself, Saccard, who would properly be appointed for this side of things? He, according to the statutes, was to run the offices, deal with income and expenditure, manage the day-to-day business, carry out the decisions of the board, and act, in short, as the executive arm of the company. These arguments seemed sound. Hamelin nevertheless still went on arguing for some time, and both Daigremont and Huret had to insist in the most pressing manner. The Marquis de Bohain remained majestically aloof. At last the engineer gave way; he was appointed chairman, and they chose as vice-chairman an obscure agronomist, the Viscount de Robin-Chagot, a former Counsellor of State, a quiet, miserly man, an excellent machine for providing signatures. As for the secretary, he was taken from outside the board, from the bank's office staff, the head of the share-issue department. And as night descended upon the large, solemn room, like a greenish shadow of infinite sadness, they decided they had done enough and done it well; then they went their separate ways, after arranging their future sessions at two a month, an ordinary meeting on the fifteenth and a plenary board on the thirtieth.

Saccard and Hamelin went up together to the workroom, where Madame Caroline was waiting for them. She saw at once from her brother's awkward manner that he had yet again, through weakness, given way; and for a moment she was very angry.

'But come on, this is unreasonable!' cried Saccard. 'Just think, the chairman is paid thirty thousand francs, a sum that will be doubled when our business develops. You're not so rich that you can scorn such a benefit... And what are you afraid of anyway?'

'Well, I'm afraid of everything,' replied Madame Caroline. 'My brother won't be here, and I personally understand nothing about money... For example, these five hundred shares you've registered in his name without his paying for them straight away, well, isn't that irregular? Wouldn't he be in trouble if things went wrong?'

Saccard began to laugh.

'Oh what a fuss about nothing! Five hundred shares, an initial outlay of sixty-two thousand five hundred francs! If he can't pay that back within six months out of the first profits then we might as well go and jump in the Seine right now, and not bother with any sort of venture... No, you can rest assured, only the inept are destroyed by speculation.'

She remained stern, in the growing darkness of the room. But two lamps were brought in, casting a bright light over the walls, with the vast maps and vivid watercolours that so often made her dream of those far-off lands. The plain still lay bare, the mountains still barred the horizon, and she called to mind the distress of that ancient world, slumbering over its treasures, a land that science was about to awaken from its filth and ignorance. What fine, great things were waiting to be achieved! Gradually she began to visualize new generations and a stronger, happier humanity springing from the ancient soil, once more beneath the plough of progress.

'Speculation, speculation,' she repeated mechanically, struggling with doubt. 'Ah! It fills my troubled heart with anguish.'

Saccard, who was well acquainted with her thoughts on the subject, had seen on her face the reflection of her hope for the future.

'Yes, speculation, why does the word frighten you?... Speculation is the very spur of life itself, the everlasting desire to struggle and go on living... If I dared to make a comparison, I could convince you...'

He laughed again, seized by scruples of delicacy. Then he dared after all, always ready to be brutal with women.

'Let's see now, do you think that without... how shall I put it?— that without lust there would be many children?... Out of every hundred children that might have been, barely one is actually produced. It's excess that produces what is necessary, isn't it?'

'Certainly,' she replied with embarrassment.

'Well, without speculation there would be no business, dear friend... Why the devil do you think I would put out my money and risk my fortune, if I didn't have the promise of some extraordinary pleasure, some sudden happiness that offers me heaven?... With the lawful and mediocre rewards of work, the prudent balance of day-to-day transactions, life is just a desert of extreme platitude, a swamp in which all energies lie dormant and stagnant; while if you forcefully set a dream ablaze on the horizon, promising that with one sou a hundred will be gained, then invite all those who lie asleep to get up and hunt for the impossible, for millions won in two hours, amid the most frightful dangers—now the race begins at once with ten times the energy, and there is such a scramble that even while sweating solely for their own pleasure, people sometimes manage to produce children, that is, living things, great and splendid things... Ah, my word! There is a lot of useless filth, but the world would end without it.'

Madame Caroline decided to laugh too; for there was no prudishness about her.

'So,' she said, 'your conclusion is that we must resign ourselves to it because it's all part of nature's plan... You're right, life isn't clean.'

She had acquired real courage at the thought that every new step forward had been made through blood and mire. You had to have the will for it. She kept her eyes fixed on the maps and drawings all around the walls, and the future took shape for her, ports, canals, roads and railways, the countryside with vast farms equipped like factories, and new towns, full of health and intelligence, where people would live to be very old and very well-educated.

'Oh, all right,' she continued gaily, 'I have to give in, as always... Let's just do some good, so that we can be forgiven.'

Her brother, who had been keeping quiet, came over and kissed her. She wagged a finger at him.

'Oh! You're a real coaxer, as I know too well... Tomorrow, when you've left us, you won't be worrying much about what's happening here; and once you've arrived and got stuck into your work everything will be fine, you'll be dreaming of triumph, while back here everything might be cracking up under our feet.'

'Ah, but', Saccard exclaimed jokingly, 'it's been decided that he's leaving you here beside me as a constable, ready to nab me if I misbehave!'

All three burst out laughing.

'And I would nab you too, you can count on it! Remember what you've promised, to us of course, and to so many others, dear old Dejoie for instance, whom I recommended to you... Ah, and our neighbours too, these poor Beauvilliers ladies whom I saw today overseeing the washing of some clothes by their cook, no doubt to reduce their laundry bills.'

For a moment all three stayed chatting very amicably, and final arrangements were made for Hamelin's departure.

As Saccard was going back down to his office his valet told him a woman was insisting on waiting for him, even though he had told her there was a meeting and Monsieur would doubtless be unable to see her. As he was tired Saccard's first reaction was anger, and he ordered the valet to send her away; then, feeling he owed a debt to his success and fearful of changing his luck if he closed his door, he thought better of it. The flow of callers was growing every day, and this crowd of people was intoxicating.

The office was lit by a single lamp and he could not see his visitor clearly.

'I've been sent by Monsieur Busch, Monsieur...'

Anger kept Saccard on his feet, and he didn't ask her to sit down. In that reedy voice, in that impossibly huge body, he had recognized

Madame Méchain. Some shareholder this, a woman who bought securities by the pound!

She calmly explained that Busch had sent her to get information about the share-issue of the Universal Bank. Were any shares still available? Would it be possible to get some, along with the bonus for members of the syndicate? But all that, surely, was just a pretext, a way of getting in to see the house, to find out what was happening here and see how he himself was doing; for her narrow eyes, like holes drilled in the fat of her face, were ferreting about everywhere then turning their gaze back on him, probing him down to his very soul. Busch, after waiting patiently for quite a while, giving the great affair of the abandoned child plenty of time to mature, was now ready to act and had sent her to spy out the land.

'There are none left,' Saccard replied brutally.

She realized she would learn nothing more from him, and it would be unwise to try anything. So that day, without giving him time to push her out, she moved to the door herself.

'Why don't you ask me for some shares for yourself?' Saccard went on, intending to be offensive.

In her lisping voice, her shrill voice, with its mocking tone, she replied:

'Oh, that's not my style of business... I just wait.'

At that moment he caught sight of the huge, worn leather bag she always had with her and shuddered. On a day when everything had gone like clockwork, a day when he had been so happy to see the birth of the bank so long desired, was this rascally old woman to be the wicked fairy, the sort that casts spells on princesses in their cradles? He felt that bag of hers to be full of depreciated shares and unbank-able bonds, that bag she had brought right into the offices of his new-born bank; and he somehow understood that she was threatening him, that she would wait as long as it took to bury his own shares in it when the bank collapsed. She was the crow, cawing as it sets off with the marching army and follows it to the evening of carnage, then hovers and swoops down, knowing there will be plenty of dead to eat.

'Au revoir, Monsieur,' said La Méchain as she left, breathless and perfectly polite.

CHAPTER V

A MONTH later, in early November, the installation of the Universal Bank was not yet completed. Carpenters were still busy on the woodwork, and painters were finishing the puttying of the enormous glass roof with which the courtyard was now covered.

The cause of the delay was Saccard, forever dissatisfied with the meanness of the establishment, and prolonging the work with his demands for luxury. Unable to push back the walls to satisfy his perpetual dream of hugeness, he had ended up losing his temper, leaving Madame Caroline with the task of getting rid of the contractors. So it was she who was supervising the placing of the last cash desks, of which there was an extraordinary number. The courtyard, now transformed into the central hall, was surrounded by cash desks: each had its own grille, severe and imposing, with its own brass plate inscribed in black. In short, the conversion, even if carried out in a rather limited space, was very well done: on the ground floor were those departments that needed to be in constant contact with the public, the various cash desks, issuing offices, all the day-to-day operations of the bank; and on the upper floor the bank's internal mechanisms, management, correspondence, accounts, offices for staff and some for dealing with disputes. In all, within that limited space more than two hundred employees were at work. And what was striking, from the moment one entered, even in all the commotion of workmen hammering in the last of the nails, while gold tinkled in the tills, was that air of severity, an air of antique probity, vaguely reminiscent of a sacristy, that no doubt derived from the premises, from this old, dark, and silent house in the shadow of the trees of the next-door garden. It felt as if one were entering a house of religion.

One afternoon, coming back from the Bourse, Saccard himself felt this, much to his surprise. That consoled him for the lack of decorative gilding. He told Madame Caroline of his satisfaction:

'Ah well, after all, for a beginning it's quite nice. It has a homely feeling, it's a real little chapel. Later on we'll see... Thank you, my lovely friend, for all the trouble you're taking while your brother's away.'

And as it was a principle of his to make use of all unforeseen circumstances, he now devoted himself to developing the austere appearance of the establishment, demanding that his employees conduct themselves like young priests; they spoke only in measured tones, and received and paid out money with a quite clerical discretion.

In all his tumultuous life Saccard had never thrown himself so heartily into so much activity. From seven o'clock in the morning, before all his employees, even before the office-boy had lit the fire, he was in his office going through the mail, answering the most urgent letters. Then, until eleven o'clock it was one long gallop—of friends and important clients, stockbrokers, kerb traders, jobbers, a whole horde of financial agents, not to mention the procession of various department heads coming for orders. Saccard himself, as soon as he had a minute of respite, would get up and make a rapid inspection of the various offices, where employees lived in terror of these sudden appearances, which always happened at different times of the day. At eleven o'clock he went up to have lunch with Madame Caroline, ate heartily and drank similarly, with the ease of a thin man who could do so without any problem, and the full hour he spent there was not wasted, for this was the time when he, as he put it, quizzed his beautiful friend, that is, asked her opinion on men and on things, though he was rarely ready to profit by her great good sense. At midday he went out to the Bourse, as he liked to be one of the first there, to see people and chat. But he did not openly speculate, he was just there as if at a natural meeting-place, where he was certain to encounter clients of his bank. However, his influence was already perceptible, he had returned to the Bourse victorious, a man of substance, supported now by real millions; and those in the know spoke quietly to each other while looking in his direction, whispering outlandish rumours and predicting his imminent sovereignty. Towards half-past three he was always back at the bank, attending to the tiresome chore of signing, so practised now in this mechanical movement of his hand that his mind was left free, and he could talk as he wished, send for employees, give answers, and settle deals without ceasing to sign. Until six o'clock he went on receiving visitors, then finished off the day's work and prepared that of the morrow. When he went back up to Madame Caroline it was for a meal more copious than the one at eleven o'clock, delicate fish and especially game, and his whims about the wine meant he dined with burgundy, bordeaux, or champagne in accordance with the fortunes of the day.

'Just dare to say I'm not behaving myself!' he would cry some-times, with a smile. 'Instead of chasing women and going to clubs and theatres, I live here at your side, like a good bourgeois... you must write and tell your brother, to reassure him.'

He was not quite as well-behaved as he claimed, since he had recently taken a fancy to a little singer at the Bouffes,* and he had even had his turn with Germaine Coeur who, however, had given him no satisfaction. The truth was that by the evening he was half-dead with fatigue. Anyway, he was living in such a state of desire and anxiety for success that his other appetites would remain diminished and paralysed until he could feel triumphant at having indisputably mastered fortune.

'Bah!' Madame Caroline would cheerfully answer. 'My brother has always been so well-behaved that good behaviour for him is more a natural condition than a merit... I wrote to him yesterday that I had persuaded you not to regild the boardroom. That will please him more.'

It was on a very cold afternoon in the early days of November, when Madame Caroline was just giving the head painter the order simply to clean the paintwork of the boardroom, that a servant brought her a card, saying that the person concerned was very insist-ent on seeing her. The rather grubby card bore the crudely printed name of Busch. The name was unknown to her, but she gave the order for the visitor to be sent up to her brother's study where she received callers.

If Busch had been patient for nearly six months, not using the extraordinary discovery he had made of Saccard's natural son, it was mainly for the reasons he had foreseen, the rather poor result it would be to get only the six hundred francs from the notes given to the mother, and the extreme difficulty of blackmailing Saccard to get more, say a reasonable sum of some thousands of francs. A widower, with no encumbrances, no fear of scandal—how could one terrorize him? How make him pay dearly for this ugly gift of a natural child, raised in the midst of filth, and who could turn out to be a pimp or murderer? Of course La Méchain had laboriously drawn up a long list of expenses, amounting to about six thousand francs, consisting of several loans of twenty sous to her cousin Rosalie Chavaille, the boy's mother, then the cost of the unfortunate mother's illness, her burial, the care of her grave, and finally what she herself had spent on Victor since he had become her charge, his food and clothing, all sorts of things. But if Saccard turned out to be unsentimental about his fatherhood, wasn't it likely that he would just send them packing? Nothing on earth could actually prove his paternity, except the child's resemblance to his father; and all they would get from him then would be the money for the notes—and that only if he failed to declare them nullified by the lapse of time.

On the other hand, if Busch had waited so long it was because he had just endured some weeks of appalling anxiety looking after his brother Sigismond, now bedridden, laid low by consumption. Indeed, for a whole fortnight this bustling man of so many concerns had neglected everything, simply forgetting about all the myriad tangled trails he was following, not even appearing at the Bourse, not tracking down a single debtor, not once leaving the bedside of the sick man, watching over him, caring for him, and changing him, like a mother. For all his disgusting meanness Busch had become quite prodigal, sending for the best doctors in Paris and wanting to pay the pharmacist extra for the medicines, if this could make them more effective; and since the doctors had totally forbidden any work and Sigismond refused to obey, he kept hiding his papers and books. It had become a war of wiles between the two. As soon as his guardian fell asleep, overcome with fatigue, the young man, soaked in sweat and consumed by fever, would find a stub of pencil and the margin of a newspaper and go back to his calculations, distributing wealth in accordance with his dream of justice, granting everyone a share of happiness and life. And Busch, when he awoke, would get angry at finding him in a worse condition, broken-hearted to see him devoting to his dreams what little life was left to him. He had allowed him to play with these fantasies when he was well, as one allows a child to play with puppets; but for him to kill himself with his wild, impractical ideas was really lunatic! At last, having agreed out of affection for his brother to be more sensible, Sigismond had regained some strength and was beginning to spend some time out of bed.

It was then that Busch, getting back to work, declared it was time to settle the Saccard affair, all the more so since Saccard had returned to the Bourse victorious and was once more a person of unquestionable solvency. The report from Madame Méchain, whom he had sent to the Rue Saint-Lazare, was excellent. However, he was still hesitant about attacking his man directly, and was temporizing, still trying to think of a tactic that would defeat him, when a chance word of La Méchain about Madame Caroline, the lady who ran the household, whom all the local shopkeepers had mentioned to her, set him off on a new plan of campaign. Was this lady perhaps the real mistress, the one who held the keys not only of the cupboards but of the heart? Busch often obeyed what he called the flash of inspiration, giving way to a sudden intuition and setting off in full cry on the merest hint of a scent, ready to wait until later for facts to give him certainty and resolution. And so it was that he went to the Rue Saint-Lazare to see Madame Caroline.

Up in the workroom Madame Caroline was surprised to find herself facing this big, ill-shaven man with a dull, grubby face, dressed in a handsome, greasy overcoat, with a white cravat. He inspected her thoroughly, down to her very soul, finding her to be just what he had hoped for, so tall, so healthy-looking, with her wonderful white hair which seemed to light up her still-young face with a joyous sweetness; and he was particularly struck by the expression of her rather large mouth, an expression of such goodness that he made up his mind at once.

'Madame,' he said, 'I was hoping to see Monsieur Saccard, but I was just told that he's not here...'

He was lying, he had not even asked for him, for he knew perfectly well that Saccard was out, having waited for him to leave for the Bourse.

'So I took it upon myself to call upon you, even rather preferring that, for I am not unaware of who it is I am addressing... This is a communication of such gravity and delicacy...'

Madame Caroline, who until then had not asked him to sit down, pointed him to a chair with uneasy haste.

'Speak sir, I am listening...'

Carefully lifting the skirts of his coat as if fearful of getting it dirty, Busch put it to himself, as a point definitely established, that she was sleeping with Saccard.

'The fact is, Madame, that this is not at all easy to say, and I confess that at the last minute I am still wondering whether I'm doing the right thing in telling you such a thing... I hope you will see, in this endeavour of mine, only the desire to allow Monsieur Saccard to repair the wrongs of the past...'

With a wave of the hand she set him at ease, having, for her part, realized what sort of person she was dealing with, and wanting to cut short the futile protestations. Anyway he did not insist, but related the old story in considerable detail: Rosalie seduced in the Rue de La Harpe, the child born after the disappearance of Saccard, the mother dying in debauchery and Victor left in the charge of a cousin too busy to look after him, growing up in the midst of total depravity. She listened, astonished at first at this tale she was not at all expecting, for she had imagined it was going to be about some shady financial affair; then she visibly softened, touched by the sad fate of the mother and the abandonment of the child, and deeply moved in her maternal feelings as a woman who had borne no children.

'But Monsieur,' she said, 'are you certain of these things you're telling me? Really strong proof is needed, absolute proof, in stories of this sort.'

He gave a smile.

'Oh Madame, there is blinding proof in the extraordinary resemblance of the child to Monsieur Saccard... Then there are the dates, everything fits and proves the facts without the shadow of a doubt.'

She sat there trembling, and he observed her. After a silence he went on:

'Now you understand, Madame, why I was so reluctant to address myself directly to Monsieur Saccard. For myself, I have no interest in the affair, I came only in the name of Madame Méchain, the cousin, who was placed on the track of the father by the merest chance; for, as I've mentioned, the twelve notes for fifty francs each, which were given to the wretched Rosalie, were signed with the name of Sicardot, a fact I do not presume to judge, quite excusable—my word!—in this awful life of Paris! Only, do you see? Monsieur Saccard might have misinterpreted the nature of my intervention... And that's when I had the inspiration to come and see you first Madame, and leave it entirely to you to decide what should be done, knowing your concern for Monsieur Saccard... There! You have our secret, do you think I should wait for him and tell him everything today?'

Madame Caroline's emotion was more and more evident.

'No, no. Later.'

But given the strangeness of this revelation, even she didn't know what to do. He continued to study her, pleased to see the extreme sensibility that put her in his power, and he was now adding the finishing touches to his plan, certain of getting more out of her than he would ever have got from Saccard.

'The thing is,' he murmured, 'a decision has to be made.'

'Well yes, I'll go. Yes, I'll go to this property of hers, I'll go and see this Madame Méchain and the child... It is better, much better, that I should go and see things for myself.'

She was thinking aloud, and resolving to make a thorough investigation before saying anything to the father. Later, if she was convinced, there would be time enough to tell him. Wasn't she there to watch over his house and peace of mind?

'Unfortunately it's quite urgent,' Busch went on, leading her gently to where he wanted her to be. 'The poor child is suffering, he is living in abominable surroundings.'

She had stood up. 'I shall put on my hat and go this minute.'

He also now rose from his seat, and added casually:

'I haven't said anything about the little bill that will have to be settled. The child has involved expense of course, and there's also the money lent to the mother while she was alive—oh! I don't know how much exactly. I didn't want to be involved in any of that. All the papers are over there.'

'Good, I shall see them.'

Then he seemed to be moved himself.

'Ah, Madame, if you only knew all the peculiar things I see in the course of business! It's the most honest people who have to suffer eventually for their passions, or even worse, for the passions of their relatives... I could even give you an example. Your unfortunate neighbours the Beauvilliers ladies...'

In a sudden move he had gone over to one of the windows and was directing his ardently curious gaze down into the next-door garden. He had no doubt been planning this bit of espionage ever since he came in, for he liked to know his battlegrounds. In the matter of the promissory note for ten thousand francs, signed by the Count for Léonie Cron, he had guessed right: information sent from Vendôme confirmed what he had imagined: the seduced girl, left without a sou after the death of the Count, with just her useless scrap of paper and consumed by longing to get to Paris, had ended up leaving the paper as a security with the usurer Charpier, for about fifty francs perhaps. But though he had found the Beauvilliers quickly enough, he had had La Méchain scouring Paris for six months without managing to get hold of Léonie. She had first found a job as a maid in the house of a bailiff, and he had been able to follow her through three other jobs; then, sacked for egregious misconduct, she seemed to disappear, and he had searched in vain through the gutters of the city. What exasperated him still more was that he could not try anything with the Countess until he had the girl, as a living threat of scandal. But he went on nursing the case, and he was happy to be standing there at the window, looking at the garden of the mansion, of which he had previously seen only the façade from the street.

'Do those ladies also have some trouble hanging over them?' asked Madame Caroline with anxious sympathy.

He played the innocent.

'No, I don't think so... I was simply referring to the wretched situation brought upon them by the bad behaviour of the Count... Yes, I have friends in Vendôme, I know their history.'

And as he at last decided to come away from the window he suddenly, in the midst of his pretended emotion, felt a singular backlash of feeling of his own:

'Still, when it's only money troubles! But when death enters a household...'

This time he had real tears in his eyes. He had just thought of his brother, and he was choking. She thought he must have recently lost one of his family, and out of tact asked him no questions. Until that moment she had not been deceived by the base concerns of this personage, who filled her with revulsion; but these unexpected tears convinced her far more than the cleverest tactics would have done, reinforcing her desire to go straight away to the 'Cité de Naples'.

'Madame, I can count on you then.'

'I'm going at once.'

An hour later Madame Caroline had taken a cab and was wandering about behind the Butte Montmartre, unable to find the 'Cité'. At last, in one of the deserted streets that run through to the Rue Marcadet, an old woman pointed it out to the coachman. At the entrance it was like a country lane, full of potholes, blocked by mud and refuse, pushing on into a stretch of wasteland; and only by looking hard could one just make out the wretched constructions of earth, old planks, and old sheets of zinc, spread around the inner yard like heaps of rubble. On the street a one-storey house, built of breeze-blocks but repulsively decrepit and filthy, seemed to govern the entrance as if it were a gaol. Indeed that was where Madame Méchain lived, a vigilant owner, always on the watch, exploiting in person her little population of starving tenants.

As soon as Madame Caroline had got down from the coach she saw La Méchain appear on the threshold, enormous, bosom and belly wobbling inside an old blue-silk dress frayed at the folds and cracking at the seams, and her cheeks so puffy and red that her little nose, almost invisible, seemed to be cooking between two braziers. Madame Caroline hesitated, feeling very uneasy, then the very gentle voice, with the rather shrill charm of a rustic flute, reassured her.

'Ah Madame, you've been sent by Monsieur Busch. You're here for little Victor… Come in, come in. Yes, this is indeed the Cité de Naples. The street is not listed and we don't have any numbers yet… Come in, first we need to talk about things. My word! It's so upsetting, and so sad.'

Then Madame Caroline had to accept a tattered chair in a black and greasy dining-room, in which a red stove kept the heat and the smell at a stifling level. La Méchain now went on about how lucky her visitor was to find her in, for she had so much business in Paris that she rarely returned home before six o'clock. Madame Caroline eventually had to interrupt her.

'Excuse me, Madame, I came about that unfortunate child.'

'Of course, Madame, I'll bring him to you… You know his mother was my cousin. Ah! I can certainly say I have done my duty… Here are the papers, and here are the bills.'

She went to a cupboard and pulled out a file of papers, neatly arranged in a blue folder like something from the office of a business agent. She talked on and on about poor Rosalie: she had certainly ended up living a quite disgusting life, going from one man to another, coming back drunk and bloodied after week-long binges. But after all, you had to be understanding, for she had been a good worker until the child's father dislocated her shoulder the day he took her on the staircase; and with her disability she couldn't keep herself going in a decent life just selling lemons in the market.

'You see, Madame, it was in small sums, just twenty or forty sous, that I lent her all that money. The dates are marked: 20 June, twenty sous; 27 June, twenty sous again; 3 July, forty sous. And then, look, she must have been ill at this point, because there's an endless series of forty sous… Then there was Victor and the clothes I had to get for him. I've put a "V" beside all the expenses for the boy... Not to mention that when Rosalie died—oh! so horribly, with a really filthy disease— he fell completely into my care. Then look, I've put fifty francs a month. That's very reasonable. The child's father is rich, he can easily spare fifty francs a month for his boy... Altogether that makes five thousand four hundred and three francs; and if we add the six hundred for the promissory notes we reach a total of six thousand francs... Yes, the whole lot for six thousand francs, and that's it!'

Though turning pale with nausea, Madame Caroline managed a comment.

'But the notes do not belong to you, they are the property of the child.'

'Ah, I beg your pardon, Madame,' replied La Méchain sharply, 'but I advanced money on them. To help out Rosalie I cashed them for her. You can see my endorsement on the back... In fact it's very good of me not to be claiming interest... You will think it over, my good lady, and you won't want to take a sou away from a poor woman like me.'

When the good lady, with a weary gesture, accepted the bill, La Méchain calmed down. And it was with her former fluting voice that she said:

'Now I'll send for Victor.'

But it was in vain that she sent, one after the other, three urchins who were prowling around; in vain that she planted herself in the doorway, waving her arms about: clearly Victor was refusing to budge. One of the urchins even brought back a dirty word as his answer. Then she bestirred herself, as if intending to drag him back by the ear. But she returned alone, having no doubt decided on reflection that it would be a good idea to show the boy in all his horror.

'If Madame will kindly take the trouble to follow me,' she said.

And as they walked she provided some details about the Cité de Naples, that her husband had inherited from an uncle. That husband had to be dead, no one had ever met him and she never mentioned him except to explain the source of her property. A bad business, it would be the end of her, she said, for she got more worry than profit out of it, especially now that the Prefecture was harassing her, sending out inspectors demanding repairs and improvements on the pretext that people were dying like flies there. Anyway, she was utterly determined not to spend a sou. Soon, no doubt, they'd be asking for mantelpieces with mirrors, in rooms that she was letting for only two francs a week! What she didn't mention was her own avidity about collecting the rent, throwing families out on the street the moment they failed to pay her two francs in advance, doing her own policing, and making herself so feared that homeless beggars would not have dared even to sleep leaning against one of her walls without paying.

With a heavy heart Madame Caroline looked around the yard, a devastated area pitted with potholes, which accumulations of filth had turned into a real midden. Everything was thrown into it; there was no cesspit or sewer, the yard was one ever-growing dunghill, poisoning the air; and it was lucky the weather was cold, for in the heat of the sun it exhaled pestilence. Careful where she placed her feet, Madame Caroline tried to avoid the vegetable-peelings and bones while casting an eye over the dwellings on each side, like the dens of animals: tumbledown shacks, ruined hovels, patched with the most heterogeneous materials. Several were only covered with tarred paper. Many, having no door, allowed a glimpse of black, cellar-like holes from which rose a sickening smell of penury. Families of eight or ten persons were huddled inside these charnel-houses, often without so much as a bed—heaps of men, women, and children, all rotting together like spoiled fruit, abandoned to their instinctive lusts from earliest childhood by this most monstrous promiscuity. So the yard was constantly filled with bands of puny urchins with pinched faces, wasted by hereditary scrofula and syphilis, poor creatures growing on this dungheap like wormy mushrooms, the accidental results of some embrace, with no one knowing exactly who their father might be. When an epidemic of typhoid or smallpox broke out it at once swept half of the Cité into the cemetery.

'As I was explaining, Madame,' La Méchain went on, 'Victor has not had very good models to follow, and it's time to think about his education for he is now almost thirteen... While his mother was alive of course, he saw some unsuitable things, since she didn't bother about propriety when she was drunk. She brought men in and everything took place right in front of him... And as for myself, I've never had time to watch over him closely enough on account of my business in Paris. He was always running about all day on the fortifications.* Twice I had to go and collect him because he'd been stealing—oh! only trifles. And then, as soon as he was able, he was with the little girls, his mother had shown him so much. Anyway, you'll see for yourself, he's already a man at the age of twelve. In the end, just to make him work a bit, I gave him to Mother Eulalie, a woman who sells baskets of vegetables in Montmartre. He goes to the market with her and carries one of her baskets. The trouble is she has an abscess on her thigh at the moment... But we're here, Madame, please go in.'

Madame Caroline shrank back. There, at the far end of the yard, behind a veritable barricade of filth, was one of the most disgusting holes, a hovel seemingly squashed into the ground, like a pile of rubble held up by bits of planking. There was no window. The door, an old glass door lined with a sheet of zinc, had to be kept open so that one could see at all, and the cold came in, the terrible cold. In a corner she saw a straw mattress simply thrown on the bare earth. There was no other identifiable furniture in the jumble of broken barrels, pieces of torn trellis, and half-rotted baskets acting as tables and chairs. The walls were damp and sticky. A crack, a green gap in the black roof, let in the rain just at the foot of the mattress. And the smell above all, the smell was awful, this was utter human degradation at its most bleak.*

'Mother Eulalie,' cried La Méchain, 'here's a kind lady come to see about Victor... What's wrong with the little monkey, that he doesn't come when he's called?'

A shapeless bundle of flesh stirred on the mattress, under some ragged old calico that served as a sheet; and Madame Caroline made out the body of a woman of about forty, quite naked, having no nightshirt, and so flabby and wrinkled that she looked like a half-deflated balloon. The face was not ugly, still quite fresh, framed by little blond curls.

'Ah,' she groaned, 'let her in, if she's come to do us good, for it can't just go on like this, God knows!... Just think, Madame, that I've been laid up here for a fortnight thanks to these filthy big sores digging holes in my thighs!... So, of course, there's not a sou in the place. Impossible to go on with my trade. I had two nightshirts that Victor went and sold for me; and I really think that tonight we'd have starved to death.'

Then, raising her voice:

'Come on out, little one... don't be silly, the lady doesn't mean you any harm.'

And Madame Caroline shuddered, seeing a sort of bundle that she had taken for a heap of old rags rising from a basket. It was Victor, dressed in the remains of a pair of trousers and cotton jacket, with his bare skin showing through the holes. He was in the full light of the door and she stood open-mouthed, stupefied by his extraordinary resemblance to Saccard. All her doubts vanished, the paternity was beyond question.

'I don't want anyone pestering me about going to school,' he declared.

But she went on looking at him, growing more and more uneasy. In this resemblance, which made such an impression on her, he was disturbing, this lad with one half of his face larger than the other, his nose twisted to the right and his head looking as if it had been crushed against the step in the assault in which his mother had conceived him.* Besides, he seemed prodigiously advanced for his age, not very tall, but stocky and fully developed at the age of twelve, his face already hairy, like some precocious animal. His bold, greedy eyes and sensual mouth were those of a man. And in his evident childhood, his complexion still so pure, with some delicate, even girlish elements, this virility, so startlingly manifest, was disturbing and even frightening, like something monstrous.

'Does school really frighten you so much, my dear?' Madame Caroline said at last. 'But you'd be better off there than here... Where do you sleep?'

With a gesture, he pointed to the mattress.

'There, with her.'

Put out by the frankness of his answer, Mother Eulalie stirred, seeking to explain:

'I'd made him up a bed with a little mattress, but it had to be sold. You just sleep wherever you can, you see, when everything's gone.'

La Méchain felt she should intervene, though she was perfectly aware of what went on.

'It's still not at all proper, Eulalie... and as for you, you little rascal, you could have come to sleep in my house instead of sleeping with her.'

But Victor planted himself firmly on his short and sturdy legs, squaring up in his precocious masculinity:

'Why? She's my wife!'

At this Mother Eulalie, wallowing in her soft flabbiness, decided to laugh, trying to mitigate the abomination by treating it as a kind of joke. And a tender admiration showed through in her words.

'Oh as for that, I certainly wouldn't trust him with my daughter if I had one, he's a real little man!'

Madame Caroline shuddered. She was overcome with an awful feeling of nausea. And what next? This urchin of twelve, this little monster, with this ravaged and sick woman of forty, on this filthy mattress in the middle of all these scraps and terrible stench. Oh, how destitution destroys and rots everything!

She left twenty francs and fled, taking refuge once more in the house of the owner in order to make a decision and come to a definite agreement with her. An idea had come to her in the face of such abandonment—the Work Foundation: hadn't it been created for just such cases, for the wretched children of the gutter that one could try to reform through hygiene and work? Victor had to be taken out of this sewer as quickly as possible and placed in the Foundation, to make a new life for him. She was all of a tremble with the idea. And with this decision she included a womanly delicacy: to say nothing as yet to Saccard, to wait until the monster was somewhat cleaned up before showing him to him; for she felt a sort of embarrassment for Saccard as the father of this fearful offspring, she suffered over the shame he would feel about it. A few months, no doubt, would suffice, and then she would speak to him when she was happy with the outcome. La Méchain found it difficult to understand.

'My word, Madame, just as you please... Only I want my six thousand francs right away. Victor doesn't move from here until I have my six thousand francs.'

This demand filled Madame Caroline with despair. She did not have that sum of money, and of course she did not want to ask the father for it. She argued and pleaded, but in vain.

'No, no, if I didn't have my security any more I could kiss my money goodbye. I know how it is.'

At last, since it was such a large sum and she might end up getting nothing, La Méchain reduced her demands.

'Oh well, give me two thousand francs straight away and I'll wait for the rest.'

But for Madame Caroline the problem was still the same, and she was wondering where she could find the two thousand francs when she had the idea of applying to Maxime. She didn't want to think about it further. He would surely agree to keep the secret and would not refuse the loan of such a small amount, for which his father would certainly reimburse him. So she went away, saying she would come back for Victor next day.

It was only five o'clock, and Madame Caroline was in such a fever of impatience to get this done that, on returning to her coach, she gave the driver Maxime's address in the Avenue de l'Impératrice. When she arrived the valet told her that Monsieur was dressing, but he would announce her anyway.

For a moment she felt suffocated as she waited in the drawing-room. It was a small house, but arranged with an exquisite refinement of luxury and comfort. Hangings and carpets were lavishly abundant, and a delicate scent of ambergris permeated the warm and silent rooms. It all looked pretty, tender and discreet, although there was no woman there; for the young widower, enriched by the death of his wife, had organized his life around the exclusive cult of himself, avoiding, as a young man of some experience, any new sharing. He was determined that the enjoyable life he owed to one woman was not going to be spoiled by another. Disenchanted with vice, he only partook of it now as if it were a dessert forbidden to him because of his lamentable digestion. He had long abandoned the idea of entering the Council of State, he no longer even ran race-horses, being just as sated with horses as with girls. He lived alone, idle and perfectly happy, eating up his fortune with art and caution, and with the relentlessness of a son-in-law formerly depraved and parasitic, but now settled down

The valet now returned to say: 'If Madame would please follow me, Monsieur will receive her at once in his room.'

Madame Caroline was on familiar terms with Maxime ever since he had seen her installed as a faithful housekeeper whenever he dined at his father's house. On entering the room she found the curtains drawn and six candles burning on the mantelpiece and a side-table, lighting with their quiet flames this nest of down and silk, a room too softly comfortable, fit for a beautiful courtesan, with its deep armchairs and huge bed of feathery softness. This was Maxime's favourite room, on which he had lavished every refinement, costly furniture and ornaments, marvels of the previous century, all melting and merging in the most delightful confusion of fabrics imaginable.

But the door to the adjoining dressing-room was wide open and he appeared, saying:

'What is it? What's happened?... Papa isn't dead, is he?'

After his bath Maxime had put on an elegant white-flannel suit, his skin fresh and sweet-smelling, his pretty girlish face already somewhat worn, and his eyes blue and clear over the emptiness of his mind. Through the door you could still hear the dripping of one of the bath-taps, while a powerful scent of flowers arose from the softness of warm bathwater.

'No, no, it's nothing so serious,' she replied, put out by the calmly bantering tone of the question. 'But what I have to say is rather embarrassing for me... Forgive me for dropping in on you like this...'

'It's true I am dining out, but I have plenty of time to get dressed... So, what is it then?'

He waited, and now she hesitated, stammering, struck by the great luxury and hedonistic refinement that she felt all around her. Cowardice took hold of her, she didn't have the courage now to tell the whole story. How was it possible that life, so hard for the child born of chance over there in the dunghill of the Cité de Naples, should have proved so prodigal for this one in his cultivated wealth? So much vile squalor, hunger and unavoidable dirt on one side, and on the other such a pursuit of the exquisite, such abundance, such a beautiful life. Could money then mean education, health, and intelligence? If the same human mire always existed under the surface, didn't all civilization lie simply in this superiority of smelling nice and living well?

'Oh dear, it's quite a tale! I think I'm doing right in telling you about it... Anyway I have to, as I need your help.'

Maxime listened, standing at first, then sitting down facing her as his legs quite gave way in his surprise. And when she finished:

'What! What! I'm not the only son of his—here's a horrible little brother dropping in on me out of the blue, without any warning!'

She thought he was speaking out of self-interest, and made a reference to the matter of inheritance.

'Oh! Papa's inheritance!'

And he waved his hand in a gesture of ironic indifference that she didn't understand. What on earth...? What could he mean? Didn't he believe in his father's great qualities, in the fortune he would certainly make?

'No, no, my affairs are all in order, I don't need anyone... Only, really, it's all so funny this business, I can't help laughing.'

He was indeed laughing, but vexed and vaguely uneasy, thinking only of himself, not having had time yet to work out what this event might bring him for good or ill. He felt quite detached from it all, and made a remark in which he fully and brutally expressed himself:

'In fact, I don't give a damn.'

Standing up, he went into the dressing-room and quickly returned with a tortoiseshell polisher, with which he began gently buffing his nails.

'And what are you going to do with this monster of yours? You can't very well send him to the Bastille, like the Man in the Iron Mask.'*

Then she told him about La Méchain's bills, explained her idea of sending Victor to the Work Foundation, and asked him for the two thousand francs.

'I don't want your father to know anything about it yet, and you're the only person I can ask; you must lend this money.'

But he flatly refused.

'To Papa, absolutely never! Not a sou! Listen, this is a vow, if Papa just needed one sou to get over a toll-bridge I wouldn't lend it to him. Get this clear! Some stupidities are just too stupid, and I don't intend to be ridiculous!'

Again she looked at him, disturbed by his ugly insinuations. In this emotional moment she had neither the wish nor the time to get him to explain.

'And to me...?' she went on curtly. 'Will you lend them to me, the two thousand francs?'

'To you, to you...'

He went on polishing his nails with light and pretty motions, while still examining her with his clear eyes, eyes that could probe into the very hearts of women.

'To you, yes, all right, I will lend to you... You're an innocent, you'll see I get them back.'

Then, when he had got the two notes out of a little desk and given them to her, he took her hands and held them for a moment in his own, with an air of friendly jollity, like a stepson fond of his stepmother.

'You have illusions about Papa! Oh, don't bother to deny it, I'm not trying to butt into your affairs... It's strange that women some-times seem to enjoy offering devotion; of course they have every right to take their pleasure wherever they find it... No matter, if ever you should find yourself getting little thanks for it, come and see me and we'll have a chat.'

When Madame Caroline got back to her cab, still suffocated by the soft warmth of Maxime's house and the scent of heliotrope that had permeated her clothes, she was shuddering as if she had just emerged from a house of ill-repute, and frightened too by the son's odd reticences and jocular remarks about his father, which aggravated her suspicions about a shameful past. But she didn't want to know; she had the money and she calmed down, planning what to do next day so that before nightfall the child would be rescued from his life of vice.

So in the morning she set out, having all sorts of formalities to deal with to make certain that her protégé would be admitted to the Work Foundation. Her position as secretary of the Supervisory Committee, to which the Princess d'Orviedo, the founder, had appointed ten ladies of standing, made the formalities rather easier; and by the afternoon she had only to go and collect Victor from the Cité de Naples. She took suitable garments with her; she was not free from worry that he might put up some resistance, this child who didn't want to hear any mention of school. But La Méchain, to whom she had sent a telegram and who was waiting for her on the threshold, gave her a piece of news which she said had greatly upset her in the night: Mother Eulalie had suddenly died, from what cause exactly the doctor had not been able to say—a congestion perhaps, or some dire effect of her infected blood; and the alarming thing was that the boy, sleeping beside her, had not noticed her death in the dark until he had felt the coldness of her body. He had ended the night in the house of the owner of the Cité, stunned by this drama, and plagued by a nameless fear, so he allowed himself to be dressed, and seemed happy enough at the idea of living in a house with a beautiful garden. There was nothing to keep him at the Cité any more, since 'the fatty', as he called her, was going to rot in the ground.

However, La Méchain, while making out the receipt for the two thousand francs, laid down her conditions.

'It's agreed, isn't it? I'll receive the whole of the six thousand from you in one single payment, in six months' time… otherwise, I'll go straight to Monsieur Saccard.'

'But', said Madame Caroline, 'it's Monsieur Saccard himself who will be paying you… Today I'm just standing in for him.'

The farewells of Victor and his old cousin were not affectionate, a quick kiss on the hair, and the boy hastened to get into the cab while

La Méchain, who had been reproved by Busch for accepting a mere instalment, went on dully chewing over her annoyance at losing her security.

'Now, Madame, be straight with me, otherwise I swear I'll make you sorry for it.'

On the way from the Cité de Naples to the Work Foundation on the Boulevard Bineau, Madame Caroline was only able to get a few monosyllables out of Victor, as his shining eyes gobbled up the road, the wide avenues, the passers-by, and the rich houses. He couldn't write and was barely able to read, having always abandoned school in favour of jaunts on the fortifications; and his face, that of a child who has grown up too fast, showed only the frustrated appetites of his race, an eagerness, a violent urge for pleasure, aggravated by the compost of wretchedness and abominations in which he had grown up. In the Boulevard Bineau his eyes, like those of a young wild animal, sparkled even more when, getting out of the cab, he crossed the central courtyard, with the boys' building on the right and the girls' on the left. He had already cast a searching look over the vast playgrounds planted with beautiful trees, the tiled kitchens from whose open windows came the smell of cooking, the refectories adorned with marble, long and with high ceilings like church naves—all this royal luxury that the Princess, bent on restitution, insisted on giving to the poor. Then, at the end of the courtyard, in the central block where the administrative staff were lodged, as he was taken from one department to another to be admitted with the usual formalities, he heard his new shoes clattering along the endless corridors, the huge staircases, and all those open areas flooded with air and light and palatially decorated. His nostrils quivered: all this would be his.

But when Madame Caroline came back to the ground floor to sign a document she took him down a new corridor and led him to a glass door, through which he could see a workshop in which boys of his age were standing at a bench, learning woodwork.

'You see, my dear,' she said, 'here people work, because you have to work if you want to be healthy and happy... In the evening there are classes, and I can count on you, can't I, to be good and do well at your studies...? You will be deciding your own future, a future such as you never dreamed of.'

A dark furrow crossed Victor's brow. He made no reply, and his wolfish young eyes now cast only oblique and piratical looks of envy at this prodigal display of luxury: eager to possess all this but without having to do anything for it; to conquer it and feast on it by force of tooth and nail. From that moment on he was there only as a rebel, as a prisoner, dreaming of theft and escape.

'Now everything is settled,' Madame Caroline went on, 'we'll go up to the bathroom.'

It was customary for each new boarder, on entry, to take a bath; the baths were upstairs, in little rooms next to the infirmary, which consisted of two small dormitories, one for boys and one for girls, near the linen-room. The six Sisters of Charity attached to the community reigned here, in this superb linen-room of varnished maple, with its three tiers of deep linen-presses, in this model infirmary so spotlessly bright and white, cheerful and clean as health itself. The ladies of the Supervisory Committee also came there quite often and spent an hour or two in the afternoon, not so much actually to supervise as to give the work their devoted support.

And in fact the Countess de Beauvilliers was there, with her daughter Alice, in the room between the two infirmaries. The Countess often brought Alice along, to offer her some distraction and give her the pleasure of doing charitable work. That day she was helping one of the sisters to prepare slices of bread and jam for two convalescent little girls who had been allowed a teatime snack.

'Ah,' said the Countess on seeing Victor, who had just been sat down to wait for his bath, 'here's a new boy!'

She usually behaved with some formality towards Madame Caroline, greeting her only with a nod and never speaking to her, for fear, perhaps, of being drawn into neighbourly relations. But this boy Madame Caroline was bringing to the Foundation, and the air of active kindness with which she was looking after him, doubtless touched the Countess and brought her out of her normal reserve. And they began talking quietly.

'If you only knew, Madame, from what hell I have just brought him! I recommend him to your concern, as I have recommended him to all the ladies and gentlemen.'

'Does he have any family? Do you know any of them?'

'No, his mother is dead... and now he only has me.'

'Poor boy! Ah, how very sad!'

Meanwhile, Victor was gazing avidly at the bread and jam. His eyes had lit up with ferocious desire; and from the jam, being spread by the knife, he looked upward to the slender white hands of Alice, on to her too-thin neck, and then to the whole person of this puny virgin, wasting away in the long and futile wait for marriage. If only he'd been alone with her, he'd have given her such a head-butt in the stomach, how he'd have pushed her staggering against the wall and grabbed the bread and jam from her! But the girl had noticed his ravenous eyes, and after consulting the sister with a quick glance:

'Are you hungry, my little friend?'

'Yes.'

'And you don't hate jam?'

'No.'

'So, it would suit you if I made you two slices of bread and jam that you could eat when you come out of the bath?'

'Yes.'

'A lot of jam on not a lot of bread is what you'd like, isn't it?'

'Yes.'

She was laughing and joking, but he remained serious and open-mouthed, his voracious eyes devouring her along with the bread and jam.

At that moment shouts of joy and quite a violent racket came up from the boys' playground, where four o'clock playtime was just beginning. The workrooms were emptying and the children had half-an-hour for their teatime snack and to stretch their legs.

'You see,' Madame Caroline went on, taking Victor over to a window, 'if there's work there's also play... Do you like work?'

'No.'

'But you like playing?'

'Yes.'

'Well, if you want to play, you have to work... That will all get sorted out, and you'll be sensible, I'm sure.'

He did not reply. A flush of pleasure had warmed his face at the sight of his fellows let out into the yard, jumping and shouting; and his eyes went back to the bread and jam that Alice had just finished preparing and was putting on a plate. Yes! Freedom and pleasure all the time, he wanted nothing else. His bath was ready, and he was led away.

'That's a little fellow who won't be all that easy to manage, I think,' said the sister quietly. 'I'm suspicious of them when they have an irregular face.'

'But he's not ugly,' murmured Alice, 'and you'd think he was eighteen, the way he looks at you.'

'It's true,' said Madame Caroline, with a little shiver, 'he's very mature for his age.'

Before they left, the ladies decided to allow themselves the pleasure of seeing the little convalescent girls eat their bread and jam. One of them was especially interesting, a little blonde ten-year-old, already with knowing eyes and the look of a woman, the precocious and sickly flesh of the poorest areas of Paris. Hers was the usual story: a drunken father who brought in the mistresses he'd picked up on the street and who disappeared with one of them; a mother who had taken up with another man, then another, before herself becoming a drunkard; and the little girl in the middle of it all was beaten by all these males, when they weren't trying to rape her. One morning her mother had had to drag her out of the arms of a mason she had herself brought home the previous day. And yet they still allowed this wretched mother to come and see her daughter, for it was she who had begged them to take her away, since even in her degradation she still kept an ardent maternal love. And indeed she was there, a thin wreck of a woman with yellowish skin and eyelids red with weeping, sitting beside the white bed on which her child, very clean and propped up with pillows, was daintily eating her bread and jam.

She recognized Madame Caroline, since she had once gone to Saccard for help.

'Ah Madame, here's my poor Madeleine saved once again. She's got all our misery in her blood you see, and the doctor told me she wouldn't live if she went on being knocked about at home with us... But here she has meat and wine, fresh air and peace... I beg you, Madame, please tell that good gentleman that not an hour of my life goes by when I don't bless him.'

A sob choked her, as if her heart was melting with gratitude. It was of Saccard she spoke, for, like most of the parents who had children at the Foundation, it was only Saccard she knew. The Princess d'Orviedo was never on the scene, while Saccard had long been abundantly visible, populating the Foundation, gathering up all the wretchedness of the gutter in order to see this great engine of charity, partly his own creation, getting to work as fast as possible, full of eager enthusiasm as ever, and distributing five-franc notes from his own pocket to the miserable families whose little ones he was saving. And he remained, for these wretches, the one true Saviour.

'You will tell him, won't you, Madame, that somewhere there's a poor woman praying for him… Oh, it's not that I'm religious, I don't want to lie, I've never been a hypocrite. No, between the churches and us it's all over, we don't even think of them any more, they never did us any good, going there was just a waste of time… But even so that doesn't mean there isn't something up above us, and it's somehow comforting, when someone has been kind, to call down the blessings of Heaven upon him.'

Her tears overflowed, rolling down her withered cheeks.

'Listen to me, Madeleine, listen…'

The little girl, so pale in her snow-white nightdress, licking the jam off her bread with the tip of a greedy tongue while her eyes shone with happiness, raised her head and listened carefully, without interrupting her treat.

'Every night, before going to sleep in your bed, you will put your hands together like this and you'll say: "Lord, please let Monsieur Saccard be rewarded for his goodness; may he have a long and happy life." D'you hear? You promise?'

'Yes, Mama.'

In the weeks that followed Madame Caroline lived in a state of great moral agitation. She no longer knew what to think about Saccard. The story of Victor's birth and abandonment, that unfortunate Rosalie, seized on the step of a staircase with such violence that she had been left disabled, the promissory notes signed and never paid, and the unfortunate fatherless child growing up in such filth—all of that deplorable past made her sick at heart. She thrust aside the images that arose from that past, just as she had not wanted to provoke any indiscretions from Maxime; there were certainly some bad things in earlier years that frightened her and would, she thought, have given her too much pain. But then there was this woman in tears, joining together the hands of her little girl, making her pray for this man, this Saccard, adored like the God of all goodness and in fact truly good, having really saved souls in that passionate businesslike activity of his, which became virtue when the work he was doing was virtuous. So she ended up unwilling to judge him and telling herself, to ease her conscience as a well-informed woman who had done too much reading and thinking, that in him, as in all men, there was both the best and the worst.

However, she had a secret pang of shame at the thought that he had possessed her. That still astounded her, but she reassured herself, vowing that it was over and done with, and that such a momentary surprise could never happen again. And three months went by, during which she went twice a week to see Victor, and one evening she found herself once more in the arms of Saccard, definitively his mistress and allowing it to become a settled relationship. What was happening to her? Was she, like so many others, just curious? Was it those shady love affairs of yesteryear that she had stirred up that had given her the desire for sensual knowledge? Or was it rather the child who had become the link, the fatal bond, between her, the mother through chance and adoption, and him, the father? Yes, it must have been just a distorted effect of sentiment. In her great sorrow at being childless, looking after the child of this man in such poignant circumstances must have touched her so deeply as to overthrow her will. Each time she saw him again she gave herself more freely to him, and her frustrated maternal longings lay at the heart of her abandon. Besides, she was a woman of clear common sense, and she could accept the facts of life without wearing herself out trying to explain their myriad complex causes. For her, that sort of untangling of mind and heart, that refined hair-splitting analysis, was only an entertainment for society ladies with nothing to do, no household to manage and no child to love, phoney intellectuals who try to find excuses for their sins and try to mask, with their science of the soul, the appetites of the flesh, common to duchesses and barmaids. She, with her overload of erudition, who had once wasted her time ardently longing to understand the whole vast world and join in the disputes of the philosophers, she had emerged from all that with a great disdain for those psychological pastimes that tend to serve as replacements for piano-playing and embroidery, and which, she would say with a laugh, had depraved more women than they cured. So, on those days when there seemed to be holes in her very self and she felt there had been a breakdown in her free will, she preferred, having once acknowledged it, to have the courage to accept the facts; and she relied on the work of life itself to remove the stain and repair the damage, just as the ever-rising sap of an oak tree renews both its wood and its bark. If she was now Saccard's mistress, without having intended it and without being at all sure she respected him, she picked herself up again from this fall with the thought that he was not unworthy of her, charmed as she was by his qualities as a man of action, his energy for conquest, and believing him to be kind and helpful to others. Her initial shame had disappeared in that instinctive need one has to purify one's faults, and nothing was in fact more natural and peaceful than their relationship: a liaison more of reason than passion, he happy to have her there in the evening when he was not going out, and she almost maternal with her soothing affection, her lively intelligence, and her honesty. And for this rogue of the Paris streets, scorched and toughened in every kind of financial swindle, it was really an undeserved stroke of luck, a reward stolen like everything else, to have as his own this adorable woman who at thirty-six was so young and healthy under the snowy mass of her thick white hair, a woman of such bold good sense and natural wisdom, with her faith in life just as it is, in spite of all the mud it carries in its flow.

Months went by, and it must be said that throughout all the difficult initial period of setting up the Universal Bank Madame Caroline found Saccard very energetic and very prudent. Her suspicions about shady deals, her fears that he might compromise her brother and herself, vanished entirely on seeing him constantly struggling with difficulties, exerting himself from morning to night to ensure the perfect operation of this great new engine, with its machinery grating as if about to explode; and she was grateful, she admired him. The Universal Bank was not in fact working as he would have wished, for it had to contend with the silent hostility of the major banks: ugly rumours were circulating, new obstacles constantly arose, immobilizing the capital and prohibiting big profitable ventures. So Saccard had made a virtue of the slow progress to which he had been reduced, moving forward one step at a time on solid ground, looking out for pitfalls, and too busy avoiding a fall to dare launching himself into the hazards of speculation. He was eaten up with impatience, pawing the ground like a racehorse made to trot along slowly; but never had the early days of a new bank been more honourable and correct, and the whole of the stock exchange was talking about it in astonishment.

So it was that they reached the time for the first General Meeting of shareholders. It had been fixed for 25 April.* On the 20th Hamelin arrived from the East to chair the meeting, having been hastily summoned by Saccard, who was suffocating in the restricted space of the bank. Hamelin, anyway, brought excellent news; contracts had been agreed for the formation of the United Steamboat Company, he had acquired concessions granting the exploitation of the Carmel Silver Mines to a French company; in addition there was the Turkish National Bank, for which he had just laid the foundations in Constantinople, and which would be a real branch of the Universal. As for the big question of the Asia Minor Railways, that had not yet matured so must be set aside for the present; he would have to go back to continue his research, the day after the General Meeting. Saccard was delighted and had a long conversation with Hamelin and Madame Caroline, and he had no trouble convincing them that an increase in the company's capital was an absolute necessity if they were to provide adequately for these ventures. The most important shareholders, Daigremont, Huret, Sédille, and Kolb, had been consulted and had approved the increase, so the proposal could be studied and presented to the board on the very eve of the meeting of shareholders.

This Extraordinary Meeting was a solemn affair, with all the directors present in the austere room, tinged with green by the tall trees of the adjoining Beauvilliers garden. There were normally two meetings a month; the small, but most important meeting on the 15th, when only the top people, the business executives, would attend; and the big meeting, the ceremonial meeting, around the 30th, to which everyone came, the silent directors and the merely ornamental ones, to approve what had already been arranged and append their signatures. That day the Marquis de Bohain, with his little aristocratic head, was one of the first to arrive, bringing with him, in his grand air of weariness, the approval of all the nobility of France. And the Viscount de Robin-Chagot, the vice-president, a man at once affable and avaricious, was given the task of looking out for the directors who had not been pre-advised and taking them aside to give them the orders of the manager, the real master. It was all a matter of course, and they all indicated their compliance with a nod.

At last the session began. Hamelin made known to the board the report he was to read at the Annual General Meeting. This was the big task Saccard had been working on for some time, and he had just written it up in two days, adding the notes that Hamelin had brought; and he was now modestly listening to it with an air of lively interest, as if it were all entirely new to him. The report began by outlining the transactions of the Universal Bank since its foundation: they had all been good, just minor, everyday matters, carried out from one day to the next, the usual banking routine. However, handsome profits were expected on the Mexican loan, which had been launched the month before, after the Emperor Maximilian's departure for Mexico: a very muddled loan, with crazy premiums, and Saccard bitterly regretted not having been able to get deeper into it for lack of funds. All this was no more than ordinary, but the bank had survived. For its first period, which was only three months, from its foundation on 5 October to 31 December, the total profits only amounted to slightly more than four hundred thousand francs, which had allowed the bank to pay off a quarter of the start-up expenses, pay the shareholders their five per cent, and put ten per cent into the reserve fund; in addition, the directors had taken the ten per cent granted by the company's statutes, and there remained a sum of about sixty-eight thousand francs carried over to the next financial period. But there had been no dividend. Nothing could have been more ordinary and honourable than this. It was the same with the share-prices of the Universal on the Bourse: they had slowly and steadily risen from five hundred to six hundred francs in the normal way, like the share-prices of any self-respecting bank; and over the last two months they had remained stationary, there being nothing to raise them any further in the petty everyday dealings in which the new banking-house seemed to be quietly dormant.

Then the report moved on to the future, and now there was a sudden expansion, with a vast horizon opening on to a whole series of grand ventures. The report laid particular emphasis on the United General Steamboat Company, the shares of which were to be issued by the Universal: a company with a capital of fifty million, which would have a monopoly of all the transport services of the Mediterranean and would be joined by the two main rival companies, the Phocean for the service through the Piraeus and the Dardanelles for Constantinople, Smyrna and Trebizond, and the Maritime Company for Alexandria, via Messina and Syria, as well as some minor banking institutions which would also join the association, Combarel and Co. for Algeria and Tunisia, Veuve Henri Liotard also for Algeria, via Spain and Morocco, and finally the Féraud-Giraud Brothers for Italy, via Civitavecchia for Naples and the cities of the Adriatic. In creating one single company out of all these rival firms and banks that had been killing each other off, they were taking over the whole of the

Mediterranean. Thanks to the centralization of the capital they would be able to build their own boats of unprecedented speed and comfort, the services would be more frequent, and new ports of call would be created, making the Orient a suburb of Marseilles; and what importance might not the company later acquire when, with the completion of the Suez Canal, it would be able to create services for India, Tonkin,* China and Japan! Never had there been a safer or more wide-ranging enterprise. The next thing would be the supporting of the Turkish National Bank, on which the report provided lengthy technical details, all demonstrating its unshakeable solidity. And this outline of future operations ended with the announcement that the Universal was also taking under its wing the French Carmel Silver Mines Company, with a capital of twenty million francs. Laboratory tests indicated a substantial proportion of silver in the samples of ore examined. But even more than science, the ancient poetry of the Holy Land seemed to send that silver streaming down like a miraculous rain-shower, a divine and dazzling idea that Saccard had used at the end of a sentence and with which he was well pleased.

Finally, after all these promises of a glorious future, the report concluded with the matter of the increase of capital. It would be doubled, raised from twenty-five to fifty million. The system adopted for the issue was of the utmost simplicity, so that everyone could easily understand it: fifty thousand new shares would be created and would be reserved, share by share, for the bearers of the fifty thousand initial shares; so there would not even be a public subscription. But these new shares would be five hundred and twenty francs, inclusive of a premium of twenty francs, making a total sum of one million which would be carried over to the reserve fund. It was quite fair, and indeed prudent, to impose this small tax on the shareholders, since they were being favoured in the new issue. Besides, only a quarter of the price of the shares, plus the premium, would have to be paid on issue.

When Hamelin came to the end of the report a great hubbub of approval arose. It was perfect, no further comment was required. During the whole time of the reading, Daigremont, absorbed in a careful examination of his nails, had occasionally smiled at various vague thoughts; and the deputy Huret, leaning back in his chair with his eyes closed, was half asleep, thinking himself at the Chamber of Deputies; while Kolb, the banker, had calmly, taking no pains to hide the fact, embarked on a lengthy calculation upon the sheets of paper that he, like every other director, had on the table before him. Sédille, however, anxious and distrustful as ever, decided to ask a question: what would happen to the shares abandoned by shareholders who chose not to exercise their right? Would the company hold them on its own account, and wouldn't this be illegal, since the legal declaration of increased capital could not be made by the lawyer until the whole of the additional capital had been subscribed? And if the company decided to get rid of them, to whom and how was it going to do so? But from the silk-manufacturer's first words the Marquis de Bohain, noting Saccard's impatience, cut him short, declaring in his grand and aristocratic manner that the board left such matters of detail in the devoted and competent hands of the chairman and the manager. And then only congratulations were heard, and the meeting closed in the midst of general delight.

The shareholders' meeting on the following day was the occasion for some really touching scenes. It was again held in the hall in the Rue Blanche, where a promoter of public dances had gone bankrupt; and before the arrival of the chairman, in the already crowded hall the most favourable rumours were circulating, one especially being whispered to the effect that the minister Rougon, the manager's brother, having been violently attacked by the increasingly powerful Opposition, was disposed to favour the Universal if the company's newspaper, *L'Espérance*, a former organ of the Catholic party, would defend the government. A left-wing deputy had just raised the terrible cry: 'The second of December is a crime!'* and this had resounded from one end of France to the other, like a reawakening of the public conscience. Great deeds were needed to respond to this: the imminent Universal Exhibition would create a tenfold increase in business, and huge gains would be made in Mexico and elsewhere with the triumph of the Empire at its peak. In one little group of shareholders, who were being indoctrinated by Jantrou and Sabatani, there was a great deal of laughter about another deputy who, during the discussion of the army, had proposed the extraordinary idea that a recruitment system like that of Prussia should be established in France. The Chamber had found this very funny: how deranged by terror of Prussia some people's minds must be after the Denmark affair* and the resentment that Italy nurtured against us ever since Solferino!* But the noise of individual conversations and the general hubbub of the room suddenly ceased when Hamelin and the other officials made their appearance. Saccard, even more modest here than in the board meeting, had almost disappeared, lost in the crowd; and he did no more than give the signal for applause, approving the report which presented to the assembly the accounts of the first quarter, checked and accepted by the auditors Lavignière and Rousseau, and which proposed the doubling of the company's capital. This meeting was solely competent to authorize the increase, and it did so with enthusiasm, utterly intoxicated by the millions of the United General Steamboat Company and the Turkish National Bank, and recognizing the need to bring the capital into line with the importance the Universal was going to assume. As for the Carmel Silver Mines, they were greeted with a religious thrill. And when the shareholders had separated, after votes of thanks to the chairman, the board, and the manager, they all dreamed of Carmel and that miraculous shower of silver, raining down in glory from the Holy Land.

Two days later, accompanied now by the vice-chairman Viscount de Robin-Chagot, Hamelin and Saccard returned to the Rue Sainte-Anne to declare, in the office of Maître Lelorrain, the increase of capital which, they asserted, had been entirely subscribed. The truth was that about three thousand shares, refused by the first shareholders to whom they belonged by right, remained in the possession of the company, which once more, with some juggling of the books, passed them over to the account of Sabatani. It was the same old irregularity, but aggravated, the system of concealing a certain number of its own shares in the coffers of the Universal as a sort of fighting-fund, allowing it to speculate, to throw itself into battle on the Bourse if needed, to maintain its share-prices in the event of a coalition of 'bears' intent on driving them down.

Anyway, Hamelin, although he disapproved of this illegal manoeuvre, had in the end left all the financial operations to Saccard; and there had been a conversation on the subject between the two men and Madame Caroline, but only in relation to the five hundred shares that Saccard had forced them to take in the first issue, which now, of course, were doubled in the second issue, making a thousand in all, which meant, for the payment of one-quarter of the value plus the premium, a sum of one hundred and thirty-five thousand francs, which the brother and sister insisted on paying, since they had just received an unexpected inheritance of about three hundred thousand francs from an aunt, who had died of the same fever that ten days previously had caused the death of her only son. Saccard let them do as they wished, without offering any explanation of how he was intending to pay for his own shares.

'Ah, this inheritance!' said Madame Caroline with a laugh. 'It's the first stroke of good fortune we've had... I really think you are bringing us luck. My brother has his salary of thirty thousand francs and substantial travelling expenses, and now all this money pours down on us, no doubt just because we don't really need it any more... We're rich!'

She gazed at Saccard with her good-hearted gratitude, quite conquered now, trusting in him and losing a little more of her clearsightedness with each passing day in the growing affection she felt for him. Then, carried away by her gaiety and frankness, she continued:

'No matter, if I had actually earned this money I assure you I would not be risking it in your ventures... But an aunt we scarcely knew, and money we had never thought of, it's like money found in the street, it's something that doesn't even seem quite honest, and I feel a bit ashamed about it... You understand, it's not close to my heart, I am prepared to lose it.'

'Quite so!' said Saccard, similarly joking. 'It's going to grow and will give you millions. There's nothing like ill-gotten gains for making money! Before a week is out you'll see, you'll see how the price will rise.'

And in fact Hamelin, who had had to delay his departure, was able to observe the rapid rise of the Universal share-price. By the settlement at the end of May it had passed the seven-hundred-franc rate. This was just the usual result of an increase of capital: it's the classic move, the way to whip up success and set the share-prices galloping with each new issue. But it was also due to the real importance of the ventures the bank was launching; and big yellow posters pasted up all over Paris, announcing the forthcoming opening of the Carmel Silver Mines, had further disturbed people's minds, lighting a spark of intoxication, a passion which would grow and carry away all common sense. The ground had been prepared, the Imperial compost, made of fermenting rubbish, and heated by exacerbated appetites, an extremely fertile ground for one of those mad surges of speculation which, every ten or fifteen years, choke and poison the Bourse, leaving behind them only blood and ruins. Crooked firms were already

springing up like mushrooms, big companies were promoting risky
financial ventures, an intense gambling fever was manifesting itself in
the rowdy prosperity of the reign, all that razzle-dazzle of pleasure
and luxury for which the impending Exhibition would be a last blaze
of glory, the mendacious grand finale of the show. And in the giddi-
ness of the crowd and the flurry of all the other fine ventures everywhere on offer, the Universal was at last beginning to get started, like
a powerful engine destined to madden and destroy everything in its
path, while violent hands went on wildly heating it to the point of
explosion.

When her brother had again set off for the East Madame Caroline
found herself once more alone with Saccard, taking up again their
life of close, almost conjugal, intimacy. She insisted on continuing
to manage the household, making savings for him as a loyal housekeeper, even though both their fortunes had considerably changed.
And in her good-humoured quietness, her always even temper, she
had just one worry, and that was her uneasy conscience about Victor,
her hesitation about whether she should go on concealing the existence of his son from the father. At the Work Foundation they were
very unhappy about Victor, for he was causing serious trouble. His
six months' trial was coming to an end, so was she going to produce
the little monster before he was cleansed of his vices? There were
times when she really suffered over this.

One evening she was on the point of speaking up. Saccard, more
and more frustrated at the inadequacy of the premises for the
Universal, had just persuaded the board to rent the ground floor of
the adjoining house in order to enlarge the offices, until such time as
he could dare to propose the construction of the luxurious building of
his dreams. Once more he was creating new communicating doors,
knocking down partition walls, installing new cash desks. And when
she came back from the Boulevard Bineau, distraught at the appalling
behaviour of Victor who had almost bitten off the ear of one of his
schoolfellows, Madame Caroline asked Saccard to come up with her
to their rooms.

'My dear, I have something to tell you.'

But when she saw him, one shoulder covered with plaster,
delighted at a new idea he'd just had for further enlargement, by glaz-
ing over the courtyard of the adjoining house as he had already done
in the Orviedo house, she did not have the heart to upset him with

the deplorable secret. No, she would wait a while yet, the dreadful lout had to be reformed. When faced by the suffering of others she lost all her strength:

'Ah yes, my dear, it was about that courtyard. I'd had the very same idea.'

CHAPTER VI

THE offices of *L'Espérance*, the failing Catholic paper that Saccard had
bought at Jantrou's suggestion to help launch the Universal, were in
the Rue Saint-Joseph, in a dark and damp old building of which they
occupied the first floor, at the far end of the courtyard. A corridor led
off from the antechamber, where a gaslight was always burning; on
the left was the office of Jantrou the editor, then a room that Saccard
had allocated to himself, whilst on the right were the communal journalists' room, the secretary's office, and various departmental offices.
On the other side of the landing were the administrative and cashier's
offices, linked to the journalists' room by an inner passage running
behind the staircase.

That day Jordan, who had installed himself early in the journalists'
room to finish a column without being disturbed, went out just as it
was striking four o'clock and came upon Dejoie the office-boy who, in
spite of the glorious June day outside, was avidly reading by the broad
flame of the gaslight the bulletin from the Bourse, which had just
been delivered and which he was always the first to see.

'Tell me, Dejoie, was that Monsieur Jantrou who just came in?'

'Yes, Monsieur Jordan.'

The young man paused, feeling a momentary pang that made him
pause a few seconds. In the difficult first days of his happy household
some old debts had fallen upon him; and in spite of his good luck in
finding this newspaper where he could place articles, he was going
through a period of gruelling difficulty, all the worse in that his salary
had been seized and he had, that very day, to pay another promissory
note or else see his few bits of furniture sold. Twice already he had
asked in vain for an advance from the editor, who had fallen back on
the legal distraint which tied his hands.

However, he was just making up his mind and approaching the
door when the office-boy added:

'But Monsieur Jantrou is not alone.'

'Ah! Who is with him?'

'He came in with Monsieur Saccard, and Monsieur Saccard
told me to let nobody in except Monsieur Huret, whom he's
expecting.'

Jordan took a deep breath, finding the delay a relief since asking for money was so painful for him.

'All right. I'll go and finish my article. Let me know when the editor's free.'

But as he was moving away Dejoie held him back, with a shout of extreme delight.

'You know, Universal shares have gone up to 750.'

With a gesture the young man indicated his total indifference and returned to the communal room.

Almost every day, after the Bourse, Saccard went on to the newspaper and often had meetings there in the room he had reserved for himself, dealing with some special and mysterious affairs. Jantrou, anyway, although officially only the editor of *L'Espérance*, for which he wrote political articles in a very academic, polished, and flowery language, recognized even by his enemies as of the 'purest Attic style', was Saccard's secret agent, the complaisant performer of delicate tasks. Among other things, it was he who had just organized a vast publicity campaign for the Universal. From the myriad little financial papers that existed he had selected and bought ten or so. The best of them belonged to seedy banking-houses, whose very simple tactics consisted in publishing then distributing them for two or three francs a year, a sum which did not even cover the cost of postage; they made their money in another way, dealing in the money and shares of the clients that the papers brought them. Under cover of publishing the current stock-exchange rates, the numbers drawn in the bond lotteries, and all the technical information useful to small investors, advertisements were gradually slipped in, in the form of recommendations and advice, at first modest and reasonable but soon becoming extravagant, and with cool impudence spreading ruin among their gullible subscribers. From the great heap of the two or three hundred publications that were wreaking their havoc across Paris and indeed France, Jantrou had cleverly sniffed out the ones that had not yet lied too vigorously and were not already too discredited. But the big deal he had in mind was to buy one of them, the *Cote financière*,* which had twelve years of absolute probity behind it—but such probity was likely to be expensive; he was waiting for the Universal to get richer and reach the point at which a last trumpet-blast can bring about deafening peals of triumph. His efforts, anyway, were not limited to creating a docile battalion of these special news-sheets celebrating the glories of Saccard's works in every issue; he was also contracted to the main political and literary newspapers, keeping up a flow of pleasant notes and approving articles at so much a line, and assuring their support by gifts of shares when there were new share-issues. All this in addition to the daily campaign he was running in *L'Espérance*, not a crude campaign of extravagant plaudits but including explanations and even discussions, thus slowly taking hold of the public and strangling it in a very proper manner.

That day it was to discuss the paper that Saccard had closeted himself with Jantrou. He had found in the paper that morning an article from Huret, so outrageously praising a speech Rougon had made the previous day in the Chamber that he had flown into a rage, and was waiting for the Deputy to arrive to have it out with him. Was he supposed to be working for his brother? Was he being paid to allow the policy of the paper to be compromised by such unqualified approval of the slightest acts of the minister? When he heard him mention the 'policy of the paper' Jantrou gave a silent smile. However, he heard Saccard out very calmly, gazing intently at his fingernails, since it was not over his head that the storm was threatening to break. With the cynicism of a disillusioned man of letters, he had the most absolute contempt for literature, for the front page and page two as well, as he was apt to say, indicating the pages on which articles, even his own, appeared; and he showed no real interest in anything except the advertisements. Now he looked quite brand new, in a close-fitting, elegant frock-coat with a buttonhole flourishing a brightly coloured rosette, in summer carrying a thin, light-coloured jacket over his arm, and in winter huddled in a hundred-louis* fur coat; he was taking great care of his hair, and his hats were impeccable, with a mirror-like sheen. But with all that he still had a few gaps in his elegance, the vague suggestion of a persistent uncleanliness underneath, the old grime of the disgraced professor who had tumbled from the Bordeaux lycée to the Paris Bourse, his skin saturated and stained with all the hideous filth he had endured for ten years; and similarly, even in the arrogant confidence of his new fortune he still showed some features of base submissiveness, quickly getting out of the way when gripped by a sudden fear of a kick on the backside as in former times. He was earning a hundred thousand francs a year and spending twice that, nobody knew on what, for he didn't appear to have a mistress—prey perhaps to some vile and secret vice which had got him dismissed from the university. Absinthe, in any case, was gradually destroying him, continuing its work from the infamous cafés of his former years of penury to the luxurious clubs of today, scything off his last strands of hair and giving a grey, leaden cast to his skull and face, a face in which his bushy black beard was the only remaining glory, the beard of a handsome man, still creating some illusion. When Saccard again referred to the 'policy of the paper' Jantrou interrupted him with the wearied gesture of a man who, not wishing to waste his time on futile emotions, had decided to talk about serious matters, since they were still waiting for Huret.

For some time Jantrou had been hatching a few new ideas about publicity. First he had the notion of writing a brochure of twenty pages or so on the great enterprises being launched by the Universal, giving them the appeal of a novelette, dramatized in a popular style; he would then flood the whole province with this publication, which would be distributed free even in the remotest depths of the countryside. Then he thought of setting up an agency which would create and litho-print a Bourse bulletin and send it to about a hundred of the best regional newspapers; this bulletin would either be given away or else would cost a derisory sum, and soon they would have in their hands a powerful weapon, a force with which all the rival banking houses would have to reckon. Knowing Saccard, he went on murmuring these ideas in his ear until he adopted them, made them his own, and enlarged them to such an extent that he was really re-creating them. The minutes slipped by, and the two men had dealt with the allocation of funds for publicity for the next three months, the subsidies to be paid to the main newspapers, the need to buy the silence of the terrible columnist of a hostile establishment, and what to do about the auctioning of page four of a very old and highly respected paper. And what emerged above all from their prodigality and all the money they were noisily throwing to the four winds in this way was their contempt for the public, the scorn they, as intelligent businessmen, felt for the dire ignorance of the masses, so ready to believe every tall tale, so ignorant of the complex operations of the stock exchange that even the most shameless of sales talks could excite passers-by and cause millions to rain down.

As Jordan was still trying to find another fifty lines to complete his two columns, he was interrupted by Dejoie calling him.

'Ah,' he said, 'Monsieur Jantrou is alone now?'

'No, Monsieur Jordan, not yet... but your wife is here, asking for you.'

Filled with anxiety, Jordan rushed out. For some months now, ever since the Méchain woman had discovered he was writing under his own name in *L'Espérance*, he was being pursued by Busch for the six fifty-franc promissory notes he had formerly signed over to a tailor. He would still have paid the sum of three hundred francs represented by the notes, but what exasperated him was the enormous amount of charges, the total of seven hundred and thirty francs and fifteen centimes, to which the debt had now risen. However, he had made an arrangement by which he would pay a hundred francs a month; and as he was now unable to do this, his young household having more immediate needs, the charges rose further every month and the intolerable harassment began again. At the moment he was going through another severe crisis.

'What is it?' he asked his wife when he saw her in the antechamber.

But she didn't have time to reply before the door of the editor's office was thrown open and Saccard appeared, shouting:

'Ah! At last, Dejoie—Monsieur Huret?'

The office-boy began to stammer in bewilderment.

'My word, Monsieur, he isn't here—I can't make him come any faster!'

The door was shut with an oath, and Jordan, who had taken his wife into one of the adjoining offices, was able to question her properly.

'What is it then, darling?'

Marcelle, usually so cheerful and valiant, a plump little person with her dark hair, her bright face, laughing eyes, and pleasant mouth, always looking happy even in difficult times, now seemed thoroughly upset.

'Oh, Paul, if you only knew, a man came, oh, a horrible ugly man who smelled awful and had been drinking, I think... Well, he told me it was all over and our furniture would be sold tomorrow... and he had a poster he insisted on sticking on the door downstairs...'

'But that's impossible!' cried Jordan. 'I've received nothing, there are other formalities.'

'Oh yes, but you know less about it even than I do. When papers arrive you don't even read them... So, to stop him putting up the poster I gave him two francs and ran to let you know straight away.'

They were in despair. Their poor little household in the Avenue de Clichy, their few little bits of furniture, in mahogany and blue rep, paid for with such difficulty month by month and of which they were so proud, even though they laughed about them sometimes, finding them to be in dreadful bourgeois taste! They loved it all because it had been a part of their happiness ever since their wedding-night in these two tiny rooms, so full of sunshine, looking out to the space outside stretching away to Mont Valérien;* and he had knocked in so many nails and she had so cleverly arranged Turkey-red cotton* about the rooms to give them an artistic look! How was it possible that all of that would be sold, that they would be driven out of their happy nook, where even their poverty was delightful?

'Listen,' he said, 'I was counting on asking for an advance, I shall do what I can, but I don't have much hope.'

Then, hesitantly, she told him her idea.

'This is what I had thought of... oh! I wouldn't do it without your agreement, but yes, I would like to appeal to my parents.'

He vehemently refused.

'No, no, never! You know I don't want to be obliged to them for anything.'

Certainly the Maugendres continued to behave with every propriety. But Jordan could not forget the coldness they had shown when, after his father's suicide and the crumbling of his fortune, they had consented to their daughter's long-planned marriage only because she had insisted, and had taken all sorts of wounding precautions, including their decision not to give them a sou, convinced that a fellow who wrote for the newspapers would devour everything. Their daughter would later inherit. And the Jordans, she just as much as he, had even taken a certain pride in enduring hunger without asking anything of the parents, apart from the meal they had with them once a week on Sunday evenings.

'Honestly,' Marcelle went on, 'it's ridiculous, these scruples of ours. After all, I'm the only child they have and everything will come to me one day... My father goes around telling anyone who'll listen that he's earned an income of fifteen thousand francs from his tarpaulin business at La Villette, and as well as that there's the little house they've retired to, with its lovely garden... It's stupid to give ourselves so much trouble when they have more than enough of everything. They've never been really nasty. I tell you, I'm going to go and see them.'

She was smiling cheerfully, looking quite determined and very practical in her desire to bring happiness to her husband who worked so hard, without getting anything yet from critics or public save a lot of indifference and a few slaps in the face. Ah, money! She would like to have had loads of it to bring to him by the bucketful, and it would really be stupid to be so over-delicate about it when she loved him and owed everything to him. This was her fairy-tale, her own Cinderella story: the treasures of her royal family which, with her own little hands, she would lay at the feet of her ruined prince to help him in his march towards glory and the conquest of the world.

'Look,' she said gaily, with a kiss, 'I really must be allowed to be of some use to you, you can't keep all the trouble for yourself.'

He gave way, and it was agreed that she would straight away go back up to the Rue Legendre in the Batignolles, where her parents lived, and return with the money so that he could still try to pay that very evening. And just as he was accompanying her as far as the landing, as anxious as if he were seeing her off on a very dangerous mission, they had to move aside for Huret who had arrived at last. When Jordan returned to finish his column in the contributors' room he heard a violent noise of voices coming from Jantrou's office.

Saccard, powerful now and once again the master, expected to be obeyed, knowing he had a grip on all of them through their hope of gain and terror of loss in the colossal game of fortune he was playing with them.

'Ah, so there you are!' he cried on seeing Huret. 'Was it to present the great man with a framed copy of your article that you stayed so late in the Chamber?... I've had enough, you know, of these puffs of incense you're blowing in his face, and I've been waiting for you to tell you that that's all over, in future you'll have to give us something else.'

Stunned, Huret looked at Jantrou. But the latter, determined not to cause any trouble for himself by coming to his aid, was now running his fingers through his beautiful beard, his eyes far away.

'What do you mean, something else?' Huret finally asked. 'I've been giving you what you asked for! When you took over *L'Espérance*, that established paper of Catholicism and royalty which was running such a brutal campaign against Rougon, it was you who asked me to write a series of laudatory articles to show your brother that you had no hostile intent against him, and also to indicate in this way the new policy of the paper.'

'The policy of the paper, yes indeed,' Saccard went on more vehemently, 'it's of compromising the policy of the paper that I'm accusing you... Do you think I want to become my brother's vassal? Certainly I've never stinted my admiration and grateful affection for the Emperor, I never forget the debt we all owe him and what I, in particular, owe him. But it's not attacking the Empire—on the contrary, it's doing one's duty as a loyal citizen—to point out the mistakes that are made... And that's what the policy of the paper is, devotion to the dynasty but total independence with regard to the ministers, and the ambitious personages who bustle about and fight for the favours of the Tuileries.'

And he launched into a review of the political situation to prove that the Emperor was being ill-advised. He accused Rougon of having lost his authoritative energy, his former faith in absolute power, even of flirting with liberal ideas, with the sole aim of keeping his portfolio. For himself, beating his fist against his chest, he declared himself unchangeable, a Bonapartist from the very start,* believing in the *coup d'état* and convinced that the salvation of France lay now, as always, in the genius and strength of one man. Yes, rather than helping along his brother's career, rather than letting the Emperor commit suicide by making new concessions, he would make common cause with the Catholics to halt the rapid fall he saw coming. And Rougon should take care, for *L'Espérance* could take up again its campaign in favour of Rome.

Huret and Jantrou listened, amazed at his anger, never having suspected him of such ardent political beliefs. Huret decided to try to defend the government's most recent acts.

'But look, my dear fellow, if the Empire is moving towards liberty it's because all of France is pushing firmly in that direction... the Emperor is being carried along, and Rougon has no option but to follow.'

But Saccard had already moved on to other grievances, without bothering to bring any logic into his attacks.

'And anyway, it's the same with our external situation, it's simply deplorable... Since the Treaty of Villafranca, after Solferino, Italy has borne us a grudge for not following through to the end of the campaign and not giving her the Veneto; so now she is allied with Prussia, in the conviction that the latter will help her to beat Austria... When war breaks out you'll see what ructions there'll be and what trouble we'll have; all the more so in that we made the great mistake of allowing Bismarck* and Kaiser Wilhelm* to seize the Duchies in the Denmark affair in contempt of a treaty signed by France: that was a slap in the face, there's no denying it, and all we can do is turn the other cheek... Ah! War is certain, you remember the big drop in French and Italian securities last month, when it was thought we might possibly intervene in the affairs of Germany. Within a fortnight, perhaps, Europe will be ablaze.'

Huret, more and more surprised, grew quite passionate, which was rare for him.

'You're talking just like the Opposition newspapers, but you surely don't want *L'Espérance* to fall in behind *Le Siècle** and the rest... All you need do now is insinuate, as those papers do, that if the Emperor allowed himself to be humiliated in the matter of the Duchies, and if he allows Prussia with impunity to grow ever larger it's just because he had immobilized an entire army corps for many months in Mexico. Look here now, let's be fair, Mexico is over and our troops are coming back... And really, I don't understand you my dear fellow, if you want to keep Rome for the Pope why do you seem to find fault with the hasty peace of Villafranca? Giving the Veneto to Italy means having the Italians in Rome* within two years, you know it as well as I do, and Rougon knows it too, even if he swears to the contrary from the platform...'

'Ah, you see how wily he is!' cried Saccard triumphantly. 'The Pope will never be touched, do you hear, without the whole of Catholic France rising up in his defence... We would take our money to him—yes, all the money of the Universal! I have my plans, this is very much our concern, and really, exasperating me like this you'd make me say things I'm not yet ready to say!'

Jantrou, very interested in all this, had quickly pricked up his ears, beginning to understand and trying to take full advantage of a word caught on the wing.

'In the end,' Huret resumed, 'I want to know where I stand, personally, with regard to my articles, and we need to come to an agreement... Do you want an intervention or not? If we are in favour of the principle of nationhood, what right would we have to go meddling in the affairs of Italy and Germany?... Do you want us to run a campaign against Bismarck? Yes! In the name of the threat to our frontiers...'

But Saccard, beside himself and on his feet now, burst out:

'What I want is for Rougon to stop treating me like a fool!... What? After all I've done! I buy a newspaper which was his worst enemy and make of it an organ devoted to his policies, allowing you to sing his praises month after month. And never once does the beggar give us a hand, I'm still waiting for the slightest favour from him!'

Timidly, Huret remarked that over there in the East the minister's support had greatly helped the engineer Hamelin, opening doors for him and putting pressure on certain people.

'Oh, don't bother me with stuff like that! He couldn't do otherwise... But has he ever warned me when there's going to be a rise or fall in the market, he who is so well placed to know such things? Remember, I have asked you so many times to sound him out, you who see him every day, and you have yet to bring me one real bit of useful information. It wouldn't be very hard, just one little word that you'd repeat to me.'

'No doubt! But he doesn't like doing that, he says it's skulduggery and one always ends up regretting it.'

'Come now! Does he have such scruples with Gundermann? He goes on about honesty with me and gives information to Gundermann.'

'Oh, Gundermann, no doubt! They all need Gundermann, they would never be able to get a loan without him.'

Saccard at once clapped his hands in a violent gesture of triumph.

'Now we get to it. You admit it! The Empire has sold out to the Jews, the dirty Jews. All our money is condemned to fall into their grasping claws. All the Universal can do is crumble before their omnipotence.'

And he gave vent to his hereditary hatred, repeating his accusations against that race of traffickers and usurers, marching for centuries through whole peoples, sucking their blood like the parasites of scabies and ringworm, going on even when spat upon and beaten, on to their certain conquest of the world which they will one day possess through the invincible power of gold. And he was especially furious against Gundermann, yielding to his long resentment and his unrealizable and mad desire to bring him down, and this in spite of a foreboding that Gundermann was the stumbling-block over which he would crash if it ever came to a struggle with him. Ah, that Gundermann! Inwardly a Prussian, although born in France! For of course he was on the side of the Prussians, he would gladly have supported them with his money, perhaps he even already did so in secret. Had he not dared to say, one evening in a salon, that if ever a war broke out between Prussia and France, France would be defeated!'

'I've had enough, do you understand, Huret! And get this firmly into your head, that if my brother does nothing for me I intend to do nothing for him either... When you bring me a helpful word from him—by which I mean a bit of information we can make use of—I shall let you resume your dithyrambs in his favour. Is that clear?'

It was all too clear. Jantrou, on finding once more under the political theorist the Saccard he knew, had again started to comb his beard with his fingers. But Huret, upset in his prudent Normandy-peasant scheming, looked very troubled, for he had banked his fortune on the two brothers and was anxious not to quarrel with either of them.

'You're right,' he murmured, 'let's play it down a bit, especially as we need to see how things turn out. And I promise to do all I can to win the great man's confidence. The first bit of news he gives me, I'll leap into a cab and bring it to you.'

Saccard, having played his part, was already joking.

'It's for all of you that I'm working, my good friends... For myself, I've always been ruined and I've always got through a million a year.'

And returning to the matter of publicity:

'Ah, by the way, Jantrou, you could really brighten up your Bourse bulletin a bit... Yes, you know, some jokes and puns. The public likes that sort of thing, nothing like wit to help people to swallow things... Isn't that so? A few puns!'

It was the turn of the editor to be put out. He prided himself on literary distinction. But he had to promise. And when he invented a story about some very respectable ladies who had offered to have advertisements tattooed on the most delicate parts of their person, the three men, laughing very loudly, became once more the best of friends.

Meanwhile, Jordan had at last finished his column and was very impatient to see his wife return. Some contributors arrived, and he chatted to them then returned to the antechamber. There he was slightly shocked to find Dejoie with his ear planted against the director's door, listening while his daughter Nathalie kept watch.

'Don't go in,' stammered the office-boy, 'Monsieur Saccard is still there: I thought I heard someone calling me...'

The truth was that, bitten by a fierce desire for gain since he had bought eight fully paid-up shares in the Universal with the four thousand francs of savings left by his wife, he now lived only for the joy of seeing those shares rising; and in total subservience to Saccard, gathering up his lightest remark like the words of an oracle, he couldn't resist, when he knew he was there, his need to know what Saccard really thought, what the god said in the secrecy of the sanctuary. But it was not selfishness, he was thinking only of his daughter, and he was elated by the calculation that, at the rate of seven hundred and fifty francs, his eight shares had already made him a profit of twelve hundred francs which, added to the capital, made five thousand two hundred francs. With a rise of only a hundred francs he would have the six thousand francs he dreamed of, the dowry required by the cardboard-manufacturer to allow his son to marry Nathalie. At this thought his heart melted, and he looked, with tears in his eyes, at this child he had brought up, whose real mother he had been in the happy little household they had made together since her return from the wet-nurse.

But in his embarrassment he went on talking, saying anything at all to try and cover up his indiscretion.

'Nathalie dropped in to say hello to me and just bumped into your wife, Monsieur Jordan.'

'Yes,' the girl went on, 'she was just turning into the Rue Feydeau. My goodness, she was really running!'

Her father allowed Nathalie to go out as she pleased, having confidence in her, he said. And he was right to count on her good behaviour, for she was really too cold and too determined to ensure her own happiness to compromise the long-planned marriage by any foolishness. With her slight figure and large eyes in a pale and pretty face, she loved only herself, with a selfish and smiling obstinacy.

Jordan, surprised and not understanding, cried out:

'What was that? In the Rue Feydeau?'

And he didn't have time for any other questions, for Marcelle arrived, breathless. He at once took her into the nearby office but found the law-court reporter there, so he simply sat with her on a bench at the end of the corridor.

'Well?'

'Well my dear, it's done, but it wasn't easy.'

He saw she had a heavy heart despite her satisfaction: and she told him everything, talking quickly and quietly; she had promised herself she would hold some things back from him, but in vain, for she could not keep secrets.

For some time the Maugendres had been changing their behaviour towards their daughter. She had been finding them less loving, more preoccupied, slowly taken over by their new passion—speculation. It was the usual story: the father, a stout, bald, and rather placid man with white whiskers, and the mother, lean and energetic, having earned her share in their fortune, both now living altogether too comfortably on their income of fifteen thousand francs and bored with doing nothing. He had had no other distraction than getting his money. In those days he used to thunder against every kind of gambling, and would shrug his shoulders in anger and pity at the poor fools who got themselves robbed in a heap of stupid and dirty swindles. But a little later, having been repaid a substantial sum, he'd had the idea of using it for loans to speculators;* that wasn't gambling, it was merely investment; but from that day on he had acquired the habit of carefully reading the share-prices on the Bourse after breakfast. And the evil had started there; the fever had gradually taken hold, as he watched the giddy dance of the prices and lived in that poisoned air of speculation, his imagination haunted by the idea of millions to be made in one hour, when he had spent thirty years just to earn a few hundred thousand francs. He couldn't help talking about this with his wife at every mealtime, telling her what gains he might have made if only he hadn't sworn never to gamble! And he would explain the whole operation, manipulating his funds with the cunning tactics of an armchair general, always triumphing over his imaginary opponents in the end, for he prided himself on having become a real expert in the matter of premiums and speculative loans. His wife became anxious and said she'd rather go and drown herself right away than see him risking a sou; but he reassured her, what did she take him for? He would never do that! However, an opportunity had arisen; for some time they had both been madly longing to have a little greenhouse built in their garden, for five or six thousand francs, and one evening, his hands trembling with a delightful emotion, he had placed on his wife's sewing-table the six notes needed, saying he had just won them on the Bourse: it had been a sure thing, an extravagance he promised never to repeat, and he had risked it simply because of the greenhouse. She, torn between anger and astonished delight, had not dared to reprove him. The following month he launched into some transactions in options, explaining that he had nothing to fear so long as he was limiting his loss. And anyway, what the devil! There were after all some good things to be found, it would be really stupid of him just to let others profit from them. And, inevitably, he had begun to gamble seriously, in a small way at first then gradually getting bolder, while his wife, still agitated by her anxieties as a good housewife but with her eyes lighting up at the slightest gain, went on warning him that he would die in the poor-house.

But it was Captain Chave, Madame Maugendre's brother, who particularly scolded his brother-in-law. Unable to manage on the eighteen hundred francs of his pension, he did indeed play the market but was extremely clever about it. He went to the Bourse like a clerk going to his office, working solely in cash and delighted when he took home his twenty-franc coin in the evening: his were daily, very safe transactions, so modest that they were beyond the reach of disaster. His sister had offered him a room in her house, too big now that Marcelle was married, but he had refused, wanting to be free to indulge his vices, and he occupied one room at the bottom of a garden in the Rue Nollet, where the swish of skirts was often heard. His winnings were spent on sweets and cakes for his lady-friends. He had always warned Maugendre, telling him not to speculate but to enjoy life instead; and when the latter cried: 'What about you?', he would gesture vigorously and say Oh! for him it was different; he didn't have an income of fifteen thousand francs—otherwise...! And if he was speculating, the fault lay with the filthy government that grudged old soldiers the enjoyment of their old age. His main argument against speculation was that the gambler is mathematically bound to lose: if he wins he has to deduct brokerage and stamp tax; if he loses he still has to pay these same taxes on top of his loss; so even if he wins as often as he loses he is still out of pocket for brokerage and stamp tax. At the Paris Bourse these taxes annually produce the enormous sum of eighty million francs. And he insisted on this figure, eighty million francs, collected by the state, the brokers, and the bucket-shops.

On the bench at the end of the corridor Marcelle was relating a part of this story to her husband.

'My dear, I have to say it was a bad time to arrive. Mama was quarrelling with Papa over a loss he'd made at the Bourse... Yes, it seems he's there all the time now. It seems so strange to me, he who only believed in work... Well, they were arguing, and there was a news-paper, *La Cote financière*, that Mama was shaking under his nose, shouting at him that he had no idea and that she herself had foreseen the fall. Then he went to get another paper, *L'Espérance* in fact, and tried to show her the article in which he had got his information... Just imagine, the whole house is full of newspapers, they are buried in them from morning till night, and I think—God forgive me!—that Mama is also beginning to gamble, in spite of looking angry.'

Jordan could not help laughing, so comically had she mimed the scene in her distress.

'Anyway, I told them of our hardship and asked them to lend us two hundred francs to stop the proceedings against us. And you should have heard how they protested... two hundred francs, when they had lost two thousand on the Bourse! Was I joking? Did I want to ruin them?... I've never seen them in such a state. They who used to be so good to me, who would have spent anything on earth to give me presents. They must really be going mad, for there's no sense in ruining their lives like that when they're so happy in their lovely house, with no worries and nothing to do other than enjoy at their leisure the fortune they worked so hard for.'

'I hope you didn't insist,' said Jordan.

'I certainly did insist, and then they started on you... as you see, I'm telling you everything; I had promised to keep that to myself but it just slipped out... They repeated that they had foreseen it, that writing for the newspapers was not a proper job and we'd end up in the poor-house... Then, since I was beginning to get angry too, I was just going to leave when the Captain arrived. You know he has always adored me, Uncle Chave. Faced with him they became reasonable, especially as he was exulting, asking Papa if he intended to go on get-ting himself robbed... Mama took me aside and slipped fifty francs into my hand, telling me we could gain a few days' reprieve with that, time to sort things out.'

'Fifty francs! A pittance! And did you accept?'

Marcelle tenderly took his hands, calming him down with her quiet good sense.

'Come now, don't be angry... Yes I accepted. And I so clearly understood that you would never dare take it to the bailiff that I went there myself straight away, you know, to the Rue Cadet. But just imagine! He refused to accept it, saying he had strict orders from

Monsieur Busch, and that only Monsieur Busch could stop the proceedings... Oh, that Busch! I don't hate anyone, but how he exasperates and disgusts me, that man! No matter, I ran to his house in the Rue Feydeau and he had to content himself with the fifty francs, so there we are! We can look forward to a fortnight of not being harassed.'

Jordan's face had tensed in the grip of powerful emotions, while the tears he was holding back were dampening his eyelids.

'You did all that, my little wife, you did all that?'

'Yes, I didn't want anyone pestering you any more! I don't care about having to listen to a lot of rubbish, so long as you're allowed to work in peace!'

And she was laughing now, telling him of her arrival in Busch's office, with all his filthy files, and the brutal way he had received her, threatening not to leave them so much as a rag if they didn't pay the whole debt there and then. The amusing thing was that she had given herself the treat of infuriating him by contesting his legal right to recover the debt, those notes for three hundred francs, now increased, with all the extras, to seven hundred and thirty francs fifteen centimes, when they had cost him maybe a hundred sous in some bundle of old rags. Busch was choking with rage: first of all, he had paid a lot for those notes; then there was the time he'd lost and the effort of two years' running about just to discover the signatory, and the intelligence he'd had to use in that manhunt—didn't he have to be reimbursed for all that? So much the worse for those who got themselves caught! In the end he had, after all, taken the fifty francs, since his prudent doctrine was always to compromise.

'Ah, my little wife, how brave you are, and how I love you!' said Jordan, allowing himself to kiss Marcelle even though the editorial secretary was just passing.

Then, lowering his voice:

'How much is there left at home?'

'Seven francs.'

'Good,' he replied, well pleased, 'we can manage for two days on that, and I'm not going to ask for an advance, which would anyway be refused. That's really too painful... Tomorrow I'll go and see if I can place an article with *Le Figaro*.* Ah, if only I had finished my novel and it was selling a bit...'

Marcelle now kissed him back.

'Yes, go on, we'll manage very well!... You'll come back with me, won't you? That will be nice, and for tomorrow we'll buy a smoked herring at the corner of the Rue de Clichy, where I saw some splendid ones. This evening we have bacon and potatoes.'

After asking a colleague to check his proofs, Jordan left with his wife. Saccard and Huret were also leaving. In the street a coupé was just stopping outside the newspaper office, and they saw Baroness Sandorff step out of it; she greeted them with a smile then hurried upstairs. She sometimes came in to see Jantrou. Saccard, always excited by her, with her big, bruised-looking eyes, almost decided to go back up.

Upstairs, in the editor's office, the Baroness didn't even want to sit down. She was just dropping in to say hello, simply to ask him if he knew anything useful. In spite of his suddenly changed fortunes she still treated him as she did when he used to come every morning as a jobber, bending over double to beg an order from her father, Monsieur de Ladricourt. Her father had been an appallingly brutal man, and she could not forget the kick with which he had thrown Jantrou out, in his anger at a large loss. But now that she saw Jantrou at the very source of news she had become familiar once more, trying to pump him.

'Ah well, nothing new?'

'No indeed, I don't know anything.'

But she went on looking at him, smiling, convinced that he was just unwilling to say anything. Then, to force him into making confidences, she talked about the stupid war that was going to set Austria, Italy, and Prussia in conflict.* The stock-markets were panicking, Italian holdings had fallen terribly, as had all the other stocks for that matter. And she was very worried, for she didn't know to what extent she ought to follow this movement, as she already had substantial sums involved for the next settlement day.

'Doesn't your husband keep you informed?' asked Jantrou with a laugh. 'After all, he's very well placed at the embassy.'

'Oh! My husband,' she murmured with a dismissive gesture, 'I don't get anything out of my husband any more.'

Jantrou found this even funnier, and went so far as to refer to Delcambre, the Public Prosecutor, the lover who, it was said, paid her losses when she eventually decided to pay them.

'And your friends at Court and the Palais de Justice?'

She pretended not to understand and carried on, in pleading tones, not taking her eyes off him:

'Come on, be nice... You know something.'

Once, some time ago, in his craze for everything in skirts that came his way, whether grubby or elegant, he had thought of treating himself to her—as he brutally put it—this gambling woman who was so familiar with him. But at the first word, the first gesture, she had drawn herself up, so full of loathing and contempt that he had sworn never to try again. This man, so often kicked by her father! Ah, never! She had not fallen that low.

'Be nice? Why should I be? You're not at all nice to me.'

At once she grew serious again and her eyes hardened. She was turning her back on him to leave when, out of spite and wanting to hurt her, he said:

'You just met Saccard at the door, didn't you? Why haven't you asked him, since he'll give you whatever you want?'

She immediately came back.

'What do you mean?'

'Heavens, whatever you choose it to mean... Come on, don't play the woman of mystery, I've seen you at his house and I know him!'

A feeling of revolt rose in her, all the pride of her race, still alive, surged up from the murky depths, from the mire in which her passion was steadily drowning her, day by day. But she did not lose her temper, she simply said, in a harsh and clear voice:

'Ah! As for that, my dear sir, what do you take me for? You are mad... No, I am not the mistress of your Saccard, because I chose not to be.'

He then bowed to her, with his elaborate literary man's courtesy.

'Well, Madame, you made a big mistake... Believe me, if the chance comes round again don't miss the opportunity; you, who are always chasing after useful tips, you'd find them easily enough under that gentleman's pillow. Oh my word! Yes, the nest will soon be there, you will only have to poke your pretty fingers into it.'

She decided just to laugh, as if resigned to making allowances for his cynicism. But when she shook hands with him he found her hand was quite cold. Had she really not gone beyond her unpleasant duties with the icy and bony Delcambre, this woman with such red lips, who was said to be insatiable?

The month of June went by; on the 15th Italy had declared war on

Austria.* Meanwhile, with a sudden lightning march, Prussia had invaded Hanover in under a fortnight, conquered the two Hesses, Baden, and Saxony, taking by surprise unarmed populations that were not at war, and France had made no move; well-informed people were quietly whispering at the Bourse that France had a secret agreement with Prussia, ever since Bismarck had met the Emperor at Biarritz; there was confused talk of the rewards France would gain for her neutrality. But the markets went on falling unremittingly, disastrously. When the news about Sadowa arrived like a thunderbolt on 4 July* there was a collapse of stocks of all kinds. It was believed that the war would go on relentlessly, for though Austria was beaten by Prussia, Austria had defeated Italy at Custoza;* and it was already being said that she was gathering the remnants of her army together and abandoning Bohemia. Orders to sell showered the trading-floor, but there was no sign of buyers.

On 4 July Saccard, who had gone to the newspaper offices very late, towards six o'clock, did not find Jantrou, whose passions for some time had been leading him astray: there were unexpected disappearances, binges from which he returned shattered and bleary-eyed, though it was impossible to say which, whether women or alcohol, was destroying him the more. At that time of day the newspaper office was emptying, and hardly anyone was left except Dejoie, who was dining on the corner of his table in the anteroom. After writing a couple of letters, Saccard was about to leave when Huret stormed in, red in the face and not even taking the time to close the doors behind him.

'My dear fellow, my dear fellow...' he spluttered.

He seemed to be choking, and put his two hands on his chest.

'I have just left Rougon,' he said... 'I've been running, because I didn't have a cab, but eventually I found one. Rougon has received a telegram from you know where. I've seen it... Such news! Such news!'

With a violent gesture, Saccard stopped him and rushed to close the door, having caught sight of Dejoie, who was already prowling about with his ears pricked up.

'So what is it then?'

'Well, the Emperor of Austria cedes the Veneto to the Emperor of France and accepts his mediation, so the Emperor will now address himself to the kings of Prussia and Italy to bring about an armistice.'

There was a silence.

'So it's peace then?'

'Evidently.'

Saccard, astonished and not yet able to think, let out an oath.

'Hellfire! And the whole of the Bourse still falling!'

Then, in a mechanical tone, he added:

'And this news, not a soul knows of it?'

'No, the telegram is confidential, there won't even be an announce-ment in the *Moniteur** tomorrow morning. Paris will certainly know nothing about it for at least the next twenty-four hours.'

Then came the lightning-stroke of sudden illumination. Saccard ran once more to the door and opened it to see if anyone was listening. He was beside himself, and came back and stood in front of Huret, clutching him by the lapels of his coat.

'Be quiet! Not so loud!... We are masters of this situation if Gundermann and his gang are not forewarned... Not a word, do you hear? Not to a living soul, not your friends, nor your wife!... And what a piece of luck that Jantrou isn't here! We shall be the only ones who know, we shall have time to act... Oh, I don't mean to work solely for myself! You are in on it, and our colleagues at the Universal too. But a secret cannot be kept when there are too many people involved. All is lost if there is the slightest indiscretion before the opening of the Bourse tomorrow.'

Huret, very disturbed, overwhelmed by the grandeur of the coup they were going to attempt, promised to remain absolutely silent. Then they divided up the work between them, deciding that they must begin their campaign at once. Saccard already had his hat on when a question rose to his lips:

'So it was Rougon who asked you to bring me this news?'

'Of course.'

Huret had hesitated, for he was lying: the telegram was simply lying on the minister's table and, being left alone with it for a moment, he had dared to read it. But since it was in his interest to keep the two brothers in agreement this lie seemed to him very adroit, especially since he knew they were not at all anxious to see each other and speak of such matters.

'Well, there's no denying it, he's done me a good turn this time... Let's get going!'

In the antechamber there was still only Dejoie, who had tried hard to listen but without being able to catch anything distinctly. Nevertheless he seemed to them very agitated, having scented some enormous booty in the air, so excited by this smell of money that he went to the window on the landing to watch them crossing the courtyard.

The difficulty was to act quickly but with the utmost caution. So they parted in the street: Huret was to deal with the evening kerb market, while Saccard, despite the lateness of the hour, went hunting for jobbers and brokers and other dealers, to give them orders to buy. But he wanted to split these orders up and spread them around as much as possible, for fear of arousing suspicion; and above all, he wanted to make it seem as though he was meeting the dealers by chance, rather than tracking them down at home, which would have looked odd. Luck happily came to his aid, for on the Boulevard he saw the broker Jacoby, with whom he stopped to chat and to whom he gave a very substantial order without causing too much astonishment. A few paces further on he bumped into a tall, blonde girl whom he knew to be the mistress of another dealer, Delarocque, Jacoby's brother-in-law; and since she said she was expecting him that night, he asked her to pass on to him a card with a few words scribbled in pencil. Then, knowing that Mazaud was going to a banquet with former colleagues that evening, he betook himself to the restaurant and changed the orders he had given him earlier that day. But his best stroke of luck was to be accosted, just as he was going home, by Massias, who had just come out of the Théâtre des Variétés. They walked together up to the Rue Saint-Lazare; this gave Saccard time enough to present himself as an eccentric who believed a rise was coming—oh! not immediately of course; he ended up giving Massias numerous orders for Nathansohn and various other dealers, telling him he was acting for a group of friends, which was true enough. By the time Saccard went to bed he had taken up a bullish position for orders worth more than five million francs.

At seven o'clock next morning Huret was at Saccard's house, telling him what he had managed to do at the kerb market on the pavement in front of the Passage de l'Opéra, where he had bought as much as possible but with restraint, so as to avoid causing a rise in the share-prices. His orders amounted to a million, and both men, thinking their coup to be still far too modest, resolved to continue their campaign. They still had the morning. But first they threw themselves upon the newspapers, trembling with fear that they might already have the news, a note or a mere line that would send their plans crashing. No! The Press knew nothing, the papers were full of the war, loaded with despatches and detailed accounts of the Battle of Sadowa. If no rumour emerged before two o'clock in the afternoon, if they had an hour after the Bourse opened or even just half-an-hour, they were made; they would make a clean sweep of the Jewish tribe, as Saccard put it. And they went their separate ways, each one rushing to throw further millions into the battle.

Saccard spent that morning tramping the streets and sniffing the air, with such a need to walk that he had sent away his cab after his very first call. He went to Kolb's place, where the jingling of the gold was delightful to his ears, like a promise of victory, and he had sufficient strength of will not to say anything to the banker, who as yet knew nothing. Then he dropped in on Mazaud, not to give him any new orders but just pretending to be worried about the order he had given the previous evening. There, too, ignorance reigned. Little Flory alone caused him some anxiety by the persistent way he kept hovering around, though the sole reason for this was the young clerk's profound admiration for the financial intelligence of the manager of the Universal Bank. And as Mademoiselle Chuchu was beginning to be very expensive and he was risking a few little speculations, Flory longed to know what the great man was doing so as to follow his lead.

At last, after a hasty lunch at Champeaux's, where he had the pleasure of hearing the pessimistic moanings of Moser and even Pillerault, predicting a further tumbling in the market, Saccard found himself at half-past twelve in the Place de la Bourse. He wanted, as he put it, to see everyone come in. The heat was overpowering, a fierce sun beat directly down, bleaching the steps, and the warmth bouncing off them filled the peristyle with the heavy, burning heat of an oven. The empty chairs seemed to be cracking in the fiery heat, while the speculators remained standing and sought out the slender bars of shade cast by the columns. Under a tree in the garden he noticed Busch and La Méchain, who began to chatter excitedly when they saw him; it even seemed for a moment as if they were going to approach him, but then they thought better of it; did they know something, then? These base ragpickers, always hunting through the refuse of the Bourse? He shuddered at the thought. But then a voice called his name and he recognized Maugendre and Captain Chave, sitting on a bench quarrelling, for the former was now always jeering at the wretched pettiness of the Captain's ventures, gaining a mere louis for his cash, the sort of thing he might just as well have done in some obscure provincial café after a few desperate rounds of piquet: honestly, couldn't he, that day, risk something more substantial on a safe bet? Wasn't a further fall certain, as clear as daylight? And he called Saccard to witness: wasn't it true that there'd be a further fall? As for himself, he had bet very heavily on a fall, so convinced indeed that he had staked his entire fortune. Faced by this direct question Saccard replied with smiles and vague shakings of his head, but felt remorseful at not being able to warn this poor man, whom he had known when he was so industrious and clear-headed, still selling his tarpaulins; but he had sworn himself to absolute silence and had the ruthlessness of a gambler determined not to risk disturbing his luck. Just then he was distracted by seeing the coupé of Baroness Sandorff passing by; he followed it with his eye and saw it stop, this time in the Rue de la Banque. Suddenly he thought of Baron Sandorff, Counsellor at the Austrian Embassy; the Baroness must surely know, and she was probably going to wreck everything with some misguided womanly act. He at once crossed the road and hovered round the coupé, now still and silent as if dead, with the coachman sitting stiffly on his box. But one of the windows was lowered, and he bowed gallantly and moved forward.

'Ah well, Monsieur Saccard, so we're still going down?'

He thought this might be a trap.

'Why yes, Madame,' he replied.

Then, as she was looking at him anxiously, with a certain wavering of the eyes that he had often seen in gamblers, he realized that she knew nothing. He had a rush of hot blood to his head, flooding him with delight.

'So, Monsieur Saccard, you have nothing to tell me?'

'Indeed, Madame, doubtless nothing you don't already know.'

And he left her, thinking: 'You haven't been very nice to me, and it will greatly amuse me to see you get your come-uppance. Perhaps another time it will make you more agreeable.' Never had she seemed to him more desirable; he was certain he would have her when the time was ripe.

As he returned to the Place de la Bourse the sight of Gundermann in the distance, coming out of the Rue Vivienne, set his heart a-quiver once more. Though foreshortened by the distance it was certainly he, with his slow walk and his head so straight and pale, looking at no one, as if he were alone in his royalty in the midst of the crowd. And Saccard followed him in terror, trying to interpret his every movement. Seeing him approaching Nathansohn, he thought all was lost. But the dealer moved off looking crestfallen, and hope returned. He definitely felt the banker had his usual everyday look. Then suddenly his heart leapt for joy: Gundermann had just entered the sweetshop to make his usual purchase of sweets for his little granddaughters; and that was a certain sign, for he never went there on a day of crisis.

One o'clock struck and the bell announced the opening of the Bourse. It was a memorable Bourse, one of those great days of disaster, one of those disasters caused by a rise in the market, disasters so rare that they are remembered as legendary. In the overpowering heat prices at first continued to fall. Then some sudden, isolated purchases, like the shots of skirmishers before the battle begins, aroused astonishment. But trading was still sluggish amid general distrust. Purchases increased and bids were heard on all sides, at the kerb market under the colonnade and on the balustrade; now the voices of Nathansohn under the colonnade and Mazaud, Jacoby, and Delarocque on the trading-floor made themselves heard, shouting that they would take any stock, whatever the price; and then there was a sort of tremor, an ever-increasing groundswell, but with no one daring to take a risk in the confusion of this inexplicable turnaround. Prices had slightly risen, and Saccard just had time to give new orders to Massias for Nathansohn. He also asked little Flory, who was rushing past, to hand Mazaud a card on which he instructed him to buy and go on buying; so Flory, filled with confidence after reading the card, at once followed the lead of the great man and bought on his own account. It was then, at a quarter to two, that the thunderbolt burst upon the busy Bourse: Austria was surrendering the Veneto to the Emperor—the war was over. Where did the news come from? Nobody knew, it seemed to come from every mouth, seemed to surge from the very paving-stones. Someone had brought the news and everyone repeated it, in a clamour that grew ever louder, like the surge of the equinoctial tide. Prices began to rise in furious leaps and bounds amid a frightful uproar. Before the bell rang for the closing of the Bourse they had gone up forty or fifty francs. It was an indescribable frenzy, one of those battles into which everyone rushes in confusion, soldiers and officers alike, deafened and blinded, all trying to save their skin, with no clear idea of the situation. Sweat streamed from their brows and the implacable sun beat down on the steps, pitching the Bourse into the blazing heat of a conflagration.

On settlement day, when it became possible to assess the extent of the disaster, it looked immense. The battlefield lay scattered with wreckage and wounded. Moser, the bear trader, was one of the most damaged. Pillerault had been severely punished for his weakness just this one time when he had despaired of a rise. Maugendre lost fifty thousand francs, his first serious loss. Baroness Sandorff had to deal with such heavy debts that Delcambre was said to be refusing to pay for her, and she was quite white with rage and hate at the very mention of her husband, the Counsellor at the Austrian Embassy, who had had the telegram in his hands even before Rougon and had told her nothing. But the big bankers, the Jewish Bank especially, had suffered a terrible defeat, a real massacre. It was said that Gundermann, for his part, had lost eight million francs. And that was truly amazing, how was it that he had not been warned? He, the undisputed master of the market; he, for whom ministers were no more than clerks and who held whole states in his sovereign fiefdom. It had been one of those extraordinary combinations of circumstances that create huge strokes of fortune. It was an unforeseen, idiotic collapse, beyond all reason and logic.

Meanwhile the story spread, and Saccard was seen as a great man. In one stroke, he had raked in almost the whole amount of the money lost by the bear traders. He had personally pocketed two million. The rest was going into the coffers of the Universal, or rather was going to disappear into the hands of its directors. Saccard had great difficulty persuading Madame Caroline that Hamelin's share in this booty, so legitimately wrested from the Jews, amounted to a million francs. Huret, having taken part in the operation, had cut himself a regal share. As for the others, the Daigremonts, the Bohains, they needed no persuading to accept whatever was coming to them. There was a general vote of thanks and congratulations to the eminent manager. One heart especially burned with gratitude to Saccard, that of Flory, who had gained ten thousand francs, a fortune, enough to live with Chuchu in a little apartment on the Rue Condorcet and go out in the evening to join Gustave Sédille and Germaine Coeur in expensive restaurants. At the newspaper office Jantrou, furious at not having been forewarned, had to be given a present. Dejoie alone remained melancholy, he would feel eternal regret at having scented the mysterious and vague presence of fortune in the air, all in vain.

This first triumph of Saccard's seemed like a sort of blossoming of the Empire at its apogee. He became part of the lustre of the reign, one of its glorious reflections. The very evening when he was thriving so well in the midst of shattered fortunes, and when the Bourse was no more than a desolate field of rubble, the whole of Paris was being bedecked and illuminated as if for a great victory; festivities at the Tuileries and rejoicing in the streets all celebrated Napoleon III as master of Europe, so lofty, so great, that kings and emperors chose him as arbiter in their disputes and gave him whole provinces to share out between them. In the Chamber of Deputies there had been some protests, some prophets of doom were confusedly predicting a terrible future: Prussia made stronger by all that France had tolerated, Austria defeated, and Italy ungrateful. But laughter and shouts of anger smothered these anxious voices, and Paris, the centre of the world, set all her avenues and monuments ablaze with light on the morrow of Sadowa, not yet seeing the dark and freezing nights to come, the nights with no gas, nights lit only by the red flashing of shells. That evening Saccard, overflowing with success, paced the streets, the Place de la Concorde, the Champs-Élysées, all the pavements lit by lanterns. Carried along in the growing flood of people, his eyes dazzled by the lights which were bright as day, he was able to imagine that the lights were in his honour: for was he not also the unexpected victor, the one who rose to new heights in the midst of disasters? Just one annoyance marred his joy, the anger of Rougon who, in a terrible fury, had sent Huret packing when he realized the source of the coup at the Bourse. So it wasn't the great man then, who had shown himself a good brother by sending him the news? Would he therefore have to do without that high patronage, and even be obliged to attack the all-powerful minister? Suddenly, in front of the Palace of the Legion of Honour,* which was surmounted by a huge cross of fire glowing in the blackness of the sky, Saccard boldly decided that he would indeed do so as soon as he had sufficient strength. Then, intoxicated by the chanting of the crowd and the flapping of the flags, he returned, through a blazing Paris, to the Rue Saint-Lazare.

Two months later, in September, emboldened by his triumph over Gundermann, he decided to give new momentum to the Universal.

At the Annual General Meeting held at the end of April the balance-sheet for the year 1864 had shown a profit of nine millions, inclusive of the twenty-franc premium on each of the fifty thousand new shares issued when the capital was doubled. The cost of the initial setting-up had now been completely paid off, the shareholders had been paid their five per cent, the directors their ten per cent, a sum of five million had been put into the reserve fund in addition to the regulation ten per cent; and with the remaining million it had been possible to pay a dividend of ten francs per share. It was a handsome result for a company less than two years old. But Saccard operated in feverish leaps and bounds, applying the methods of intensive farming to the financial terrain, heating and overheating the soil at the risk of burning the harvest; and he persuaded first the board of directors then the shareholders, by means of an Extraordinary General Meeting on 15 September, to accept a second increase of capital: it was doubled yet again, raising it from fifty to a hundred million francs by creating a hundred thousand new shares, reserved exclusively for existing shareholders, share for share. But this time the shares were issued at six hundred and seventy-five francs, that is, with a premium of one hundred and seventy-five francs, which was to be paid into the reserve funds. The increasing successes, the profitable deals already made, and above all the grand ventures the Universal was about to launch were the reasons given to justify this enormous increase of capital, now doubled twice over; for it was essential to give the bank an importance and strength appropriate to the interests it represented. Moreover, the result was immediate: the shares which had remained steady at the Bourse at an average rate of seven hundred and fifty rose to nine hundred francs in three days.

Hamelin, who had not been able to return from the Orient to preside at the Extraordinary General Meeting, wrote a worried letter to his sister expressing his fears about this way of driving the Universal at the gallop, in a mad rush. He had a shrewd suspicion that false declarations had once again been made in Maître Lelorrain's office. Indeed, the new shares had not all been legally subscribed, the bank had retained for itself the shares rejected by the shareholders; and since the payments had not been made, these shares had been transferred, by juggling the books, to the account of Sabatani. In addition, the use of other cover-names, names of directors and employees, had allowed the bank itself to subscribe to its own share-issue, so that it now held nearly thirty thousand of its own shares, amounting to a sum of seventeen and a half millions. Not only was this illegal but the situation could become dangerous, for experience has shown that any bank that gambles with its own stock is lost. But Madame Caroline nevertheless responded no less cheerily to her brother, joshing him that he had now become the nervous one, and it was she, formerly so suspicious, who had to reassure him. She said she was still keeping an eye on things and saw nothing shady going on but, on the contrary, was amazed at the great things, all of them clear and logical, that she was witnessing. The truth was that she, of course, knew nothing about what was being kept from her, and in addition was blinded by her admiration for Saccard and the feelings of sympathy aroused in her by that little man's activity and intelligence.

In December the share-price rose to more than a thousand francs. Then, in the face of this triumph of the Universal, the big banks began to be concerned, Gundermann was seen on the Place de la Bourse, walking as if absent-mindedly, and rather automatically, into the sweetshop to buy sweets. He had paid up his eight million loss without a murmur, and not one of his friends or family had heard a word of anger or resentment pass his lips. When he lost like this—a rare event—he would usually say that it served him right and would teach him to be less careless; and everyone smiled, for carelessness from Gundermann was scarcely imaginable. But this time the hard lesson must have lain heavy on his heart; the idea that he, so cold, so much the master of facts and men, should have been beaten by Saccard, that reckless and passionate madman, must certainly have been unbearable. So from that time on he began to watch Saccard closely, certain of getting his revenge. At once, given the widespread infatuation with the Universal, he had taken up a position as an observer convinced that over-rapid successes and dishonest prosperity always led to the worst disasters. However, the thousand-franc rate was still reasonable, and he was waiting to start to bring it down. His theory was that one could not provoke events on the Bourse, the most one could do was foresee them and profit by them once they occurred. Logic was the sole master of events, and truth, in speculation as everywhere else, was an all-powerful force. As soon as the share-prices became too inflated they would collapse: a fall was then a mathematical certainty, and he would simply be there, ready to see his calculation fulfilled and to pocket his profit. Already he had fixed on the rate of fifteen hundred francs to begin the war. So, when the share-price reached fifteen hundred he began to sell Universals, just a little at first, but slightly more at each settlement day, following a predetermined plan. There was no need for a syndicate of bear dealers; he alone would be sufficient; sensible people would clearly perceive the truth and follow his lead. That rowdy Universal, that Universal which was so rapidly taking up so much room in the market and rising up threateningly against the big Jewish banks, he would coolly wait for it to crack all by itself, then, with a shove of his shoulder, cast it to the ground.

It was said later that it was Gundermann who secretly facilitated Saccard's purchase of an ancient building in the Rue de Londres, which he intended to demolish and replace with the mansion of his dreams, the palace which would provide sumptuous accommodation for his bank. He had managed to persuade the board of directors, and the work began in mid-October.

On the very day when the first stone was laid, with great ceremony, Saccard was at the newspaper office at about four o'clock waiting for Jantrou, who had gone to take reports of the ceremony to some friendly papers, when he received a visit from Baroness Sandorff. She had first asked for the editor and then, as if by chance, had come upon the manager of the Universal, who had gallantly offered his services for whatever information she required, leading her into his own room at the end of the corridor. And there, at the first brutal attack, she surrendered like a prostitute, on the divan, resigned in advance to the event.

But a complication arose, for Madame Caroline, out shopping in Montmartre, called in at the newspaper. She sometimes dropped in like this to answer some query of Saccard's or just to get the news. Besides she knew Dejoie, having got him his job, and always stopped for a minute to chat, happy in the gratitude he showed her. That day, not having found Dejoie in the antechamber, she entered the corridor and bumped into him just as he was getting back from listening at the door. This had now become a real malady; he trembled feverishly and pressed his ear at every keyhole, trying to surprise the secrets of the Bourse. But this time what he overheard and understood had rather embarrassed him, and he smiled vaguely.

'He is here, isn't he?' said Madame Caroline, wishing to get past. Dejoie stopped her and, not having time to invent a lie, stammered:

'Yes he's there, but you can't go in.'

'What do you mean, I can't go in?'

'No, he is with a lady.'

She had turned quite white, and Dejoie, knowing nothing of the situation, with multiple winks and nods and expressive mimicry, indicated what was happening.

'Who is this lady?' she asked curtly.

He had no reason to hide the name from his benefactress, so he leaned over to whisper in her ear:

'Baroness Sandorff... Oh! She's been hanging round him for some time.'

Madame Caroline stood quite still for a moment. In the gloom of the corridor the livid pallor of her face remained invisible. She had just felt a sharp and cruel pain in her heart, of a sort she could not remember ever having felt before; and it was stupefaction at this appalling wound that rooted her to the spot. And now what would she do, break into the room? Fall upon that woman? Hit them both with a scandal?

She was still standing there, indecisive and dazed, when Marcelle, who had come to get her husband, approached her gaily. The young woman had only recently made her acquaintance.

'Ah, it's you, dear lady... Just imagine, we're going to the theatre this evening! Oh! it's quite a business, it has to be very cheap... But Paul has discovered a little restaurant where we can eat for thirty-five sous each...'

Jordan arrived and interrupted his wife with a laugh.

'Two courses, a carafe of wine, and as much bread as you like!'

'And', Marcelle went on, 'we're not taking a cab; it's such fun to walk home when it's very late!... And since we're rich this evening, we'll get an almond cake for twenty sous to take home... Such a celebration! A fantastic treat!'

She went away full of delight, on her husband's arm. And Madame Caroline, who came back with them to the antechamber, had now recovered enough strength to smile.

'Have a lovely time,' she murmured in a tremulous voice.

Then she also left. She loved Saccard, and this caused her both astonishment and pain, as if it were a shameful wound she was unwilling to reveal.

CHAPTER VII

Two months later, on a mild, grey November day, Madame Caroline went up to the workroom straight after lunch to get to work. Her brother, now in Constantinople, and busy with his grand Oriental railways project, had asked her to look up the notes he had made on their first trip, and then to draw up a sort of report, to serve as a historical record; and for a good two weeks now, she had been trying to get totally absorbed in this task. It was so warm that day that she let the fire go out and opened the window, and before sitting down again, she gazed for a moment at the tall, bare trees in the garden of the hotel Beauvilliers, purplish against the pale sky.

She had been writing for almost half-an-hour when the need for a particular document took her off on a long search among the files piled up on the table. She got up and rummaged among some other papers, then went back with her hands full, and sat down again. And as she sorted through a few loose pages, she came upon some religious pictures, an illustrated view of the Holy Sepulchre* and a prayer framed by the instruments of the Passion,* a sovereign guarantee of salvation in those moments of distress when the soul is in peril. Then she remembered that her brother, like the pious grown-up child that he was, had bought these images in Jerusalem. Her feelings suddenly overcame her, and her cheeks became wet with tears. Ah, that brother of hers, so intelligent, so unappreciated for so long, how lucky he was to have his faith, and not want to smile at this naive, chocolate-box picture of the Holy Sepulchre, how fortunate to be able to find serene strength in his belief in the efficacy of this prayer with its sugary verses. She could see him now, too trusting, too easily taken in perhaps, but so upright, so steady, so free from rebellion or conflict. She, on the other hand, no longer a believer, had endured two months of suffering and struggle, her mind burned by reading and battered by arguments, and how passionately she had wished in her hours of weakness, that she had remained simple and ingenuous like him, able to soothe her bleeding heart by repeating three times, morning and evening, that childish prayer framed by the nails, the lance, the crown, and the sponge of the Passion!

In the days that followed the brutal accident through which she

had learned of Saccard's affair with Baroness Sandorff, she had
steeled herself, by a great effort of will, to resist the urge to keep
watch on them and find out more. She was not the wife of this man,
nor did she wish to be the passionate mistress, jealous enough to provoke a scandal; and the worst of it was that she still could not bring
herself to refuse him, in the intimacy of their everyday life. This was
because of the quiet, simply affectionate way in which she had at first
viewed their affair: a friendship that had inevitably led to her giving
herself, as often happens between a man and a woman. She was no
longer twenty, and she had acquired a great deal of tolerance after the
harsh experience of her marriage. At thirty-six, as she was so sensible, and believed herself to be quite without illusions, couldn't she
just shut her eyes to things and behave more like a mother than a
lover toward this friend, to whom she had surrendered herself late in
life, in a momentary moral lapse, this friend, who was himself well
past the age of romantic heroes? She had frequently remarked that
people often attached too much importance to these sexual relations,
sometimes mere encounters, which were then allowed to complicate
their entire lives. But then she was the first to smile at the immorality
of her remark, for didn't that mean that all sins were permitted, and
every woman could belong to every man? And yet so many women
are sensible enough to accept sharing with a rival, that the good-
natured character of current practice seems better than the jealous
demand for sole and total possession! But these were all just theoret-
ical ways of making life bearable; and although she forced herself into
abnegation, continuing to be the devoted housekeeper, the unusually
intelligent servant, willing to offer her body when she had already
given her heart and mind, it was all in vain, for her body and her
passion rose in revolt, and she suffered dreadfully from not knowing
everything, not violently breaking with Saccard, and flinging in his
face the terrible wrong he had done her. She had, however, mastered
herself sufficiently to be able to hold her tongue, remaining calm
and continuing to smile, and never in her whole existence, harsh as it
had been, had she felt the need of so much strength.

For a moment longer, with the smile, sad but full of tenderness, of
a non–believer, she gazed at the sacred images she still held in her
hands. But she was no longer seeing them, she was trying to work out
what Saccard might have been doing the day before, and what he was
doing this very day, in an endless and irresistible churning of her

mind, which instinctively returned to this inquisition, once she allowed it to be less than fully occupied. He seemed anyway to be leading his usual life, his mornings spent dealing with his managerial responsibilities, his afternoons at the Bourse, and in the evening dinner engagements, first-nights, a life of pleasure, and a few theatre girls, about whom she felt no jealousy. But she had the feeling that he had some new interest, something that occupied the hours he had previously spent in other ways—it was that woman, no doubt, and meetings with her somewhere she would not allow herself to know about. All this made her suspicious and distrustful, and she began once more, in spite of herself, to 'act the policeman', as her brother had laughingly called it, even about the affairs of the Universal, that she had quite ceased to keep an eye on, so great for a time had been her confidence in Saccard. Certain irregularities now struck her forcibly and upset her. Then she found to her surprise that she didn't really care, and didn't have the strength to speak up or act, so totally gripped was she by the one anguish, that betrayal she had tried to accept, but which was choking her. Ashamed to feel tears overcoming her again, she hid the pictures away, mortally regretting that she could not get on her knees to find comfort in a church, and weep for hours until she had no more tears to shed.

After ten minutes, Madame Caroline had calmed down and was working on the report again when the valet came in to tell her that Charles, a coachman who had been dismissed the day before, was insisting on speaking to her. Saccard himself had engaged him but had caught him stealing from the oat store. She hesitated, then agreed to see him. Tall, good-looking, clean-shaven, and swaying his hips with the confident, conceited air of a man that women spend money on, Charles came in, full of insolence.

'Madame, I've come about my two shirts that the laundress has lost and refuses to account for. Madame surely can't imagine that I can simply accept such a loss... and since Madame is the person in charge, I want Madame to reimburse me for my shirts... Yes, I want fifteen francs.'

Madame Caroline was very strict on such household matters. She would perhaps have given him the fifteen francs, just to avoid an argument. But the effrontery of the man, caught red-handed the day before, quite revolted her.

'I owe you nothing, and shan't give you a sou... Besides, Monsieur warned me about you and absolutely forbade me to do anything for you.'

At this, Charles took a step forward, threateningly.

'Ah, so that's what Monsieur said! I thought as much, and Monsieur was wrong, because now we'll have some fun... I'm not so stupid as not to have seen that Madame is his mistress...'

Flushing, Madame Caroline stood up to send him away. But he didn't give her the chance, and went on:

'And perhaps Madame will be happy to know where Monsieur goes from four o'clock to six, two or three times a week, when he's sure of finding a certain person alone...'

She had suddenly turned very pale, as if all her blood was flowing back to her heart. She made a violent gesture, as if to force back into his throat this information she had been avoiding for the last two months.

'I absolutely forbid you...'

But he shouted over her.

'It's Madame the Baroness Sandorff... She is kept by Monsieur Delcambre, and to enjoy her in comfort, he rents a little ground-floor apartment in the Rue Caumartin, in a building with a fruit-stall in front, near the corner of the Rue Saint-Nicolas... And Monsieur goes along to take his place while it's still nice and warm...'

She had reached for the bell to get the man thrown out, but he would certainly have carried on speaking in front of the servants.

'Oh, when I say warm!... I have a friend there, Clarisse, the chambermaid, and she has watched them together, and seen her mistress, a real icicle of a woman, doing all sorts of filthy things with him...'

'Be quiet you wretch!... Here, take your fifteen francs.'

And with a gesture of unspeakable contempt, she gave him the money, realizing it was the only way to get rid of him. And indeed, he at once became quite polite again.

'For myself, I only want to help Madame... The building with the fruit-stall. The steps at the back of the courtyard... Today is Thursday, and it's four o'clock, if Madame wants to catch them...'

She pushed him toward the door, her lips tightly pressed together, her face livid.

'All the more so today, when Madame would perhaps witness something really amusing... Not likely Clarisse is going to stay in such a place! And when one has had good masters, one leaves them a little souvenir, isn't that so? ... Good afternoon, Madame.'

At last he was gone. Madame Caroline stood stock still for a few seconds trying to understand, and realizing what sort of scene awaited Saccard. Then, drained of strength, she gave a long groan and slumped over her work-table, while the tears that had been choking her for so long flowed freely.

This Clarisse, a skinny blonde girl, had simply betrayed her mistress, offering Delcambre the chance to surprise her with another man in the very apartment he was paying for. She had first asked for five hundred francs, but as he was very miserly, she'd been forced to haggle, and finally settled for two hundred francs to be paid cash in hand, the moment she opened the bedroom door for him. She herself slept in the apartment, in a little room behind the dressing-room. The Baroness had taken her on for the sake of discretion, to avoid having the concierge in to do the housework. Most of the time Clarisse lived a life of idleness in the empty apartment, with nothing to do in between the assignations, just keeping out of the way and disappearing as soon as Delcambre or Saccard arrived. It was in this building that she had met Charles, who for a long time had been coming in at night to share with her the big bed in the master bedroom, with the sheets still in disarray from the day's debauchery, and it was indeed she who had recommended Charles to Saccard as a solid, honest fellow. Since his dismissal, she had shared in his resentment, especially since her mistress was not playing fair with her, and she had found another job which would pay her five francs a month more. At first Charles had wanted to write to Baron Sandorff, but she had thought it would be more amusing and more lucrative to arrange a surprise with Delcambre. So that Thursday, with everything prepared for her big plan, she waited.

At four o'clock, when Saccard arrived, Baroness Sandorff was already there, stretched out on the chaise longue in front of the fire. She was usually very punctual, like a businesswoman who knows the value of her time. On the first few encounters, Saccard had felt disillusioned at not finding the ardent lover he had hoped for in this woman, with her dark hair, bruised eyelids, and the provocative allure of a wild Bacchante. She was like marble, tired of her useless quest for a sensation that never happened, wholly absorbed by her gambling, the stress of which at least warmed her blood. Then, having felt that she was curious, free of disgust, and resigned even to revulsion, if she thought it might offer some new thrill, he had depraved her to the point where she would give him caresses of any and every sort. She talked about the stock exchange, prised bits of information out of him, and as she had been winning—chance no doubt playing its part—since their affair began, she regarded Saccard rather as a lucky charm, something you pick up and kiss, even if it's dirty, because it brings you luck.

Clarisse had made such a big fire that day that they didn't get into bed, preferring the extra pleasure of staying on the chaise longue in front of the leaping flames. Outside, night was about to fall. But the blinds were closed, the curtains carefully drawn, and two large lamps with frosted-glass globes and no shade, threw their stark light upon them.

Saccard had hardly entered the room before Delcambre, in turn, alighted from his carriage. The Public Prosecutor Delcambre, a personal acquaintance of the Emperor, and on his way to becoming a minister, was a thin, sallow man of about fifty, tall and solemn in stature, his clean-shaven face deeply furrowed, and severely austere. His rugged nose, like an eagle's beak, seemed as devoid of weakness as of forgiveness. As he mounted the steps at his usual pace, measured and grave, he had the same cold and dignified air as he had in the courtroom. No one in the building knew him, for he generally came only at night. Clarisse was waiting for him in the tiny antechamber.

'If Monsieur will just follow me, and I strongly urge Monsieur to make no noise.'

He hesitated—why not enter by the door that opened directly into the bedroom? But she explained very quietly that it would almost certainly be bolted, so they would need to break it down, and if she were forewarned, Madame would have time to rearrange herself. No! What she wanted was to let him catch her just as she herself had seen her one day, when peering through the keyhole. To this end she had devised a very simple plan. Her own room had formerly communicated with the dressing-room by a door now kept locked, and since the key had been thrown into a drawer, she had only had to retrieve it, and reopen the door; so, thanks to this unused and forgotten door, it was possible, without making any noise, to enter the dressing-room, which was separated from the bedroom simply by a screen. Madame would certainly not be expecting anyone to come in from there.

'Just trust me, Monsieur. Don't I have every reason for this to succeed?'

She slipped through the half-open door, disappearing for a second, leaving Delcambre by himself in her tiny maid's bedroom, with its unmade bed and its bowl of soapy water; Clarisse had already sent off her trunk in the morning, so as to be ready to leave as soon as the job was done. Then she came back, closing the door quietly behind her.

'Monsieur will need to wait a while. It's not time yet. They're just talking.'

Delcambre remained dignified, not uttering a word, but standing there quite still under the slightly mocking glances the girl directed at him. However, he was tiring, and a nervous tic was twitching all the left-hand side of his face, as repressed anger flooded up to his brain. Beneath the icy severity of his professional mask, the hidden raging male, with ogre-like appetites, now secretly began to growl with anger at this flesh that was being stolen from him.

'Let's get on with it, let's get on with it,' he repeated, hardly knowing what he was saying, his hands trembling feverishly.

But when Clarisse, after disappearing once more, returned with a finger to her lips, she begged him to wait a little longer.

'I assure you, Monsieur, be sensible, otherwise you'll miss the best of it... In a moment or two they'll really be at it.'

And Delcambre, his legs suddenly giving way, had to sit for a moment on the maid's little bed. Night was falling, and he stayed there in the dark, while the chambermaid, listening carefully, captured every slightest sound from the bedroom, sounds which he also heard, but so amplified by the buzzing in his ears that they seemed like the tramping of an army on the march.

At last he felt Clarisse's hand groping along his arm. He understood, and without a word gave her an envelope into which he had slipped the promised two hundred francs. And she walked in first, drew aside the dressing-room screen, and pushed him into the bedroom, with the words:

'Look! There they are!'

In front of the roaring fire with its glowing coals, Saccard was lying on his back on the edge of the chaise longue, wearing nothing but his shirt, which was rolled up, right up to his armpits, exposing, from his feet all the way to his shoulders, his dark skin which age had covered with animal-like hair, while the Baroness was on her knees, completely naked and toasted quite pink by the flames; and the two big lamps lit them both up with so brilliant a light that the slightest details stood out, thrown into extravagant relief.

Gaping and gasping at this unnatural *flagrante delicto*, Delcambre had stopped, while the two others, as if thunderstruck and stupefied at seeing this man coming in from the dressing-room, remained quite still, with wild, staring eyes.

'Ah, you filthy pigs!' the Public Prosecutor at last stammered out. 'Pigs! Pigs!'

It was the only word he could find, and he kept repeating it, emphasizing it each time with the same jerky gesture to give it more force. The woman had now leapt up, frantic at her nakedness, turning this way and that, looking for the clothes she had left in the dressing-room, where she couldn't go and get them; and having managed to grab a white petticoat which was lying there she covered her shoulders with it, gripping the two ends of the waistband between her teeth, to pull it round her neck and over her bosom. The man, who had also got up from the chaise longue, pulled down his shirt, looking very put out.

'Pigs!' Delcambre repeated again. 'Pigs! And in this room that I'm paying for!'

And shaking his fist at Saccard, growing more and more furious at the idea that these filthy activities were taking place on furniture bought with his money, he raged at them.

'This place is mine, you filthy pig! And this woman is mine—you are a pig and a thief!'

Saccard, who wasn't angry, would have tried to calm him down, feeling very embarrassed at being caught like this in his shirt, and thoroughly annoyed by the whole affair. But the word 'thief' offended him.

'Lord! Monsieur,' he replied, 'when one wants to have a woman all to oneself, the first thing you do is give her what she needs.'

This allusion to his meanness was the ultimate provocation for Delcambre. He became unrecognizable, frightening, as if the human animal, all the hidden priapism within him, was bursting out through his skin. That face, so dignified and cold, had suddenly turned red and was swelling, bulging, protruding like the muzzle of a furious beast. His rage was releasing the carnal brute within, in the awful pain of all this stirred-up filth.

'Needs? Needs?' he spluttered. 'What she needs is the gutter...
Ah! The slut!'

And he made such a violent gesture at the Baroness that she took
fright. She had remained standing, motionless, only managing to
hide her bosom with the petticoat by leaving her belly and thighs
exposed. Realizing that this display of her guilty nudity was enraging
him further, she retreated to the chaise longue and sat on it, with her
legs together and knees drawn up in such a way as to hide as much as
she could. Then she just stayed there, without a gesture or word, her
head lowered, casting sly, sidelong glances at the battle, a female
being fought over by men, waiting to become the prize of the victor.

Saccard had bravely thrown himself in front of her.

'At least you're not going to strike her!'

The two men were now face to face.

'Come now, Monsieur,' Saccard went on, 'this has got to stop. We
can't go on rowing like cabbies... It is indeed true, I am Madame's
lover. And I tell you again, if you paid for the furniture here, I have
paid for...'

'For what?'

'Lots of things: the other day for instance, the ten thousand francs
owing on her old account with Mazaud that you had absolutely
refused to pay... I have the same rights as you. A pig, possibly! But a
thief? Oh no! You will withdraw that word.'

Beside himself, Delcambre shouted:

'You are a thief, and I'm going to smash your face in if you don't
clear off this instant.'

But now Saccard too was growing angry. As he pulled his trousers
back on, he protested:

'Ah, that's enough, you're seriously annoying me now! I shall go if
and when I choose... And it certainly won't be a fellow like you
who'll frighten me away!'

And when he had put his boots back on, he firmly stamped his feet
on the carpet, and said:

'There, I'm all fixed now, and here I stay.'

Choking with rage, Delcambre moved nearer, his face thrust
forward.

'Filthy pig, will you get out!'

'Not before you, you old scoundrel!'

'And if I give you a good slap across the face!'

'Then I'll give you a good kick somewhere else.'

Nose to nose and teeth bared, the two men barked at each other. Quite forgetting themselves, making a nonsense of their education, caught in the flow of filthy mud in this rut they were fighting over, the magistrate and the financier were reduced to rowing like drunken carters, hurling appalling words at each other, seeking ever-fouler language. Their voices were strangled in their throats, they were frothing at the mouth with filth.

On the chaise longue, the Baroness was still waiting for one of them to throw the other one out. Now that she had calmed down and was thinking of the future, the only thing still bothering her was the presence of the chambermaid, whom she knew to be waiting behind the dressing-room door, enjoying the scene. As the girl craned her neck, with a satisfied chuckle at hearing these gentlemen saying such disgusting things, the two women caught sight of each other, the mistress huddled up in her nudity, the servant standing there all neat and tidy, with her little flat collar; and they exchanged a look that blazed with the age-old hatred of female rivals, in that equality that levels farm-girls and duchesses, when they have no clothes on.

But Saccard too had seen Clarisse. He angrily finished getting dressed, pulled on his waistcoat, turned back to fling another insult into Delcambre's face, pulled on the left sleeve of his coat, yelling another insult, then the right sleeve with yet more, and more again, hurling them out by the bucketful. Then suddenly, to bring things to an end:

'Clarisse! Come on in!... Open the doors, open the windows, so the whole house and the whole street can hear! Monsieur the Public Prosecutor wants people to know he's here, and I'm going to make sure they do!'

Turning pale, Delcambre stepped back when he saw him moving towards one of the windows as if to undo the catch. This terrible man was quite capable of carrying out his threat, since he didn't give a hoot about scandal.

'Ah! You scoundrel, you scoundrel,' murmured the magistrate. 'You make a great pair, you and that trollop. I leave her to you...'

'That's right, clear off! You're not wanted here... At least her bills will get paid and she won't have to moan about poverty any more... Here! Do you want six sous for the omnibus?'

At this insult, Delcambre paused for a moment in the doorway of the dressing-room. He had now regained his tall, lean stature and his pallid face, furrowed by rigid lines. He stretched out his arm, and made a vow:

'I swear you'll pay for this... Oh! I'll get back at you, just look out!'

Then he disappeared. Immediately behind him came the sound of a skirt hurrying away; it was the chambermaid who, fearing a row, was making her escape, greatly amused at the thought of what fun it had been.

Saccard, still shaken, and shuffling his feet, went and closed the doors, then returned to the bedroom, where the Baroness still sat as if glued to her chair. He strode around, poked a falling ember back into the fire; and only then noticing her, so strangely and scantily clad, with that petticoat over her shoulders, he now behaved with great decorum.

'Come, get yourself dressed, my dear... and don't be upset. It's a stupid business, but it's nothing, nothing at all... We'll meet again here, the day after tomorrow, and sort things out, all right? I have to go now, I have an appointment with Huret.'

And as she was at last putting her underwear back on, and he was just leaving, he called out from the antechamber:

'And remember, if you buy any Italian stock don't do anything silly! Only buy if they're offering a premium.'

Meanwhile, at that very moment, Madame Caroline was sitting with her head slumped over the work-table, sobbing. The brutal information from the coachman, this betrayal of Saccard's that she could no longer ignore, stirred up in her all the suspicions and all the fears she had tried to keep buried. She had forced herself to remain serene and hopeful about the dealings of the Universal, and blinded by her feelings, had colluded in all the things she was not being told, the things she didn't try to find out. Now she reproached herself with savage remorse for the reassuring letter she had written to her brother at the time of the last Annual General Meeting; for she knew, now that jealousy had reopened her eyes and ears, that illegalities were still happening and constantly getting worse; the Sabatani account had grown, and under cover of this frontman the bank was speculating more and more; in addition there were the massive and mendacious advertisements, the foundations of sand and mud on which they were building the whole colossal enterprise, while its rapid, almost miraculous rise filled her with more terror than joy. What worried her above all was the terrible pace of it all, the way the Universal was being urged along at such a gallop, like an engine crammed with coal, launched along diabolical rails until the point when everything would shatter and explode in one final crash. She wasn't naive, nor was she a simpleton, easily fooled; even if she was ignorant about technical banking operations, she well understood the reason for this overdoing of things, this feverish pace, all intended to intoxicate people, and whirl them into the epidemic madness of the dancing millions. Every morning had to produce a rise in the price, people had to be made to believe in ever-greater success, in monumental cash desks, enchanted cash desks, that took in streams of gold and sent back rivers, oceans of gold. Her poor brother, so gullible, so beguiled and enthused— was she really going to let him down, abandon him to this flood that threatened one day to drown them all? She despaired at her inertia and helplessness.

Twilight now was darkening the workroom, not even lit by a glow from the now dead fire, and in the deepening shadows, Madame Caroline wept even more. It was feeble to cry like this, for she knew full well that such a flood of tears did not come from anxiety over the dealings of the Universal. Saccard alone was driving this terrifying gallop, lashing the beast with such ferocity and extraordinary lack of moral conscience, even at the risk of killing it. He was the sole culprit, and it made her shudder when she tried to see into his mind, into the dark soul of this money-man, that soul unknown even to himself, in which darkness hid further darkness, in an infinite mire of every kind of degeneracy. What she couldn't yet see clearly she already suspected, and it made her tremble. But the gradual discovery of so many lesions, and the fear of some catastrophe to come, would not have had her weeping helplessly at her table like this, but rather would have made her pull herself together in her need to resist and recover. She knew herself, she was a fighter. No, if she sobbed so hard, like a sickly child, it was because she loved Saccard, and because Saccard, at that very moment, was with another woman. And that admission she was forced to make to herself filled her with shame and redoubled her tears until they almost choked her.

'To have so little pride, my God!' she stammered aloud. 'To be so weak and wretched. To be so incapable of doing what I need to do!'

Just then, in the darkness of the room, she was astonished to hear a voice. It was Maxime who, familiar with the house, had let himself in.

'Hello, what are you doing, sitting here weeping in the dark?'

Embarrassed at being caught like this, she struggled to control her sobbing, while he went on:

'I beg your pardon, I thought my father was back from the Bourse… A lady asked me to bring him to dinner with her.'

But the valet then brought in a lamp, put it on the table, and withdrew. The whole of the vast room was illuminated by the gentle light from the lampshade.

'It's nothing,' Madame Caroline tried to explain, 'just one of those little upsets that women sometimes have, though I'm generally more stable.'

And dry-eyed, sitting up straight, she was already smiling, valiant and mettlesome as ever. For a moment, the young man looked at her, sitting so proudly, with her large, clear eyes and firm mouth, her face full of noble kindness, softened and made especially charming by her dense crown of white hair; and he thought how young she still looked, with her white hair and equally white teeth, an adorable woman, who had become beautiful. Then he thought of his father, and shrugged his shoulders with a mixture of pity and scorn.

'It's because of him, isn't it? He's the one who's got you into such a state.'

She tried to deny it, but she was choking, and her eyes once more filled with tears.

'Ah! My dear lady, I told you that you had illusions about Papa and that they wouldn't do you any good… It was inevitable that he'd devour you too!'

Then she remembered the day when she had gone to Maxime to borrow the two thousand francs to pay for Victor's release. Hadn't he then promised to talk to her, when she wanted to know more? Wasn't this her opportunity to question him, and learn all about the past? An irresistible need drove her on: now that she had started on the downward path, she had to go all the way. That was the only brave thing to do, the only thing worthy of her, and useful for everyone. But finding such an interrogation repugnant, she changed the subject, as if wanting to break off the conversation.

'I still owe you two thousand francs,' she said. 'I hope you don't mind too much having to wait for them?'

He made a gesture indicating that she could have all the time she wanted. Then, suddenly, he added:

'By the way, how is that monster, my little brother?'

'He's making me despair, I haven't told your father anything yet... I should so like to scrub him up a bit, so the poor thing might be loved!'

Maxime gave a disturbing laugh, and when she looked at him enquiringly:

'Lord! I think you're just giving yourself unnecessary bother. Papa won't understand all the trouble you've taken... Family problems are nothing new to him!'

She was still looking at him, so very proper in his self-centred enjoyment of life, so thoroughly cynical about human relations, even those created by pleasure. He had smiled to himself, enjoying the hidden malice of his last remark. And she realized she was getting very close to the secrets of these two men.

'You lost your mother when you were very young?'

'Yes, I hardly knew her... I was still in school in Plassans when she died here in Paris... Our uncle, Dr Pascal, kept my sister Clotilde with him in Plassans, and I've only ever seen her once since then.'

'But your father remarried?'

He hesitated. His eyes, so clear and empty, had clouded over with a slight reddish mist.

'Oh! Yes, yes, remarried... a magistrate's daughter, a Béraud du Châtel... Renée, not a mother to me, but a good friend...'

Then, with a certain familiarity, he sat down beside her:

'Look, you have to understand Papa. He's no worse—God knows!—than the rest. But his children, his wives, in fact everyone and everything around him, all come second to money... Oh, let's be clear, it's not that he loves money like a miser, wanting to have a whole heap of it and hide it in a cellar. No! If he wants to make it gush out from everywhere, and if he doesn't care what sources he taps, it's just to see it flowing around him in torrents, it's for all the enjoyment he can get out of it, in luxury, pleasure, and power... What can you do? It's in his blood, and he'd sell us both, you, me, anyone at all, if we were part of some deal. And he would do all that quite unthinkingly, as a man of quality, for he really is the poet of the million, money simply makes him mad, makes him a scoundrel—oh! a scoundrel on a grand scale!'

This was just what Madame Caroline had thought, and she nodded in agreement as she listened to Maxime. Ah! Money! Money the corrupter, the poisoner, shrivelling souls, driving out all goodness, affection and love for others. Money alone was the great culprit, the promoter of all human cruelty and filth. At this moment, she cursed it and loathed it, with all the indignant revulsion of her nobility of soul and her womanly probity. If only she had the power, she would have destroyed all the money in the world, as one would crush disease underfoot to save the world's health.

'And your father remarried,' she repeated after a silence, in a slow, embarrassed voice, caught in a confused awakening of memories. Who was it had mentioned this story to her? She couldn't tell: a woman no doubt, some friend from the time of her first moving in to the Rue Saint-Lazare, when the new tenant had arrived to occupy the first floor. Wasn't it something about a marriage for money, a shameful bargain that had been struck, and then later on hadn't some crime entered the household, tolerated and even thriving, a monstrous kind of adultery, almost incest?

'Renée', Maxime went on very quietly, as if in spite of himself, 'was only a few years older than me.'

He had raised his head and was looking at Madame Caroline; and with sudden abandon, and an irrational surge of confidence in this woman who seemed so robust and reasonable, he related the past, not as a coherent narrative but in bits, in incomplete, seemingly involuntary admissions that she had to stitch together. Was it an old rancour against his father that he was thus settling? That rivalry that had existed between them, and still made them strangers to each other, even now, with nothing in common? He made no accusations against him and seemed incapable of anger, but his quiet laugh turned into a sneer, and he spoke of these abominations with an unpleasant and sneaky pleasure in blackening his father by raking up so many vile events.

And thus it was that Madame Caroline learned the terrible story from beginning to end: Saccard selling his name, taking money to marry a girl whom someone had seduced; Saccard, with his money and wild and dazzling life, finally making that sick, grown-up child quite unbalanced; Saccard in need of money, and requiring a signature from her, accepting the love affair of his son and his wife under his own roof, shutting his eyes to it, like a good patriarch, happy for people to enjoy themelves. Money, money the king, money the god, reigning high above blood, above tears, adored in its infinite power far above any vain human scruples. And as money grew ever greater, and Saccard was revealed to her with all that diabolical greatness, Madame Caroline was seized by a real terror, frozen and distraught at the thought that she, like so many others, belonged to this monster.

'There!' said Maxime, ending his story. 'It hurts me to see you like this, but it's better for you to be warned. And don't let it make you fall out with my father. I'd be really sorry to see that, because it would again be you who'd end up weeping over it, not him… So now do you understand why I refuse to lend him a sou?'

As she made no reply, struck to the heart and unable to speak, he stood up, and glanced at a mirror, with the tranquil ease of a good-looking man, certain of the propriety of his life. Then he came back to her.

'You see? Such things age one very quickly… I decided to settle down right away, so I married a girl who was sick, and who died, and today I can swear that no one will make me do stupid things ever again… No! You see, Papa is incorrigible, because he has no moral sense.'

He took her hand, and feeling how cold it was, held it for a moment in his own.

'I'm going now, since he's still not back… But don't take it so hard! I thought you were so strong! And say thank-you to me, for the only really stupid thing is to be duped.'

He was at last leaving when he paused at the door with a laugh, and added:

'I was forgetting—tell him Madame de Jeumont wants him to come to dinner… You know, Madame de Jeumont, the one who slept with the Emperor for a hundred thousand francs… And have no fear on that score, for however mad Papa may be, I dare to hope he's not capable of paying that sort of price for a woman!'

Once alone, Madame Caroline did not move. She just sat, crushed, on her chair, in the suddenly heavy silence of the vast room, gazing fixedly at the lamp with eyes widened. It was as if a veil had suddenly been torn away: what she had been refusing to see clearly until then, what she had only tremulously suspected, she now saw it all, in all its hideous crudeness, with no possible mitigation. She saw Saccard stripped naked, with his ravaged money-man's soul, a soul complicated and murky in its decay; he really knew no ties nor barriers, just pursuing his appetites with the unbridled instincts of a man who recognizes no limit save his own impotence. He had shared his wife with his son, sold his son, sold his wife, sold everyone who came within his reach; he had sold himself, and he would sell her too, would sell her brother, and turn their hearts and minds into cash. He was no more than a money-maker, one who threw things and beings alike into the melting-pot to turn them into money. In a brief moment of lucidity she saw the Universal sweating money from every pore, forming a lake, an ocean of money, in the midst of which, suddenly, with a terrible cracking noise, the whole enterprise sank to the bottom. Ah! Money! Horrible money that soils and devours everything!

With an angry movement Madame Caroline got up. No, no! It was monstrous, it was over, she could not stay with this man any longer. His betrayal of her she would have forgiven; but she felt sickened by all this filth in his past, and she shook with terror at the threat of further crimes yet to come. She simply had to leave at once if she didn't want to be spattered with mud herself, and crushed beneath the wreckage. And she felt a need to go far away, very far, to rejoin her brother in the Orient, a need to disappear even more than a need to warn him. To get away, get away immediately! It was not yet six o'clock, she could catch the express for Marseilles at seven fifty-five, for she felt it quite beyond her to set eyes on Saccard again. She would buy what she needed in Marseilles before going on board. Just some underwear in a trunk, a spare dress, and she would be off. She would be ready in a quarter of an hour. Then the sight of her work on the table, the report she had begun, made her pause for a moment. What was the use of taking all that, since everything was bound to collapse, being rotten at the base? She began, nevertheless, to put the documents and notes carefully away, out of her good housewifely habit of never leaving things in a mess. That task took her a few minutes, and calmed down the initial fever of her decision. And she was quite self-possessed again, casting a final glance around the room before leaving it, when the valet reappeared and handed her a bundle of newspapers and letters.

Madame Caroline automatically looked at the addresses, and recognized in the pile a letter for her from her brother. It had been sent from Damascus, where Hamelin was then occupied with the planned branch-line from that city to Beirut. At first, she started to skim through it, standing near the lamp, promising herself she would read it slowly later, in the train, but every sentence gripped her attention, she was unable to skip a single word, and eventually she sat down again at the table, and gave herself over entirely to reading the long and exciting twelve-page letter.

Hamelin appeared to be having one of his happier days. He thanked his sister for the latest good news she had sent him from Paris, and he was now sending her even better news, for everything was going very well. The first balance-sheet of the General United Steamboat Company promised to be splendid, for the new steamboats were proving very successful, thanks to their excellent equipment and improved speed. He jokingly added that people travelled on them just for pleasure, and described the sea-ports as being overrun by people from the West; he couldn't go anywhere off the beaten track, he wrote, without bumping into someone from the Paris boulevards. The Orient really had been opened up to France, just as he had predicted. Soon towns would spring up again on the fertile slopes of Lebanon. But above all, he painted a very vivid picture of the remote Carmel Gorge, where the silver mine was now fully operative. That wild site was becoming more human, for springs had been discovered in the gigantic pile of fallen rocks that blocked the valley to the north, and fields were being created; wheat was replacing the mastic trees, while a whole village had already been built close to the mine, simple wooden huts at first, just shacks for the workers, but now small stone-built houses with gardens, the beginnings of a city which was going to keep on growing for as long as the deposits of ore were not exhausted. About five hundred inhabitants lived there, and a road had just been built, linking the village to Saint-Jean-d'Acre. From dawn to dusk the digging machines were roaring, waggons started up with a loud cracking of whips, women sang and children played and shouted here in this desert, where once the only sound that had broken the death-like silence was the slow beating of eagles' wings. The scent of myrtles and broom still filled the air, so warm and deliciously pure. Finally Hamelin went on at length about the first railway line he was to open, from Bursa to Beirut via Angora and Aleppo. All the formalities had been concluded in Constantinople, and he was very pleased with some excellent modifications he had made to the planned route for the difficult passage through the Taurus mountains; he wrote of the mountain-passes and the plains that lay at the foot of the mountains with the rapture of a scientist who had found new coal mines and could already see the country covered with factories. His guidelines were in place, the location of the stations had been decided, some of them in totally isolated spots; with one town here and another further off, new towns would grow up around these stations, each placed at the crossing of natural highways. The seed was already sown for the future harvests of men and great things, and it was all germinating; within a few years it would be a new world. He ended with a tender kiss for his beloved sister, happy to associate her with this resurrection of a people, telling her that she was an important part of it, she who for so long had helped him, with her courage and her robust strength.

Madame Caroline had finished the letter, which now lay open on the table, and she was lost in thought, her eyes once more fixed upon the lamp. Then, without thinking, she looked up, scanning the walls, pausing at each of the maps, and every watercolour. In Beirut, the residence of the managing director of the General United Steamboat Company had now been built, with vast warehouses all around it. At Mount Carmel, the floor of that savage gorge, choked with bushes and rocks, was now being populated like the gigantic nest of a new race. In the Taurus range, levellings and new outlines were altering the horizons, opening up a path for the development of trade. And before her eyes, from these sheets pinned on the wall, with their geometric lines and faded colours, arose a whole image of that far-off country, visited so long ago and loved so much for its eternally blue sky and fertile soil. She saw once more the terraced gardens of Beirut, the valleys of the Lebanon, full of olive groves and mulberry trees, and the plains of Antioch and Aleppo with their vast orchards of delicious fruit. She could see herself once more with her brother in their continual journeying through that wonderful country where incalculable wealth was being wasted, unrecognized or spoiled, in a land of idleness and ignorance, with no roads, no industry, no agriculture and no schools. But now it was all springing to life in an extraordinary burst of new vigour. In this vision of the Orient of tomorrow, she could already see prosperous cities, cultivated fields and happy people. She could see them, she could hear the noisy work on the building-sites, and she saw that this ancient dormant land, now reawakened, was giving birth.

Madame Caroline then had the sudden conviction that money was the manure in which this humanity of tomorrow was growing. Various phrases of Saccard's came back to her, fragments of theories about speculation. She recalled his idea that without speculation there would be no great lively and fertile ventures, just as without lustfulness there would be no children. That excess of passion, and that base expenditure and wasting of life, were all necessary for the very continuation of life. If her brother was rejoicing and singing of victory far away, where construction work was under way and buildings were springing from the ground, it was because in Paris money was pouring down, rotting everything in the madness of speculation. Money, poisonous, destructive money, became the ferment of all social vegetation, providing the necessary compost for the accomplishment of the great works that would bring nations together and create peace on the earth. She had cursed money, but now she was falling into a terrified admiration of it: for was it not money that alone had strength enough to raze a mountain, fill up a stretch of sea, and at last make the earth habitable for men, delivered from toil and now merely the drivers of machines? From money, which did so much evil, everything good was being born. Now she didn't know what to think, shaken to the roots of her being, already resolved not to leave after all, since there seemed to be such complete success in the East, and the battle was here in Paris; but she could not yet be calm, with her heart still bleeding.

Madame Caroline rose, and went to lean her brow against the pane of one of the windows overlooking the Beauvilliers garden. Night had fallen and she could only see a faint light in the little side-room where the Countess and her daughter lived, to avoid getting the other rooms dirty, and having to spend money on heating. Behind the thin muslin curtains she could just make out the profile of the Countess, mending some garment with her own hands, while Alice painted watercolours, which she knocked off by the dozen, and must be selling in secret. They had a stroke of bad luck when their horse had fallen sick, so they had been tied to the house for two weeks, determined not to be seen out on foot, but shrinking from hiring a carriage. But in that poverty, so heroically concealed, one hope now kept them going with more courage, and that was the continued rise of the Universal shares and the already very considerable gains which they could see falling upon them in a dazzling shower of gold on the day they decided to sell with the share-price at its peak. The Countess was promising herself a genuinely new dress, and dreaming of giving four dinner parties a month in the winter, without having to live on bread and water for a fortnight. Alice no longer just laughed with her look of affected indifference when her mother spoke about her marriage, but listened, with slightly trembling hands, beginning to think it might even happen, that she too might come to have a husband and children. And Madame Caroline, looking at the little lamp that cast its light on them, felt a great wave of calmness rising up to her, and compassion, as she recalled the remark that money, even the mere hope of money, was enough to give happiness to these poor creatures. If Saccard made them rich, wouldn't they bless his name, and wouldn't he always be, in their eyes, a good and charitable man? So goodness was everywhere, even in the worst of people, for they are always good for someone, and even in the midst of general execration, a few humble voices will be thankful and adoring. This reflection made her think of the Work Foundation, while her eyes went on staring blindly at the darkness of the garden. The day before, acting on Saccard's behalf, she had handed out toys and sweets to celebrate a birthday, and she gave an involuntary smile at the memory of the children's noisy delight. For the past month they had been happier about Victor at the Foundation; she had read some satisfactory reports about him during her long, twice-weekly discussions about the institution with Princess d'Orviedo. But as the recollection of Victor suddenly came to mind, she was astonished at having quite forgotten him in her crisis of despair, when she was thinking of leaving. Could she really have abandoned him like that, undermining the good deed she had accomplished with so much difficulty? A feeling of gentleness rose from the obscurity of the tall trees, filling her ever more deeply with a wave of inexpressible renunciation and divine tolerance, which seemed to make her heart grow bigger, while down below, the poor little lamp of the Beauvilliers ladies continued to shine like a star.

When Madame Caroline got back to her table she gave a slight shiver. What was that about? She was cold! And that amused her—she who always boasted of spending the whole winter without a fire! It was as if she had just emerged, rejuvenated and strong, with a steady pulse, from an ice-cold bath. This was how she felt on getting up in the morning when she was in the bloom of health. Then she decided to put another log on the fire, and when she saw the fire had gone out, she resolved to light it again herself rather than ring for the

servant. It was quite hard work, as she had no firewood, but she managed to get the logs to catch, just using old newspapers that she
burned one after another. Down on her knees in front of the hearth,
she found she was laughing at herself. For a moment she stayed there,
surprised and happy. So another of her great crises was now over,
and she still had hope, but of what? She still had no idea, just the
inevitable unknown, that lies at the end of life, at the end of humanity. Just being alive had to be enough, and life would always bring
healing for the wounds that it caused. Once again she recalled the
disasters of her existence, her dreadful marriage, her hard times in
Paris, her abandonment by the only man she had loved, and yet after
every calamity she had rediscovered the vital energy, the immortal
joy that set her on her feet again, even among the ruins. Hadn't
everything just collapsed on her? She had lost all esteem for her lover
in the face of his frightful past; she was like the sainted women who,
faced by loathsome wounds, go on dressing them night and morning,
never expecting them to heal. She would continue to belong to him,
knowing that he belonged to others, and not even seek to win him
back from them. She would live on hot coals, in the breathless forge
of speculation, with the constant threat of a final catastrophe, in
which her brother might lose both his honour and his life. And yet
here she stood, almost carefree, as if squarely facing up to danger on
the morning of a beautiful day, enjoying the exhilaration of battle.
Why? For no good reason, for the simple pleasure of living. As her
brother was always telling her, she was invincible hope.

When Saccard returned, he found Madame Caroline buried in her
work, finishing, in her firm hand, a page of the report on the Oriental
railways. She raised her head and gave him a tranquil smile, while he
touched with his lips her beautiful, radiant white hair.

'You've been very busy, my dear?'

'Oh, just one thing after another! I saw the Minister of Public
Works, met up with Huret again, then I had to go back to see the
minister, but there was only a secretary there... In the end I did get
his promise for our overseas concerns.'

In fact, since leaving Baroness Sandorff, he had hardly stopped for
breath, entirely occupied with business affairs, and carried away by
his customary zeal. She passed him Hamelin's letter, which delighted
him; and she watched as he exulted over the coming triumph, telling
herself that she would henceforth keep a close eye on him, to try to

prevent the follies he was certain to commit. However, she couldn't manage to be severe.

'Your son came with an invitation for you from Madame de Jeumont.'

He protested.

'But she wrote to me!... I forgot to tell you I was going there this evening... That really is a chore, when I'm so tired!'

And he left, after once more kissing her white hair. She went back to her work, with her friendly smile, full of indulgence. Wasn't she simply a friend, who gave herself to him? Her jealousy made her feel ashamed, as if she had somehow further sullied their relationship. She intended to be above any anguish at sharing, quite free of the carnal selfishness of love. Belonging to him, knowing he belonged to others, was of no importance. And yet she loved him, with all her brave and charitable heart. It was a triumph of love that this Saccard, this bandit of the financial streets, should be loved so absolutely by this adorable woman, because she saw him as brave and dynamic, creating a world, creating life.

CHAPTER VIII

IT was on 1 April that the Universal Exhibition of 1867 opened,* with great celebrations and ostentatious splendour. It was the start of the grand season of the Empire, a season of supreme festivity that would turn Paris into the hostelry of the world, a gaily beflagged hostelry, full of music and song, with feasting and fornication in every room. Never had any regime at the height of its power summoned the nations of the world to so colossal a spree. The long procession of emperors, kings, and princes from the four corners of the earth set forth for the Tuileries, which blazed with light like the finale of a theatrical extravaganza.

It was just then, a fortnight after the opening of the Exhibition, that Saccard opened the monumental mansion he had always wanted as the majestic new home of the Universal Bank. It had only taken six months to build, for work had gone on day and night, never wasting an hour, achieving a miracle only possible in Paris; and the façade now stood there in all its flowery ornamentation, like a cross between a temple and a music-hall, with such a lavish display of opulence that passers-by stopped on the pavement to gaze at it. Inside, it was utterly sumptuous, as if the millions in the coffers were streaming out along the walls. A grand staircase led up to the boardroom, resplendent in red and gold, like the auditorium of an opera house.* There were carpets and hangings everywhere, and offices equipped with furniture of dazzling wealth. In the basement, where the share offices were, huge safes were fixed, showing gullets deep as ovens behind plate-glass that allowed the public to see them lined up there like the barrels in storybooks, full of countless fairy treasures. And the nations and their kings on their way to the Exhibition, could come and file past: it was all ready, the new building was waiting to dazzle them and catch them, one after another, in that irresistible snare of gold, blazing in the sun.

Saccard was enthroned in the most sumptuous of the offices, with Louis-Quatorze furniture in gilded wood, covered in Genoese velvet. The staff had just been increased again: there were now more than four hundred employees. This was the army that Saccard commanded, with all the pomp of a tyrant who was both adored and obeyed, for he was very generous with his rewards. In reality, in spite of being nominally just the manager, it was he who ruled, above the chairman of the board, indeed even above the board itself, which merely ratified his orders. Madame Caroline was now constantly on the alert, busily finding out about his decisions, in order to try to counter them if necessary. She disapproved of this new establishment, which was far too magnificent, and yet could not entirely condemn it in principle, for in the happy days of her tender confidence in Saccard, she had recognized the need for a larger building, and had joshed her brother for being worried about it. The fear that she acknowledged, and her argument against all this luxury, was that the bank was losing its air of respectable integrity and lofty, religious gravity. What would customers, used to the monkish restraint and sober half-light of the ground-floor in the Rue Saint-Lazare, make of this in the Rue de Londres,* with its many floors, all so lively and noisy, and flooded with light? Saccard had replied that they would be struck with admiration and respect, and those who were bringing in five francs, once they were filled with self-esteem and intoxicating confidence, would produce ten from their pockets. And it was he, with his brutal flashiness, who was proved right. The success of the building was prodigious, creating a stir more effective than even the most extraordinary of Jantrou's advertisements. Well-off, pious people from the quiet parts of the city, and needy country priests just off the train that morning, all gaped in beatitude at the door, and came out flushed with pleasure at having funds in such a building.

In truth, what was especially worrying Madame Caroline was that she was no longer able to be constantly there in the Bank, carrying on her supervision. She could scarcely do more now than go to the Rue de Londres at infrequent intervals, on some pretext or other. She was living alone in the workroom, hardly seeing Saccard except in the evenings. He had kept his apartment, but the whole of the ground floor was closed up, as were the first-floor offices; and the Princess d'Orviedo, with her deliberate indifference to any even legitimate gain, was not even trying to find a new tenant, glad in fact to be relieved of her nagging remorse about having that banking-house, that money-shop, installed in her building. The empty house, echoing to the sound of every passing carriage, was like a tomb. All Madame Caroline could hear now was the vibrant silence rising through the ceilings from the closed counters, from which, for two years, she had heard the faint, incessant tinkling of gold. The days seemed all the more heavy and long. She was, however, doing a lot of work, still kept busy by her brother who, from the East, was sending her various bookkeeping tasks. But sometimes she would pause in her work and listen, with instinctive anxiety, needing to know what was happening down below; and there was nothing, not so much as a whisper, just the desolation of the cleared rooms, now empty, dark and securely locked. Then she would feel a little cold shiver, and stay uneasily lost in thought for a few minutes. What was happening in the Rue de Londres? Was it perhaps at this very second that the crack was appearing, the crack that would bring the whole edifice down?

There was a rumour, quite vague and insubstantial as yet, that Saccard was preparing a further increase in the bank's capital. He wanted to raise it from a hundred million to a hundred-and-fifty million. And this was a moment of special excitement, the inevitable moment when all the prosperity of the reign, the vast works that had transformed the city, the frenzied circulation of money and the wild extravagances of luxury, were bound to end in a frantic fever of speculation. Everybody wanted a share in it, risking their fortune on the gaming-table, hoping to see it increased tenfold so they could enjoy themselves like so many others suddenly made rich overnight. The banners of the Exhibition flapping in the sunshine, the illuminations, the bands playing on the Champ-de-Mars, crowds from the entire world flowing along the streets, all completed the intoxication of Paris in a dream of inexhaustible wealth and sovereign domination. During the long evenings, from this huge, festive city, dining out in exotic restaurants, and changed into a colossal fairground, with pleasure everywhere for sale beneath the stars, there rose an ultimate spasm of madness, the blithe and voracious frenzy that grips great capital cities on the edge of destruction. And Saccard, with his cut-purse flair, had so well recognized this general craze, this urge to throw money to the winds, to empty one's pockets and one's body, that he had just doubled the funds destined for advertising, urging Jantrou to make the most deafening din. Ever since the opening of the Exhibition, the Universal had been getting paeans of praise every day in the press. Every morning there was a new clashing of cymbals to attract the attention of the public: some extraordinary news item, the story of a woman who had lost a hundred shares in a cab; an extract from a journey in Asia Minor, claiming that Napoleon I had

predicted the bank in the Rue de Londres; a big leading article in
which the political role of the bank was considered in relation to the
impending solution of the Orient question;* and there were continual
notes in the financial journals, all under orders and marching together
in a solid phalanx. Jantrou had set up yearly contracts with the minor
financial papers, by which he had a column in each issue, and he used
this column with an amazingly fertile and varied imagination, sometimes going so far as to launch an attack on the bank in order to enjoy
the triumph of winning the day in the end. The famous pamphlet
he'd been planning had just been launched on the world, in a million
copies. His new agency had also been created, and under the pretext
of sending a financial news bulletin to the provincial newspapers, it
was making itself absolute master of the market in all the important
towns. And finally *L'Espérance*, under his skilful management, was daily
acquiring more and more political importance. Particular interest
had been aroused by the series of articles that followed the decree of
19 January in which the address was replaced by the right to interpellation,* a further concession from the Emperor in his move towards
greater liberty. Saccard, who inspired the articles, did not yet have
them openly attack his brother, who had after all remained a minister
of state, resigned, in his passionate attachment to power, to defending
today what he had condemned the day before; but Saccard was clearly
watching, keeping a close eye on the false position of Rougon, caught
as he was in the Chamber between the Third Party,* hungrily waiting
to take over from him, and the clericals who had allied themselves
with the authoritarian Bonapartists against the liberalization of the
Empire; insinuations were already beginning; the paper was again
supporting militant Catholicism, and remarking sourly on each one
of the minister's acts. Now that *L'Espérance* had gone over to the
Opposition, its popularity was assured, as the expression of a spirit of
revolt that would end up carrying the name of the Universal to the
four corners of France and the world.

Then, after the formidable surge of publicity, in that over-excited
atmosphere, ripe for every kind of folly, the probable increase of the
bank's capital and the rumour of a new issue of fifty millions, stirred
even the most sensible to fever-pitch. From humble dwelling to aristocratic mansion, from the concierge's lodge to the drawing-rooms of
duchesses, heads were set afire and infatuation became blind faith,
heroic and ready for battle. People reeled off the great things the

Universal had already achieved, the first dazzling successes, the unhoped-for dividends, such as no company had ever distributed in its early days. They recalled the excellent idea of the United Steamship Company, so quick to yield magnificent results, its shares already carrying a premium of a hundred francs; the Carmel Silver Mines with its miraculous product, mentioned during Lent at Notre-Dame by a revered preacher, who called it a gift from God to faithful Christians; another company created for the exploitation of immense coalfields, and yet another which was going to carry out periodic felling in the vast forests of Lebanon, and lastly, the establishment of the unshakeably solid Turkish National Bank in Constantinople. Without a single failure, this constantly increasing success that turned everything the bank touched into gold, along with a large number of prosperous companies already providing a sure base for future operations, justified the rapid increase of capital. Then there was the future, opening out in overheated imaginations, a future so full of even greater enterprises that it necessitated the call for the fifty millions, the mere announcement of which was sufficient to wreak havoc in people's brains. So the scope for rumours, from Stock Exchange or drawing-rooms, was limitless, but the next great undertaking, the Oriental Railway Company, stood out from the other projects, and was the subject of every conversation, derided by some and exalted by others. Women especially were passionate about it, generating enthusiastic propaganda in favour of the idea. In boudoirs and at gala dinners, behind potted plants in bloom, at the late tea-hour,* and even in the bedroom, charming creatures could be found catechizing their menfolk: 'Really? You have no Universals? But they're the thing! Hurry up and buy Universals if you want to be loved!' It was the new Crusade they said, the conquest of Asia which the crusaders, Peter the Hermit and Saint Louis,* had been unable to achieve, but which these ladies were now taking under their wing, with their little gold purses. They all claimed to be well informed, speaking in technical terms of the main line which was going to be opened first, running from Broussa to Beirut, via Angora and Aleppo. Later there would be the branch line from Smyrna to Angora, through Erzerum and Sivas, and later still, a line from Damascus to Beirut. And they smiled and winked and whispered that there would perhaps be another, in the distant future, from Beirut to Jerusalem through the ancient coastal cities of Sidon, Saint-Jean-d'Acre, Jaffa, and then—Heavens! Who could say?—There might be a line from Jerusalem to Port Said and Alexandria. Not to mention the fact that Baghdad was not far from Damascus, and if a railway line got that far, then one day would see Persia, India, and China, all acquired for the West. It seemed that with just one word from their pretty lips, the rediscovered treasures of the Caliphs shone once more, as in a wonderful tale from the *Arabian Nights*. The dream jewels and gems rained down into the coffers of the Rue de Londres, while the incense from Carmel gave off the vague and delicate atmosphere of biblical legend, lending a touch of the divine to the eager appetites for profit. Was this not Eden Regained, the Holy Land delivered, and religion triumphant in the very cradle of humanity? And they would stop, refusing to say any more, their eyes shining with what had to be kept hidden—what could not even be whispered. Many of them did not know what it was, but pretended to know. It was the mystery, it was what would perhaps never happen, or what would one day burst upon the world like a thunderbolt: Jerusalem bought back from the Sultan and given to the Pope, with Syria as his kingdom; the Papacy with a budget provided by a Catholic bank, the Treasury of the Holy Sepulchre which would keep it safe from political disturbances, and finally Catholicism rejuvenated, freed from all compromise, finding a new authority and ruling the world from the summit of the mountain on which Christ died.

In the morning, in his luxurious Louis-Quatorze office, Saccard now had to defend his door, when he wanted to work, for there was an assault upon it, a procession like that of a court attending a king's levée, a procession of courtiers, businessmen, supplicants of all sorts, clustering around his omnipotence in a frenzied mixture of adoration and begging. One morning during the first days of July, he was especially merciless, giving orders that nobody should be allowed in. While the antechamber was crammed with people, a crowd which, in spite of the usher, insisted on waiting, hoping against hope, Saccard had shut himself in with two department heads to finish planning the new share-issue. After looking at several suggestions, he had just decided on an arrangement which, thanks to the new issue of a hundred thousand shares, would allow the complete release of the two hundred thousand old shares, on each of which only one hundred and fifty francs had been paid; to reach this end, the share-issue reserved for shareholders only, at the rate of one new share for two old ones, would be priced at eight hundred and fifty francs, to be paid immediately, that is, five hundred francs for the capital, and a premium of three hundred and fifty francs for the proposed release.* But complications arose, for there was still a big hole to be filled, a fact that made Saccard very edgy. The noise of the voices in the antechamber irritated him. This Paris, grovelling at his feet, all this homage that he normally received with a despot's amiable informality, on that day simply filled him with contempt. And when Dejoie, who sometimes acted as usher in the morning, took it upon himself to walk round, and appear at a little door from the passageway, he greeted him with fury.

'What? I told you nobody, nobody, d'you hear?... Here, take my walking-stick, plant it at my door and let them kiss that!'

Quite unmoved, Dejoie ventured to insist.

'I beg your pardon, Monsieur, it's the Countess de Beauvilliers. She begged me, and as I know Monsieur likes to be nice to her...'

'Ah!' cried Saccard in fury. 'She can go to the devil along with all the rest!'

But then he thought better of it, and with a gesture of suppressed anger, said:

'Let her in, since I'm fated not to get any peace!... Through this little side-door, so the whole herd doesn't come in with her.'

Saccard greeted the Countess with the prickliness of a man still rather annoyed. Even the sight of Alice, who accompanied her mother, and her air of quiet seriousness, did not calm him. He had sent the heads of department away, and was thinking only of when he could call them back and get on with his work.

'I beg you, please be quick, Madame, I am dreadfully busy.'

The Countess, always slow to speak, with her air of sadness as of a fallen queen, stopped short in surprise.

'But Monsieur, if I'm disturbing you...'

He had to ask them to be seated, and the girl, the braver one, was the first to sit down with a resolute air, while her mother went on:

'Monsieur, I've come for some advice... I am in the most painful state of indecision, and I feel I shall never be able to make up my mind by myself...'

She reminded him that when the bank was founded, she had taken a hundred shares, which had been doubled at the first increase of capital, and doubled again at the second increase, which now meant four hundred shares on which, including the premiums, she had paid eighty-seven thousand francs. To pay this sum, above and beyond her savings of twenty thousand francs, she had had to borrow seventy thousand francs on her farm, Les Aublets.

'And now', she continued, 'I have a buyer for Les Aublets... so, if there is indeed going to be a new share-issue, I could place our entire fortune in your bank.'

Saccard was calming down now, flattered to see these two poor ladies, the last of a great and ancient race, standing before him, so anxious and trusting. He rapidly told them all about it, with facts and figures.

'Yes, quite right, a new share-issue, I'm just dealing with it... The share-price will be eight hundred and fifty francs, with the premium... Well now, we're saying you have four hundred shares, so you'll be allocated two hundred new ones, for which you'll need to pay one hundred and seventy thousand francs. But all your shares will be released, and you will have six hundred shares totally your own, with nothing further owing.'

They didn't understand, so he had to explain how the premium would release the shares, and they remained rather pale, faced by these big numbers, and discomfited at the thought of the boldness of the risk they would be taking.

'In terms of money,' the mother eventually murmured, 'that would be all right... I am being offered two hundred and forty thousand francs for Les Aublets, which was formerly worth four hundred thousand, so when the money already borrowed is paid back, we would have just enough to make the investment... But oh! what a terrifying thing, to see this fortune moved around like this, and our whole existence put at risk!'

Her hands were trembling, and there was a silence, during which she reflected on the chain of events that had taken first her savings, then the seventy thousand francs she had borrowed, and was now threatening to take her entire farm. Her innate respect for landed property, for ploughed fields, grasslands, and forests, and her repugnance for trafficking in money, that base Jewish activity, unworthy of her race, came back to her, filling her with anguish at this moment of decision, when everything was about to be concluded. Her daughter gazed at her in silence, with pure and ardent eyes.

Saccard gave her an encouraging smile.

'Indeed, it's clear you will need to have confidence in us... but the figures are there. Just examine them and there's no more room for hesitation... Let's say you go ahead, you'll then have six hundred shares, which, when released, will have cost you a total of two hundred and fifty-seven thousand francs. In fact, they are quoted today at an average of thirteen hundred francs, which makes a total for you of seven hundred and eighty thousand francs. You have already more than tripled your money... And that will go on, you'll see how the price will rise after the flotation! I promise you a million before the end of the year.'

'Oh, Mama!' said Alice with a sigh, as if in spite of herself.

A million!—The house in the Rue Saint-Lazare freed of its mortgages, cleansed of the grime of poverty! The household set back on a proper footing, delivered from the nightmare of keeping a carriage but not having enough to eat! The daughter married, with a respectable dowry, able at last to have a husband and children, that joy granted to the lowliest poor woman of the streets. And the son, who was being killed by the climate of Rome, released from all that, able once more to maintain his rank while waiting to serve that grand cause which now made so little use of him. The mother re-established in her high position, able to pay her coachman, not needing to worry about adding an extra dish to her Tuesday dinners, no longer having to condemn herself to fasting for the rest of the week! That million blazed before them; it was salvation, it was their dream.

The Countess, quite won over, turned towards her daughter, to share in the decision.

'Well, what do you think?'

But the daughter said nothing more, slowly closing her eyelids to dim the shining of her eyes.

'Yes, I know,' her mother went on, smiling in her turn, 'I was forgetting that you want me to be absolute mistress in this matter... But I know how courageous you are, and everything you hope for...'

Then, turning to Saccard:

'Ah, Monsieur, people speak so highly of you!... We can't go anywhere without someone telling us some lovely and very touching stories about you. It's not only the Princess d'Orviedo but all my friends, who are full of enthusiasm for your work. Many of them envy me for being one of your first shareholders, and if people listened to the advice of those friends, they'd sell their very beds to buy your shares!'

Pleasantly joking, she added:

'I find them a little mad, yes indeed, a little bit mad! It's no doubt because I'm no longer young enough... My daughter is one of your admirers. She believes in your mission, and campaigns for it in all the salons we visit.'

Saccard, quite charmed, looked at Alice, and at that moment she was so animated, so vibrant with her faith that she seemed to him really pretty, in spite of her sallow complexion and her rather skinny, already withered neck. So he felt himself to be great and good, thinking he had made the happiness of this poor creature, who became pretty at the mere hope of a husband. Then in a low and faraway voice, she said:

'Oh, it's so splendid, that far-off conquest... Yes, it's a new era, with the cross shining forth...'

It was the mystery, it was what remained unspoken, and her voice sank lower still, fading into a gasp of rapture. Saccard, in any case, was silencing her with a friendly gesture, for he would not allow anyone to speak in his presence of the grand affair, the supreme and hidden goal. His gesture indicated that one must always aim towards it, but never speak of it. In the sanctuary, the censers were swinging in the hands of the few initiates.

After a moment of tender silence, the Countess at last stood up.

'Ah well, Monsieur, I am convinced, I shall write to my lawyer to say I accept the offer for Les Aublets... May God forgive me if I do wrong!'

Saccard, also standing now, declared in a voice of deeply felt gravity:

'It is God himself who inspires you, Madame, be assured of it.'

As he was accompanying the ladies to the passageway, to avoid the still-overcrowded antechamber, he met Dejoie, who was hovering about with an embarrassed air.

'What is it? Not another person, I trust?'

'No, no, Monsieur... If I dare ask Monsieur's advice... It's for myself...'

And he manoeuvred so skilfully that Saccard found himself back in his study, while the other remained very deferentially in the doorway.

'For you?... Ah yes, of course you too are a shareholder... Well, my lad, take the new shares which will be reserved for you, even if you have to sell the shirt off your back to buy them. That's the advice I give all my friends.'

'Oh, Monsieur, it's all too much for me, my daughter and I don't aim that high… At the start, I bought eight shares with the four thousand francs of savings my poor wife left us; and I still have just those eight, because—d'you see?—when it came to the other share-issues, in which the capital was doubled twice over, we didn't have the money to take the shares we were allocated… No, no, that's not the point, one must not be greedy!—I just wanted to ask Monsieur, without offence, if Monsieur thinks I should sell.'

'What! That you should sell?'

Then Dejoie, with all sorts of anxious and respectful circumlocutions, explained his situation. At the rate of thirteen hundred francs, his eight shares represented a sum of ten thousand four hundred francs. He was therefore well able to give Nathalie the six thousand francs needed for the cardboard manufacturer. But after seeing the continual rise of the shares, he had acquired an appetite for money, then came the idea, vague at first, then overwhelming, of having his own share in it, to get a little income of six hundred francs, which would allow him to retire. But a capital of twelve thousand francs, added to his daughter's six thousand francs, made the enormous sum of eighteen thousand francs, and he despaired of ever reaching that figure, for he had worked out that to do that, he would have to wait for the rate to reach two thousand three hundred francs.

'You understand, Monsieur, that if it's not going to rise any more, I'd rather sell, because Nathalie's happiness must come first, mustn't it?… On the other hand, if it all goes up again, what a heartbreak it will be if I've sold…'

Saccard exploded.

'Ah! You really are stupid, my lad!… Do you think we're going to stop at thirteen hundred? Am I selling?… You'll have your eighteen thousand francs, I can assure you. And now get going! And get rid of all those people in there; tell them I've gone out.'

When he was alone again, Saccard was able to call back the two department heads and finish his work in peace.

It was decided that an Extraordinary General Meeting should be held in August to vote the new increase in capital. Hamelin, who was to chair it, landed in Marseilles in the last days of July. For two months, his sister, in each of her letters, had been urging him more and more insistently, to come back. In the midst of the bank's emphatic success, more apparent day by day, she had the sense of a lurking danger, an irrational fear she dared not even mention; and she wanted her brother to be there, to take account of things for himself, for she was beginning to doubt her own judgement, fearing she would have no strength against Saccard, would let herself be blinded to such a point as to let down the brother she loved so much. Shouldn't she have confessed her affair to him, the affair that he was very far from suspecting, in his innocence as a man of faith and science, moving through the world like a sleepwalker? This idea was extremely painful for her, and she let herself drift into cowardly compromises; she was arguing with duty, which very clearly commanded her to tell all, now that she knew Saccard and his past, so that her brother might be on his guard. In her hours of strength, she promised herself she would get things sorted out once and for all, and not abandon the unfettered management of such large sums of money to criminal hands in whose grip so many millions had already cracked and crumbled away, bringing ruin to so many people. It was the only possible sound and honest course worthy of her. Then her clarity of mind faded and she weakened and temporized, now finding that the only grounds for complaint were irregularities common—so Saccard affirmed—to all banking houses. Perhaps he was right to tell her with a laugh that the monster that frightened her was success, that resounding Parisian success that strikes like a thunderbolt, and which left her trembling as if from the shock and anguish of a catastrophe. She didn't know where she stood any more, there were times when, full of that infinite affection she still felt for Saccard, she admired him even more, even though she could no longer esteem him. Never would she have believed her heart could be so complicated, she felt herself to be very much a woman, and feared she might lose the power to act. That was why she was so pleased at her brother's return.

It was on the very day of Hamelin's return that Saccard decided to see him in the workroom, where they were certain not to be disturbed, to show him the resolutions that the board would be asked to approve before putting them to the vote in the General Meeting. But by tacit agreement, the brother and sister anticipated the agreed time of the meeting, and alone together, were able to talk freely. Hamelin had come back very cheery, delighted at having successfully arranged the complex railway deal in that Eastern country, so sleepy and idle, so strewn with political, administrative, and financial obstacles. At last success was complete, the first work was about to begin and construction-sites would be opening on all sides as soon as the company had been properly set up in Paris. He showed such enthusiasm, such confidence in the future, that this became a new reason for keeping silent, since it hurt her so much to spoil his delighted joy. However, she did express some doubts, and warned him against the infatuation that was transporting the public. He stopped her and looked her straight in the eye; did she know of anything shady? Why didn't she speak of it? And she didn't speak, unable to articulate anything definite.

Saccard, who had not yet seen Hamelin, threw his arms around him when they met, and kissed him with the exuberance of a man from the Midi. Then, when Hamelin had confirmed the news given in his recent letters, and given him details of the complete success of his long journey, Saccard became effusive.

'Ah, my dear chap, this time we shall be the masters of Paris, the kings of the market!... I too have worked to some purpose; I've had an amazing idea. You shall see.'

Without more ado, he outlined his plan to take the capital from a hundred to a hundred and fifty million, by issuing a hundred thousand new shares, and in this way to release all the shares, the old as well as the new. He was launching the new shares at eight hundred and fifty francs, thus creating, with the premium of three hundred and fifty francs, a reserve which, with the addition of the monies already put aside at each distribution, would reach the figure of twenty-five million; and he needed now only to find an equal sum to obtain the fifty million necessary for the release of the two hundred thousand old shares. And that was where his amazing idea came in; it was to draw up a balance-sheet of the approximate profits of the current year, profits which, in his view, would reach a minimum of thirty-six million. From this he could easily take the twenty-five million he needed. And the Universal would therefore, after 31 December 1867, have a definitive capital of one hundred and fifty million in the form of three hundred thousand fully paid-up shares. The shares would be unified and made payable to bearer to facilitate their free circulation on the market. It was the ultimate triumph, the stroke of genius.

'Yes, genius!' he cried. 'That is not putting it too strongly.'

Somewhat dazed by all this, Hamelin was flicking through the pages of the plan, examining the figures.

'I don't much care for this hastily drawn up balance-sheet,' he said at last. 'These are real dividends you're going to be giving your share-holders, since you're releasing their shares; and it's essential to be certain that all these sums have really been gained: otherwise we could justifiably be accused of issuing fictitious dividends.'

Saccard got angry.

'What! But I am lower than the estimates! Just see whether I haven't been reasonable; won't the Steamship Company and Carmel and the Turkish Bank bring in greater profits than those I've listed? You bring me news of victory from those countries, where everything is going well and prospering, and then you quibble about the certainty of our success!'

Hamelin smiled, and calmed him with a gesture. Yes, yes, he had faith in it. But he liked things to take their regular course.

'Indeed,' said Madame Caroline gently, 'what's the point of hurry-ing? Couldn't we wait until April for this increase in capital?... Or else, since you need twenty-five million more, why not issue the shares at a thousand or twelve hundred francs straight away, which would avoid the need to anticipate the profits of the next balance-sheet?'

Saccard looked at her, stunned for a moment, astonished that she should have thought of that.

'No doubt, at eleven hundred francs instead of eight hundred and fifty, the hundred thousand shares would produce exactly the twenty-five millions.'

'Well then,' she went on, 'that's the solution. You need have no fear that the shareholders will complain. They will be just as willing to give eleven hundred as eight hundred and fifty.'

'Oh yes! They'll give whatever we like, and even fight over who will give most. They're like madmen, they'd tear down the building just to give us their money.'

But suddenly he regained his self-possession, with a violent start of protest.

'But what are you going on about? I don't want to ask them for eleven hundred francs, emphatically not! That would really be too stupid and too simple... Try to understand that in these financial matters, it is vital to excite the imagination. The great idea is to take the money out of people's pockets before it has even got there. They at once imagine that they are not giving it but receiving it as a gift. And then, don't you see the colossal effect this anticipatory balance-sheet will have when it appears in all the newspapers, with its profit

of thirty-six million announced in advance with a great fanfare?...
The Bourse will catch fire, we'll be quoted at over two thousand, and
we're going up and up, and there'll be no stopping us!'

He was standing up, gesticulating, stretching himself up on his
little legs, so that he actually seemed to grow taller, gesturing into the
stars, like the poet of money, undaunted by bankruptcies and ruins.
This was his instinctive system, the urge and impulse of his whole
being, to whip his business affairs ferociously onward, driving them
along feverishly at a double-quick gallop. He had pushed success to
the limit, kindling people's greed with this lightning march of the
Universal: three share-issues in three years, the bank's capital leaping
from twenty-five to fifty, a hundred, then a hundred-and-fifty million,
in a progression that seemed to promise miraculous prosperity. And the
dividends too proceeded in leaps and bounds: nothing in the first year,
then ten francs, then thirty-three francs, then the thirty-six million
bringing the release of all the shares! And all this in the deceitful
overheating of the whole machine, in the midst of fictitious subscriptions of shares, of shares kept by the company to create the impression they had been fully paid-up, all under the impact of speculation
on the Bourse, where every increase in capital created an exaggerated
rise in the share-price.

Hamelin, still absorbed in his scrutiny of Saccard's plan, had not
supported his sister's remarks. He shook his head and returned to
matters of detail.

'No matter! Your anticipatory balance-sheet* is simply not right,
when the profits indicated have not yet been made... I'm not talking
now about our ventures, although they too can be afflicted by cata-
strophic events, like any other human endeavour... But I see here the
Sabatani account, three thousand or so shares, representing more
than two million. You have placed these on the credit side, but they
ought to be on the debit side, since Sabatani is only our man of straw.
Just between ourselves, we can say this, can't we?... And wait a
moment! I can also see the names of several of our employees, and
even some of our directors, all men of straw. Oh, I see what you're
doing, you don't need to tell me. It makes me tremble, to see that
we're keeping such a large number of our own shares. Not only do we
get no cash, but we paralyse ourselves, and we'll end up one day
simply destroying ourselves.'

Madame Caroline looked on approvingly, for he was at last giving voice to all her own fears, uncovering the cause of that vague unease of hers which grew ever greater with the growing success.

'Ah, gambling!' she murmured.

'But we are not gambling!' cried Saccard. 'It's quite allowable for us to support our share-prices, and we'd really be stupid if we didn't see to it that Gundermann and others don't devalue our stock by going for a fall against us. They haven't quite dared to do so yet, but it can happen. That's why I'm glad to have a certain number of our shares in hand, and I warn you, if it becomes necessary I'm even ready to buy some, yes! I'll buy some myself, sooner than let them drop by a centime!'

He had spoken these last words with extraordinary vehemence, as if he were vowing to die rather than suffer defeat. Then, with an effort, he calmed down and began to laugh with a rather forced air of affability.

'Oh look, it's starting up again, all that distrust! I thought we'd had that out once and for all, on these matters. You had agreed to place yourselves in my hands, so let me get on with it! All I want is to make your fortune, a great, great fortune!'

He paused and lowered his voice, as if himself alarmed at the enormity of his desire.

'Shall I tell you what I want? I want to see the rate at three thousand francs.'

He waved his hand as if pointing it out in mid-air, that triumphant rate of three thousand francs, seeing it rising up like a star, and setting the horizon of the Bourse on fire.

'That's mad,' said Madame Caroline.

'Once the rate goes past two thousand francs,' Hamelin declared, 'every new rise will be a danger; and as for me, I warn you I shall sell my shares to avoid having anything to do with such madness.'

But Saccard just began humming a tune. People always say they'll sell, but they don't do it. He would make them rich in spite of themselves. He was smiling once more, in a very tender and slightly mocking way.

'Put your trust in me, it seems to me I've not done too badly for you... Sadowa alone brought you a million.'

It was true, the Hamelins had forgotten that; they had accepted that million, fished out of the murky waters of the Bourse. They remained silent for a moment, turning pale, with that disturbance of the heart felt by people still honest, but who are no longer certain they have done what they ought to have done. Had they themselves become tainted with the leprosy of speculation? Were they too growing corrupt in this feverish atmosphere of money, in which their concerns forced them to live?

'No doubt,' the engineer finally murmured, 'but if I had been there...'

Saccard did not let him finish.

'Oh come on! No need for remorse: it's just money won back from those dirty Jews!'

At this, all three of them laughed. And Madame Caroline, who had sat down, made a gesture of tolerance and resignation. Could one simply allow oneself to be eaten and not eat others? It was just life. One would need excessively sublime virtues, or the temptation-free solitude of the cloister.

'Come, come,' Saccard continued gaily, 'don't seem to be spitting on money: first of all, that's stupid, and anyway it's only the powerless who despise power... It would be illogical to kill yourselves with work to make others rich, without taking out your own legitimate share. Otherwise you might just as well go to bed and sleep!'

He was in control now, and would not let them utter another word.

'You know you will soon be pocketing a pretty sum!... Wait!'

And with the exuberance of a schoolboy, he rushed over to Madame Caroline's table, and picked up a pencil and a sheet of paper, on which he began to scribble figures.

'Wait! I'm making up your account. Oh, I know it already!... At the start you had five hundred shares, doubled once, then doubled again, so now you have two thousand. So after our next share-issue, you'll have three thousand.'

Hamelin tried to interrupt.

'No, no, I know you have enough money to pay for them, with the three hundred thousand francs of your inheritance on the one hand, and your million from Sadowa on the other... Look! Your first two thousand shares cost you four hundred and thirty-five thousand francs, the other thousand will cost you eight hundred and fifty thousand francs, a total of twelve hundred and eighty-five francs... So, you will still have fifteen thousand francs left to live on, not to mention your salaries of thirty thousand francs, which we're going to raise to sixty thousand.'

They both listened in some bewilderment, and in the end became passionately interested in these figures.

'You can see very well that you're quite honest, that you're paying for what you get... but all that is just trivial. This is what I wanted to get at...'

He stood up again, waving his sheet of paper triumphantly.

'At the rate of three thousand, your three thousand shares will give you nine million.'

'What? A rate of three thousand!' they cried, with a gesture of protest against his obstinate persistence in this madness.

'Yes, of course! I forbid you to sell before that. I shall be able to stop you, yes indeed, by force if necessary, by the right that one has to prevent one's friends from doing something stupid... And as for the rate of three thousand, I must have it, and I will have it.'

What response could there be to this terrible man, whose shrill voice, like the crowing of a cock, proclaimed his triumph? They laughed once more, and simply shrugged their shoulders. They declared they were quite unworried, for that fantastic rate would never be reached. Saccard, however, had gone back to the table, where he was making further calculations, this time on his own account. Had he paid, would he pay, for his three thousand shares? That remained very hazy. In fact he must be in possession of an even greater number of shares, but it was difficult to know; for he himself was also one of the company's straw men, and how could one distinguish, in such a heap of shares, which ones were actually his? His pencil went on endlessly producing line after line of figures. Then, in one lightning stroke, he crossed it all out and crumpled up the paper. That and the two million collected from the mire and blood of Sadowa was his share.

'I have an appointment, so I'll leave you now,' he said, picking up his hat, 'but everything's agreed, isn't it? In a week, there'll be the board of directors, then immediately afterwards, the Extraordinary General Meeting, for the vote.'

When Madame Caroline and Hamelin were alone again, tired and alarmed, they looked at each other in silence for a moment.

'What's to be done?' Hamelin said at last, responding to his sister's unspoken thoughts. 'We are in it and we have to stay in it. He's right to say it would be silly of us to refuse this fortune... As for me, I've always considered myself nothing more than a man of science, bringing water to the mill, and I think I have brought it, clear and abundant water, in the shape of excellent business deals, to which the company owes such rapid success. So, since there's nothing I can be reproached for, let's not be discouraged, let's get to work!'

Madame Caroline rose unsteadily from her chair, stammering.

'Oh! All that money... all that money...'

And, choked by an overpowering emotion at the thought of those millions that were going to fall upon them, she laid her head on his shoulder and wept. No doubt it was joy, her happiness at seeing him at last worthily rewarded for his intelligence and his work; but it was also pain, pain for which she could not easily account, a mixture of shame and fear. He made a joke of it, and they once more assumed a cheerful mood, yet a certain unease still lingered, a vague feeling of dissatisfaction with themselves, an unspoken remorse for a shameful complicity.

'Yes, he's right,' Madame Caroline repeated, 'it's the same for everyone. That's life.'

The board of directors met in the new room in the sumptuous building of the Rue de Londres. No longer the damp drawing-room slightly tinged with the green from the next-door garden, but a huge room, lit by four windows overlooking the street, and with a high ceiling and majestic walls, adorned with large paintings and gleaming with gold. The chairman's seat was a real throne, dominating the other chairs which stood in line, superb and grave, as if for a meeting of royal ministers, around an immense table with a cover of red velvet. And on the monumental white-marble fireplace in which, in winter, enormous logs were burned, was a bust of the Pope, a fine and kindly face which seemed to smile mischievously at finding itself there.

Saccard had managed to get his hands on all the members of the board by, for the most part, simply buying them. Thanks to him the Marquis de Bohain, involved in a backhander bordering on a swindle and caught with his fingers in the till, had been able to stifle the scandal by paying back the company he had robbed; so he was now Saccard's humble servant, while continuing to carry his head high, like the flower of the nobility and the most handsome ornament of the board. Huret too, ever since Rougon had sacked him over the theft of the telegram announcing the ceding of the Veneto, had devoted himself entirely to the fortunes of the Universal, representing the bank at the Legislative Assembly and fishing on its behalf in the muddy waters of politics, while keeping the major part of his shameless and shady deals, which one day could land him in Mazas.* And Viscount de Robin-Chagot, vice-chairman of the Board, was receiving a hundred thousand francs of secret bonus for giving his signature without hesitation during Hamelin's long absences; and the banker Kolb was also getting paid for his passive compliance, through being allowed to use the Universal's power overseas, even going so far as to involve the bank in his arbitrage deals; and Sédille the silk-merchant, himself shaken by a terrible settlement day, had managed to borrow a large sum, that he had been unable to pay back. Only Daigremont still retained his absolute independence of Saccard, a fact that sometimes worried the latter, although the amiable fellow remained charming, inviting him to his parties, and he too signed everything without comment, with the easy grace of the sceptical Parisian who finds everything is quite all right, so long as he's making money.

That day, in spite of the exceptional importance of the session, the work of the board was conducted just as speedily as on other days. It had become a matter of habit; all the real work was done in the little meetings on the fifteenth of the month, while the big meetings at the end of the month simply approved the resolutions, with much ceremony. So great now was the indifference of the directors that, as the minutes threatened to be the same banal account of constant approval for every meeting, it had been necessary to invent some scruples and comments for the directors, a wholly imaginary discussion that no one was surprised to hear being read out at the following meeting, and which they all signed with perfect seriousness.

Knowing the good news, the great news, that Hamelin was bringing, Daigremont had rushed forward to shake his hand.

'Ah, my dear Chairman, how happy I am to congratulate you!'

Everyone gathered round eagerly welcoming him, even Saccard himself, as if he had not yet seen him, and when the session began, when Hamelin started reading the report that he was to deliver to the General Meeting, they listened—which they never normally did. The excellent results already achieved, the magnificent promise for the future, the ingenious increasing of the capital, which at the same time released the old shares, everything was greeted with admiring nods of the head. And nobody thought of asking for further details. It was perfect. When Sédille pointed out an error in one of the figures, it was even agreed that his remark be omitted from the minutes, so as not to spoil the beautiful unanimity of the meeting, and in their enthusiasm, they all signed rapidly, one after another, without further comment.

The meeting was already over, people were standing up, laughing and joking, surrounded by the glittering gold adornments of the room. The Marquis de Bohain was describing a hunt at Fontainebleau; while Deputy Huret, who had been to Rome, was telling how he had brought back with him the blessing of the Pope. Kolb had just disappeared, rushing off to an appointment. And the other directors, the minor figures, were receiving quiet instructions from Saccard on the position they were to take at the next meeting.

But Daigremont, irritated by Viscount de Robin-Chagot's exaggerated praise of Hamelin's report, grasped the manager's arm as he went by, and whispered in his ear:

'Not too rapid a rise, eh?'

Saccard stopped dead and looked at him. He remembered how hesitant he had originally been about bringing him into the affair, knowing him to be unreliable in business matters.

'Ah, if you're with me, follow me!' he replied very loudly, so that everyone could hear.

Three days later, the Extraordinary General Meeting was held in the Grand Function Room of the Hotel du Louvre. For such a solemn occasion, the poor, rather bare room in the Rue Blanche had been rejected, for they wanted a festive hall, still warm, as if between an official banquet and a wedding ball. It was necessary, according to the articles of association, to be possessed of at least twenty shares to be admitted, and there were more than twelve hundred shareholders there, representing more than four thousand votes. The entry formalities, presentation of cards, and signing of the register took nearly two hours. A hubbub of happy chatter filled the room, in which one could see all the directors and many of the senior employees of the Universal Bank. Sabatani was there, in the middle of a group, talking about the Orient, his native land, in a caressing and languorous tone, telling wondrous stories, as if over there one had only to bend down to pick up silver, gold and precious stones; and Maugendre, who had decided in June to buy fifty shares in Universal at twelve hundred francs each, convinced that they would rise, was listening to him open-mouthed, delighted at the flair he had shown; Jantrou, meanwhile, who had fallen into a life of utter depravity since becoming rich, was sniggering to himself, his mouth twisted in an ironic sneer, showing the after-effects of the previous night's debauchery. After the appointment of the officers, when Hamelin, as rightful chairman, had opened the meeting, Lavignière, re-elected as auditor and who, after his report, was to be raised to the status of director, fulfilling his dream, was invited to read a report on the company's financial position as it would be on 31 December: this, in order to comply with the statutes, was a way of checking in advance the anticipatory balance-sheet that was to be presented. He recalled the previous balance-sheet, presented at the ordinary meeting in April, that magnificent balance-sheet showing a net profit of eleven-and-a-half million, which, after allowing for the five per cent for shareholders, ten per cent for the directors, and ten per cent for the reserve fund, had still permitted the distribution of a dividend of thirty-three per cent. Next, he demonstrated, with a deluge of figures, that the sum of thirty-six million, given as the rough total of the profits of the current year, far from striking him as exaggerated, was well below the most modest expectations. He did this, no doubt, in good faith, and he must have conscientiously examined the documents submitted for his inspection; but nothing is more illusory, for to study a set of accounts with any thoroughness, it is necessary to create an entirely new set. In any case, the shareholders were not listening. A few devotees, Maugendre and some other minor figures who represented only one or two votes, drank in each and every figure, amid the persistent rumble of conversation. Auditors' reports were not of the slightest importance. A reverential silence fell only when Hamelin, at last, rose to his feet. Applause broke out even before he opened his mouth, in homage to his zeal, and the obstinate, courageous genius of this man who had travelled so far to seek out barrels of gold to empty over Paris. From this point on, there was nothing but ever-growing success, almost glory. There was applause at a reminder of the previous year's balance-sheet, on which Lavignière had been unable to make himself heard. But the estimates for the next balance-sheet aroused special delight: millions for the United Steamships, millions for the Carmel Silver Mines, millions for the Turkish National Bank; the list seemed endless, the thirty-six millions fell into place easily and naturally, and poured down, thundering like a waterfall. Then the horizon opened out further on to future operations. The Oriental Railway Company made its appearance: first, the central main line on which work was about to begin, then the branches, the whole network of modern industry cast over Asia, the triumphant return of humanity to its cradle, the resurrection of a world; while in the dim distance, between the sentences, loomed the matter that remained unspoken, the mystery, the crowning of the edifice, which would astonish the peoples of the world. And there was a totally unanimous response when Hamelin, in conclusion, began to outline the resolutions he was going to submit to the vote of the meeting: the raising of the capital, the issuing of a hundred thousand new shares at eight hundred and fifty francs, and the release of the old shares, thanks to the premium on the new shares, and the profits of the next balance-sheet, on which they could draw in advance. A storm of bravos greeted this brilliant idea. Above the heads of the audience, the fat hands of Maugendre could be seen, clapping with all their might. In the front rows, the directors and the bank's staff were making a huge uproar, led by Sabatani, who was standing up and shouting 'Bravo! Bravo!' as if at the theatre. All the resolutions were enthusiastically accepted.

However, Saccard had organized a little incident, which now occurred. Aware that he was being accused of gambling, he wished to remove even the slightest suspicions of any distrustful shareholders who might be there in the hall.

Jantrou, primed by Saccard, rose to his feet. And in his thick voice:

'Mr Chairman, I believe I speak for many of the shareholders when I ask whether it is firmly established that the bank holds none of its own shares.'

Hamelin, who had not been forewarned, was disconcerted for a moment. He turned instinctively to Saccard, who until then had stayed out of sight in his seat, but he now rose, stretching himself up to increase his height, and replied in his strident voice:

'Not one, Mr Chairman!'

Bravos, for no obvious reason, broke out again at this response. If he was fundamentally lying, it was nevertheless true that the Bank did not hold a single share in its own name, since Sabatani and others were covering for it. And that was all, the applause went on, and the meeting broke up with much gaiety and noise.

In the days that followed, the report of the meeting in the newspapers produced a huge effect on the Bourse, and on the whole of Paris. Jantrou had kept a last surge of advertisements for this moment, the most deafening fanfare blown for some time on the trumpets of publicity; and there was even a joke going around to the effect that he had had the words 'Buy Universals' tattooed on the most secret and delicate parts of good-hearted ladies, launching them too into circulation. Besides, he had just, at last, made his great coup, the buying of *La Cote financière*, that old, respectable paper with a twelve-year history of impeccable honesty. It had been expensive, but its serious readers, the nervous bourgeois, and the prudent holders of large fortunes, all the self-respecting world of money, were won over. In a fortnight, the rate on the Bourse had risen to fifteen hundred; and in the last week of August, it rose by successive leaps to two thousand. The general infatuation had grown even stronger, and it got worse with every hour, in an epidemic of speculation fever. People were buying and buying, even the most sensible, in the conviction that the rate would continue to rise, would go on rising indefinitely. It was the opening up of the mysterious caves of the *Arabian Nights*, and the immeasurable wealth of the Caliphs was being delivered to the greed of Paris. All the dreams, whispered for months, were now, it seemed, being realized for an enchanted public: the cradle of humanity reoccupied, the ancient historical cities of the coast, resuscitated from their sand; Damascus, Baghdad, then India and China would be exploited by the invading troop of French engineers. That conquest of the East that Napoleon had failed to achieve with the sword would be accomplished by a financial company with an army of pickaxes and wheelbarrows. Asia was being conquered by force of millions, for a return of billions. The women's crusade was especially triumphant, in little, intimate five-o'clock meetings, and grand midnight receptions, whether at table or in the boudoir. They had foreseen it all: Constantinople was taken, soon they would have Broussa, Angora, and Aleppo, and later on, Smyrna, Trebizond, all the cities besieged by the Universal, until in the end they would have the last one, the sacred city, the one they did not name, and which seemed like the Eucharistic promise of that far-off expedition. Fathers, husbands and lovers, bullied by the passionate ardour of the women, now only went to give orders to their brokers with the repeated cry of 'It's the will of God.'* Then there was the frightening horde of the humble, the tramping crowds that follow great armies, as the passion moved down from drawing-room to kitchen, from bourgeois to workman and peasant, and hurled into this mad gallop of millions, poor subscribers with only one, two, three, four, or ten shares, concierges on the point of retiring, old spinster ladies living with their cat, provincial pensioners on a budget of ten sous a day, country priests impoverished by their almsgiving—the whole gaunt and hungry mass of people with tiny incomes, that a catastrophe on the Bourse carries off like an epidemic, and at one stroke lays in a communal paupers' grave.

And this exaltation of the Universal shares, this ascension, carrying them up as if on a divine wind, seemed to harmonize with the louder and louder music from the Tuileries and the Champ-de-Mars, and the continual festivities with which the Exhibition was driving Paris mad. The flags flapped more noisily in the heavy air of the warmer days, and there was no evening when the blazing city did not sparkle under the stars like some colossal palace, in the depths of which, debauchery went on until dawn. Joy had spread from house to house, the streets were an intoxication, a cloud of animal vapours, cooking-smells from the feastings, the sweat of couplings, all rolling away to the horizon, carrying over the rooftops the nights of Sodom, Babylon, and Nineveh.* Ever since May, emperors and kings had been coming on pilgrimage from the four corners of the earth in endless processions, nearly a hundred sovereigns, princes, and princesses. Paris was filled to the brim with Majesties and Highnesses; it had welcomed the Emperor of Russia and the Emperor of Austria, the Sultan and the Viceroy of Egypt, and had thrown itself under the wheels of the carriages just to see close-up the King of Prussia, followed by Count von Bismarck like a faithful hound. Jubilant salvos were continually thundering through the Invalides,* while the crowds, crammed into the Exhibition, made a great popular success of Krupp's huge and sombre cannon that Germany had put on show.* Almost every week the Opéra lit up its chandeliers for some official gala. In the smaller theatres and in the restaurants, people could hardly breathe, and the pavements were not wide enough now for the overflowing torrent of prostitution. Napoleon III decided to distribute in person the awards for the sixty thousand exhibitors, in a ceremony that excelled all others in its magnificence, like a glorious halo glowing on the brow of Paris, the resplendence of the reign, in which the Emperor appeared, in a fairy-tale lie, as master of Europe, speaking with calmness and strength, and promising peace. That same day, news had come to the Tuileries of the appalling catastrophe of Mexico,* the execution of Maximilian, French blood spilt and French money spent, all for nothing; and the news was concealed in order not to cast a blight on the festivities. It was a first death-knell on the evening of this splendid day, still dazzling in the sun.

Then, in the midst of all this glory, it seemed as if the star of Saccard was also rising to its greatest brilliance. At last he had achieved what he had sought for so many years, he had fortune as his slave, a thing of his own to dispose of as he would, to keep under lock and key, a living reality! So many times his coffers had been full of lies, so many millions had flowed through them, leaking out through all sorts of unseen holes! No, this was no longer the deceptive façade of wealth, this was the genuine royalty of gold, solid and enthroned on sacks full of gold; and he had this royalty of his, not thanks to the economies of a long line of bankers, like a Gundermann; he flattered himself proudly that he had conquered it for himself, like a soldier of fortune who seizes a kingdom at one stroke. In the time of the land-deals in the Europe district* of Paris, he had often risen very high, but never had he felt Paris so thoroughly conquered, so humble at his feet. And he recalled that day when, eating at Champeaux's, ruined once again, and no longer believing in his star, he had cast hungry eyes upon the Bourse, suddenly in a fever to start everything all over again, to conquer again, in a fury of revenge. So, now he was once again the master, what an appetite he had for enjoyment! First, as soon as he felt all-powerful, he dismissed Huret, and ordered Jantrou to launch an article against Rougon, in which the minister would find himself unambiguously accused, in the name of the Catholics, of playing a double game on the Roman question.* This was a definitive declaration of war between the brothers. Ever since the September Convention of 1864,* and especially after Sadowa, the clerical party had decided to show intense anxiety over the position of the Pope; and from now on *L'Espérance*, resuming its former Ultramontane political stance, violently attacked the liberalization of the Empire, begun with the decrees of 19 January. One of Saccard's comments went around the Chamber: he had said that despite his profound affection for the Emperor, he would resign himself to Henri V,* rather than allow the revolutionary spirit to lead France into catastrophe. Then, his victories making him ever more audacious, he no longer concealed his plan of attacking the big Jewish banks in the person of Gundermann, whose billion he meant to pound and batter until a final assault and capture. The Universal had grown so miraculously that supported as it was by the whole of Christendom, why should it not become, in a few more years, the undisputed mistress of the Bourse? And with a warlike swagger Saccard presented himself as a rival, as a neighbouring king of equal power; while Gundermann phlegmatically went on watching and waiting, with not so much as an ironic smile, seeming simply interested in the continual rise of the shares, as a man whose entire strength lies in patience and logic.

It was his passion that took Saccard so high, and his passion that would cast him down. In order to satisfy his appetites, he would like to have discovered a sixth sense to indulge. Madame Caroline had reached the point of being able to go on smiling, even when her heart was bleeding, and she remained a friend, who listened to him with a sort of wifely deference. Baroness Sandorff, whose bruised eyelids and red lips were so deceptive, was beginning to lose her charm for him, with her icy coldness even in the midst of his perverse experiments. And besides, he had himself never known any grand passion, he was too busy, in his world of money, using his nerves in other ways, and paying for love by the month. So when, on the heap of his new millions, he thought of women at all, he thought only of buying himself an expensive one, to show her off to the whole of Paris, just as he might have bought himself, simply out of vanity, a very large diamond pin for his cravat. Then, wouldn't it be an excellent bit of publicity? When a man can pay a lot for a woman, doesn't that mean he must have a considerable fortune? His choice at once fell on Madame de Jeumont, at whose house he had dined two or three times with Maxime. She was still very beautiful at thirty-six, with a regular, grave and Junoesque beauty, and she had a great reputation due to the fact that the Emperor, for one night with her, had paid a hundred thousand francs, not to mention a decoration for her husband, a man of propriety who had no other role in life than to be his wife's spouse. The two lived a life of ease and were received everywhere, in the ministries and at court, keeping themselves afloat with a few rare and select deals, restricting themselves to no more than three or four nights a year. Everyone knew how hideously expensive it was and how extremely distinguished the clientele. Saccard, who was particularly excited by the thought of having a taste of the Emperor's morsel, bid as high as two hundred thousand francs, since the husband had at first pulled a face at this shady former financier, finding him too slight a personage and of compromising immorality.

It was around this time that little Madame Conin flatly refused to take her pleasure with Saccard. He often went to the stationery shop in the Rue Feydeau, always needing to buy order-books and very attracted by this adorable blonde, all pink and plump, with her pale, silky hair, so fluffy, a little curly lamb, graceful, beguiling, and always cheerful.

'No, I don't want to. Never with you!'

When once she had said 'never', that was it, nothing ever made her change her mind over a refusal.

'But why? I saw you with someone else coming out of the house in the Passage des Panoramas...'

She blushed, but went on looking him straight in the eye. That house, kept by an old lady who was a friend of hers, was indeed the place she used for her rendezvous, when some whim made her give in to a gentleman from the Bourse, at those hours when her good soul of a husband was pasting up his registers, and she was out and about in Paris, always on stationery business.

'You know perfectly well, that young man Gustave Sédille is your lover.'

With a pretty gesture, she protested. No, no, she had no lover. No man could boast of having had her more than once. What sort of person did he think she was? Once, yes, from time to time, for pleasure, without its being of the slightest significance! And they all remained her friends, very grateful, and very discreet.

'Is it because I'm no longer young?'

But with a new gesture, and still with a laugh, she seemed to say that for her, being young was of no importance at all! She had yielded to men less young than he, less good-looking too, often indeed to some wretched poor devils.

'Why then? Just tell me why!'

'My word, it's simply... that I don't fancy you. With you, never!'

She was still just as amiable, and sorry to have to refuse.

'Come on,' he went on, brutally, 'it can be as much as you want... do you want a thousand, two thousand francs, for just one time?'

Each time he raised his offer, she shook her head gently.

'Do you want... Come now, do you want ten thousand? Do you want twenty thousand?'

Gently, she interrupted him, placing her little hand on his.

'Not ten, not fifty, not a hundred thousand! You could go on and

on like that, but it would still be no, always no... You can see I don't
wear any jewels. Oh, I've been offered them, I've been offered lots of
things, money, all sorts of things! But I don't want anything, isn't it
enough in itself, when it gives pleasure?... But just understand that
my husband loves me with all his heart, and I too am very fond of
him. He's a very decent man, my husband. So, I'm certainly not
going to kill him by causing him pain... What do you expect me to do
with your money, since I can't give it to my husband? We are not badly
off, we shall retire one day with a tidy sum; and if those gentlemen are
all so well disposed as to continue to buy their supplies from us, that
I gladly accept... Oh, I'm not pretending to be more disinterested
than I really am. If I were single I'd think about it. But one more thing,
you can't imagine that my husband would take your hundred thousand
francs after I had slept with you... No! No! Not for a million!'

And she dug in her heels. Saccard, exasperated by this unexpected
resistance, went on badgering her for nearly a month. She bowled
him over, with her laughing face and her big eyes full of tenderness
and compassion. What! So money could not buy everything! This
woman others had enjoyed for nothing, and he could not have her,
even at a crazy price! She said no, and she meant it. In all his triumph,
he suffered cruelly over this, as if it cast a doubt over his power, a
secret disillusion about the power of money, which until then he had
thought absolute and sovereign.

But one evening his vanity experienced the most intense enjoyment. It was the high point of his existence. There was a ball at the
Ministry of Foreign Affairs, and he had chosen this event, celebrating
the Exhibition, to make known to the public his good fortune of one
night spent with Madame de Jeumont; for it was always agreed, in
the deals of this beautiful person, that the buyer would have the right,
just once, to exhibit his good luck in such a way that the affair could
have all the publicity desired. So towards midnight, in the rooms
where bare shoulders were crushed among the men's black evening-
jackets, under the blazing light of the chandeliers, Saccard made his
entrance with Madame de Jeumont on his arm, and her husband following. When they appeared, groups broke up to make way for this
two hundred thousand-franc whim on display, this scandal of uncon-
trolled appetite and lunatic extravagance. There were smiles and
whispers, amusement, and no indignation, in the intoxicating scent
of the corsages and the distant lulling of the orchestra. But at the end

of one of the rooms, a quite different group was gathered inquisitively around a colossus, dressed in the dazzling and superb white uniform of a cuirassier.* It was Count von Bismarck, his tall figure towering above the heads of all, laughing heartily, with his big eyes, prominent nose, and powerful jaw, adorned by the moustaches of a barbarian conqueror. After Sadowa, he had given Germany to Prussia; the treaties of alliance* against France, denied for so long, had been signed months before, and the war which had almost broken out in May over Luxembourg* was now inevitable. When the triumphant Saccard went through the room, with Madame de Jeumont on his arm, and her husband following, Count von Bismarck stopped laughing for a moment to watch them passing, with the curiosity and ironic amusement of a kindly giant.

CHAPTER IX

MADAME CAROLINE found herself alone once more. Hamelin had stayed in Paris until the beginning of November for the formalities required for the definitive constitution of the company, with a capital of one hundred and fifty millions; it was he, too, who went, at Saccard's request, to make the legal declarations stating that all the shares had been subscribed and the capital paid, which was not true. Then he left for Rome where he was to spend two months, having some important matters to study there, matters he kept to himself—doubtless his great dream of the Pope in Jerusalem, as well as another, more substantial and practical project, the transformation of the Universal into a Catholic Bank supported by the interests of the whole of Christendom, a simply enormous machine intended to crush the Jewish banks and sweep them out of the universe; from there he meant to turn back to the Orient again, to deal with the work on the railway from Broussa to Beirut. He went away happy about the rapid success of the bank, convinced of its unshakeable solidity and with only a vague anxiety about its excessive success. So on the eve of his departure, in conversation with his sister, he firmly recommended just one thing: that she should resist the general infatuation and sell their shares if the price went beyond two thousand two hundred francs, since he intended to make a personal protest against the continual rise, which he judged to be foolish and dangerous.

Once she was on her own, Madame Caroline felt even more troubled by the hothouse atmosphere in which she was living. Towards the first week of November, the price of two thousand two hundred was reached, and all around her there was rapture, with cries of thankfulness and unlimited hope. Dejoie was brimming over with gratitude; the Beauvilliers ladies now treated her as an equal, as a friend of the god who was going to restore their ancient house. A concert of benedictions arose from the happy crowd of investors, great and small alike, daughters with dowries at last, the poor suddenly rich, their retirement secure, and the rich burning with the insatiable joy of being even richer. With the Exhibition over and Paris intoxicated with pleasure and power, it was a unique moment, a moment of belief in happiness, a conviction of endless good luck. All the stocks and shares had risen, even the weakest found credulous takers, and the market was flooded with a plethora of highly dubious companies, choking it almost to the point of apoplexy, while underneath lay a resounding emptiness, the real exhaustion of a reign that had greatly enjoyed itself and spent billions on public works, fattening in the process huge financial houses, whose gaping coffers were splitting open on all sides. In this giddy whirl the first sign of any cracking meant disaster. And it was doubtless an anxious foreboding of this sort that made Madame Caroline so alarmed at each new leap in the price of Universals. No bad rumours were going round, only a slight ripple of movement from the astonished and daunted short-sellers. And yet she was definitely uneasy, something seemed already to be undermining the whole edifice; but what? Nothing showed up clearly, and she was obliged to wait, in the dazzle of the ever-growing triumph, in spite of those minor rumbles of disturbance that precede catastrophes.

Besides, Madame Caroline now had another worry. At the Work Foundation they were at last satisfied with Victor, who had become silent and sly; and if she had not already told Saccard of the whole affair it was because of an odd feeling of embarrassment, that made her put off telling him from day to day, suffering over the shame he would feel. On the other hand, Maxime, to whom, at around this time, she returned the two thousand francs out of her own pocket, was greatly amused by the fact that Busch and La Méchain were still demanding their four thousand: these people were robbing her, he said, and his father would be furious. After that she turned a deaf ear to the repeated demands of Busch, who was insisting on being paid the full amount of the promised sum. After innumerable vain efforts he at last grew angry, especially since his old idea of blackmailing Saccard had come back to him, given Saccard's new situation, that elevated situation in which Busch thought the fear of scandal placed him at his mercy. So one day, exasperated at getting nothing out of such a promising affair, he decided to contact Saccard directly, and wrote asking him to drop into his office to take a look at some old papers found in a house on the Rue de la Harpe. He mentioned the number of the house, and made such clear reference to the events of the past that Saccard, gripped by anxiety, could not fail to obey the summons. But in fact the letter was delivered to the Rue Saint-Lazare and fell into the hands of Madame Caroline, who recognized the writing.

Trembling, she briefly wondered whether to run straight away to see Busch and persuade him to give up. Then she told herself that he was perhaps writing on some other matter entirely, and in any case this was one way to get it over with, and she was even glad, perturbed as she was, that someone else should have to tell the story. But in the evening, when Saccard came home and opened the letter in her presence, she saw him simply take on a serious expression and thought it must be some financial problem. However, Saccard had in fact experienced a considerable shock and a tightening of the throat at the thought of falling into such filthy hands, sensing some vile machination. He calmly put the letter in his pocket and decided he would go to the suggested meeting.

Some days went by, it was the second fortnight in November, and every morning Saccard put off the visit, dazed by the torrent of events carrying him along. The rate of two thousand three hundred francs had just been passed and he was delighted, but still felt that at the Bourse some resistance was forming and growing, as the mad rise continued; clearly some short-sellers were taking up a position, engaging in the battle, timidly thus far, in mere preliminary skirmishes. On two occasions he had felt obliged to give orders to buy, using frontmen, so that the steady rise of the market rates would not be interrupted. The practice of the bank buying its own shares, gambling on them and thus devouring itself, was getting under way.

One evening, stirred up by his passion, Saccard could not help talking to Madame Caroline about it.

'I really think things are hotting up. We are proving too strong, getting in their way too much... I can scent Gundermann, this is his strategy: he'll keep on selling at regular intervals, so much today, so much tomorrow, gradually increasing the amount until he makes an impact on us...'

She interrupted him in her grave voice:

'If he's holding Universals, he's quite right to sell.'

'What? He's quite right to sell?'

'Yes indeed. My brother told you, a market price over two thousand is absolutely crazy.'

At this he looked at her and exploded, quite beside himself:

'Well, sell then, just dare to sell your own shares!... Yes, play against me, since you want me to be defeated.'

She reddened slightly, for just the day before she had indeed sold a thousand of her shares in obedience to her brother's orders, and with a certain feeling of relief herself, as if this sale were an act of tardy honesty. Since he did not question her directly she did not admit what she had done, and was all the more embarrassed when he added:

'In fact I'm sure there were some defections yesterday. A whole parcel of shares came on to the market, and the price would surely have faltered if I hadn't intervened. That's not how Gundermann operates. His methods are slower, but more devastating in the long run... Ah! My dear, I am quite confident, but I can't help trembling a little, for defending one's life is nothing, the worst thing is defending one's money and the money of others.'

Indeed, from that moment on Saccard was no longer his own man. He belonged to the millions he was making, still triumphant but always on the verge of being beaten. He no longer had time to go and see Baroness Sandorff in the little apartment on the Rue Caumartin. The truth was that she had wearied him, with the deception of her ardent eyes, and that coldness which even his most perverse endeavours had failed to overcome. Besides, a misadventure had befallen him, the same that he had inflicted on Delcambre: one evening, thanks this time to the stupidity of a chambermaid, he had entered just at the moment when the Baroness lay in the arms of Sabatani. In the stormy discussion that followed, he calmed down only after a total confession, in which she admitted to mere curiosity, culpable of course but so understandable. That Sabatani, all the women talked about him as if he were such a phenomenon, they whispered about this enormous thing of his, and she had not been able to resist the desire to see for herself. And Saccard forgave her when, in answer to a brutal question from him, she had replied—My word! It wasn't that astonishing after all. He now rarely saw her more than once a week, not because he felt any rancour but simply because he was finding her boring.

Baroness Sandorff, sensing that he was breaking away from her, returned to her former doubts and uncertainties. Ever since she had been sharing his secrets in their hours of intimacy, she had been gambling almost on certainties and winning a great deal, sharing in his good luck. Now she could see he was no longer willing to answer her questions, and she even feared he might lie to her; and whether it was that her luck had changed, or whether he had indeed deliberately sent her off on a false track, it happened that she lost one day, while following his advice. Her confidence was badly shaken. If he could mislead her like that, who was now going to be her guide? And the worst of it was that the signs of hostility to the Universal at the Bourse, so slight at first, were now growing day by day. As yet it was only rumours, nothing specific was being said and no actual fact was damaging the soundness of the bank. But it was being suggested that there must be something wrong, that there was a worm in the fruit. None of this, however, prevented the increasingly amazing rise of the stock.

After an unsuccessful deal in Italians, the Baroness grew decidedly anxious, and decided to visit the offices of *L'Espérance* to try to get Jantrou to talk.

'Come on, what's going on? You of all people must know... Universals have just gone up again by twenty francs, yet there was a rumour—no one could tell me exactly what, but certainly something not good.'

But Jantrou was equally puzzled. Placed as he was at the very source of rumours, starting them himself when necessary, he jokingly compared himself to a clockmaker living in the midst of hundreds of clocks, but never knowing the right time. Thanks to his advertising agency he was in everybody's confidence, but had no single, solid opinion he could rely on, for the various pieces of information he received were so contradictory they cancelled each other out.

'I know nothing, nothing at all.'

'Oh, you just won't tell me.'

'No, on my word of honour, I know nothing! In fact I was thinking of coming to see you to ask you about it! So Saccard isn't being nice to you any more?'

She made a gesture which confirmed what he had suspected: an end to an affair of which they had both grown weary, the sulking woman and the cooled-off lover no longer talking to each other. For a moment he regretted not having played the role of the well-informed man in order to have her at last, as a treat for himself as he put it, this little Ladricourt, whose father had so enjoyed kicking him. But he felt that his time was not yet come, and he went on looking at her and thinking aloud.

'Yes, it's annoying, I was counting on you... Because, don't you think? If there's going to be some disaster, we need to know in good time to be able to cope with it... Oh, I don't think it's urgent, things are still very solid. But, one sees such odd things...'

Even as he gazed at her, a plan was taking shape in his head.

'Look,' he suddenly went on, 'since Saccard is leaving you, you should get friendly with Gundermann.'

She was startled for a moment.

Then: 'Why Gundermann?... I know him a little, I've met him at the Roivilles and at the Kellers.'

'All the better if you know him already... Go and see him on some pretext, chat with him, try to become his girlfriend... Just imagine that—be the girlfriend of Gundermann and rule the world!'

He sniggered at the licentious images he conjured up with a gesture, for the Jew was well known for his coldness, and nothing could be more complicated or more difficult than trying to seduce him. The Baroness, taking his meaning, smiled silently without showing any annoyance.

'But', she repeated, 'why Gundermann?'

Jantrou then explained that Gundermann must certainly be directing the group of short-sellers who were beginning to manoeuvre against the Universal. That he knew; he had proof. Since Saccard was not being helpful, didn't simple prudence suggest making friends with his adversary, without, however, actually breaking with him? With a foot in each camp one could be sure of being on the side of the victor on the day of battle. He proposed this act of treachery in a kindly way, simply as a man offering good advice. If he had a woman working for him, he would sleep better.

'Eh? What do you say? Let's work together... We'll keep each other informed, and share everything we get to know.'

As he then took hold of her hand, she drew it away with an instinctive movement, misreading his intentions.

'No, no, that's not what I meant, for we shall now be comrades... Later you'll be wanting to reward me.'

With a laugh, she now abandoned her hand to him and he kissed it. She had already lost her contempt for him, forgetting the lackey he had been, and no longer seeing on him the marks of the vile debauchery into which he had sunk, with his ravaged face, his handsome beard reeking of absinthe, his new frock-coat covered with stains, and his shiny hat scratched by the plaster of some foul staircase.*

The Baroness went to see Gundermann the very next day. Ever since Universal shares had reached two thousand francs, he had indeed been conducting a short-selling campaign, though with the

utmost discretion, never going to the Bourse, not even having an official
agent there. His reasoning was that a share is worth, first of all, its
issue value, then the interest it can bring, which depends on the prosperity of the company and the success of its undertakings. So there is
a maximum value that it should not reasonably go beyond, and if it
does go beyond that, because of public infatuation, then the rise is
artificial and the wise course is to bet on a fall, with the certainty that
it will happen. Despite his conviction, and his absolute faith in logic,
he was still surprised by Saccard's rapid achievements and his suddenly
increased power, which was beginning to alarm the big Jewish banks.
This dangerous rival had to be cut down as soon as possible, not only
to recoup the eight million lost after Sadowa, but above all, to avoid
having to share the sovereignty of the market with this terrible adventurer, whose reckless actions seemed to be successful against all good
sense, as if by miracle. And Gundermann, full of contempt for passion,
exaggerated even further his phlegmatic attitude as a mathematical
gambler, with the cold obstinacy of a numbers man, still selling in spite
of the continuing rise, and losing ever greater sums at each settlement,
but always with the serenity of a wise man simply putting his money
in the savings bank.

When the Baroness was at last able to get in to see him, in the midst
of all the turbulence of the clerks and jobbers, the showers of papers
to sign and telegrams to read, she found the banker suffering from a
horrible cold, which was tearing at his throat. However, he had been
there since six o'clock that morning, coughing and spluttering, utterly
exhausted but still standing firm. That day, on the eve of a foreign
loan, the huge room was invaded by a flood of visitors even more
impatient than usual, who were being very hastily received by two of
his sons and one of his sons-in-law. Meanwhile, on the floor near the
narrow table he had kept for himself, well back in the embrasure of a
window, three of his grandchildren, two girls and a boy, were fighting
with shrill cries over a doll whose one arm and one leg lay beside
them, already torn off.

The Baroness at once announced her pretext:

'Monsieur, I have taken it upon myself to see you personally with
my request... It's a lottery for charity...'*

He didn't let her go on, for he was very charitable and always
bought two tickets, especially when ladies he had met in society took
the trouble to bring them to him. But he had to ask her to wait a

moment, as a clerk had brought him the papers of some deal or other. Enormous numbers were rapidly exchanged.

'Fifty-two million, you were saying? And the credit was how much?'

'Sixty million, Sir.'

'Ah well, take it up to seventy-five million.'

He was just getting back to the Baroness, when a word he overheard in a conversation his son-in-law was having with a jobber made him rush over to him.

'But not at all! At the rate of five hundred and eighty-seven fifty, that makes ten sous less per share.'

'Oh, Monsieur,' said the jobber, humbly, 'it would only make forty-three francs less.'

'What! Forty-three francs! But that's enormous! Do you think I steal money? Everyone should get what's due. That's all I know!'

At last, to be able to talk in peace, he decided to take the Baroness into the dining-room, where the table was already laid. He was not fooled by the pretext of the charity lottery, for he knew of her affair, thanks to a whole police-force of obsequious informers, and he easily guessed that she had come on some serious matter. So he came straight to the point.

'Come now; tell me what you have to say to me.'

She affected surprise. She had nothing to say, she only wanted to thank him for his kindness.

'So you haven't been given some message for me?'

And he seemed disappointed, as if he had thought for a moment that she had come on a secret mission from Saccard, about some scheme or other from that madman.

Now that they were alone, she looked at him with a smile and that falsely ardent air of hers, by which men were so futilely excited.

'No, no, I have nothing to say to you, and since you are so kind, I might rather perhaps have something to ask of you.'

She leant over towards him, brushing against his knee with her delicate gloved hands. She told him about herself, spoke of her deplorable marriage to a foreigner who had never understood either her nature or her needs. And she explained how she had taken to gambling in order to maintain her position in society. And finally she told of her solitude, and her need for advice and guidance on the frightening terrain of the Bourse, where any false step can cost one dear.

'But', he interrupted, 'I thought you already had someone.'

'Oh, someone,' she murmured with a gesture of deep disdain. 'No, no, there's no one, I have no one… it's your advice I'd like to have, you the master, the god. And really it wouldn't cost you much just to be my friend and say a word to me, just a word from time to time. If you only knew how happy you'd make me, and how grateful I'd be—oh! with my whole being.'

She drew even closer, wrapping him in her warm breath, and the fine and powerful scent her whole body exhaled. But he remained very calm, not even drawing back, his flesh being quite dead, without a twinge of excitement to suppress. While she was speaking, he, whose digestion was also destroyed, and who lived on a milk diet, was taking some grapes, one by one, out of a fruit-bowl on the table and eating them mechanically, the only debauch he sometimes allowed himself, in his most sensual moments, knowing he would pay for it with days of suffering.

He gave the sardonic smile of a man who knows he is invincible, when the Baroness, as if forgetfully, in the ardour of her plea, at last laid on his knee her little seductive hand with its predatory fingers, supple as a nest of snakes. Smiling, he took that hand and removed it, nodding a thank-you as if refusing a useless gift. And without wasting any more time he went straight to the point:

'Look, you are very charming. And I'd like to be helpful to you… So, my beautiful friend, on the day you bring me a piece of good advice, I promise to do the same for you. Come and tell me what's going on, and I'll tell you what I'm going to do… That's a bargain, right?'

He had got up, and she had to go back with him into the big room. She had perfectly well understood the bargain he was offering: espionage and treason. But she chose not to reply, and took it upon herself to talk once more about her charity lottery; while he, with a mocking nodding of his head, seemed to add that he didn't really need any help, for the logical and inevitable outcome would happen anyway, even if perhaps a little later. And when at last she left, he was already caught up again in other matters, in the extraordinary tumult of this great money market, amid the procession of market people, the rushing about of the clerks, and the playing of the grandchildren, who had just torn the doll's head off, with shouts of triumph. Gundermann sat down at his narrow table and, absorbed in the contemplation of a sudden new idea, became deaf to everything.

Baroness Sandorff twice went back to the offices of *L'Ésperance* to give Jantrou an account of her actions, but he was not there. At last Dejoie let her in one day, when his daughter Nathalie was chatting with Madame Jordan on a bench in the corridor. It had been raining torrents since the day before; and in this damp, grey weather the mezzanine of the old building, deep in the dark well of the courtyard, seemed dreadfully melancholy. The gas was lit in the murky twilight. Marcelle, waiting for Jordan, who was out hunting for money to pay a new instalment to Busch, was listening with a melancholy air to Nathalie, who was chattering away like a conceited magpie, with her harsh voice and the angular gestures of a girl grown up too fast in Paris.

'You understand, Madame, Papa doesn't want to sell. A certain person is urging him to sell, trying to frighten him into it. I shan't name the person, for it's hardly her role to go around frightening people... Now it's I who am stopping Papa from selling... Sell? Not likely, when it's still going up! You'd have to be really stupid, wouldn't you?'

Marcelle simply answered: 'No doubt.'

'The shares, you know, are at two thousand five hundred,' Nathalie went on. 'I keep the accounts, for Papa can hardly write... So, with our eight shares, that already makes twenty thousand francs. Eh? Isn't that nice!... At first, Papa wanted to stop at eighteen thousand, because that was the sum he wanted: six thousand francs for my dowry and twelve thousand for him, a little income of six hundred francs that he would really have earned, after all this excitement... But say, isn't it lucky he didn't sell? For now there are two thousand francs more!... So now we want more, we want an income of at least a thousand francs. And we shall have it, Monsieur Saccard has said so... He is so nice, Monsieur Saccard!'

Marcelle could not help smiling.

'So you're not intending to get married any more?'

'Oh yes, yes, as soon as the shares stop rising... We were in a hurry, especially Theodore's father, because of his business. But after all, one can hardly block up the source when the money's coming through. Oh, Theodore understands, especially since if Papa has a better income, there's that much more capital to come our way in due course. My goodness! It's worth considering... And there you are, we are all waiting. We've had the six thousand francs for months, so we could get married, but we prefer to let the francs multiply… Do you read the articles about the shares in the newspapers?'

And, without waiting for an answer, she added:

'Myself, I read them in the evening. Papa brings me the news-papers… He has read them already and I have to reread them for him… We could go on and on reading them, it's so lovely, the things they promise. When I go to bed my head is full of them, and I dream of them in the night. And Papa, too, tells me that he sees things that are very good omens. The day before yesterday we both had the same dream, about shovelling up five-franc coins in the street. It was very funny.'

Once again she stopped short to ask: 'How many shares do you have?'

'We don't have any,' Marcelle replied.

Nathalie's little face, with her pale blonde hair flying around it, took on an expression of immense pity. Ah, the poor souls who had no shares! And when her father called her to ask her to deliver a pack-age of proofs to a reporter on her way back up to the Batignolles, she took herself off with the amusing self-importance of a capitalist who, almost every day now, went down to the newspaper office to learn the stock-market prices as soon as possible.

Left by herself on the bench, Marcelle sank into a melancholy reverie, she who was usually so cheerful and stalwart. Lord! How dark it was, and how dismal! And her poor husband pacing the streets in this torrential rain! He had such contempt for money, was so uncomfortable at the mere idea of concerning himself with it, that it cost him a huge effort to ask for money even from those who owed it to him. Lost in thought, and deaf to everything, she began to relive her day since waking, this bad day; whilst the feverish work of the newspaper went on all around her, the rushing about of reporters, the hustle and bustle of news items coming in, doors slamming and bells ringing.

First of all, at nine o'clock, when Jordan had just left to cover an investigation into an accident, Marcelle, who had barely had time to wash and was still in her chemise, was amazed to see Busch descend-ing on them along with two very dirty-looking men, perhaps bailiffs, or else bandits, she hadn't been able to decide. That abominable Busch, no doubt taking advantage of the fact that there was only a woman there, declared that they were going to seize everything, if she didn't pay up immediately. She had argued in vain, having no knowledge of any of the legal formalities; he maintained with such vigour that the judgement had been notified, and the notice displayed, that she ended up quite distraught, believing these things might be possible without one's knowing about them. But she did not give up, explaining that her husband would not even be back for lunch and that she would not allow them to touch anything until he was there. There then ensued the most painful of scenes between these three undesirable persons and the not fully dressed young woman, with her hair down on her shoulders, the men already making an inventory of everything, and she closing the cupboards, and throwing herself in front of the door, to try to stop them taking anything out. Her poor little lodging that she was so proud of, her few bits of furniture that she had polished until they shone, and the Turkish bedroom curtain she had put up herself! She kept shouting, with fierce courage, that they would have to walk over her dead body; and she yelled out that Busch was a scoundrel and a thief, yes, a thief who had no shame even about demanding seven hundred and thirty francs and fifteen centimes, not to mention new costs, for a debt of three hundred francs, a debt bought for a hundred sous as part of a heap of rags and old iron! To think that they had already paid four hundred francs in instalments, and that this thief now spoke of carrying off their furniture as payment for the three hundred or so francs he still wanted to steal from them! And he knew perfectly well that they were honest people who would have paid him straight away if only they had the money. And he was taking advantage of her being on her own, to frighten her and reduce her to tears, unable to answer back, ignorant of legal procedure as she was. You scoundrel! You thief! You thief! Busch, now furious, shouted even more loudly than she did, fiercely beating his breast: Wasn't he an honest man? Hadn't he paid for the debt with good money? He had the law on his side and meant to see the thing through. However, when one of the two very dirty-looking men began opening the cupboard drawers in search of linen, Marcelle took on such a terrible air, threatening to rouse the whole house, and the street, that the Jew calmed down a bit. At last, after another half-hour of sordid argument, he had agreed to wait until the next day, swearing angrily that he would then take everything, if she did not keep her word. Oh, what a burning shame she still felt, to have had those horrible men in their home, wounding all her tender feelings, all her modesty, as they rummaged about even in her bed, making such a stink in that happy bedroom that she had to leave the window wide open after they'd gone!

But another even greater grief lay in wait for Marcelle that day. She had thought of running straight away to her parents to borrow the money, so that when her husband returned in the evening, she could save him from despair, and be able to make him laugh at the events of that morning. She could already see herself describing the great battle, the ferocious assault upon their household, and the heroic way in which she had repulsed the attack. Her heart was beating fast as she entered the little house in the Rue Legendre, that comfortable house in which she had grown up, but where she thought she would now find only strangers, so different and so icy was the atmosphere. As her parents were just sitting down to eat, she had accepted their invitation to join them, to try to make them more friendly. Throughout the meal, the conversation remained stuck on the rise of the Universals, their price having gone up twenty francs just the day before; and she was astonished to find her mother more feverish, more grasping even than her father, though she, at the start, had quivered with fear at the very thought of speculation; but now, with the ferocity of a woman converted, it was she who, desperately eager for a great stroke of luck, chided him for his timidity. From the very first course, she had lost her temper, amazed that he was talking of selling their seventy-five shares at the unhoped-for price of two thousand five hundred and twenty francs, which would have made them a handsome profit of a hundred and eighty-nine thousand francs, more than a hundred thousand francs above the purchase price. Sell! When *La Cote finan-cière* was promising a price of three thousand francs! Was he going mad? For after all, *La Cote financière* was long known for its honesty, and he himself had often said that if you followed that paper, you had nothing to worry about! Ah, no! Absolutely not, she was not going to let him sell! She would rather sell their house to buy more shares! And Marcelle, silent, felt a pang at the heart on hearing all these huge sums flying about with such passion, and wondered how she was going to dare to ask for a loan of five hundred francs in this house taken over by gambling, this house in which she had seen the steadily rising flood of financial newspapers which were now drowning it in the intoxicating dreams of their advertisements. At last, when the time came for dessert, she had risked it: they needed five hundred francs, or they were going to be sold up, surely her parents could not abandon them in this disaster. Her father had at once bowed his head, with an embarrassed glance at his wife. But her mother was already firmly refusing. Five hundred francs! Where were they expected to find them? All their capital was tied up in their dealings; and besides, she returned to her old diatribes: when you married a pauper, a man who wrote books, you had to accept the consequences of your folly, not try to fall back as a burden on your family. No! She didn't have a sou to offer idlers who affect a fine contempt for money, dreaming only of devouring that of other people. And she had allowed her daughter to leave in despair, with a heart bleeding from finding her mother unrecognizable, that mother who had once been so sensible and kind.

Once out in the street Marcelle had walked along like one unaware of her surroundings, looking at the ground as if she might find money there. Then she had suddenly thought she might appeal to Uncle Chave, and immediately called in at the ground-floor apartment in the Rue Nollet, before the opening of the Bourse, so as not to miss him. She could hear some whisperings and some girlish laughter. However, once the door was opened, she had found the captain alone, smoking his pipe, and he was terribly sorry, even angry with himself, as he exclaimed that he never had a hundred francs to hand, since he always, day by day used up, pig that he was, the little that he won on the Bourse. Then, after hearing of the refusal of the Maugendres, he thundered against them, the wretched scoundrels, he didn't even see them any more, now the rise of their shares had driven them mad. Just the other week, hadn't his sister called him a penny-pincher, ridiculing his caution as a speculator just because, in a friendly spirit, he had been advising her to sell? That was one person he wouldn't be weeping over, when she came a cropper!

Marcelle, out in the street once more with empty hands, had to resign herself to going to the newspaper office to tell her husband what had happened that morning. Busch absolutely had to be paid. Jordan, whose book had not yet been accepted by any publisher, had at once launched himself into a hunt for money, all through the muddy Paris of that rainy day, with no idea of where to seek help— from friends, the newspapers for which he wrote, or from some chance meeting. Although he had begged her to go back home, Marcelle was so anxious that she had preferred to stay there on that bench and wait for him.

After his daughter had gone, Dejoie, seeing Marcelle by herself, brought her a paper.

'Perhaps Madame would care to read this, to pass the time.'

But she refused with a wave, and as Saccard was just arriving, put on a brave face and gaily explained that she had just sent her husband off on an errand in the neighbourhood, a tiresome errand she had unloaded on him. Saccard, who had kindly feelings for this 'little household', as he called them, absolutely insisted that she come into his office to wait more comfortably. Marcelle refused, saying she was fine where she was. He ceased to insist when, to his surprise, he found himself suddenly face to face with Baroness Sandorff, coming out of Jantrou's office,. They just smiled at each other, with an air of amiable understanding, in the manner of people who greet each other formally to avoid displaying their relationship.

Jantrou, in the course of their conversation, had just told the Baroness that he no longer dared advise her. He was growing more and more perplexed at the solidity of the Universal, in spite of the efforts of the 'bears'; Gundermann would no doubt win, but Saccard could last quite a while yet, and there might still be much to gain by staying with him. He had persuaded her to play for time and stay on good terms with both. The best plan was to try always to be amiable enough to learn the secrets of the one, either keeping them to herself and profiting by them, or else selling them to the other, according to which was more profitable. And all this without any dark plotting, presented as if in jest, while the Baroness, with a laugh, promised to cut him in on the deal.

'So she's forever closeted with you now, it's your turn, is it?' said Saccard with his usual brutality, as he went into Jantrou's office. Jantrou affected astonishment.

'Who do you mean?... Ah, the Baroness!... But my dear sir, she adores you. She was just saying so.'

With the gesture of a man who is nobody's fool, the old pirate stopped him there. And he gazed at Jantrou, wrecked as he was by vile debauchery, and thought that if the Baroness had yielded to her curiosity about Sabatani's physique she might well have also wanted a taste of the vice of this old ruin.

'Don't defend yourself, my dear chap. When a woman starts playing the market, she would go for the doorman round the corner, if he could bring her an order.'

Jantrou was very hurt, and merely laughed, while still insisting on explaining the presence of the Baroness, who had come, he said, about a publicity matter.

Anyway, with a shrug of his shoulders, Saccard had already dropped the subject of the woman, of no interest as far as he was concerned. Remaining standing, walking back and forth, then planting himself at the window to watch the grey rain endlessly falling, he vented his joy and agitation. Yes, the Universal had again gone up twenty francs the day before! But how the devil was it that sellers were still persisting? For the rise would have gone up to thirty francs, without a whole package of shares that had fallen on the market as soon as the Bourse opened. What he didn't know was that Madame Caroline had again sold a thousand of her shares, herself now struggling against the unreasonable rise, as her brother had ordered her to do. Saccard could hardly complain about the ever-increasing success, and yet he was agitated that day, trembling inwardly with ill-defined fear and anger. He exclaimed that the dirty Jews had sworn to defeat him, and that scoundrel Gundermann had just placed himself at the head of a syndicate of short-sellers to bring him down. He had been told of it at the Bourse, there was talk of a sum of three hundred million, intended by the syndicate to cover the short selling. Ah, the robbers! And what he did not repeat aloud were the other rumours going around, growing clearer day by day, rumours that questioned the solidity of the Universal, and already alleged some facts, some signs of approaching difficulties; without yet, it's true, having at all shaken the blind confidence of the public.

But the door was pushed open and Huret appeared, with his simple, straightforward air.

'Ah! There you are, you Judas!' said Saccard.

Having learned that Rougon was definitely going to abandon his brother, Huret had joined up again with the minister; for he was convinced that once Saccard had Rougon against him, catastrophe was inevitable. To obtain his pardon, he had re-entered the household of the great man, once more running errands for him and exposing himself in his service to insults and kicks on the backside.

'Judas,' Huret repeated, with the sly smile that sometimes lit up his crude peasant features, 'well, at any rate, a good-natured Judas, who comes to give a disinterested piece of advice to the master he betrayed.'

But Saccard, as if refusing to understand, shouted, simply to confirm his trumph:

'Eh? Two thousand five hundred and twenty yesterday, two thousand five hundred and twenty-five today.'

'I know, I just sold.'

Immediately, the anger Saccard had been hiding beneath his jesting manner exploded.

'What? You sold?... Ah, well, that's it then! You leave me for Rougon, and you join up with Gundermann!'

The Deputy gazed at him in bewilderment.

'Why with Gundermann?... I'm simply looking after my own interests! You know I'm not a reckless fellow. No, I don't have the stomach for it, I prefer to realize as soon as there's a nice profit. And perhaps that's why I have never lost.'

He was smiling again, like a prudent and sensible Norman who simply, unhurriedly, gathers in his harvest.

'One of the directors of the company!' Saccard expostulated. 'So who can be expected to have faith in us? What must people think, seeing you selling like that while the price is still rising? Good Lord! I'm not surprised now if people claim our prosperity is artificial and that the day of our downfall draws nigh... These gentlemen are selling, so let's all sell! It's a panic!'

Huret, without a word, made a vague gesture. Basically he didn't care, he had seen to his own business. His only concern now was to carry out the mission with which Rougon had entrusted him, as decently as possible, with not too much bother for himself.

'As I was saying, my dear chap, I came to give you a disinterested piece of advice... Here it is. Be sensible, your brother is furious, he will totally abandon you if you allow yourself to be defeated.'

Holding back his anger, Saccard didn't move a muscle.

'It was he who sent you to tell me that?'

After a brief hesitation, the Deputy thought it best to admit the fact.

'Ah well, yes, it was he... Oh, don't go thinking the attacks in *L'Espérance* played a part in his irritation. He is above such matters of wounded vanity. No! But truly, just think how much your newspaper's Catholic campaign must be hampering his current policies. Ever since those unfortunate complications with Rome he has had the whole of the clergy on his back, and he has just been forced to have a bishop condemned for abuse of his position... And you choose to attack him just at the moment when he's struggling to avoid being overwhelmed by the liberal movement arising from the 19 January reforms,* which he agreed to apply, as one might say, simply in order to keep them prudently under control... Come now, you're his brother, do you think he's likely to be pleased?'

'Indeed,' Saccard mockingly replied, 'it's really nasty of me... There's that poor brother of mine who, in his rage to remain a minister, goes on governing in the name of the very principles he formerly fought against, and takes it out on me because he can no longer keep his balance between the Right, annoyed at having been betrayed, and the Third Party, hungry for power. Only a short time ago, to calm the Catholics, he uttered his famous 'Never!'—swearing that never would France allow Italy to take Rome from the Pope. And now, in his terror of the liberals, he would like to give them a pledge too, and deigns to think of cutting my throat just to please them... Just a week or so ago Émile Ollivier gave him a real shaking in the House...'

'Oh!' Huret interrupted, 'he still has the confidence of the Tuileries, the Emperor has sent him a diamond medallion.'*

But with a violent gesture, Saccard responded that he was not fooled.

'The Universal is too powerful now, isn't it? A Catholic bank that threatens to invade the whole world and conquer it with money, just as it was previously conquered by faith, can such a thing be tolerated? All the freethinkers and all the freemasons, striving to become ministers, feel the chill of it in their bones... Perhaps there is also some loan to be fixed up with Gundermann. What would happen to a government if it didn't allow itself to fall prey to these dirty Jews?... And so my idiot of a brother, just to hang on to power for another six months, will throw me to the dirty Jews, to the liberals, and all the rest of the scum, in the hope that they'll give him a bit of peace while they're devouring me... Well, go back and tell him I don't give a damn about him...'

He straightened up his short body, rage at last bursting through his irony like a warlike blast of trumpets.

'Get this clear, I don't give a damn about him. That's my answer and I want him to know it.'

Huret had dropped his shoulders. When dealings became heated he just opted out. After all, in all this he was only a messenger.

'All right, all right! He will be told… You are going to break your neck, but that's your affair.'

There was a silence. Jantrou, who had remained absolutely silent, pretending to be wholly absorbed in the correction of a packet of proofs, raised his eyes in admiration at Saccard. How splendid he was, the bandit, in his passion! These scoundrels of genius sometimes triumph, at this level of recklessness, when the intoxication of success carries them away. And Jantrou, at this moment, was on Saccard's side, convinced of his good fortune.

'Ah, I was forgetting,' Huret began again, 'it seems that Delcambre, the Public Prosecutor, detests you… And one thing you don't yet know is that the Emperor this morning appointed him Minister of Justice.'

Suddenly Saccard paused. With darkened face, he at last commented:

'Another nice bit of goods! Ah! So they've made a minister of that object! And what's that to me?'

'Well,' Huret went on, exaggerating his air of simplicity, 'if a misfortune should befall you, as happens to everyone in the business world, your brother doesn't want you counting on him to defend you against Delcambre.'

'But damn it all!' Saccard shouted. 'When I tell you that I don't give a damn for the whole mob of them, Rougon, Delcambre, and you too come to that!'

At that moment, fortunately, Daigremont came in. He never called at the newspaper office, so it was a surprise to everyone, which cut short the violent encounter. With perfect politeness he shook hands all round with a smile, and the flattering affability of the man of the world. His wife was giving an evening reception at which she would sing, and he had come simply to invite Jantrou in person, hoping for a good review. But the presence of Saccard seemed to delight him.

'How are things, great man?'

Without answering, Saccard asked: 'Tell me, you haven't been selling, have you?'

'Selling! Oh no, not yet!'—and his laugh was very sincere, he really was made of more solid stuff than that!

'But one must never sell, in our position!' cried Saccard.

'Never! That's what I meant. We are all in it together, you know you can count on me.'

Daigremont's eyelids drooped, and he looked to one side while he answered for the other directors, Sédille, Kolb, the Marquis de Bohain, as well as for himself. Everything was going so well, it was really a pleasure to be all in agreement, in the most extraordinary success the Bourse had seen for fifty years. And he had a charming remark for each of them, then went away repeating that he was counting on all three of them for the soirée. Mounier, the tenor from the Opéra, would be singing with his wife. Oh, it would be quite an event!

'So,' Huret asked, he too now preparing to leave, 'is that all the answer you're giving me?'

'Indeed it is!' Saccard curtly replied.

And he made a point of not going down with him, as he usually did. Then, when he was alone again with the editor of the newspaper:

'This is war, my dear fellow! There is no more need for caution, just thump the whole bunch of crooks!... Ah, I'm now going to be able to fight the battle my way!'

'All the same, it's pretty rough,' commented Jantrou, who was beginning to feel perplexed again.

Out in the corridor, on the bench, Marcelle was still waiting. It was hardly four o'clock and already Dejoie had lit the lamps; darkness was falling so early under the grey, relentless downpour of rain. Every time Dejoie went past he found something to say to try to cheer her up. Anyway the comings and goings of the contributors were now increasing, and the sound of voices burst out from the next room in all the mounting feverishness of creating the newspaper.

Marcelle, suddenly looking up, saw Jordan before her. He was soaked, and looked quite shattered, with the trembling lips and slightly crazy eyes of those who have pursued a hope for a long time without attaining it. She at once understood.

'So you got nothing?' she asked, turning pale.

'Nothing, my darling, nothing at all... Not anywhere, just not possible...'

She simply let out a low moan that expressed the bleeding of her heart.

'Oh, my God!'

At that moment Saccard came out from Jantrou's office and was astonished to find her still there.

'What, Madame, your truant husband has only just got back? I told you to come and wait in my office.'

She stared at him, a sudden thought having just awoken in her large, desolate eyes. She did not stop to reflect, she yielded to that wild courage that drives women forward under the impulse of passion.

'Monsieur Saccard, I have something to ask you... If you don't mind, we could now go into your office...'

'But certainly, Madame.'

Jordan, who feared he had guessed her intentions, tried to hold her back, stammering: 'No, no!...' in her ear, in the sick anguish that always afflicted him where money was concerned. She broke away and he had to follow her.

'Monsieur Saccard,' she resumed, as soon as the door was closed, 'my husband has been rushing about for the last two hours trying to find five hundred francs, and he doesn't dare to ask you for them... So it is I who am asking you...'

And then, with vigour, and the droll expressions of a lively and resolute young woman, she described the happenings of the morning, the brutal entry of Busch, the invasion of her room by the three men, telling how she had managed to repel the assault, and the promise she had made to pay up that very day. Oh, the wounds money makes for humble folk, the great suffering created by shame and helplessness, life itself constantly under threat, all for a few wretched hundred-sou coins!

'Busch,' Saccard repeated, 'it's that old scoundrel Busch who has you in his claws...'

Then with charming affability, turning to Jordan, who sat silent and pale in unbearable discomfort, he said:

'Well, I'll advance you the five hundred francs. You should have asked me straight away.'

He had sat down at the table to write a cheque when he stopped, with a sudden thought. He remembered the letter he had received, and the visit he had to make, which he had been putting off from day to day, in annoyance at the shady business he scented. Why shouldn't he go straight away to the Rue Feydeau, taking advantage of the opportunity now he had a pretext?

'Listen, I know this scoundrel of yours very well... It will be better for me to go in person to pay him, and see if I can't get your notes back for half the price.'

Marcelle's eyes now shone with gratitude.

'Oh, Monsieur Saccard, how kind you are!'

And to her husband:

'See? You great ninny, Monsieur Saccard didn't eat us up!'

In an irresistible impulse Jordan threw his arms round her neck and kissed her, for it was she that he thanked most of all for being more active and skilful than he in these difficulties that paralysed him.

'No, no,' said Saccard, when the young man at last shook his hand, 'the pleasure is all mine, you are very sweet, the two of you, to love each other so much. Go on home in peace!'

His carriage, which was waiting for him, took him in two minutes to the Rue Feydeau, in this muddy Paris, in the bustling of umbrellas and the splashing of puddles. But at the top of the stairs he rang in vain at the old door with flaking paint, on which a brass plate displayed the word: 'Litigation' in big black letters; it did not open, and there was no movement from inside. And Saccard was just about to leave when, in his frustration, he beat the door violently with his fist. Then halting footsteps were heard and Sigismond appeared.

'Ah! It's you!... I thought it was my brother coming back, having forgotten his key. I never answer the doorbell... He won't be long, you can wait for him if you really want to see him.'

With the same painful and faltering steps he returned, followed by the visitor, to the room he occupied, looking out on the Place de la Bourse. It was still full daylight up in these heights, above the mist with which the rain filled the streets below. The room was bleak and bare, with its narrow iron bed, its table and two chairs, its few planks loaded with books, and no furniture. In front of the fireplace, a little stove, untended and forgotten, had just gone out.

'Sit down, Monsieur. My brother said he was only going out and coming back straight away.'

But Saccard refused the chair, looking at him and seeing the progress the tuberculosis had made upon this tall, pale youth with the eyes of a child, eyes drowning in dreams, so strange beneath the energetic obstinacy of the brow. Between the long curls of his hair, his face was extraordinarily hollowed out, as if elongated and dragged towards the tomb.

'You've been ill?' he asked, not knowing what to say. Sigismond made a gesture of total indifference.

'Oh, just the same. Last week was not good, because of this filthy weather. But anyway, things are all right... I don't sleep any more, I can still work, and I've a slight fever that keeps me warm... Ah, there is so much to be done.'

He had gone back to the table, on which a book in German stood open. He went on:

'Forgive me for sitting down, but I've been awake all night reading this book which I received yesterday... A great work indeed, ten years of the life of my master, Karl Marx, the book on capital that he had been promising us for so long!... And now here it is, here is our Bible!'*

His curiosity aroused, Saccard moved to take a look at the book, but the sight of its Gothic characters* immediately put him off.

'I'll wait until it's translated,' he said with a laugh.

The young man, shaking his head, seemed to say that even when translated it would be properly understood only by a few initiates. It was not a work of propaganda. But what forceful logic, and what a triumphant abundance of proofs, demonstrating the inevitable destruction of our present society based on the capitalist system! Once the ground was cleared the rebuilding could begin.

'So, it's the clean sweep?' Saccard asked, still joking.

'In theory, yes absolutely!' replied Sigismond. 'Everything I explained to you a while ago, the whole revolutionary process, is all in there. It only remains for us to bring it about in fact... But you are all blind if you don't see the great advances the idea is making hour by hour. So, with your Universal, in three years you've moved around and centralized hundreds of millions, and you don't seem to have the slightest inkling that you are driving us straight into collectivism... I've followed your business with passionate interest, yes, from this quiet, out-of-the-way room I have studied its growth day by day and know it as well as you do yourself, and I tell you it's a wonderful lesson you're giving us, for the collectivist state will only have to do what you do, take you over in one go after you've taken over the smaller companies one by one, and thus fulfil the ambition of your extravagant dream, which is to absorb all the capital of the world, to be the sole bank—isn't that so?—to be the one general depository of public wealth... Oh, I greatly admire you! I would let you continue if I were the master, for you are beginning our work, like a forerunner of genius!'

He smiled with his pale invalid's smile, noticing the attentiveness of his interlocutor, who was very surprised to find him so well acquainted with the business of the day and very flattered too by the intelligent praise.

'But', Sigismond went on, 'on that happy morn when we take you over in the name of the nation, replacing your private interests with those of all, making your great machine for sucking up the wealth of others into the very regulator of social wealth, we shall begin by abolishing this.'

He had found a sou among the papers on his table and held it up between two fingers, as the intended victim.

'Money!' cried Saccard. 'Abolish money! What utter madness!'

'We shall abolish cash money... You must realize that metal money has no place, no justification in the collectivist state. For all remuneration, money is replaced by work vouchers; and if you think of money as a measure of value, we have an alternative which will stand perfectly well in its stead, one that we shall obtain by establishing the average day's labour in our workplaces... It has to be destroyed, this money that masks and encourages the exploitation of the worker, allowing him to be robbed by reducing his wage to the smallest sum needed to prevent him starving to death. Is it not appalling, the way the possession of money builds up private fortunes, bars the way to fruitful circulation, and creates scandalous kingships that powerfully rule both the financial market and social production? All our crises, all our anarchy, arise from this. It must be killed, money must be killed off!'

But Saccard was getting annoyed. No more money, no more gold, no more of those shining stars that had illuminated his whole life! Wealth for him had always taken the form of that dazzle of new coins, raining down through the sunshine like a spring shower and falling like hail on the ground, covering it with heaps of gold that you stirred with a shovel just to see their brightness and hear their music. And they were going to abolish that joy, that reason for fighting and living!

'That's idiotic, that is—idiotic!... Never, do you hear?'

'Why never? Why idiotic?... Do we make use of money in the family economy? There all you see is common effort and exchange... So, what's the use of money when society is nothing other than one great family, governing itself?'

'I tell you it's mad!... Destroy money? But money is life itself! There would be nothing left. Nothing!'

Saccard walked up and down, beside himself. And in his anger, as he passed by the window, he looked out to make sure the Bourse was still there, for this terrible young man had perhaps blown it away. It was still there, though very blurred in the depths of the oncoming night, as if melted under the shroud of rain, a pale and spectral Bourse, almost vanishing into a smoky greyness.

'Anyway, I'm really stupid to be arguing about this. It's impossible... Go on, abolish money, I'd like to see you try.'

'Bah,' Sigismond muttered, 'everything gets abolished, everything changes and disappears... For instance, we have already seen the form of wealth change once before, when the value of land went down and landed fortunes, big estates, fields and woods declined in favour of securities and industrial wealth, stocks and shares, and today we are observing the precocious decay of the latter, a sort of rapid depreciation, for it's certain that the value of money is being debased, and the norm of five per cent return per annum is no longer reached... The value of money is declining then, so why shouldn't it disappear altogether? Why shouldn't a new form of wealth come in to govern social relations? It's the wealth of tomorrow that our work-vouchers will provide.'

Sigismond had become absorbed in contemplation of the sou, as if dreaming that he was holding the last coin of past ages, a stray sou that had survived the old dead society. What joys and sorrows had worn away the humble metal! And he had fallen into the sadness of eternal human longing.

'Yes,' he went on quietly, 'you are right, we shall not see these things. It will take years and years. Can we even know whether love of one's fellow men will have enough vigour in it to replace egoism in the organization of society?... And yet I hoped the triumph would be sooner, I should so like to have been there to see that dawn of justice.'

For a moment, bitterness over the illness from which he suffered broke his voice. He, who in his denial of death, treated it as though it did not exist, made a gesture as if to push it away. But he was already becoming resigned once more.

'I have completed my task, I shall leave my notes in case I don't have time to draw out of them the complete work of reconstruction I have envisaged. The society of tomorrow must be the mature fruit of civilization, for if we do not keep the good side of emulation and control, then all is lost... Ah, that society, how clearly I see it now, at last created and complete, such as I have managed to set it up after so many sleepless nights! Everything is foreseen, everything is resolved, and at last there is sovereign justice and absolute happiness. It's all there on paper, mathematical and definitive.'

And he stretched out his long, emaciated hands over the scattered notes, and exulted in this dream of the billions won back and equitably shared among all, in this joy and health he was restoring to suffering humanity with a stroke of the pen, he who neither ate nor slept, and was simply dying, needing nothing, in that bare room.

But a harsh voice made Saccard start.

'What are you doing here?'

It was Busch, who had come back and now looked askance at the visitor like a jealous lover, in his constant fear that someone would make his brother talk too much and provoke a fit of coughing. Anyway, he did not wait for an answer but started scolding in despair, like a mother.

'What! You've let your stove go out again! I just ask you, is that reasonable in such damp weather?' He was already on his knees, in spite of the heaviness of his large body, breaking up some kindling and relighting the fire. Then he went to get a broom and tidied things up, asking anxiously about the medicine his brother had to take every two hours. He was not content until he had persuaded him to stretch out on his bed.

'Monsieur Saccard, if you'd like to come into my office...'

Madame Méchain was there, sitting on the only chair. She and Busch had just made an important visit in the neighbourhood, and were delighted with its successful outcome. At last, after a long and desperate wait, they had been able to make a start on one of the affairs they most cared about. For three years La Méchain had scoured the streets searching for Léonie Cron, that seduced girl for whom the Count de Beauvilliers had signed a note promising ten thousand francs, payable on her majority. In vain had she appealed to her cousin Fayeux, the collector of revenues in Vendôme, who had bought the note for Busch in a pile of old debts, part of the estate of one Charpier, a grain merchant and occasional moneylender. Fayeux knew nothing, he wrote only to say that the girl Léonie Cron must be in service with a bailiff in Paris, that she had left Vendôme more than ten years before and never come back, and he couldn't even question one of her relatives, for they were all dead. La Méchain had found the bailiff and managed to trace Léonie from there to a butcher, then a lady of ill-repute, then a dentist; but after the dentist the thread suddenly

broke, the trail came to an end—now it was like looking for a needle
in a haystack, a fallen woman lost in the mire of huge Paris. In vain
had she done the rounds of the employment agencies, visited seedy
boarding-houses, rummaged about in haunts of debauchery, always
on the watch, looking about her and asking questions as soon as the
name Léonie struck her ear. And this girl she had gone so far afield to
search for, she had just that very day, by chance, laid hands on her in
the Rue Feydeau, in the local brothel, where La Méchain had been
pursuing a former tenant of the Cité de Naples who owed her three
francs. A stroke of genius had enabled her to sniff her out and recognize her under the distinguished name of Léonide, just when the
madam in a high-pitched voice was calling her to the salon. Busch,
being notified, had at once gone back to the house with La Méchain
to negotiate; and this fat girl, with her coarse black hair falling over
her eyebrows and her flat, flabby face, of vile vulgarity, had at first
surprised him; then he had recognized what must have been her special charm, especially before ten years of prostitution, delighted
anyway that she had fallen so low and become so abominable. He had
offered her a thousand francs if she ceded to him her rights on the
promissory note. She was stupid, she had accepted the bargain with
childlike joy. Now at last they would be able to pursue the Countess
de Beauvilliers, they had the weapon so long sought, a weapon of an
even unhoped-for degree of ugliness and shame!

'I was expecting you, Monsieur Saccard. We need to talk... You
received my letter, no doubt?'

In that tiny room, full of papers and already dark, lit only by one
feeble, smoky lamp, La Méchain, still and silent, did not budge from
the only chair in the room. Still standing, and not wanting to look as
if he had come in answer to a threat, Saccard at once embarked on the
Jordan affair, in a harsh and contemptuous tone.

'Excuse me, I came to settle a debt for one of my contributors...
young Jordan, a very charming fellow whom you are pursuing most
cruelly, with a truly revolting ferocity. This very morning, it seems,
you conducted yourself with his wife in a manner any gentleman
would find shameful...'

Shocked at being attacked in this way when he was expecting to
take the offensive, Busch lost his grip on things and, forgetting the
other matter, became annoyed over this one.

'The Jordans, you've come about the Jordans... There's no such thing as wife or gentlemanly behaviour in business. When people owe, they pay, that's all I know... Wretched pests who've been messing me about for years, from whom I've had the devil's own job getting four hundred francs, sou by sou!... Oh yes, by God, I'll sell them up, I'll throw them on to the street tomorrow morning if I don't get, this evening, right here on my desk, the three hundred francs and fifteen centimes they still owe me.'

When Saccard deliberately, to drive him mad with rage, said that he had already been paid forty times over for that bill, which had surely cost him less than ten francs, Busch did indeed choke with anger.

'There we go again! That's what you all say... But there are also the expenses, aren't there? This debt of three hundred francs that has risen to more than seven hundred... is that my fault? When people don't pay, I sue. And if justice is expensive, too bad! It's their fault!... So, when I've bought a ten-franc debt, I should just get repaid the ten francs, and that would be the end of it, eh? And what about my risks? My comings and goings, my mental efforts—yes! and all my research? Indeed, now, with regard to this Jordan affair, you can ask Madame here. It's she who has been in charge of it. Ah! She has done so much walking, approached so many people, used up lots of shoe-leather climbing the stairs of all the newspapers, from which she was often driven away like a beggar, without even being given the address she wanted. We have been nursing this affair for months, we have dreamed about it, worked on it like one of our masterpieces, it has cost me a crazy amount, even at only ten sous an hour!'

He was getting carried away, and with a sweeping gesture pointed to the folders filling the room.

'I have papers here for debts of twenty million, owed by people of all ages and every level of society, debts both tiny and colossal... Do you want them for a million? I'll give them to you. When you remember that there are debtors here that I've been tracking for a quarter of a century! To get a few miserable hundreds of francs, sometimes even less, I wait for years, I wait for them to be successful or to inherit... The rest, the unknown ones, the most numerous, lie sleeping there— look!—in that corner, all that huge pile. That's the rubbish, or rather the raw material, out of which I have to make my living, after heaven only knows what complications of searching and worrying!... And you're asking me, when at last I get hold of a solvent one, not to squeeze him dry? Ah, no, you'd think I was too stupid—you certainly wouldn't be that stupid yourself!'

Without waiting for any further discussion, Saccard drew out his wallet.

'I'm going to give you two hundred francs, and you're going to give me the Jordan papers, with a receipt showing everything fully paid.'

Busch leaped up in exasperation.

'Two hundred francs, never!... It's three hundred and thirty francs and fifteen centimes... and I want the centimes.'

But in an even voice, with the tranquil assurance of a man who knows the power of money visibly offered and displayed, Saccard repeated two or three times:

'I'm going to give you two hundred francs...'

And the Jew, convinced at heart that it was sensible to compromise, finally agreed, with a cry of rage and tears in his eyes.

'I am too weak. What a wretched occupation!... Upon my word! I am stripped and robbed... Go on! While you're at it, don't hold back, take some more, yes! Rummage about in this heap, for your two hundred francs!'

Then when he had signed a receipt and written a note for the bailiff, who was now holding the documents, Busch stood panting for a moment in front of his desk, so shaken that he would have let Saccard leave, were it not for La Méchain, who had not thus far made a gesture or uttered a word.

'And the other matter?' she asked.

He suddenly remembered, he was going to get his revenge. But everything he had prepared, his story, his questions, the cunningly planned unfolding of the interview, all were forgotten in his haste to get to the point.

'That matter, yes indeed... I wrote to you, Monsieur Saccard. We have an old account to settle...'

He had stretched out his hand to take down the Sicardot folder, which he opened out in front of him.

'In 1852 you stayed in lodgings on the Rue de la Harpe, and you signed twelve promissory notes of fifty francs each to a certain Rosalie Chavaille, then sixteen years old, whom you assaulted one evening on the stairs... Here they are, those notes. You never paid a single one of them, for you went off, leaving no address, before the payment of the first one fell due. And what is even worse is that you signed with a false name, Sicardot, the surname of your first wife…'

Saccard, now very pale, was listening and staring. Suddenly, in an unspeakable spasm, his whole past was conjured up, he had a sensation of something crumbling, of a huge, confused mass falling upon him. In the alarm of that first moment he lost his head, and stammered:

'How do you know?… How did you get this?'

Then with trembling hands, he hastened to pull his wallet out once more, just wanting to pay and get these upsetting documents back.

'There aren't any costs, are there?… It's six hundred francs… Oh, there's a great deal I could say, but I'd rather just pay, with no further discussion.'

And he held out the six banknotes.

'Not so fast!' cried Busch, pushing aside the money. 'I haven't finished… Madame, here, is Rosalie's cousin, and these papers are hers, it's in her name that I am seeking reimbursement… The unfortunate Rosalie was disabled as a result of your violence. She had a great deal of misfortune and died in atrocious penury in the house of Madame, who had taken her in… Madame, if she chose to, could tell you a few things…'

'Terrible things!' emphasized La Méchain in her reedy voice, at last breaking her silence.

Alarmed, Saccard turned towards her; he had forgotten she was there, slumped in a heap like a huge, half-empty wineskin. He had always found her disturbing, with her unsavoury trade as a bird of prey devouring devalued securities; and now there she was again, mixed up in this unpleasant story.

'No doubt, poor thing, it's very unfortunate,' he murmured. 'But if she's dead, I don't really see… Anyway, here are the six hundred francs.'

For a second time, Busch refused to take the money.

'Excuse me, but you don't know everything yet; she had a child… Yes, a child now in his fourteenth year, a child who looks so very like you that you cannot deny him.'

Stunned, Saccard repeated several times: 'A child, a child…'

Then, with a sudden movement putting the six banknotes back in his wallet, now quite reassured and cheery:

'Ah! Come on, do you take me for a fool? If there's a child I shan't give you a sou… The child is his mother's heir, and it's he who shall have all that, along with whatever else he wants. A child, well, that's very nice, it's very natural, there's nothing wrong with having a child. On the contrary, I'm really pleased about it. Honestly! That makes me feel quite young... Where is he, so I can go and see him? Why didn't you bring him to me at once?'

Now Busch, stupefied in his turn, thought about his long hesitation and the endless care taken by Madame Caroline to avoid revealing Victor's existence to his father. And quite taken aback, he launched into the most violent and complicated explanations, letting everything out all at once, the six thousand francs claimed by La Méchain for Victor's keep and the money lent to Rosalie, the two thousand francs Madame Caroline had paid on account, the appalling instincts of Victor, and his entry into the Work Foundation. And it was Saccard now who shuddered at each new detail. What! Six thousand francs! but how could he know, on the contrary, whether they had not robbed the child? A down-payment of two thousand francs! And they had had the audacity to extort two thousand francs from a lady who was a friend of his! But it was theft, an abuse of trust! The little chap, clearly, had been badly brought up, and they wanted him to pay the people responsible for that bad upbringing! Did they take him for an idiot?

'Not a sou!' he cried. 'Do you hear? Don't expect to get a single sou out of my pocket!'

Busch, his face pale, had stood up in front of the table.

'We'll see about that. I'll take you to court.'

'Don't talk nonsense. You know perfectly well that the courts don't deal with matters of this sort... And if you hope to blackmail me, that's even more stupid, because as far as I'm concerned I don't give a damn what you do. A child! I can assure you, I find it very flattering.'

And as La Méchain was blocking the doorway, he had to push past her, and even step across her, to get out. She was choking, but in her piping voice she yelled out to him in the stairway:

'You scoundrel! You heartless wretch!'

'You'll be hearing from us,' Busch shouted as he slammed the door shut.

Saccard was in such a state of excitement that he told his coachman to go back at once to the Rue Saint-Lazare. He was impatient to see Madame Caroline, and he approached her without any embarrassment and scolded her right away for having given them the two thousand francs.

'But my dear friend, one never gives money away like that... Why the devil did you act without consulting me?'

Astonished that he already knew the whole story, she remained silent. It had indeed been Busch's handwriting that she had recognized, and now she had nothing more to hide, since someone else had taken on the burden of revealing the secret. However, she still hesitated, embarrassed for this man who was interrogating her and seemed so much at ease.

'I wanted to spare you some suffering... That unfortunate child was in such a state of degradation!... I would have told you a long time ago, but for a feeling...'

'What feeling?... I confess, I don't understand.'

She did not try to explain herself or excuse herself any more; normally so courageous about life, she was overcome by a wave of sadness, a weariness of everything; while he went on exclaiming, seeming delighted, truly rejuvenated.

'The poor little fellow! I shall really love him, I assure you... You did well to send him to the Work Foundation to get him cleaned up a bit. But we're going to take him out of there, we'll get teachers for him... Tomorrow I'll go and see him, yes tomorrow, if I'm not too busy.'

The following day there was a board meeting, and two days went by, then the week, without Saccard's managing to find a free minute. He still talked about the child quite often, while putting off his visit, giving in to the flood-tide which was carrying him along. In the first days of December the rate of two thousand seven hundred francs was reached in the midst of the unhealthy fit of extraordinary fever still overwhelming the Bourse. What was worse was that alarming reports had multiplied, and that the rise went on wildly, in an atmosphere of intolerable and growing unease: now the inevitable catastrophe was being openly predicted, and the price went on rising, rising relentlessly, thanks to the obstinate force of one of those prodigious infatuations which are impervious to evidence. Saccard now was just living in the extravagant fiction of his triumph, as if wearing a halo from the shower of gold he was scattering down on Paris, but still shrewd enough to sense that the ground beneath his feet was undermined, cracking up, and threatening to collapse under him. So, although he remained victorious at each settlement, he continued to be enraged by the short-sellers, whose losses must already be frightful. What possessed these dirty Jews to persist like this? Wasn't he at last going to destroy them? And he was especially exasperated in that he said he could sniff out others alongside Gundermann who were playing Gundermann's game, other sellers, even troops from the Universal perhaps, traitors who had gone over to the enemy, shaken in their faith and hastening to realize their gains.

One day when Saccard was expressing his annoyance about this to Madame Caroline, she felt impelled to tell him everything.

'You know, my dear, I too have sold... I have just sold our last thousand shares at the rate of two thousand seven hundred.'

He was utterly shattered, as if by the blackest of treacheries.

'You have sold! You! Even you! My God!'

She had taken his hands, and was pressing them, truly grieved, but reminding him that she and her brother had warned him. Her brother, still in Rome, had been writing letters full of mortal anxiety about that exaggerated rise, which he could not account for, and which at all costs had to be stopped, for fear of falling into an abyss. Only the day before, she had received a letter from him giving her formal instructions to sell. And she had sold.

'You! You!' Saccard kept repeating. 'It was you fighting against me, you I sensed in the shadows! It was your shares I had to buy back!'

He did not fly into a rage as he usually did, and she suffered all the more from his dejection, she would have liked to reason with him, to persuade him to abandon this merciless battle that could only end in massacre.

'My dear, listen to me... Remember that our three thousand shares have produced more than seven and a half million. Isn't that an unhoped-for, extravagant profit? Personally, all that money horrifies me, I can't believe it belongs to me... But anyway, it's not a matter just of our personal interests. Think of the interests of all those who have placed their fortune in your hands, the frightening number of millions you are risking in this game. Why keep on with this senseless rise? Why stimulate it further? People all around are saying that it will inevitably end in catastrophe... You can't just keep on rising, there's no shame in letting the shares revert to their real value, then the company will stand firm, and everything will be put right.'

But he had angrily leapt to his feet.

'I want the rate at three thousand... I have bought, and I shall go on buying, even if it kills me... Yes, let me be killed, and everything along with me, if I don't reach the rate of three thousand, and keep to it!'

After the settlement of 15 December the share price rose to two thousand eight hundred, two thousand nine hundred. It was on the 21st that the rate of three thousand and twenty francs was announced at the Bourse, amid the commotion of a demented throng. There was no more truth or logic, the very idea of value was corrupted to the point of losing any real meaning. It was rumoured that Gundermann, contrary to his normal habits of prudence, had embarked on fearful risks; for months he had been working towards a fall, and every fort-night, as the rise went on by leaps and bounds, his losses had grown in parallel; and people were beginning to say he might well come a real cropper. Brains were all turned upside-down, people were expecting wonders.

And at that supreme moment, when Saccard, at the summit, felt the earth tremble beneath him and secretly felt the dread of a fall, he was king. When his carriage arrived in the Rue de Londres, stopping outside the triumphant palace of the Universal, a valet came running out, spreading a carpet that rolled down from the steps of the vestibule to the pavement, and down to the very gutter; Saccard then deigned to alight from his coach, and made his entrance, like a sovereign spared from contact with the common paving of the streets.

CHAPTER X

At the end of that year, on the day of the December settlement, the great hall of the Bourse was already full at half-past twelve, with an extraordinary commotion of voices and gestures. Excitement had been mounting for weeks, culminating now in this last day of conflict, with a feverish mob in which there were already rumblings of the decisive battle about to be fought. Outside it was freezing hard; but the slanting rays of a bright winter sun came in through the high windows, brightening up the whole of one side of the bare hall, with its stern pillars and sombre vaulting, all made even more chilly by the dreary allegorical pictures on the walls; heating-pipes along the whole length of the arcades puffed out their warm breath into the cold draughts coming from the continual opening of the reinforced doors.

The 'bear' Moser, even more anxious and jaundiced-looking than usual, bumped into the 'bull' Pillerault, standing arrogantly on his long, heron-like legs.

'You know what they're saying?'

But he had to raise his voice to make himself heard in the growing clatter of talk, a regular, monotonous rumble, like the clamour of floodwater endlessly pouring along.

'They say we'll have war in April... That's how it's bound to end, with all these massive armaments. Germany won't want to give us time to apply the new army law* the Chamber is about to vote on... and anyway, Bismarck...'

Pillerault burst out laughing.

'Oh, do let up about your Bismarck!... I spent five minutes talking to him myself this summer when he was here. He seems a very decent chap... If you're still not satisfied after the thundering success of the Exhibition, what more do you want? Eh? My dear fellow, the whole of Europe is ours!'

Moser shook his head in despair. Then, though he was continually interrupted by the jostling of the crowd, he continued to speak of his fears. The market was too prosperous, with an excessive prosperity, of no more real worth than the surplus fat of obesity. Thanks to the Exhibition, too many new businesses had sprung up, people had got too carried away, there was now a sheer mania for gambling on the market. Universals, for instance, at three thousand and thirty, wasn't that just crazy?

'Ah, now we're getting to it,' cried Pillerault.

And moving closer, emphasizing each syllable, he said: 'My dear chap, by this evening they'll be up to three thousand and sixty... you'll all be knocked sideways, I'm telling you...'

Moser, easily impressionable though he was, gave a little hiss of defiance. And he gazed into the air to underline his false tranquillity of soul, pausing for a moment to look intently at the heads of some women who were leaning over, up there in the telegraph gallery,* astonished at the spectacle in this room that they were not allowed to enter. There were shields bearing the names of towns, while capitals and cornices stretched away up there in a colourless perspective, stained here and there with yellow where rain had leaked in.

'Aha! It's you!' Moser went on, lowering his head as he recognized Salmon standing in front of him, smiling his eternal and profound smile. Then, somewhat disturbed, taking that smile as approval of Pillerault's comments:

'Well, if you know something, tell us. My own reasoning is simple. I'm with Gundermann, because, well, Gundermann is Gundermann, isn't he?... With him things always turn out right.'

'But', said Pillerault with a snigger, 'how do you know Gundermann is short-selling?'

At this, Moser's eyes widened with alarm. For some time everyone had been saying in the Bourse that Gundermann was out to get Saccard, and that he was promoting short-selling against the Universal, until he could finally cripple it at some month's end, with a sudden effort, when the time was ripe for crushing the market with his millions; and if this session already looked so turbulent, it was because everyone thought, and kept repeating, that the battle was at last going to take place that very day, one of those merciless battles in which one of the two armies is left on the field, destroyed. But could you ever be sure, in this world of lies and trickery? Even the most certain things, the most firmly predicted, could, at the slightest breath, become subjects of anguished doubt.

'You're denying the evidence,' Moser murmured. 'Of course I haven't seen the orders, and one can't be certain of anything... eh? Salmon, what do you think? Gundermann really can't give up, damn it!'

He didn't know what to think, faced with Salmon's silent smile that seemed to narrow with an extreme subtlety.

'Ah!' Moser went on, indicating with his chin a large man who was passing by, 'if only that man chose to speak, I'd have no problem. He sees things clearly.' It was the famous Amadieu, still living on his success with the Selsis mines, shares he had bought at fifteen francs in an idiotic fit of obstinacy, and later sold for a profit of about fifteen million, without his having foreseen or calculated anything at all, but just by chance. He was revered for his great financial abilities, he had a real court of followers who tried to catch his slightest word in order to place their money in the direction it seemed to indicate.

'Bah!' cried Pillerault, caught up in his favourite theory of reckless gambling. 'The best thing is still to do whatever you fancy, come what may... It's all just luck. Either one has luck or one doesn't. So there's no point in thinking about it. Every time I've actually thought about it I've almost lost my shirt... Look, as long as I can see that gentleman over there, firmly at his post, and looking ready to devour everything in sight, I shall go on buying.'

With a wave he had pointed out Saccard, who had just arrived and settled into his usual place beside the pillar of the first archway on the left. Like all the heads of important companies, he had his own recognized place, where employees and clients could be certain of finding him on the days when the Bourse was open. Only Gundermann made a point of never setting foot in the great hall; he didn't even send an official representative; but one could tell he had his army there, and as an absent and sovereign master, he reigned through the vast legion of jobbers and brokers who carried his orders, not to mention the others he had working for him, so numerous that any man present might be one of his mysterious soldiers. And it was against this elusive, but everywhere active, army that Saccard was fighting, in person and out in the open. Behind him, on the corner of the pillar, was a bench, but he never sat on it, staying on his feet for the two hours of the market, as if disdainful of fatigue. Sometimes, relaxing a moment, he would lean his elbow against the stone, which long rubbing had darkened and polished up to the height of a man; and in the dull bareness of the monument, this was even a characteristic feature, this band of shiny dirt, on the doors, on the walls, on the stairs, in the hall, a filthy underlay of the accumulated sweat of generations of gamblers and thieves. Very elegant, very correctly dressed, like all the market men, in his fine cloth and dazzling linen, Saccard, amid those walls with black borders, had the amiable and relaxed look of a man with no worries.

'You know,' said Moser, lowering his voice, 'some say he's supporting the rise by making large purchases. If the Universal is speculating on its own shares, it's done for.'

But Pillerault protested:

'Another bit of gossip!... How can you tell for sure who's buying and who's selling?... He's here for the clients of his company, which is quite natural. And he's also here on his own account, for he must be speculating too.'

Moser, anyway, did not insist. Nobody at the Bourse would yet have dared to state positively the terrible campaign conducted by Saccard, all the buying he had done on behalf of the bank under cover of frontmen like Sabatani, Jantrou, and others, especially his own employees. There was just a rumour going round, whispered from ear to ear, always denied but always springing up again, though without any possible proof. Saccard had at first been cautious in his support of the market price, reselling as soon as he could, to avoid tying up too much capital and loading the coffers with shares. But now he was being dragged along by the struggle; he had foreseen that he might need, that day, to make excessive purchases if he wanted to remain master of the battlefield. He had given his orders and now affected the smiling tranquillity of any ordinary day, despite his uncertainty about the final outcome and the worry he felt at thus proceeding further and further down a path he knew to be appallingly dangerous.

Suddenly Moser, who had been prowling about behind the back of the famous Amadieu, who was deep in conversation with a small, sly-looking man, came back very excited, stammering:

'I heard him, heard him with my own ears... He said that Gundermann's orders to sell were for more than ten million... Oh! I'm selling, I'm selling, I'd sell my very shirt!...'

'Heavens! Ten million!' muttered Pillerault, in a slightly changed tone. 'The knives are really out.'

And in the ever growing clamour, intensified by all the individual conversations, there was now no other subject than the ferocious duel between Gundermann and Saccard. It was impossible to make out the words, but this was the very substance of the noise, this alone that made so loud a roar; the calm and logical obstinacy of the one selling, and the feverish passion to keep on buying that was suspected in the other. Conflicting reports were circulating, at first murmured, but ending up as trumpet-blasts. As soon as they opened their mouths, some were shouting to make themselves heard above the din; while others, full of mystery, were bending close to the ears of their inter-locutors, speaking very quietly, even when they had nothing to say.

'Ah! I'm keeping to my position, going for a rise!' said Pillerault, already reassured. 'With such lovely sunshine, everything will go up again.'

'Everything's going to collapse,' said Moser, stubbornly doleful. 'Rain is not far off, I had a really bad night last night.'

But the smile of Salmon, who was listening to each of them in turn, became so narrowed that both became unhappy, without any possi-bility of certainty. Could that devil of a man, so extraordinarily able, so deep, and so discreet, have found a third way of playing the market, being neither bull nor bear?

Saccard, at his pillar, could see the throng of flatterers and clients growing around him. Hands continually stretched out towards him, and he shook them all with the same happy ease, putting a promise of triumph into each squeeze of his fingers. Some ran up to him, exchanged a word or two, and went off again, delighted. Many stayed on obstinately, refusing to leave him in their pride at being in his group. He would often show kindness towards people, even when he couldn't remember the names of those who were speaking to him. He did not recognize Maugendre, for instance, until Captain Chave told him his name. The Captain, now reconciled with his brother-in-law, was urging him to sell, but Saccard's handshake was enough to inflame Maugendre with unlimited hope. Then there was Sédille, the great silk-merchant and one of the directors of the bank, who wanted to consult him for a moment. His business was going downhill, and his entire fortune was so tied in with the Universal that if the price dropped it would mean ruin for him; anxious and consumed by his passion, and worried too about his son Gustave, who was not doing at all well at Mazaud's, he was in need of reassurance and encourage-ment. With one tap on his shoulder, Saccard sent him away full of faith and ardour. Then there was quite a procession: Kolb the banker, who had taken his profits some time ago, but was trying to keep on the right side of fortune; the Marquis de Bohain, with his lordly air

of haughty condescension, who affected to go to the Bourse solely
out of curiosity and through having nothing better to do; and even
Huret, incapable of nursing a grudge, and supple enough to remain
friends with people until the very day they were finally swallowed
up, was there to see if there was anything left for him to pick up. But
Daigremont appeared and everyone moved aside. He was very influential, and people noticed his affability and the confident and friendly
way he joked with Saccard. The 'bulls' were radiant, for he had a
reputation as a man who knew his way about, shrewd enough to get
out of a business at the first sign of cracks in the floor; so it became
certain that Universals were not cracking yet. Others too were walking about and simply exchanging glances with Saccard; these were
his own men, the employees who were there to give his orders, and
who were also buying for themselves in the mania for gambling, the
epidemic that was decimating the staff in the Rue de Londres, always
on the watch, with an ear at every keyhole in the hunt for tips.
Sabatani passed by twice, with the soft grace of his mixed Italian and
Oriental blood, affecting not even to see Saccard, while Jantrou,
standing a few paces away with his back turned, seemed absorbed in
reading the dispatches from the foreign stock-exchanges pinned up
on wire-meshed frames. Massias the jobber, running as usual, bumped
into the group and gave a little nod, doubtless a reply about some
swiftly performed commission. As the opening-hour approached, the
endless shuffling of feet, and the double movement of the crowd,
back and forth across the room, filled it with the deep upheavals and
roaring of a high tide.

They were waiting for the first price to be announced.

Mazaud and Jacoby had just come out from the brokers' room on
to the trading-floor side by side, with an air of conventional confra-
ternity. Yet they knew they were adversaries in the merciless struggle
which had been going on for weeks, and which could end with the
ruin of one of them. Mazaud, short, with the slim figure of a handsome man, had a bright vivacity in keeping with his good luck thus
far—luck that had led to his inheriting his uncle's business at the age
of only thirty-two, while Jacoby, a former manager, had only become
a broker by virtue of seniority, thanks to clients who supported him,
and had the stout belly and heavy gait of his sixty years—a tall man,
bald and grizzled, he had the broad face of a cheery, pleasure-loving
fellow. And both of them, with their notebooks in their hands, were

chatting about the fine weather as if they were not holding, on those pages, the millions they would be exchanging like gunshots in the murderous fight between offer and demand.

'A fine frost, eh?'

'Oh indeed, it was so pretty I even came on foot!'

When they reached the trading-floor, its vast circular basin as yet free of the cast-off papers and cards that get thrown down there, they paused a moment, leaning on the red-velvet balustrade that goes around it, continuing to exchange banal and inconsequential remarks, while also keeping an eye on their surroundings.

The four gated aisles formed a cross, a sort of four-branched star with the trading-floor at its centre; this was the sacrosanct area closed to the public; and between the branches, at the front, there was, on one side, another section for the clerks dealing in cash, overlooked by the three quoters* perched on high chairs in front of their huge registers; on the other side, a smaller open section, known as the 'guitar', no doubt on account of its shape, allowed employees and speculators to have direct contact with the brokers. Behind, in the angle formed by two other branches, in the midst of the crowd was the market for government stocks, where each broker was represented, as in the cash market, by a special clerk, each with his own distinctive notebook; for the brokers around the trading-floor are concerned exclusively with forward trading, totally given over to the great, frenetic task of speculation.

But Mazaud, seeing Berthier, his authorized clerk, trying to get his attention in the left-hand aisle, went over to exchange a few quiet words with him, the authorized clerks being allowed only in the aisles, at a respectful distance from the red-velvet balustrade which was not be touched by any profane hand. Every day Mazaud came to the Bourse with Berthier and his two clerks, one for cash deals and one for government stock, usually accompanied by the settlement clerk as well as the telegraph clerk, the latter always being little Flory, whose face was disappearing more and more under his bushy beard, leaving only the tender sparkle of his eyes. Since gaining ten thousand francs in the aftermath of Sadowa, Flory, driven to distraction by the demands of Chuchu, who was now both capricious and rapacious, was speculating wildly on his own account, without any calculation, just copying the moves of Saccard, which he followed with blind faith. The orders he knew about and the telegrams that passed through his hands were a sufficient guide for him. And now, as he was running down from the telegraph office on the first floor, both hands full of telegrams, he had to send one of the attendants to call Mazaud, who left Berthier and came over to the guitar.

'Monsieur, do I need to go through them and classify them today?'

'Yes of course, if they're arriving en masse like this... What's all that?'

'Oh, Universals, purchase orders, almost all of them.'

The broker, with a practised hand, flicked through the telegrams, obviously pleased. Very much involved with Saccard, whom he had been carrying over* for some time for considerable sums of money, and having that very morning received from him huge orders to buy, he had ended up as the official broker for the Universal. Although not greatly worried thus far, he still found it reassuring to see the continuing infatuation of the public and the obstinate buying, in spite of the extravagant rise in the price. One name stood out for him in the signatories of the telegrams: that of Fayeux, the revenue-collector of Vendôme, who must have acquired an extremely large clientele of small buyers among the farmers, pious ladies and priests of his province, for not a week went by without his sending telegram after telegram like this.

'Give all that to the cash-clerk,' Mazaud told Flory, 'and don't wait for the telegrams to be brought down to you, eh? Stay up there and take them yourself.'

Flory went and leaned over the balustrade of the cash section, shouting loudly: 'Mazaud! Mazaud!'

It was Gustave Sédille who came, for in the Bourse employees lose their own names, using only the name of the broker they represent. Flory, too, was called Mazaud. After leaving the office for nearly two years, Gustave had just gone back to it, to try to persuade his father to pay his debts, and that day, in the absence of the head clerk, he found himself in charge of the cash section, which greatly amused him. Flory leant over to whisper in his ear, and both agreed to buy for Fayeux only on the last quotation, after using his orders for their own speculation, buying and selling in the name of their usual frontman so as to pocket the difference, since a further rise seemed certain.

Meanwhile, Mazaud came back to the trading-floor. But at every step, an attendant passed him a card with an order scribbled in pencil on it, from some client who had not been able to reach him. Each broker had his own card, of a special colour—red, yellow, blue or green—so it could be easily recognized. Mazaud's were green, the colour of hope, and the little green slips kept on accumulating between his fingers, as the attendants went to and fro, taking the cards at the end of the aisles, from the hands of clerks and speculators, all of them having a ready stock of these cards in order to save time. As he paused once more by the velvet balustrade, he again found Jacoby, who was also holding a constantly growing fistful of cards, red cards, the bright red of spilt blood; orders, no doubt, from Gundermann and his followers, for everyone knew that in the massacre being prepared Jacoby was the agent for the bears, the chief operator for the Jewish banks. He was now chatting with another broker, Delarocque, his brother-in-law, a Christian married to a Jewish woman, a big, stocky, ruddy-faced man, now very bald, a frequenter of clubland, and known to be the receiver of the orders of Daigremont, who had recently fallen out with Jacoby, as he had previously done with Mazaud. The story Delarocque was telling, a rather coarse story about a woman who had returned home to her husband in a state of undress, made his little eyes twinkle and blink, while in excited mimicry he waved his notebook about, bulging with cards, blue ones, the tender blue of an April sky.

An attendant came to tell Mazaud: 'Monsieur Massias is asking for you.'

Mazaud at once returned to the end of the aisle. Massias, the jobber, wholly in the pay of the Universal, was bringing him news from the kerb market, which was already operating under the peristyle despite the terrible cold. Some speculators were venturing out anyway, going back into the hall from time to time to get warm; while the kerb-market dealers, huddled in thick overcoats, with their fur collars turned up, stayed at their posts, in a circle as usual, beneath the clock, so animated, shouting and gesticulating so much that they didn't feel the cold. And little Nathansohn was one of the most active, well on the way to becoming an important person, favoured by good luck ever since the day when, resigning his post as a petty employee of the Crédit Mobilier, he had had the idea of renting a room and opening a trading-desk.

Speaking quickly, Massias explained that as prices had seemed to waver under the impact of the load of shares with which the bears were pounding the market, Saccard had just decided to operate in the kerb market, in order to influence the first official quotation on the trading-floor. Universals had closed the previous evening on three thousand and thirty francs; and he had given Nathansohn an order for a hundred shares that another of the kerb market brokers was to offer at three thousand and thirty-five francs. This would give an increase of five francs.

'Good! That price will reach us,' said Mazaud.

And he came back to the group of brokers, all of whom were now present. All sixty were there* already, doing business among themselves in spite of the regulations, at the average price of the day before while waiting for the official bell. Orders given at a prearranged price had no influence on the market, since they had to wait until that price was quoted, while 'best price' orders, whose execution was freely left to the judgement of the broker, determined the constant up or down movements of the quotations. A good broker needed to be both shrewd and prescient, with a quick brain and agile muscles, for speed was often the key to success; and in addition he needed to be very well connected in the banking world, gathering information from just about everywhere, and seeing telegrams from the French and foreign stock exchanges before anyone else. And he also had to have a strong voice, to be able to shout loudly.

But then one o'clock struck, the peal of the bell passing like a gust of wind over the surging sea of heads; and the last vibration had not died away before Jacoby, his two hands pressed down upon the velvet, was bellowing in the loudest voice of them all:

'I have Universals! I have Universals!'

He named no price, waiting to be asked. The sixty had drawn near and formed a circle round the trading-floor, on which a few discarded slips already made splashes of bright colour. Face to face, they stared at each other, feeling each other out like duellists before the fight, very eager to see the first quotation established.

'I have Universals!' repeated Jacoby's thundering bass voice. 'I have Universals!'

'What price Universals?' asked Mazaud, in a voice not strong but so high-pitched that it rose above that of his colleague, just as the sound of the flute is heard above a cello accompaniment. And Delarocque proposed the quotation of the day before.

'At three thousand and thirty, I take Universals.'

But immediately another broker went higher:

'At three thousand and thirty-five, send me Universals.'

It was the kerb-market price arriving, preventing the deal that Delarocque must have had in mind: a purchase on the trading-floor and a quick sale at the kerb market to pocket the rise of five francs. So Mazaud made his decision, certain of Saccard's approval:

'At three thousand and forty, I take...! Deliver Universals at three thousand and forty!'

'How many?' asked Jacoby.

'Three hundred.'

Both wrote a line in their notebooks and the deal was done, the first quotation fixed, with a rise of ten francs on the price of the previous day. Mazaud moved away, to give the figure to the quoter who had the Universal on his books. Then, for twenty minutes, the floodgates were open; quotations for the other stocks had also been fixed, and the whole assorted heap of business brought in by the brokers was being transacted, without much variation in prices. And meanwhile the quoters, perched on high, caught between the din of the trading-floor and that of the cash market, which was also feverishly busy, could scarcely manage to enter all the new quotations the brokers and clerks were constantly throwing at them. Further back, the market for government stocks was also furiously busy. Now the market was open, it was no longer simply a matter of the crowd roaring with the unremitting noise of rushing water; above that tremendous rumbling there now rose the strident shouts of offers and demands, a characteristic yapping that rose and fell, and paused only to start again in tormented shrieks of varying strength, like the cries of thieving birds caught in a storm.

Saccard, standing beside his pillar, was smiling. His court had grown even bigger; the rise of ten francs on Universals had set the whole Bourse in a flutter, for a crash on settlement day had long been forecast. Huret had drawn near, along with Sédille and Kolb, loudly claiming to regret his prudence, which had made him sell his shares once the price reached two thousand five hundred; while Daigremont, looking quite detached, with the Marquis de Bohain on his arm, was cheerily telling him why his stable had been defeated in the autumn races. But above all, Maugendre was triumphantly pouring scorn on Captain Chave, who was still obstinately pessimistic, saying they had better wait to see how it would all end. And the same scene was being played out between the boastful Pillerault and the woeful Moser, the one radiant about this mad rise, the other clenching his fists and talking of this obstinate, idiotic rise, as if it were some mad animal that in the end would have to be put down.

An hour went by, the quotations remained much the same, and business continued on the trading-floor, as new orders and telegrams came in, but less intensely than before. About half way through each session of the Bourse, there would be this sort of slowing-down, a calmer spell of ordinary business before the decisive battle over the final quotations. But Jacoby's bellowing could still be heard, interspersed with Mazaud's shrill cries, both of them hard at work on options. 'I have Universals at three thousand and forty, of which fifteen... I take Universals at three thousand and forty, of which ten... How many? Twenty-five... deliver!' These were no doubt the orders from Fayeux that Mazaud was carrying out, for in order to limit their losses, many provincial speculators bought and sold options before finally committing themselves. Then suddenly a rumour went around, and spasmodic shouts were heard: Universals had just dropped five francs; then, in swift succession, they dropped ten francs, then fifteen francs, and fell down to three thousand and twenty-five.

Just then Jantrou, who had come back after a brief absence, told Saccard that Baroness Sandorff was there in her coupé in the Rue Brongniart, and was asking him if she should sell. Coming just at the moment when the price was wobbling, this question exasperated Saccard. In his mind's eye he could see again the motionless coachman perched on his box, and the Baroness studying her notebook behind the closed windows, as if she were at home. And he replied:

'Tell her to stop bothering me! And if she sells, I'll strangle her!'

Massias came rushing up at the announcement of the fall of fifteen francs as if answering an alarm-call, feeling he would be needed. Indeed, Saccard, who had prepared a stratagem to make sure of the last quotation—a telegram that was to be sent from the Lyons Stock Exchange, where a rise was certain—was beginning to grow anxious at the non-arrival of the telegram; and this unexpected fall of fifteen francs could bring disaster.

Massias, astutely, did not stop in front of Saccard but nudged him with his elbow and inclined his ear to receive the order:

'Quick, to Nathansohn, four hundred, five hundred, whatever it takes.'

This was all done so quickly that only Pillerault and Moser noticed. They at once rushed after Massias to find out what was happening.

Since he had been in the pay of the Universal, Massias had acquired enormous importance. People would attempt to sound him out and try to read over his shoulder the orders he was carrying. And he was himself now making splendid gains. With his smiling affability, this unlucky fellow, ill-used by fortune as he had been until now, was quite astonished; he now declared that this dog's life at the Bourse was after all quite bearable, and he no longer said one had to be a Jew to get on.

At the kerb market, in the freezing air of the peristyle that the pale mid-afternoon sun did little to warm, Universals had fallen less rapidly than on the trading-floor. And Nathansohn, forewarned by his brokers, had just effected the deal that Delarocque had failed to make: buying in the main hall at three thousand and twenty-five, he had sold again under the colonnade for three thousand and thirty-five. This had taken less than three minutes, and he had made sixty thousand francs. The purchase had already made the price rise in the hall to three thousand and thirty, thanks to the levelling effect that the two markets, the official one and the tolerated one, have on each other. There was an endless gallop of clerks, elbowing their way through the throng, from the hall to the peristyle. However, the price in the kerb market was just about to drop, when the order that Massias brought to Nathansohn maintained it at three thousand and thirty-five then raised it to three thousand and forty-five; while in consequence, the stocks on the trading-floor came back to the first quotation. But it was difficult to keep it there, for the strategy of Jacoby and the other agents acting for the bears was to save the really big sales until the end of the session, so that they could use them to crush the market and bring about a collapse in the disarray of the last half-hour. Saccard so clearly understood the danger that with a pre-arranged signal he alerted Sabatani, standing just a few steps away, smoking a cigarette with the unconcerned and languid air of a ladies' man; he at once, with serpentine suppleness, made his way to the guitar, where, while listening intently to all the prices, he went on sending orders to Mazaud on the green cards of which he had a considerable stock. In spite of all this, the attack by the bears was so fierce that Universals once again went down five francs.

The clock struck the third quarter; there was only a quarter of an hour left before the closing bell. The crowd was now whirling about and screaming as if lashed by some hellish torment; the trading-floor was snarling and howling, with a harsh clanging like the smashing of pots and pans, and it was just then that the incident so anxiously awaited by Saccard occurred.

Little Flory, who, since the opening of the Bourse, had been running down from the telegraph office every ten minutes with his hands full of telegrams, reappeared once more, pushing his way through the throng, this time reading a telegram with which he seemed highly pleased.

'Mazaud! Mazaud!' called a voice.

And Flory, naturally, turned his head, as if he were responding to his own name. It was Jantrou who wanted to hear the news. But the clerk, in too great a hurry, pushed past him, full of delight at the thought that the Universal would finish with a rise; for the telegram announced that the share-price was rising at the Lyons Stock Exchange, where purchases of such importance had been made that the effect was bound to be felt on the Paris Bourse. Indeed, other telegrams were already arriving, a large number of brokers were receiving orders. The result was immediate and considerable.

'At three thousand and forty, I take Universals,' Mazaud was repeating in his shrill, birdlike voice.

And Delarocque, overwhelmed with orders, raised the bid by five francs more.

'At three thousand and forty-five, I take...'

'I hold, at three thousand and forty-five,' bellowed Jacoby. Two hundred, at three thousand and forty-five.'

'Deliver!'

Then Mazaud himself went higher.

'I take at three thousand and fifty.'

'How many?'

'Five hundred. Deliver!'

But the din was now so dreadful, with all this epileptic gesticulating, that the brokers themselves could no longer hear each other. And caught up in the professional frenzy that possessed them, they continued their work by gestures, since the resonant bass of some voices did not carry, while the fluting of others thinned into nothingness. Enormous mouths could be seen opening, without any distinct sound coming out of them; all the talking was being done by hands alone; an outward gesture meant an offer, and an inward gesture acceptance; fingers raised indicated quantities, and a nod or a shake of the head said yes or no. It was like one of those fits of madness that can seize a crowd, and was intelligible only to the initiated. Up above, women were leaning their heads over the telegraph gallery, stupefied and horrified at this extraordinary spectacle. In the government-stocks market, it was almost like a brawl, with a furious central group resorting to fisticuffs, while the public, crossing this side of the room in both directions, pushed into the groups that were constantly breaking up and forming again in a continual turmoil. Between the cash market and the main trading-floor, above the tempest-tossed sea of heads, there were now only the three quoters, sitting on their high chairs, floating above the waves like wreckage, with the big white patch of their registers, while they were tugged hither and thither by the rapid fluctuation of the prices being thrown at them. In the cash section especially, the jostling was at its worst, it was a solid mass of heads of hair, without faces, like a dark swarm, lightened only by the little white pages of the notebooks waving about in the air. And on the trading-floor around the basin, now filled with a multicoloured floral display of crumpled cards, one could see the grey of hair, the glistening of bald heads, the pallor of agitated faces, and hands feverishly outstretched, a whole dancing pantomime of bodies moving more freely, all seeming ready to devour each other if the balustrade had not held them back. This last-minute madness had also reached the public, people were being crushed in the hall, in a huge shuffling of feet, like the stampede of a great herd let loose in too narrow a passage; and in the great blur of frock-coats, only the silk hats gleamed, under the diffused light from the high windows.

Then suddenly the sound of a bell rang out through the tumult. Everything calmed down, gestures stopped in mid-air, voices fell silent in the cash market, the government-stock market, and on the trading-floor. There remained only the dull roar of the crowd, like the even voice of a torrent returning to its bed and its normal flow. And in the last of the agitation, the last quotations were circulating; Universals had risen to three thousand and sixty a rise of thirty francs over the previous day. The defeat of the bears was complete; the settlement was once again going to be disastrous for them, for the differences of the fortnight would cost a substantial amount.

For a moment, before leaving the hall, Saccard stretched up as though the better to take in the crowd around him in one glance. He was really bigger, so uplifted by his triumph that the whole of his little figure swelled and grew longer, became enormous. The person he seemed to be looking for over the heads of the crowd was the absent Gundermann, the Gundermann he would like to have seen defeated, grimacing and begging for mercy; and he was determined that at least all those unknown agents of the Jew, all the filthy Jews who were there, full of resentment, should see him thus transfigured, in the glory of his success. This was his great day, the day people still talk about, as they do about Austerlitz and Marengo.* His clients and his friends had rushed to him. The Marquis de Bohain, Sédille, Kolb, and Huret were shaking his hand, while Daigremont, with the false smile of his worldly affability, was congratulating him, knowing that at the Bourse death often follows such victories as these. Maugendre would have kissed him on both cheeks in his excitement, though exasperated to see Captain Chave just shrugging his shoulders. But the most complete, even religious, adoration came from Dejoie, who had run from the newspaper office to learn what the last quotation had been, and now stood quite still, a few steps away, rooted to the spot by tenderness and admiration, his eyes glistening with tears. Jantrou had disappeared, no doubt gone to take the news to Baroness Sandorff. Massias and Sabatani were panting and beaming, as if on the triumphant evening of a great battle.

'Well, what did I tell you?' cried the delighted Pillerault. Moser, with a long face, made vague, threatening noises.

'Yes, yes, but he laughs longest who laughs last... Mexico will have to be paid for; affairs in Rome are even more confused since Mentana,* and Germany is going to fall upon us one of these fine mornings... Yes, yes, and these fools, the higher they go, the further they'll fall. Ah, it's all up now, you'll see!'

Then, as Salmon this time continued to look at him gravely, he added:

'That's your view, isn't it? When everything's going too well, it means everything's going to crash.'

But now the hall was emptying, and soon the only thing left would be the cigar-smoke in the air, a bluish cloud, thickened and yellowed by all the dust flying about. Mazaud and Jacoby, now restored to normality, had returned together to the brokers' office, the latter more upset at his own losses than by the defeat of his clients; while the former, who didn't speculate, was full of delight at the last quotation, so valiantly fought for. They talked to Delarocque for a few minutes, exchanging their engagements, holding in their hands their little books full of notes, notes that their settlement clerks would go through that very evening to process the deals that had been made. Meanwhile, in the clerks' office, a low room with big pillars, rather like a badly kept classroom, with rows of desks and a cloakroom at the far end, Flory and Gustave Sédille, who had gone there to get their hats, were noisily engaged in merry chatter while waiting to find out the average quotation, which was calculated by the clerks of the syndicate, according to the lowest and highest of the quotations. Towards half-past three, when the poster had been put up on one of the pillars, they both neighed like horses, clucked like hens, and crowed like roosters, in their satisfaction at the splendid result they had achieved with their manoeuvres on Fayeux's orders to sell. It meant a pair of diamond earrings for Chuchu, who was now tyrannizing Flory with her demands, and six months payment in advance for Germaine Coeur, whom Gustave had been foolish enough to entice definitively away from Jacoby, who had just taken up with a horsewoman from the Hippodrome on a monthly basis. The noise continued unabated in the clerks' room, with all sorts of silly tricks and throwing about of hats, like the romping of schoolboys in the playground. And on the other side, under the peristyle, the kerb market was hastily finishing its business, and Nathansohn, delighted with his dealings, was making his way down the steps through the last of the speculators, who were still lingering there in spite of the now intense cold. By six o'clock, this whole world of gamblers, brokers, dealers and jobbers, once they had calculated their gains or losses, and others had prepared their brokerage bills, would all get dressed up and, with their distorted view of money, complete the dizziness of the day in restaurants and theatres, fashionable soirées, and mistresses' boudoirs.

That evening, the fun-loving Paris that stays up late talked of nothing but the tremendous duel between Gundermann and Saccard. The women, quite caught up in speculation, through enthusiasm and fashion, made ostentatious use of technical terms like 'settlement' and 'option', 'carry-over' and 'close', without necessarily understanding them. People talked especially about the critical situation of the short-sellers, who, for so many months, had been paying larger and larger sums at each settlement to cover ever greater differences as Universals just went up and up beyond any reasonable limit. Some were certainly gambling without cover, and getting carried over, being unable to deliver the shares; they kept on and on, still betting on a fall, hoping for a sudden collapse of the market; but in spite of all the carrying-over, which became ever more expensive as money grew more scarce, the bears, exhausted and crushed, were going to be annihilated if the rise went on. It was true, though, that the situation of the all-powerful Gundermann, reputed to be their chief, was quite different, for he had his billion in his cellars, his inexhaustible troops that he could go on sending out to be massacred, no matter how long and murderous the campaign. This was his invincible strength, being able to keep on short-selling, with the certainty that he would always be able to pay the differences, until the day when the inevitable fall would give him victory.

People talked about it, calculating what large sums he must already have seen swallowed up, when, on the 15th and 30th of every month, he sent forth sacks of gold that melted in the fire of speculation, like lines of soldiers mown down by bullets. Never before had he experienced, in the Bourse, so fierce an attack on his power, which he intended to be sovereign and indisputable; for, if he was, as he liked to repeat, a simple money-merchant, not a gambler, he was fully aware that to remain that merchant, the first in the world, in control of the public fortune, he had to be absolute master of the market; and he fought not for immediate gain but for his very royalty, and his life. Hence the cold obstinacy, the wild grandeur of the struggle. He was seen on the boulevards or along the Rue Vivienne, with his pale, impassive face, walking, as ever, like an exhausted old man, but without the slightest trace of any anxiety. He believed only in logic. Once the shares of the Universal went above the two-thousand-franc mark, it was the beginning of madness, and at three thousand it was sheer lunacy; they were bound to fall, just as a stone thrown in the air inevitably drops; and he was waiting. Would he go right to the end of his billion? Around Gundermann people throbbed with admiration, but also with the desire to see him at last devoured; while Saccard, who provoked a more tumultuous enthusiasm, had on his side the women, the smart salons, and the whole fashionable world of gamblers, who had been pocketing handsome profits ever since they started coining money with their faith, and trading on Mount Carmel and Jerusalem. The forthcoming ruin of the big Jewish banks had been decreed; Catholicism was going to acquire the empire of money, as it had that of souls. But if his troops were making huge gains,

Saccard himself was running out of money, emptying his coffers to make his continual purchases. Of the two hundred million available, almost two-thirds were now tied up: this was a prosperity too great, an asphyxiating, suffocating triumph. Any company that tries to be mistress of the Bourse in order to preserve the price of its shares is a company doomed. So indeed, at the start, Saccard had only intervened with caution. But he had always been the man of imagination, seeing things on too grand a scale, transforming his shady and risky deals into epic poems; and this time, with this really colossal and prosperous enterprise, he had moved into extravagant dreams of conquest, with an idea so mad, so huge, that he did not even formulate it clearly to himself. Ah, if only he had had millions, endless millions, like those dirty Jews! The worst of it was that he could see the end of his troops, only a few more millions left for massacre. Then, if the fall should come, it would be his turn to pay the differences; and being unable to produce the shares, he would have to ask to be carried over. For all his victory, the tiniest speck of grit could wreck his vast machine. There was some vague awareness of this even among the faithful, those who believed in the rise the way they believed in God. This was what was exciting Paris still more, all the confusion and doubt that accompanied this duel between Saccard and Gundermann, this duel in which the victor was bleeding to death, this hand-to-hand struggle between two fabulous monsters, trampling underfoot the poor devils who dared to join in their game, and threatening to strangle each other upon the heap of ruins they were piling up beneath them.

Suddenly, on 3 January, on the morrow of the day when the accounts of the last settlement had been paid, Universals went down by fifty francs. This caused some commotion. In fact everything had gone down; the market, driven too hard for so long, and impossibly inflated, was now cracking all over; the collapse of two or three crooked companies had made quite a din; anyway, people should have been used to these violent fluctuations, for prices sometimes varied by several hundreds of francs even in the course of one day's Bourse, going crazy, like the needle of a compass in a storm. But in the great shudder that ensued, everyone sensed the beginning of the debacle. Universals were going down, the cry went around, spreading into a great clamour made of astonishment, hope, and fear.

The very next day Saccard, firmly at his post and smiling, raised the price by thirty francs by means of substantial purchases. But on the 5th, despite his efforts, the fall was forty francs. Universals were now down to three thousand. And from then on, every day brought another battle. On the 6th, Universals went up again. On the 7th and 8th they went down once more. There was an irresistible movement, dragging them gradually into a slow fall. The bank was to be the scapegoat, it was to pay for the folly of all, for the crimes of other less prominent enterprises, for the proliferation of shady ventures, over-heated by advertising, springing up like monstrous mushrooms in the putrefied compost of the reign. But Saccard, who now couldn't sleep, and who every afternoon took up his battle-post beside the pillar, was living as if hallucinated by a still-possible victory. Like an army commander convinced of the excellence of his plan, he yielded ground only inch by inch, sacrificing his last soldiers and emptying the bank's coffers of their last bags of gold to bar the way to his assailants. On the 9th, he still won a signal advantage: the bears trembled and retreated, would the settlement of the 15th once again be fattened by their losses? And Saccard, already without resources, reduced to launching paper into circulation, now dared, like those starving people who in the delirium of their hunger see huge feasts before them, to acknowledge to himself the prodigious and impossible goal he was aiming at, the gigantic idea of buying back every one of his shares, to hold the short-sellers, bound hand and foot, at his mercy. That had just been done for a minor railway company, when the issuing bank had gathered up the entire market; and the vendors, unable to deliver, had surrendered like slaves, forced to offer up their fortune and their person. Ah! If only he had been able to hunt down and frighten Gundermann to the point where he could hold him, powerless and unable to sell! If only he had seen him one morning bringing his billion, and begging him not to take it all, but to leave him ten sous for the daily milk on which he lived! But for that to happen, seven to eight hundred millions were needed. Saccard had already cast two hundred million into the abyss, and he needed to line up five or six hundred more. With six hundred million he could sweep away the Jews, he could become the king of gold, the master of the world. What a dream! And it was so simple, any idea of the value of money was totally abolished at this level of fever, it was merely a matter of moving pawns about on the chessboard. During his sleepless nights, he raised the army of six hundred millions and had them all killed for his glory, so he stood victorious at last in the midst of disasters, on the ruins of everything.

Unfortunately, on the 10th Saccard had a terrible day. At the Bourse he remained splendidly light-hearted and calm. But never had there been a war of such silent ferocity, with every hour bringing new slaughter, and ambushes on every side. In these covert and cowardly financial battles, in which the weak are quietly disembowelled, there are no more bonds of any sort, no kinship, no friendship, only the atrocious law of the strong, those who eat so as not to be eaten. So Saccard felt absolutely alone, with no other support than his own insatiable appetite which kept him on his feet, ceaselessly devouring. He particularly dreaded the afternoon of the 14th, when the replies on the options would come in. But he still managed to find enough money for the three days before, and the 14th, instead of bringing a crash, strengthened Universals, which, on the settlement day of the 15th, closed at two thousand eight hundred and sixty francs, only one hundred francs down on the last quotation of December. Having feared a disaster, Saccard now affected to believe this was a victory. In reality it was the bears who, for the first time, were winning, at last receiving the differences instead of paying them, as they had done for months; and in this reversed situation, Saccard had to get Mazaud to carry him over, and from then on, Mazaud found himself heavily involved. The second fortnight of January would be decisive.

Ever since he had been fighting like this, with daily shocks casting him down into the abyss, then up again, Saccard had felt, every evening, a frantic need for mind-numbing entertainment. He could not be alone; he dined out, and ended his nights beside some woman. Never before had he burned up his life in this way, turning up everywhere, doing the rounds of the theatres and nightclubs, spending ostentatiously, with the extravagance of a man with too much money. He avoided Madame Caroline, who embarrassed him with her reproaches, always telling him about the anxious letters she was receiving from her brother, and herself despairing about his bullish campaign, so alarmingly dangerous. He was seeing more of Baroness Sandorff, as if this cold perversion in the new little ground-floor apartment in the Rue Caumartin could provide a sufficient change of scenery to allow him the hour or so of forgetfulness necessary for the relaxation of his overtaxed, exhausted brain. Sometimes he hid out there to examine some papers, or reflect on certain matters, glad to be able to assure himself that there no one would disturb him. Sleep would often overtake him, and he would nod off for an hour or two, the only delicious hours of unconsciousness he had; and the Baroness then had no hesitation about going through his pockets and reading the letters in his wallet; for he had become totally silent with her, not a single useful tip could she get out of him, and when she did get a word out of him, she was convinced he was lying, so she no longer dared to follow his suggestions in her speculation. It was by stealing his secrets in this way that she had acquired certainty about the financial problems with which the Universal Bank was now struggling, with a whole vast system of kite-flying, raising money on credit, with accommodation bills* that the bank was discreetly discounting abroad. One evening Saccard, waking too soon, caught her in the act of going through his wallet and slapped her as one might a prostitute caught filching money from the waistcoat of her clients; and since that time he had taken to beating her, which enraged them and wrecked them, then calmed both of them down.

However, after the settlement of 15 January, which had cost her about ten thousand francs, the Baroness began to nurture a plan. She became obsessed with it, and eventually went and asked Jantrou's advice.

'My word, I think you're right,' he replied, 'it's time to go over to Gundermann... Go and see him then and tell him, since he promised that the day you gave him a useful piece of advice, he would give you one in return.'

On the morning when the Baroness turned up, Gundermann was in a filthy humour. Just the day before, Universals had risen again. Would he never be rid of it, this voracious beast that had swallowed so much of his gold, and still refused to die! It could even go up again, once more closing on a rise on the 31st of the month, and he was reproaching himself for ever having entered this disastrous conflict, when he might perhaps have done better just to get on with the new bank from the start. Shaken in his usual strategy, and losing faith in the inevitable triumph of logic, he would, at that instant, have resigned himself to beating a retreat if he could have done so without losing everything. Such moments of discouragement were rare for him, though even the greatest captains have experienced them, even on the eve of victory, when men and things seem to be willing them to succeed. This disturbance of his normal, powerful clear-sightedness resulted from the fog that eventually arises from those mysterious operations of the Bourse, which it is never possible to lay at the door of anyone in particular. Certainly Saccard was buying, was speculating. But was he doing it for real clients? Or was it for the company itself? In the end Gundermann couldn't tell, surrounded as he was by all the different bits of gossip he was getting from everywhere. The doors of his huge office were being slammed, all his staff were trembling at his rage, and he greeted the jobbers so brutally that their usual procession turned into a gallop of disarray.

'Ah, it's you!' said Gundermann to the Baroness, without the slightest touch of courtesy. 'I don't have time to waste with women today.'

She was so disconcerted that she abandoned everything she had prepared to say, and just blurted out the news she was bringing.

'What if it could be proved to you that the Universal has run out of money after the huge purchases it has made, and that it has been reduced to discounting its accommodation bills abroad, in order to continue its campaign?'

The Jew suppressed a shiver of joy. His eyes remained lifeless, and he replied in the same growling tones:

'That's not true.'

'What do you mean, not true? I have heard with my own ears, seen with my own eyes.'

She decided to convince him by explaining that she had held in her hands the notes signed by frontmen. She named them, and named also the bankers who, in Vienna, Frankfurt, and Berlin, had discounted the bills of credit.* Gundermann's correspondents would be able to inform him, and he would see she wasn't bringing him any airy gossip. She further maintained that the company had bought its own shares, with the sole aim of keeping the price rising, and that two hundred millions had already been swallowed up.

Listening to her with his gloomy air, Gundermann was already planning the next day's campaign, working with such quick intelligence that in a few seconds he had distributed his orders and calculated the amounts. Now he was certain of victory, knowing full well from what filth this information came, and full of contempt for the pleasure-loving Saccard, who was stupid enough to trust himself to a woman and allow himself to be betrayed.

When she had finished, he raised his head and looked at her with his big, lifeless eyes:

'Well now, why should what you're telling me be of any concern to me?'

She was quite astonished, so calm and unconcerned did he seem.

'But I thought, as you were short-selling...'

'I? Who told you I was short-selling? I never go to the Bourse, I don't speculate... None of that is of any interest to me!'

And his voice was so guileless that the Baroness, shaken and alarmed as she was, would have ended up believing him, had it not been for certain inflections of irony in the naivety of his response. Clearly he was laughing at her, in his absolute disdain as a man totally free of desire, with no more use for women.

'So, my good friend, as I am very busy, if you don't have anything more interesting to tell me...'

He was showing her the door. Furious now, she turned on him:

'I trusted you, I spoke first... and fell into a trap... You promised me, if I was helpful to you, you would in turn help me, and give me some advice...'

He stood up, interrupting her. He, who never laughed, gave a little snigger, so thoroughly was he enjoying this brutal fooling of a young and pretty woman.

'Some advice, well, I don't refuse that, my good friend... Listen to me carefully. Don't gamble, don't ever gamble. It will make you ugly, a gambling woman is not a pretty sight.'

And when she had left, beside herself with rage, he shut himself up with his two sons and his son-in-law, allocated the roles they would play, and sent messages to Jacoby and other brokers, to prepare the great coup of the following day. His plan was simple: to do what, in his ignorance of the actual situation of the Universal, prudence had prevented him from daring until now; to crush the market under enormous sales, now he knew the Universal was at the end of its resources and incapable of holding the price up. He was going to bring forward the formidable reserves of his billion, like a general who wants to get the battle over, and has learned the weak point of the enemy from spies. Logic would triumph, all securities that rise above the real value they represent are doomed.

Indeed, that very day, Saccard, sensing danger with his natural flair, went to see Daigremont. He was in a fever, he felt that this must surely be the time for striking hard at the bears, if he didn't want to be definitively beaten by them. And his gigantic idea was tormenting him, that colossal army of six hundred million still to be raised in order to conquer the world. Daigremont greeted him with his usual amiability, in his princely mansion, surrounded by valuable pictures, and all the dazzling luxury paid for by his fortnightly profits from the Bourse, though no one really knew what actual substance lay behind the lavish decor, always liable to be whisked away by some whim of fortune. So far, Daigremont had not betrayed the Universal, refusing to sell and affecting an air of absolute confidence, enjoying his stance as a good gambler, betting on a rise, out of which he was anyway making a considerable profit; and he had been pleased with himself for not flinching, even after the bad settlement of the 15th, convinced, as he kept telling everyone, that the rise would restart, but keeping his eyes open, ready to go over to the enemy at the first serious sign of trouble. Saccard's visit, the extraordinary energy he displayed, and the enormous idea he outlined, of scooping up everything on the market, filled him with real admiration. It was mad, but then the great men in war and finance, aren't they often just madmen who succeed? And Daigremont formally promised to come to his aid the very next day at the Bourse. He had already taken up strong positions, and he would see his agent Delarocque, to take up some more; not to mention the friends he would visit, a whole syndicate, as it were, that he would bring in as reinforcements. This new army corps could be estimated, he thought, at about a hundred million, immediately available. That would be enough. Saccard, radiant, certain of victory, at once drew up the battle plan, a flanking movement of rare audacity, a strategy borrowed from the most celebrated captains; first, at the opening of the Bourse, a simple skirmish to attract the short-sellers and give them confidence; then, when they had obtained a first success and the prices were falling, Daigremont and his friends would arrive with their heavy artillery, all those unexpected millions suddenly appearing from behind a ridge, attacking the short-sellers in the rear and overwhelming them. They would be crushed, massacred. The two men left each other after much handshaking and triumphant laughter.

An hour later, as Daigremont, who was dining out, was about to get dressed, he received another visit, from Baroness Sandorff. In her consternation, she had suddenly had the idea of consulting him. At one time she had been thought to be his mistress, but in fact there had never been anything between them except a very free man–woman comradeship. They were both too feline, and understood each other too well to manage the deception involved in a liaison. She told him her fears, her visit to Gundermann, and his response, but she lied about the surge of treachery that had inspired her conduct. Daigremont was most amused, and enjoyed frightening her even more, pretending to be quite shaken, and almost believing that Gundermann was telling the truth when he swore he was not short-selling, for indeed, can one ever tell? The Bourse is a real forest, a forest on a dark night, in which people can only grope their way along. In all that darkness, if you're foolish enough to take heed of everything, however inept and contradictory, that you're told, then you're sure to break your neck.

'So,' she asked anxiously, 'I ought not to sell?'

'Sell? Why would you? What madness! Tomorrow we shall be the masters, Universals will go up to three thousand one hundred: just hold on, whatever happens: you will be happy with the closing price... I can't say any more.'

The Baroness had just left, and Daigremont was at last getting dressed, when a ring at the doorbell announced a third visit. Ah! Not another! He would not receive this one. But when he was handed the card of Delarocque, he at once called out to let him in, and as the broker, looking very disturbed, seemed to hesitate to speak to him, Daigremont sent away his valet, himself putting the finishing touches to his white tie in front of a tall mirror.

'My dear chap!' said Delarocque with the easy familiarity of a man of the same social circle. 'Look, I'm counting on your friendship, all right? This is rather delicate... Just imagine, Jacoby, my brother-in-law, has just been kind enough to warn me of an attack that is being prepared. Gundermann and the others have decided to break the Universal at tomorrow's Bourse. They are going to throw the whole lot on to the market... Jacoby has his orders... he came running to tell me...'

'Heavens!' cried Daigremont, turning pale.

'You understand, I'm holding some very strong positions, betting on a rise, yes, up to about fifteen millions, enough to wipe me out entirely... So, do you see? I've hired a cab and I'm doing the round of my main clients. It's not at all correct, but the intention is good...'

'Heavens!' Daigremont repeated.

'So, my good friend, as you are speculating without cover, I came to ask you to cover me, or else to abandon your position.'

'Abandon it, yes, abandon it, my dear chap... Oh, no, I don't stay

with companies that are crumbling, that's just useless heroism...
Don't buy, sell! I have about three millions' worth with you, sell, sell
it all!'

And as Delarocque was hurrying away, saying he had other clients
to see, Daigremont seized his hands and pressed them vigorously.

'Thank you, I shall never forget this. Sell, sell everything.'

Once more alone, he called his valet back to attend to his hair
and beard. Ah, what a lesson! This time he had almost let himself be
bamboozled, like a child. That's what came from associating with a
madman!

That evening, at the eight o'clock kerb market, the panic began.
That market was held at that time on the pavement of the Boulevard des
Italiens, at the entrance of the Passage de l'Opéra; it was only the kerb
market, operating in the midst of a shady throng of option-dealers,
jobbers, and seedy speculators. Street-hawkers were going round,
and collectors of cigar-ends were crawling about among the tramping
feet of the different groups. The Boulevard was quite blocked by this
obstinate herd, packed together, sometimes carried along by the flow
of passers-by, sometimes split up, but always forming again. That
evening nearly two thousand people were standing there, thanks
to the mildness of the weather, with the cloudy, misty sky now promising rain, after the earlier dreadful cold. The market was very busy,
Universals were being offered on all sides, and prices were falling
rapidly. Soon, of course, rumours began circulating, and a new anxiety set in. What was happening? With voices lowered, people named
the likely sellers, according to the jobber who gave the order, or the
broker who executed it. Since the big players were selling like this,
something really serious must be in the wind. And from eight o'clock
until ten, there was a mad rush; all the canny speculators abandoned
their positions, there were even some who just had time to change
from buyers into sellers. All went off to bed in a fever of unease, as on
the eve of great disasters.

Next day, the weather was appalling. It had rained all night, a fine
icy rain was swamping the city, now transformed by the thaw into a
cesspit of yellow, liquid mud. By half-past twelve, the Bourse was
already clamouring under this downpour. The crowd sheltering
under the peristyle, and in the hall, was enormous; and the hall, with
all the umbrellas dripping on to the floor, soon found itself turned
into a vast puddle of muddy water. The walls exuded black filth, and

from the glass roof there came only a dim and reddish light, of desperate melancholy.

With all the ugly rumours going around, extraordinary stories that were seriously disturbing, the eyes of all, from the moment they entered the room, searched out Saccard and stared at him. He was at his post, standing by the usual pillar; and he looked the same as on other days, the days of triumph, with his air of pleasant good humour and absolute confidence. He was well aware that Universals had dropped by three hundred francs the day before at the evening kerb market; he could sense a huge danger, he was expecting a furious assault from the short-sellers; but his battle-plan seemed to him unbeatable; Daigremont's flanking movement, the unexpected arrival of a fresh army of millions, must surely sweep everything before it, and once again assure him of victory. He had no further resources; the coffers of the Universal Bank were empty, he had scraped out everything, down to the last centime—but he was not despairing; he had been carried over by Mazaud yet again, he had won him over to such an extent, telling him of the support of Daigremont's syndicate, that the broker had again accepted his purchase orders for several millions without any cover. The strategy they had agreed on was not to let the prices fall too far at the opening of the Bourse, but to fight to support them pending the arrival of the reinforcements. So great was the excitement that Massias and Sabatani, abandoning useless pretences, now that the true situation was on everyone's lips, went quite openly to talk to Saccard, then both ran to take his new orders, one to Nathansohn under the peristyle, and the other to Mazaud, who was still in the brokers' room.

It was ten minutes to one, and Moser, who arrived looking pale after a liverish attack which had kept him awake all the previous night, remarked to Pillerault that everybody, that day, looked jaundiced and sickly. Pillerault, restored by the approach of disasters, began boasting like a knight-errant and gave a loud laugh:

'My dear fellow, you're the one who's sick. Everyone is very happy. We are about to give you one of those thrashings that are not easily forgotten.'

The truth was, however, that in the general anxiety, the whole room remained gloomy, under the reddish light, and this was especially noticeable in the subdued rumble of the voices. No longer was it the tumultuous roar of the days when prices were rising, that agitation,

that din of an all-conquering tide, overflowing on all sides. There was
no more running, no more shouting—people sidled along and spoke
quietly, as if in a house where someone lay ill. Although there was a
considerable crowd, and one could hardly breathe when trying to
move around, there was only a desolate murmuring, a whispering
about the current fears, and some quiet exchanges of appalling news.
Many remained silent, their faces drawn and livid, and eyes widened,
desperately scanning the faces of others.

'Nothing to say for yourself, Salmon?' asked Pillerault, full of
aggressive irony.

'Of course not!' muttered Moser. 'Like all the rest, he has nothing
to say, he's frightened.'

Indeed, on that day, the silences of Salmon upset no one, for everyone was in the same state of profound and mute anticipation.

But it was especially around Saccard that a stream of clients had
gathered, trembling with anxiety, longing for a word of comfort. It
was later noticed that Daigremont had not shown his face, nor had
Deputy Huret, doubtless forewarned, since he was once more
Rougon's devoted lackey. Kolb, surrounded by a group of bankers,
pretended to be absorbed in a big arbitrage. The Marquis de Bohain,
quite above the vicissitudes of fortune, calmly walked around with
his pale, aristocratic little head, certain of winning in any event, since
he had told Jacoby to buy as many Universals as he had asked Mazaud
to sell. And Saccard, besieged by the crowd of others, the devout and
the naive, presented an especially amiable and reassuring face to
Sédille and Maugendre who, with trembling lips, and tearful, pleading
eyes, were looking for hope of triumph. He shook them firmly by the
hand, putting into the grip of his hand an absolute promise of victory.
Then, like a man who is invariably happy, and beyond the reach of
any danger, he began to bewail a triviality.

'You find me quite upset. A camellia got left out in my courtyard
in this severe cold, and it died.'

Word went around, and people lamented the unfortunate camellia.
What a man, that Saccard! With his calm assurance, his ever-smiling
face, with nobody able to tell if it was only a mask covering frightful
worries that would have tortured anyone else.

'What a creature! Isn't he splendid?' Jantrou muttered in the ear of
Massias, who had just come back.

Just then Saccard, a memory suddenly coming back to him at this supreme moment, called Jantrou, remembering the afternoon when they had both seen Baroness Sandorff's coupé drawn up in the Rue Brongniart. Was it there again today, on this day of crisis? And was the coachman, perched on high, keeping stock-still, as the rain pelted down, while the Baroness, behind the closed windows, waited to hear the prices?

'Yes, certainly, she is there,' Jantrou answered quietly, 'and heartily with you, determined not to retreat one step... We are all here, stoutly at our posts.'

Saccard was happy to hear of this fidelity, though he had doubts about the disinterestedness of the lady, and the others. Anyway, in the blindness of his fervour, he still believed he was marching to victory, with his whole nation of shareholders behind him, that nation of humble folk and high society, all intoxicated and fanatical, pretty women and servants, all alike in the same surge of faith.

At last the bell rang out, with the wail of an alarm over that agitated sea of heads. And Mazaud, who was giving orders to Flory, hurried back to the trading-floor, while the young clerk rushed to the telegraph office, very worried on his own account, for, though he had been making a loss for some time, stubbornly following the fortunes of the Universal, he was that day risking a decisive move, based on the expectation of Daigremont's intervention, which he had heard about from behind a door at the office. The trading-floor was as nervous as the hall; the brokers, ever since the last settlement, had been feeling the ground shaking beneath their feet, amid symptoms of such gravity as to alarm even them with all their experience. Already there had been some partial collapses, the market, exhausted and overburdened, was showing cracks on all sides. Was this then going to be one of those great cataclysms of the sort that happens every ten or fifteen years, one of those crises that hit speculation when it reaches the point of acute fever, when it decimates the Bourse, and sweeps through like a wind of death? In the government stocks and in the cash market, the shouting sounded choked, the jostling was getting rougher, and above it all were the dark and high silhouettes of the quoters, waiting, pen in hand. And at once, Mazaud, his hands gripping the red-velvet balustrade, saw Jacoby on the other side of the circular area, shouting in his deep voice:

'I have Universals... At two thousand eight hundred, I have Universals...'

That was the closing price on the kerb market of the night before; and to check the fall, Mazaud thought it wise to buy at that price. His shrill voice rose above all the others:

'At two thousand eight hundred, I take... three hundred Universals, deliver!'

So the first quotation was fixed. But it proved impossible to maintain. Offers flooded in on all sides. He struggled desperately for half-an-hour, with no other result than slightly to slow down the rapid fall. He was surprised to find he was not being supported from the trading-floor. So what was happening to Nathansohn, from whom he was expecting orders to purchase? It was only later that he learned of Nathansohn's clever tactics; while buying for Saccard, he was selling on his own account, having got wind of the real situation through his Jewish flair. Massias, himself very involved as a buyer, ran up, panting, to give news about the disaster on the trading-floor to Mazaud, who lost his head and decided to shoot his bolt, releasing in one stroke all the orders he had been keeping back to execute one by one, pending the arrival of the reinforcements. That sent the price up a little: from two thousand five hundred it went back to two thousand six hundred and fifty, with the sudden mad leaps that happen on tempestuous days; and once again, for a moment, hope, boundless hope, arose in the minds of Mazaud, Saccard, and all those who were in the secret of the battle-plan. Since the price was already going up, they had won the day, the victory would be crushing when the reserves came out on the flank of the short-sellers, changing their defeat into a devastating rout. There was a movement of intense joy, Sédille and Maugendre looked as if they would kiss Saccard's hand, and Kolb drew near, while Jantrou disappeared, running off to take the good news to Baroness Sandorff. And at that moment the radiant little Flory was seen searching everywhere for Sabatani, now acting as his intermediary, to give him new orders to purchase.

But two o'clock had just struck, and Mazaud, who was bearing the brunt of the attack, was again weakening. He was more and more surprised at the delay of the entry into battle of the reinforcements. It was high time for them to arrive, so what were they waiting for, to release him from the untenable position which was draining him? Although, out of professional pride, he kept his face impassive, he could feel a great chill rising to his cheeks, and feared he might be turning pale. Jacoby, thundering on, went on throwing offers at him in bundles, one after another, but he was no longer picking them up. And it was no longer at Jacoby that he was looking; his eyes were turned now in the direction of Delarocque, Daigremont's broker, whose silence he could not understand. Stout and stocky, with his russet beard, smiling beatifically after some festivity of the night before, Delarocque seemed quite calm, while waiting so inexplicably. Wasn't he going to pick up all these orders, and save everything through the purchase orders with which the order-books he was holding must be bulging?

Suddenly, in his guttural, slightly hoarse voice, Delarocque threw himself into the fight.

'I have Universals… I have Universals…'

And in a few minutes he offered several millions' worth. Some voices responded. The share-price was collapsing.

'I have at two thousand four hundred… I have at two thousand three hundred… How many? Five hundred, six hundred… Deliver!'

What was he saying? What was happening? Instead of the expected help, was this a new enemy army, suddenly appearing out of nearby woods? Just like Waterloo, when Grouchy did not arrive;* and it was treachery that completed the rout. In the face of these deep and new masses of sellers, coming in at the gallop, a fearful panic set in.

At that moment, Mazaud felt death pass over his face. He had carried over Saccard for too large an amount, and he had the distinct sensation that the Universal, in its collapse, was breaking his back. But his handsome, dark face, with its small moustache, remained stolid and impenetrable. He bought some more, exhausting the orders he had received, with his young-cockerel voice crowing just as shrilly as it had in success. And facing him, his opposite numbers, Jacoby bellowing and Delarocque apoplectic, despite their effort at indifference, showed some signs of anxiety; for they could see that he was now in great danger, and if he went bust, would he pay them? Their hands gripped the velvet of the balustrade, while their voices kept on shouting, as if mechanically, out of professional habit, while their fixed stares reflected all the dreadful anguish of this drama of money.

Then, during the last half-hour, it was disaster, the rout steadily worsening, and carrying people away in a gallop of confusion. After extreme confidence and blind infatuation came the reaction of fear, all now rushing to sell, if there was still time. A hail of orders to sell beat upon the trading-floor, all one could see was order-slips raining down; and these huge blocks of shares, scattered pell-mell like this, accelerated the fall, made it a real collapse. The prices, going down and down, fell to one thousand five hundred, to one thousand two hundred, to nine hundred. There were no more buyers, nothing was left, the ground was strewn with corpses. High above the dark swarm of frock-coats, the three quoters seemed like mortuary clerks, registering deaths. By a singular effect of the wind of disaster blowing through the room, all agitation had come to a stop and the noise had died down, as in the stupor of a great catastrophe. A frightening silence reigned when, after the ringing of the closing bell, the closing price of eight hundred and thirty francs became known. And the rain went on stubbornly streaming down the windows, which now let in only a sort of sickly twilight; the hall, under the dripping umbrellas and trampling of feet, had become a cesspit, like the muddy floor of an ill-kept stable, littered with all sorts of torn papers; while the trading-floor displayed the bright, multicoloured slips, the green, the red, the blue, thrown away in handfuls, in such quantities that day that the vast basin was overflowing.

Mazaud had gone back to the brokers' room at the same time as Jacoby and Delarocque. He went up to the bar and, consumed with a raging thirst, drank a glass of beer, and gazed at the huge room, with its cloakroom, its long central table with the chairs of the sixty brokers ranged around it, the red-velvet hangings, all the banal and faded luxury which made it look like the first-class waiting-room of a large railway-station; he looked at it with an astonished air, as a man might, who had never really seen it before. Then, as he was leaving, without a word, he shook hands with Jacoby and Delarocque in the usual way, but all three were pale beneath their appearance of everyday normality. He had told Flory to wait for him at the door, and he found him there, along with Gustave, who, having definitively left the office a week ago, had come along simply out of curiosity, always smiling and leading a life of pleasure, without ever wondering whether his father, on the morrow, would still be able to pay his debts; while Flory, looking very wan, was struggling to talk, and making idiotic grimaces, under the impact of the fearful loss he had just made, of about a hundred thousand francs, with no idea where to find the first sou of it. Mazaud and his clerk disappeared into the rain.

But in the hall, panic had raged above all around Saccard—this

was where the war had done most damage. Without at first understanding, he had faced up to the danger and watched the whole rout.
Where did that noise come from? Wasn't that Daigremont's troops
arriving? Then, when he had heard the prices collapsing, still unable
to grasp the cause of the disaster, he had stiffened himself, ready to
die on his feet. An icy chill rose up from the ground to his skull, he
sensed something irreparable, this was his defeat for ever; and no base
regret for money, or anger about pleasures lost, had any part in his
pain; he bled only for his humiliation at being vanquished, and for the
dazzling, definitive victory of Gundermann, consolidating once more
the omnipotence of that king of money. At this moment Saccard was
really superb, his whole slight figure braving destiny with unblinking
eyes, his face stubbornly set, standing alone against the flood of
despair and resentment that he could already feel rising against him.
The whole room was seething, surging towards his pillar; fists were
clenched, mouths were muttering curses; and he had kept on his lips
an unconscious smile, that could easily seem a provocation.

First, in a sort of mist, he made out Maugendre, with a face of
mortal pallor, as Captain Chave led him away on his arm, saying over
and over that he had told him how it would be, with the cruelty of a
minimal gambler, delighted to see the big players come a cropper. Then
there was Sédille, with drawn face and the mad look of a merchant
whose business is crumbling, who came like a good fellow, though
with trembling hands, to shake Saccard's hand, as if to say he bore
him no grudge. At the first sign of danger, the Marquis de Bohain
had moved away, going over to the triumphant army of short-sellers,
telling Kolb, who was also prudently keeping his distance, about the
worrying doubts he had had about Saccard ever since the last shareholders' meeting. Jantrou, quite distraught, had disappeared again,
running as fast as he could to take the closing price to Baroness
Sandorff, who would surely have a hysterical fit in her carriage, as she
was apt to do on days when she lost heavily.

There too, facing the still silent and enigmatic Salmon, were
Moser the short-seller and the bullish Pillerault;, the latter, in spite of
his ruin, remained provocative, with his proud face, while the former,
having made a fortune, was spoiling his victory with worries about
the future.

'You'll see, in the spring, we'll be at war with Germany. All this
has a bad smell, and Bismarck is watching and waiting.'

'Oh, do stop all that! Once again I made the mistake of giving things too much thought... Too bad! I just need to start all over again, and all will be well.'

So far, Saccard had not weakened. But hearing someone behind him mention Fayeux, the collector of revenues in Vendôme, with whom he had had dealings for a number of petty shareholders, the name had caused him some distress, reminding him of the enormous mass of humble folk, wretched little investors who would be crushed to pieces under the wreckage of the Universal. Then, suddenly, the sight of Dejoie, distraught and deathly pale, sharpened that distress, with this one poor man whom he knew, seeming to personify all the rest of the humble folk now ruined. At the same time, in a sort of hallucination, the pale and desolate faces of the Countess de Beauvilliers and her daughter arose before him, gazing at him in despair with their wide eyes full of tears. And at that moment, Saccard, the pirate, with a heart toughened by twenty years of banditry, Saccard, who took pride in never having felt his legs give way and who had never once sat down on the bench right there beside the pillar, this same Saccard experienced a moment of real weakness, and had to let himself sink down upon it for a moment. Crowds still surged around, almost suffocating him. He raised his head to get some air, and was at once on his feet, for he recognized, up in the telegraph gallery, looking down on the hall, La Méchain, towering over the battlefield with her enormous fat person. Her old black-leather bag lay beside her on the stone balustrade. Waiting to fill it up with worthless shares, she was watching out for the dead, like the voracious crow that follows armies until the day of massacre.

Saccard then, with a firm step, went away. His entire being seemed to him empty; but by an extraordinary effort of will, he went forward, erect and steady. But his senses seemed to have been blunted, he could no longer feel the ground, he seemed to be walking on a thick woollen carpet. His eyes too were clouded by mist, and his ears buzzing with noise. As he went out of the Bourse and down the steps, he no longer recognized people, they were just phantoms floating around him, vague shapes and stray sounds. Did he not see the broad grimacing face of Busch go by? Did he not pause for a moment to chat with Nathansohn, who was very much at ease, and whose weakened voice seemed to come from far away? Were not Sabatani and Massias walking with him, amid the general consternation? He seemed to see himself once more with a large group around him, perhaps Sédille and Maugendre again, all sorts of faces that faded away, and kept changing. And as he was about to go away, and disappear into the rain and the liquid mud submerging Paris, he repeated in a shrill voice to all that phantom throng, making it a last point of honour to show his freedom of spirit:

'Ah! How very upset I am about that camellia that got left out in my courtyard, and died of the cold!'

CHAPTER XI

MADAME CAROLINE, horrified, sent a telegram that very evening to her brother, who still had one more week in Rome; and three days later, rushing to the scene of danger, Hamelin arrived in Paris.

There was a fierce encounter between Saccard and the engineer, right there in the workroom where formerly their venture had been discussed and decided on with so much enthusiasm. During those three days, the collapse at the Bourse had horribly worsened, and Universal shares had gone down, fall after fall, even to below par, to four hundred and forty francs; and the fall was continuing, the whole edifice was crumbling hour by hour.

Madame Caroline listened in silence, not wanting to intervene. She was full of remorse, accusing herself of complicity, for it was she who, after promising to watch over things, had let it all happen. Instead of contenting herself with merely selling her shares to try to hamper the rise, shouldn't she have found some other recourse, like warning people, taking some action, in short? Adoring her brother as she did, her heart bled for him, seeing him compromised in this way, with his great ventures undermined and his whole life's work called in question; she suffered all the more in that she felt she had no right to judge Saccard: hadn't she loved him? Was she not his, through that secret bond, the shame of which she now felt more than ever? Placed as she was between these two men, she was being torn apart in a violent struggle. On the evening of the catastrophe, she had launched out at Saccard in a great fit of frankness, emptying her heart of all the reproaches and fears it had been gathering for so long. Then, seeing him smiling, still tenacious and unvanquished, and thinking of how much strength he needed to keep standing up, she had felt she had no right, when she had been so weak with him, to finish him off by hitting him when he was down. And taking refuge in silence, showing blame only by her attitude, she wanted to be merely a witness.

But Hamelin, he who was normally so conciliatory, so detached from everything other than his work, this time grew angry. He made an extremely violent attack on speculation; the Universal had succumbed to the madness of speculation in a frenzy of sheer lunacy. Of course he was not one of those who claimed that a bank can simply let its shares go down, as, for instance, a railway company can: railway companies have their mass of equipment, equipment that makes money, whereas the bank's real equipment is its credit, so it is in dire trouble the moment its credit wobbles. But there was a question of proportion. If it was necessary, even wise, to keep the share-price at two thousand francs, it was crazy and completely criminal, to push it up, to try to put it up to three thousand and even beyond. As soon as he arrived, Hamelin had insisted on the truth, the whole truth. It was now impossible to lie to him, to tell him what he had allowed them to announce in his presence at the last shareholders' meeting, that the company did not possess a single one of its own shares. The books were there and he easily saw through the lies they held. For instance, Count Sabatani; he knew that this frontman concealed the activities of the bank itself, and he was able to follow month by month Saccard's mounting fever over the last two years, starting timidly, buying only with moderation, then driven on to larger and larger purchases, reaching the enormous figure of twenty-seven thousand shares costing nearly forty-eight milllion francs. Wasn't that mad, a madness of such impudence it seemed to take people for fools, with such enormous transactions attributed to Sabatani? And Sabatani was not the only one, there were other men of straw, bank employees, even directors, whose purchases, entered as carried over, exceeded twenty thousand shares, these too representing nearly forty-eight million francs. Indeed, that was just the completed purchases; to these must be added the fixed-term purchases,* made in the course of the last January settlement, representing a sum of sixty-seven-and-a-half million for more than twenty thousand shares, of which the Universal would have to take delivery; in addition, ten thousand other shares at the Lyons Stock Exchange, which made another twenty-four million. All of this, when added up, showed that the bank was holding nearly a quarter of the shares it had issued, and had paid for those shares the appalling sum of two hundred million francs. That was the abyss into which it had sunk.

Hamelin's eyes filled with tears of grief and rage. He had so successfully laid the foundations for his great Catholic bank in Rome, the Treasury of the Holy Sepulchre, which in the coming days of persecution, would allow the Pope to be royally installed in Jerusalem, in the legendary glory of the Holy Land: a bank that would put the new kingdom of Palestine beyond the reach of political disturbance, basing its budget, with the guarantee of the country's own resources, on a series of share-issues that Christians the world over would vie with each other to buy! And all of that was now foundering, thanks to the imbecile madness of speculation. Hamelin had gone away, leaving behind him an admirable state of affairs, with millions aplenty, and a bank enjoying so fast and so great a prosperity that it had astonished the world; and less than a month later, he returned to find the millions had melted away, and the bank was wrecked, reduced to dust, nothing left but a black hole, over which fire seemed to have passed. His stupor grew, he violently demanded explanations, trying to understand what mysterious power had driven Saccard to strive so relentlessly against the colossal edifice he had built, destroying it stone by stone on one side, while on the other he claimed to be completing it.

Saccard, without getting angry, gave a very clear reply. After the first hours of turmoil and despair, he had recovered his self-possession, standing sturdily on his own two feet, with his indomitable hopefulness. Treachery had made the catastrophe terrible, but all was not lost, he would raise it all up again. Besides, if the Universal had enjoyed such rapid prosperity, wasn't that due to the very methods for which he was now being reproached? The creation of the syndicate, the successive increases of capital, the early balance-sheet of the last shareholders' meeting, the shares kept by the bank and, later, the shares bought en masse, so wildly. It was all of a piece. Accepting the success meant also accepting the risks. When you overheat a machine, it sometimes bursts. For the rest, he acknowledged no fault, he had simply done, but with more intelligence and vigour, what every manager of a bank does; and he had not abandoned his brilliant idea, his gigantic idea, of buying up the entirety of the shares and bringing down Gundermann. He had lacked the money, that was all. Now they must start again. A shareholders' meeting had been called for the following Monday, and he was certain of his shareholders, he said: they would be willing to make the necessary sacrifices, he was convinced that at a word from him they would all bring him their money. Meanwhile, they would manage on the little sums that the other financial houses, the big banks,* were advancing every morning for the day's urgent needs, to avoid too sudden a collapse which would endanger them too. Once the present crisis was over, everything would start again and be splendid once more.

'But', Hamelin objected, already calmed by this smiling tranquillity of Saccard's, 'can't you see the tactics behind the help being offered by our rivals? It's a way of protecting themselves first, and then of slowing down our fall to make us fall further... What worries me is that I see Gundermann in all this.'

In fact Gundermann was one of the first to offer help, to avoid the immediate declaration of bankruptcy, with the extraordinary practical common sense of a man who, having been forced to set fire to a neighbour's property, hastens thereafter to bring pails of water to prevent the destruction of the whole neighbourhood. He was above resentment, and the only glory he cared about was being the premier money-merchant of the world, the richest and the most shrewd, having succeeded in sacrificing all his passions to the continuous increase of his fortune. Saccard made an impatient gesture, exasperated by this evidence of the victor's wisdom and intelligence.

'Oh, Gundermann is playing Mister Magnanimous, and thinks he's wounding me with his generosity.'

Silence fell, and it was Madame Caroline, who had not spoken until now, who at last went on:

'My friend, I've let my brother speak to you as he needed to do, in the legitimate grief he has felt on learning all these deplorable things... But our situation, his and mine, seems clear, and it seems to me impossible—it is, isn't it?—that he should find himself compromised if this affair were to turn out decisively badly. You know at what price I sold our shares, no one can say that he pushed for a rise to get a bigger profit from his holdings. Besides, if there is a catastrophe we know what we have to do... I confess I don't have your obstinate hopefulness. But you're right, we must fight until the last minute, and you can be sure my brother will certainly not discourage you from that.'

She was very moved, once more captured by tolerance towards this man with his obstinate vivacity, but trying not to show this weakness, for she could no longer close her eyes to the execrable things he had done and would surely do yet again, with all the dishonest passion of an unscrupulous brigand.

'Certainly,' declared Hamelin, weary and incapable of further resistance, 'I am not going to paralyse you when you're fighting to save us all. You can count on me if I can be of help.'

And once more, at this last hour, facing the most terrible threats,

Saccard reassured them, winning them over again and leaving them with these words, full of promise and mystery:

'Sleep easy... I cannot say more, but I am absolutely certain I can get everything back on track again before the end of another week.'

This remark, which he did not explain, he repeated to all the associates of the bank, and all the clients who came to him, frightened or even terrified, seeking advice. For three days now, there had been an endless gallop through his office in the Rue de Londres. The Beauvilliers, the Maugendres, Sédille, and Dejoie all came, one after another. He received them very calmly, with a soldierly air, and with vibrant words that put courage back in their hearts; and when they spoke of selling, of realizing at a loss, he got angry, shouted at them not to do anything so stupid, promising on his honour, to get back to the quote of two thousand or even three thousand francs. In spite of all the mistakes that had been made, they all still had blind faith in him: if only he could be set free to rob them again, he would sort everything out and in the end make them all rich, as he had sworn to do. If no accident occurred before Monday, and if he was given time to call an Extraordinary General Meeting, no one doubted that he would pull the Universal safe and sound out of the ruins.

Saccard had thought of his brother Rougon, that was the all-powerful help he had indicated without giving any further explanation. On meeting the traitor Daigremont face to face and bitterly reproaching him, he had received only this response: 'But my dear chap, it wasn't I who abandoned you, it was your brother.' Of course the man was within his rights, since he had only joined the company on condition that Rougon was in it, and Rougon had been formally promised; so it was not at all astonishing that he should pull out when the minister, far from being in it, was at war with the Universal and its manager. This was at least an excuse to which there was no answer. Struck by this, Saccard realized what a huge mistake he had made by quarrelling with his brother who alone could defend him, and make him so sacred an object that no one would dare to bring about his ruin, knowing the great man was behind him. For Saccard's pride, this was one of the hardest moments, when he decided to beg Deputy Huret to intervene on his behalf. But he still maintained a threatening attitude, refusing to disappear, and demanding help as if it were a right, from Rougon, who had more to lose than he did from a scandal. The next day, as he awaited Huret's promised visit, Saccard only received a note, in which he was told in vague terms not to be impatient and to count on a happy outcome later on, if circumstances permitted. He had to content himself with these few lines, which he regarded as a promise of neutrality.

But the truth was that Rougon had just taken the firm decision to finish once and for all with this diseased member of his family, who had been embarrassing him for years with the perpetual terror of unsavoury events, and he preferred to be at last done with him for good. If catastrophe came, he was resolved to let things take their course. Since he would never get Saccard to go voluntarily into exile, the simplest solution, surely, was to force him to leave the country, helping him to take flight after a thorough condemnation. A sudden scandal, quickly swept under the carpet, and that would be an end of it.

Besides, the minister's position was becoming difficult ever since he had declared to the Legislative Assembly, in a passage of memorable eloquence, that France would never allow Italy to take possession of Rome. Heartily applauded by the Catholics, he had been severely attacked by the increasingly powerful Third Party,* and he could see the time coming when the latter, supported by the Liberal Bonapartists, were going to force him out of power, unless he also gave them some sort of pledge. And the pledge, if circumstances so decreed, would be the abandonment of the Universal Bank, which, under the patronage of Rome, had become disturbingly powerful. Finally, what had clinched his decision was a secret message from his colleague in the Ministry of Finance, who, being about to float a loan, had found Gundermann and all the Jewish bankers very reticent, intimating that they would refuse their capital as long as the market remained uncertain for them, and open to adventurers. It was a triumph for Gundermann. Better the Jews, with their accepted sovereignty of gold, than the Ultramontane Catholics as masters of the world, if they became the kings of the Bourse!

It was later related that the Minister of Justice, Delcambre, with his relentless grudge against Saccard, had had Rougon sounded out about the conduct to be followed with regard to his brother if justice had to intervene, and had received only the heartfelt cry: 'Ah, if he'll just get rid of him for me, I'll light a special candle for him!'

After that, with Rougon abandoning him, Saccard was done for. Delcambre, who ever since he got into power had just been waiting for the opportunity, at last had him on the margin of the law, on the very edge of the vast net of the judiciary, needing now only a pretext to launch his police and his judges against him.

One morning Busch, furious at not having acted sooner, took himself off to the Palais de Justice. If he didn't hurry, he would never now get out of Saccard the four thousand francs still owed to La Méchain on the famous bill of expenses for little Victor. His plan was simply to create an appalling scandal, accusing Saccard of the abduction of a child, which would allow the exposure of all the filthy details of the rape of the mother, and the abandonment of the child. Such a prosecution of the manager of the Universal, in all the heightened emotions of the bank's current crisis, would rouse the whole of Paris; and Busch still hoped that Saccard would pay up at the first threat. But the surrogate who had been appointed to receive him, a nephew of Delcambre, listened to his story with an air of impatience and boredom: No, no! Nothing serious could be done with such gossip, this did not fall under any article of the law. Disconcerted, Busch grew angry, and was speaking of his long and patient wait, when the magistrate suddenly interrupted him on hearing him say that he had pushed his good-will towards Saccard to the point of depositing funds on credit in the Universal. What? He had funds compromised in the certain failure of that institution, and he was taking no action? Nothing could be simpler; he had only to make a charge of embezzlement, for the law was already aware of fraudulent transactions which were going to result in bankruptcy. This was what would deal a terrible blow, not the other story—that melodrama about a girl who drank herself to death, and a child brought up in the gutter. Busch listened with a grave, attentive face, launched on this new path, pulled towards an act he had not originally intended, but whose decisive consequences he could foresee: Saccard under arrest, and the Universal receiving its death-blow. Simple fear of losing his money would have made him decide at once. He liked nothing better than disasters and the opportunity to fish in troubled waters. Yet he hesitated, saying he would think about it and come back later, and the surrogate Public Prosecutor had to thrust the pen into his hand, and make him write out, there and then in his office, on his desk, the charge of embezzlement, which, as soon as Busch had gone, he carried off in a ferment of zeal to his uncle, the Minister of Justice. The deed was done.

Next day, at the bank in the Rue de Londres, Saccard had a long interview with the auditors and the appointed administrator, to draw up the balance-sheet he wanted to present to the shareholders' meeting. In spite of the loans from the other financial houses, it had proved necessary to close the counters and suspend all payments, in the face of increasing demands. This bank, which only a month before, had nearly two hundred millions in its coffers, had been able to reimburse its desperate clients only the first few hundreds of thousands of francs. Bankruptcy had been officially declared by a Commercial Court, after a summary report given the day before by an expert called in to examine the books. In spite of everything, Saccard, as if unaware, with an extraordinary mixture of blind hopefulness and obstinate bravura, was still promising to save the situation. And indeed, that very day he was awaiting a response from the floor of the Bourse about fixing a rate of compensation, when the usher came in to tell him that three gentlemen were waiting to see him in an adjoining room. This was perhaps salvation, so Saccard rushed off happily, only to find a police superintendent, accompanied by two constables, who immediately arrested him. The summons had just been issued after perusal of the expert's report, pointing out irregularities in the accounts, and particularly after the accusation of abuse of trust from Busch, who claimed that funds he had deposited in the bank had been misappropriated. At the same time Hamelin was being arrested at his home in the Rue Saint-Lazare. This time it really was the end, as if every hatred and every kind of ill-luck had relentlessly worked against them. The Extraordinary General Meeting could not now take place: the life of the Universal Bank was over.

Madame Caroline was not at home at the time of her brother's arrest, and he could do no more than leave her a few hastily scribbled lines. When she returned home, she was aghast. Never had she thought even for a moment that anyone could think of prosecuting her brother, so entirely free did he seem of any shady dealings, his innocence seemingly proved by his long absences. The day after the bankruptcy, the brother and sister had stripped themselves of all they possessed, in order to increase the assets,* wanting to remain as naked, coming out of this adventure, as when they had gone into it; and the sum was considerable, nearly eight million, in which the three hundred thousand francs inherited from an aunt had also been swallowed up. Madame Caroline immediately threw herself into all sorts of activities and appeals; she now lived with the sole purpose of improving the lot, and preparing the defence, of her poor dear Georges, bursting into tears, despite her courage, whenever she thought of him, innocent as he was, behind bars, stained by this fearful scandal, his life in ruins and soiled for ever. He, so gentle and weak, with the piety of a child, and, apart from his technical work, the ignorance of 'a big ninny', as she used to say. At first she had raged against Saccard, sole cause of the disaster, creator of their adversity, whose execrable handiwork she could now reconstruct and clearly judge, from those very first days when he had teased her so merrily for reading the Code, to these final days when, with the severe consequences of failure, all the irregularities had to be paid for, irregularities she had foreseen and allowed to happen. Then, tortured by remorse for the complicity that haunted her, she fell silent, and tried to avoid openly concerning herself with him, doing her utmost to act as if he did not exist. When she had to pronounce his name, it seemed as if she were speaking of a stranger, an adversary, whose interests were quite other than hers. She, who visited her brother almost every day at the Conciergerie,* had not even requested a permit to go and see Saccard. And she was very brave, still living in their apartment in the Rue Saint-Lazare, receiving all comers, even those who arrived with insults on their lips, transformed now into a businesswoman, determined to salvage whatever she could of their honesty and happiness.

During the long days she spent in this way in the workroom, where she had lived such lovely days of work and hope, one sight particularly distressed her. When she drew near a window and looked down upon the house next door, it was with a pang at her heart that she saw, behind the windows of the little room where the two poor women lived, the pale profiles of the Countess de Beauvilliers and her daughter Alice. These February days were very mild, so she saw them frequently, walking slowly, with heads bent, along the alleys of the mossy, winter-ravaged garden. The crash had been terrible for these two lives. The unhappy ladies who, a fortnight before, had been in possession of eighteen hundred thousand francs through their six hundred shares, would today be able to get only eighteen thousand for them, now that the shares had fallen from three thousand francs to thirty. Their entire fortune had been lost, swept away at a stroke: the twenty thousand francs for the dowry, so painfully saved by the Countess, the seventy thousand francs, first borrowed on the farm at Les Aublets, then the two hundred and forty thousand francs from the sale of Les Aublets, when it had actually been worth four hundred thousand. What was to become of them, when the many mortgages on their house already ate up eight thousand francs a year, and they had never been able to reduce the household expenses to less than seven thousand, despite all their miserliness and the sordid miracles of economy they achieved to keep up appearances and maintain their status? Even if they sold their shares, how could they now live, how meet all their needs, with just eighteen thousand francs, the final debris from the shipwreck? One necessity imposed itself, one that the Countess had not yet been able to face with resolution: to leave their house, since it was impossible to pay the interest, abandon it to the mortgagees rather than waiting until the latter put the house up for sale, retire at once to some quiet little lodging and there live a restricted and obscure life until the last crust of bread was gone. If the Countess still resisted, it was because this meant a tearing away of her whole person, the death of what she had believed herself to be, the crumbling of that edifice of her race that for years, with heroic obstinacy, she had upheld with her trembling hands. The Beauvilliers in rented accommodation, no longer under the ancestral roof but living in the houses of others, in the acknowledged penury of the defeated—wasn't that, really, enough to make one die of shame? So she went on struggling.

One morning Madame Caroline saw the two ladies doing their washing in the little shed in the garden. The old cook, now almost helpless, was no longer much use to them; during the recent cold weather they had had to look after her; and it was the same story with the cook's husband, who was porter, coachman and valet all in one; it was now only with great difficulty that he swept the house, and kept the old horse on its feet, stumbling now and wrecked by age, as he was himself. So the ladies had resolutely applied themselves to the housework, the daughter sometimes leaving her watercolours to make the thin broths on which the four people were frugally living, the mother dusting the furniture, mending the clothes and shoes, thinking she was making some minute economy in the use of dusters, needles and thread now that it was she who was using them. But as soon as a visitor arrived it was quite a sight to see the way they both fled, throwing off aprons, having a quick wash, and reappearing as the ladies of the house, with white and idle hands. Viewed from the street, their lifestyle had not changed: their honour was intact, the carriage came out properly equipped to take the Countess and her daughter on their visits, and the fortnightly dinners still brought together the same guests as every winter, with not one dish less on the table nor one candle less in the candelabra. Only someone who was able, like Madame Caroline, to look down into their garden could know what terrible days of fasting followed all that show, that illusory façade of a vanished fortune. When she saw them, down there in that damp well of a garden, squashed between neighbouring houses, walking with their mortal melancholy under the greenish skeletons of the centenarian trees, she was seized by immense pity, and would leave the window, her heart torn with remorse, as if she felt she had been Saccard's accomplice in causing this wretchedness.

Then, on another morning, Madame Caroline felt a sadness more direct, and even more painful. A visit from Dejoie was announced, and she bravely insisted on seeing him.

'Well, my poor Dejoie...'

But she stopped in alarm when she saw the pallor of the former office-boy. His eyes seemed lifeless, his face was distraught, and formerly very tall, he had shrunk, as if folded up.

'Come now, you must not let yourself be demoralized by the thought of all that money being lost.'

And then he spoke, in a slow voice:

'Oh, Madame, it's not that... Of course, in the first moment it was a hard blow, because I had got used to thinking we were rich. When you're winning, it goes to your head, it's as if you were drunk... But Lord! I was already resigned to going back to work, and I'd have worked so hard I would have managed to make up the sum again... But, you can't imagine...'

Fat tears rolled down his cheeks.

'You can't imagine... She's gone...'

'Gone? Who's gone?' asked Madame Caroline in some surprise.

'Nathalie, my daughter. Her marriage had fallen through, and she was furious when Théodore's father came to tell us that his son had waited too long, and he was going to marry a haberdasher's daughter who was bringing him nearly eight thousand francs. That, of course, I understand—that she should be angry at being left with no money, and no prospect of marriage. But I loved her so much! Even last winter, I would get up in the night to tuck in her blankets. And I went without tobacco so she could have prettier hats, and I was a real mother to her, I brought her up, I only lived for the pleasure of seeing her, in our little apartment.'

His tears were choking him, and he broke into sobs.

'So it's all the fault of my ambition... If I had sold, as soon as my eight shares gave me the six thousand francs for the dowry, she would have been married by now. But there, do you see? The price kept going up, and I thought of myself; first I wanted to get an income of six hundred, then eight hundred, then a thousand francs; all the more eagerly in that my little girl would later inherit that money... To think that at one moment, when the price was three thousand, I had twenty-four thousand francs in hand, enough to give her a dowry of six thousand, and retire, myself, with an income of nine hundred francs. No! I wanted a thousand, isn't that stupid? And now it's not even two hundred francs... Ah, it's my fault! I'd have done better to throw myself in the river.'

Madame Caroline, very moved by his grief, let him relieve his feelings. But she still wanted to know more.

'So she's gone, my poor Dejoie, but gone where?'

Then he looked embarrassed, and a faint flush rose to his pallid face.

'Yes, gone, disappeared, three days ago. She had become acquainted with a gentleman who lived across the street from us—oh! a very proper gentleman, a man of forty... So, she has run away.'

While he gave some details, searching for words, tripping over his tongue, Madame Caroline could see Nathalie again in her mind's eye, slim and blonde, with the frail grace of a pretty girl of the Paris streets. She had noticed especially her wide eyes, so tranquil and so cold, with the extraordinary limpidity of egoism. The child had allowed herself to be adored by her father, happy to be idolized, and behaving well as long as it was in her interests to do so, incapable of a stupid fall for as long as she was expecting a dowry, a marriage, and a counter in a little shop, where she could have played the queen. But to go on with a penniless life, living in rags with her good old father, having to go back to work—ah, no, she had had enough of that dreary life, now unrelieved by hope! And she had gone, had coldly put on her boots and her hat, and gone elsewhere.

'Oh Lord!' Dejoie went on, stammering. 'She didn't have much fun at home, it's true, and it's annoying for a nice girl to be wasting her youth, getting bored... But even so, she has been very hard. Just think of it! Not even saying goodbye to me, not a scrap of a letter, not the tiniest promise to come back and see me now and then... She just shut the door and that was that. You see, my hands are trembling,

I've been like a wounded animal ever since. It's too much for me, I keep on looking for her in the house. After so many years, dear Lord, how is it possible that I don't have her with me any more, and never shall again, my poor little child!'

He had stopped crying, and his bewildered grief was so distressing that Madame Caroline seized hold of both his hands, finding no other comfort for him than to keep repeating:

'My poor Dejoie, my poor Dejoie…'

Then, to distract him, she went back to the failure of the Universal. She blamed herself for having let him buy shares, and severely criticized Saccard, without naming him. But suddenly the former office-boy became animated. Bitten by the gambling bug, he was still passionate about it.

'Ah, Monsieur Saccard, he was so right to stop me selling. It was a splendid business, and we'd have beaten them all, but for the traitors who let us down… Ah, Madame, if Monsieur Saccard were here, things would be different. It was death for us when they put him in prison. And it's only he who could save us… I told the judge: "Monsieur, give him back to us, and I'll trust him again with my fortune and my life, because, you see, that man, he's like God himself! He can do whatever he wants."'

Madame Caroline gazed at him, quite stupefied. What! Not a word of anger or reproach? This was the ardent faith of a believer. What powerful influence could Saccard have had on the whole flock, to keep them under such a yoke of credulity?

'In fact, Madame, I came here just to tell you that, and you must forgive me if I told you about my own troubles, because I'm not very steady in my head just now… When you see Monsieur Saccard, please tell him we are still with him.'

He went away with faltering steps, and for a moment she felt a horror of life. That unhappy man had broken her heart. Against the other man, the one she didn't name, she felt a fresh surge of anger, the force of which she rammed down inside herself. Besides, visitors were now arriving, she had hordes of them that morning.

Among the flow of people, the Jordans especially upset her again. They had come, Paul and Marcelle, like a loving couple who always acted together in serious matters, to ask whether there was really nothing more their parents, the Maugendres, could get out of their shares in the Universal. On that side the disaster was irreparable.

Before the great battles of the last two settlements, the former tarpaulin-manufacturer already held seventy-five shares, which had cost him about eighty thousand francs—a splendid deal, since at one moment, with the price at three thousand francs, the shares represented two hundred and twenty-five thousand. But the awful thing was that in the passion of the fight, he had gambled without cover, believing in the genius of Saccard, and had gone on buying, with the result that the frightful differences he had to pay, more than two hundred thousand francs, had just swept away the last remnants of his fortune, that income of fifteen thousand francs, that he had earned with thirty years of hard work. Now he had nothing, he would hardly be able to clear all his debt, even after selling his little house in the Rue Legendre, of which he had been so proud. And in this disaster, Madame Maugendre had certainly been more guilty than he.

'Ah, Madame,' Marcelle explained, with her sweet face, even in the midst of catastrophe, still fresh and smiling, 'you can't imagine how Mama changed! She, so prudent, so thrifty, the terror of the servants, always at their heels picking over their accounts, she had taken to speaking only in terms of hundreds of thousands; she kept urging Papa on—oh! he was much less brave, deep down, and would have listened to Uncle Chave if she hadn't driven him mad with her dream of winning the big prize, the million... They got caught up in speculation at the start through reading the financial papers, and it was Papa who first got enthusiastic about it; indeed, to begin with he used to hide what he was doing; then once Mama went into it too, despite having for so long professed a good housekeeper's hatred of all gambling, it all blazed up, it didn't take long. How is it possible that the passion for winning can change decent people to such an extent!'

Jordan broke in, amused by the recollection of the face of Uncle Chave, evoked by his wife's mention of him.

'And if you had only seen Uncle's serenity in the midst of these catastrophes! It was just what he had predicted, he was triumphant in his tight military collar. Not one day was he absent from the Bourse, not one day did he fail to make his tiny gamble on the cash market, content every evening to carry off his fifteen- or twenty-franc coin, like a good worker who has resolutely done his day's work. All around him millions were crumbling on every side, gigantic fortunes were being made and unmade in the space of two hours, gold was raining down in bucketfuls amid flashes of lightning, and he went on calmly making his little living, his little gains for his little vices... He is the cleverest of the clever, and the pretty girls of the Rue Nollet have continued to get their cakes and sweets.'

This allusion, made with great good humour, to the pranks of the Captain, succeeded in amusing the two ladies. But right away, the sadness of the situation returned to their minds.

'Alas, no, declared Madame Caroline, 'I don't think your parents will get anything out of their shares. It seems to me it's all over. The shares are at thirty francs now, and they'll fall down to twenty francs or even a hundred sous... Oh Lord! Poor old folk, at their age, and so used to comfort, what will become of them?'

'Well,' Jordan replied with simplicity, 'they will need to be looked after... We are not exactly rich yet, but things are beginning to get better, and we shan't be leaving them out on the street.'

He had just had a stroke of luck. After so many years of thankless work, his first novel, issued first as a newspaper serial, then taken up by a publisher,* suddenly looked like being a great success, and he was now rich to the tune of several thousand francs, with every door opening for him, and he longed to get back to work, certain of achieving fortune and glory.

'If we can't take them in, we shall rent a little apartment for them. We'll manage to sort it out!'

Marcelle, gazing at him with boundless tenderness, was shaken by a slight tremor:

'Oh! Paul, Paul, how good you are!' And she began to sob.

'Calm yourself, my dear, I beg you,' said Madame Caroline, over and over, concerned and astonished. 'You mustn't grieve so.'

'No, let me be, I'm not grieving... But, honestly, this is all so stupid! I just ask you, when I married Paul, shouldn't Mama and Papa have given me the dowry they had always promised? But on the pretext that Paul no longer had any money, and that I was stupid to insist on keeping my promise to him, they didn't give us a centime... Ah, much good has it done them! They could have had it back now, my dowry! That at least would not have been swallowed up by the Bourse!'

Madame Caroline and Jordan couldn't help laughing. But that did not comfort Marcelle, who went on crying all the harder.

'And anyway, that's not all... When Paul suddenly became poor,

I had a dream of my own. Yes! I dreamed I was a princess, like the ones in fairy-tales, and one day I would bring my ruined prince heaps and heaps of money, to help him to be a great poet... And now he has no need of me, now I am nothing but a burden, along with my family! It's he who will have all the trouble, and he who will be giving all the gifts... Ah, it really breaks my heart!'

Paul had quickly caught her up in his arms.

'What are you saying, my silly goose! Does a wife need to bring anything? You bring yourself, your youth, your love, your good humour, and there's not a princess in the world who could bring more!'

This at once calmed her, happy to be loved so much, and feeling it was indeed silly to be crying. Jordan went on:

'If your mother and father are willing, we'll find them a place in Clichy, where I've seen some ground-floor apartments with gardens, that were not too dear... Our apartment, our little nest, filled as it is by our few sticks of furniture, is very nice, but it's too small; all the more so since we're going to need a bit more room...'

And smiling again, turning towards Madame Caroline, who was very touched by this family scene, he added:

'Ah yes! We are going to be three, no reason not to admit it, now I'm at last earning a living!... So you see, Madame, yet another gift she's giving me, she who's been weeping over bringing me nothing!'

Madame Caroline, in the incurable despair of her sterility, looked at the slightly blushing Marcelle, whose increased girth she had not previously noticed. And now it was her own eyes that were full of tears.

'Ah, my dear children, love one another, you are the only sensible ones, the only happy ones!'

Then, before taking his leave, Jordan related some details about the newspaper, *L'Espérance*. With his instinctive horror of business matters, he spoke of the office of *L'Espérance* as a sort of extraordinary cavern, echoing with the hammers of speculation. The entire staff were gamblers, from the manager to the office-boy, and he alone—he added with a laugh—had not engaged in speculation, so was out of favour, and treated with contempt by all. Anyway, the collapse of the Universal, and especially the arrest of Saccard, had just killed the newspaper dead. The contributors had taken flight, while Jantrou, in dire straits, held on stubbornly, hanging on to this bit of debris, still trying to live off what was left of the shipwreck. It was all over for him, his three years of prosperity had totally ruined him, with his monstrous over-indulgence in everything that can be bought, like those starvelings who die of indigestion when at last they sit down to a meal. And the curious thing, though logical enough, was the final downfall of Baroness Sandorff, who had become the mistress of this man, as she tried in her desperation to get her money back in the confusion of the catastrophe.

On hearing the name of the Baroness, Madame Caroline turned slightly pale, while Jordan, who knew nothing of the rivalry of the two women, went on with his story.

'I don't know why she gave herself to him. Perhaps she thought he would supply her with information, thanks to his connections as a publicity agent. Perhaps she simply rolled down to him by the laws of gravity, falling ever lower and lower. In the passion for gambling there is a sort of destructive ferment I've often observed, that corrodes and rots everything, and changes even the proudest and most well-brought-up person into a mere rag of humanity, a scrap of rubbish that gets swept into the gutter… In any case, if that old scoundrel Jantrou had always bitterly remembered the kicks on the backside he is said to have received from the Baroness's father, when he went long ago to ask for orders, he has had his vengeance now; for when I went back to the newspaper to get paid, I pushed a door open too suddenly, and came upon an altercation, and with my own eyes I saw Jantrou giving Sandorff a resounding slap in the face… Oh! A drunkard like that, sunk in alcohol and vice, striking that society lady with such loutish brutality!'

With a gesture of pain, Madame Caroline silenced him. It seemed to her as if these excesses of degradation were bespattering her too.

Marcelle, very lovingly, had taken her hand before leaving.

'At least, don't think, dear Madame Caroline, that we came here to bother you. Paul, in fact, vigorously defends Monsieur Saccard.'

'Why certainly!' the young man replied. 'He has always been good to me. I shall never forget the way he rid us of that terrible Busch. And anyway, he is a very considerable person… When you see him, Madame, tell him that our little family is still deeply grateful to him.'

When the Jordans had left, Madame Caroline made a gesture of silent anger. Grateful? Why? For the ruin of the Maugendres! These Jordans were like Dejoie, going away with the same words of excuse and good wishes. And yet these people did know! He was no ignoramus, this writer who had travelled through the world of finance, full of so fine a contempt for money. Her own rebellion continued, and grew stronger. No! There was no possible pardon, there was too much mud. Jantrou's slapping of the Baroness did not avenge her. It was Saccard who had corrupted everything.

That same day, Madame Caroline was to go and see Mazaud about some documents she wanted to add to her brother's file. She also wanted to know what his attitude would be, if the defence should call him as a witness. The appointment was not until four o'clock, after the Bourse; and being alone at last, she spent more than an hour and a half sorting out the information she had already obtained. She was beginning to see more clearly into this heap of ruins; in the same way as on the day after a fire, when the smoke has cleared and the embers have ceased to glow, one sorts through whatever's left, still hoping to find the gold of melted jewels.

At first she had wondered where the money could have gone. In that swallowing-up of two hundred million, if some pockets had been emptied, it followed that other pockets must have been filled. However, it seemed certain that the 'bears' had not raked in the whole sum, a terrible leakage had carried away at least a third. On days of catastrophe at the Bourse, it seems the very ground drinks up money, some wanders away, and a little of it sticks to every finger. Gundermann alone must have pocketed about fifty million. Next came Daigremont, with twelve or fifteen. The Marquis de Bohain was also cited, having once again been successful with his classic coup; having played for a rise with Mazaud he refused to pay up, while he had gained almost two million with Jacoby, with whom he had been playing for a fall; but this time, even knowing that the Marquis had, like any common crook, put all his possessions in his wife's name, Mazaud, in despair over his losses, was talking of taking legal action against him. Almost all the directors of the Universal had cut themselves a handsome slice of the profits, some, like Huret and Kolb, by realizing at the top price before the collapse, and others, like the Marquis and Daigremont, by treacherously going over to the 'bears'; and besides, in one of its last meetings, when the company was already in serious trouble, the board had had each of its members credited with more than a hundred thousand francs. Indeed, on the trading-floor Delarocque, and especially Jacoby, were thought to have made huge personal profits, which had already been swallowed up into the two gaping and unfillable chasms created, in the case of the former, by his appetite for women, and in the latter by his passion for gambling. It was also rumoured that Nathansohn had become one of the kings of the kerb market, thanks to a gain of three million that he had made by playing on his own account for a fall, while playing for a rise for Saccard; and his extraordinary stroke of luck was that, committed as he was to large purchases in the name of the Universal, which was no longer paying, he would certainly have been ruined if there had not been a forced clearing of debts, making the whole kerb market, now declared insolvent, a gift of the more than a hundred million francs it owed. Such a lucky and clever fellow, that little Nathansohn! And what a happy turn of events—it made you smile—by which you keep all your profits, without paying for any of the losses.

But the figures were still vague, and Madame Caroline could not arrive at a correct estimation of the profits, for the transactions of the Bourse are carried on with a great deal of mystery, and professional secrecy is strictly observed by the brokers. Nothing could have been learned even from the order-books, for they contain no names. She tried in vain to discover how much had been carried off by Sabatani, who had mysteriously disappeared after the last settlement. That was yet another ruinous blow hitting Mazaud hard. It was the usual story: the shady client, accepted at first with misgivings, who deposits a small security of two or three thousand francs and gambles only modestly for the first few months, then, when the meagreness of the cover has been forgotten, and he has become a friend of the broker, he absconds after some act of banditry. Mazaud was talking of 'posting'* Sabatani, as he had formerly 'posted' Schlosser, a crook out of the same stable, part of that endless band of robbers who make use of the market to cover their activities in the same way that bandits once used the woods. And the Levantine, that mixture of Italian and Oriental, with his velvety eyes, and endowed, it was said, with a phenomenon that women inquisitively whispered about, had gone off to skim some other stock market—Berlin, some said—waiting until the Paris Bourse had forgotten him, and he could return to be accepted once more, ready, given the general tolerance, to perform the same trick.

The next list Madame Caroline had drawn up was of the disasters. The crash of the Universal had been one of those terrible shocks that shake the foundations of a whole city. Nothing had remained steady and solid; cracks were appearing in neighbouring institutions, and every day brought new collapses. The banks were crumbling one after another, with a sudden clatter like stretches of wall still standing after a fire. People listened in silent dismay to this noise of things falling, and wondered where the ruins would stop. What struck Madame Caroline to the heart was not so much the bankers, the companies, the financiers and financial establishments destroyed and carried away in the storm, as all the poor people, the shareholders, and even speculators, whom she had known and loved, and who were among the victims. After the defeat, she was counting her dead. And it wasn't just her poor Dejoie, the incredibly stupid and lamentable Maugendres, or the sad Beauvilliers ladies. Another drama that had greatly upset her was the bankruptcy of Sédille the silk manufacturer, which had been declared the day before. Having seen him at work as a director, the only one, she said, that she would have trusted with ten sous, she declared him to be the most honest man in the world. What a frightening thing, this passion for gambling! A man who had spent thirty years establishing, with his work and integrity, one of the soundest businesses in Paris, and who now, in less than three years, had so damaged it, so undermined it, that in one stroke it had crumbled into dust! What bitter regrets he must have for the laborious days of yesteryear, when he still believed in fortune being made by long effort, before one first lucky gain had made him scorn all that, consumed by the dream of acquiring in one hour on the stock market the million that takes the whole lifetime of an honest tradesman! And the Bourse had taken everything, leaving the wretched man struck down, disgraced, incapable and unworthy of taking up business again, and with a son whom penury would perhaps turn into a swindler—Gustave, that soul of joy and festivity, living on the basis of forty to fifty thousand francs of debt, and already compromised in an ugly story of promissory notes made out to Germaine Coeur. Another poor devil who distressed Madame Caroline was Massias the jobber, though, heaven knows, she was not often disposed to be sentimental about those go-betweens serving deception and theft! But she had known him too, with his big, laughing eyes, and that look of his, like a good dog unjustly whipped, as he raced around Paris to snatch up a few meagre orders. If he too had for a moment imagined himself one of the masters of the market, after making a conquest of fortune, following in

Saccard's footsteps, what a dreadful awakening he had had from his dream, finding himself quite knocked down, a broken man! He had debts of seventy thousand francs, and he had paid, when he might have claimed gambling-exemption* as so many others had done; but by borrowing from friends and pledging his entire life, he had been sublimely and uselessly stupid enough to pay—uselessly, in so far as nobody showed any gratitude, and some even shrugged their shoulders at him behind his back. His rancour was directed only against the Bourse; he had returned to his former disgust with his sordid job, insisting that you had to be a Jew to succeed in it, but resigning himself to carrying on, since he was already in it, and still had the stubborn hope of making his fortune after all, as long as he still had his keen eye and good legs. But the unknown dead, the victims with no name and no history, especially filled Madame Caroline's heart with infinite pity. They were legion, scattered in remote thickets and overgrown ditches, dead or wounded bodies breathing their last in anguish, behind every tree-trunk. What fearful, silent dramas there were, in this host of unfortunate people of modest means, timid shareholders who had put all their savings into one stock; retired concierges, pale spinster ladies living with their cats, provincial pensioners with their obsessively regulated lives, country priests impoverished by their charitable giving, all these little people with a budget of a few sous— so much for milk, so much for bread—a budget so precise and restricted that even two sous less meant disaster! And suddenly, nothing left, life cut short and swept away; old, trembling hands, bewildered and groping in the dark, incapable of work; all these humble, quiet existences thrown at one stroke into the horror of want! A hundred desperate letters had arrived from Vendôme, where Fayeux, the collector of revenues, had aggravated the disaster by taking flight. Holding money and shares for the clients on whose behalf he operated at the Bourse, he had begun a terrible gambling spree for himself; and having lost, but not intending to pay, he had disappeared with the few hundred thousand francs he had still kept his hands on. All around Vendôme, in farms far from anywhere, he had left destitution and tears. The crash had reached everywhere, even the humblest cottages. As after great epidemics, were they not always the most pitiable victims, these ordinary people, neither rich nor poor, people with limited savings? Savings that would be replaced only after years of hard work by their sons.

At last Madame Caroline went out to visit Mazaud; and while she walked down towards the Rue de la Banque, she thought of the repeated blows that had been hitting the broker over the last fortnight. There was Fayeux, who had robbed him of three hundred thousand francs; Sabatani, who had left an unpaid account of almost double that sum; the Marquis de Bohain and Baroness Sandorff, who had refused to pay, between the two of them, more than a million francs' worth of differences; and Sédille, whose bankruptcy carried away about the same amount, not to mention the eight million owed him by the Universal, the eight million carried over for Saccard, that dreadful loss, the abyss into which the anxious Bourse hourly expected to see him sink. Twice already Mazaud's downfall had been rumoured. And with fate's relentlessness, a further misfortune had just occurred, one that was going to be the last straw; the clerk Flory had been arrested two days before, convicted of having embezzled a hundred and eighty thousand francs. Little by little the demands of Mademoiselle Chuchu, the former variety artiste, the skinny grasshopper from the Paris streets, had grown: first it was jolly parties, of no great expense; then the apartment in the Rue Condorcet; then jewels and lace; and what had led the unfortunate and tender lad astray was his first winnings of ten thousand francs after Sadowa, that special luxury, money so quickly gained, so quickly spent, those winnings that had called for more, and then still more, in his feverish passion for the woman so dearly bought. But the extraordinary thing about this story was that Flory had robbed his employer simply to pay the gambling debt he owed another broker; a singular piece of honesty, due to fright at the prospect of immediate 'posting', and hoping, no doubt, to hide the theft and replace the money by some miraculous means. In prison he had wept a great deal, in an awful reawakening of shame and despair, and it was said that his mother, who had arrived that morning from Saintes to see him, had had to take to her bed at the home of the friends with whom she was staying.

What a strange thing is luck, thought Madame Caroline, as she crossed the Place de la Bourse. The extraordinary success of the Universal, that rapid rise into triumph, conquest and domination in less than four years, then the sudden crumbling, and that colossal edifice that took less than a month to be reduced to dust—all this she still found stupefying. And wasn't that also the story of Mazaud? Surely no man had ever seen destiny smile on him to such an extent.

A stockbroker at thirty-two, already very rich through his uncle's death, the happy husband of a charming wife who adored him, and had given him two lovely children, he was also a good-looking man, occupying a place on the trading-floor that every day grew in importance thanks to his connections, his energy, his really surprising flair, and even his shrill voice, that piping voice, that had become as famous as the thundering bass of Jacoby. And suddenly, the whole situation had started to crack, and he had found himself on the edge of the abyss, into which a mere breath was now enough to hurl him. And yet he had not gambled, still protected by his ardour for work and his youthful anxiety. While still battling faithfully, he had been struck down through inexperience, passion, and having too much faith in others. Anyway, there was a great deal of sympathy for him, and it was claimed that if he could keep his nerve, he might yet be able to survive.

When Madame Caroline had gone up to the main office, she clearly smelled the scent of ruin, and felt the shudder of secret anguish in the now bleak offices. As she went through the cash office, she saw about twenty people, quite a crowd, waiting there, while the money-cashier and the shares-cashier still honoured the establishment's commitments, but with slower hands, like men emptying the last drawers. The settlement office, seen through a half-open door, looked asleep, with its seven clerks reading their newspapers, having only a very few transactions to deal with since the Bourse was now idle. Only the cash office showed some signs of life. It was Berthier, the authorized clerk, who received her, himself looking very upset and pale, amid the misfortunes of the house.

'I don't know whether Monsieur Mazaud will be able to receive you, Madame... He isn't very well, he caught a chill, insisting on working all through the night with no fire, and he has just gone down to his home on the first floor, to rest a while.'

Then Madame Caroline insisted.

'Please, Monsieur, arrange for me to have a few words with him... It may be vital for saving my brother. Monsieur Mazaud knows that my brother never took part in the operations in the Bourse, and his testimony could be of great importance... In addition, I have to ask him about some figures, only he can give me information about certain documents.'

Berthier, still very hesitant, at last asked her to go into the broker's office.

'Wait there a moment, Madame, I'll go and see.'

And indeed, Madame Caroline felt the cold in that room very keenly. The fire must have gone out the day before, and no one had thought of relighting it. What struck her even more was the impeccable order, as if the whole night and all the morning had been spent emptying cupboards, destroying useless papers, and filing those that had to be kept. Nothing was lying about, not a file, not even a letter. On the desk, neatly arranged, were only the inkstand, the pen-rack, and a large blotter, and in the middle, a bundle of Mazaud's slips, green slips, the colour of hope. In the bareness of the room an infinite sadness seemed to hang, along with the heavy silence.

After a few minutes, Berthier reappeared.

'Oh dear, Madame, I rang twice and I don't dare go on... As you go down, see whether you should ring yourself. But I advise you to come back another time.'

Madame Caroline had to give up. However, on the first-floor landing, she still paused, even stretched out her hand towards the doorbell. And she was at last about to go away, when cries, sobs, and a muffled commotion in the depths of the apartment stopped her. Suddenly the door was opened, and a frightened-looking servant rushed out and disappeared down the stairs, stammering:

'Oh my God! My God! Monsieur...'

Madame Caroline had remained stock-still before that open door, from which emerged, quite distinctly now, a wail of dreadful grief. And she turned cold, as she guessed, and then clearly envisaged, what had happened here. At first she decided to take flight, but she couldn't, overwhelmed with pity, and drawn on, feeling the need to see, and to bring her own tears to the scene. She went in, finding all the doors wide open, and reached the drawing-room.

Two servants, the cook and the chambermaid no doubt, were craning their necks into the room, with terrified faces, and stammering:

'Oh, Monsieur! Oh my God! My God!'

The dying light of the grey winter day filtered weakly through a gap in the thick silk curtains. But it was very warm, and large logs, almost burnt through, were glowing in the fireplace, lighting up the walls with their red reflection. On one of the tables, a bunch of roses, a royal bouquet for that season, which the broker had brought his wife the day before was opening out in that hothouse warmth, its flowers filling the whole room with their scent. It seemed to be the very scent of the refined luxury of the apartment, the sweet smell of good luck, wealth, and happiness in love, which for four years had flourished in this place. And there, in the red reflection of the fire, lay Mazaud, stretched out on the edge of the sofa, his head shattered by a bullet, his clenched hand still gripping the revolver; while standing in front of him, his young wife, who had run to the scene, was making that wailing sound, that continuous wild scream that could be heard from the stairway. When the shot rang out, she had been holding her little boy of four-and-a-half in her arms, and his little hands had clung tightly to her neck in fright, and her little girl, already six years old, had followed her, clinging to her skirt, huddled against her; and the two children, hearing their mother's desperate screams, were screaming too. Madame Caroline at once tried to lead them away.

'Madame, I beg you, Madame... Don't stay here...'

She herself was trembling, and feeling faint. She could see the blood still flowing from the hole in Mazaud's head, and falling, drop by drop, on to the velvet of the sofa, then down on to the carpet. On the floor was a large and spreading stain. And she felt as if this blood was reaching her, bespattering her feet and hands.

'Madame, I beg you, please follow me...'

But, with her son hanging round her neck, and her daughter pressed to her waist, the unhappy woman did not hear, did not move, standing rigid, fixed to the spot with such force that no power on earth could have uprooted her. All three were blond, with skin of milk-like freshness, the mother looking as delicate and innocent as the children. And in the stupor of this death of their happiness, in this sudden destruction of the joy which was meant to last for ever, they continued their great cry, the scream that seemed to carry all the fearsome sufferings of humankind.

Then Madame Caroline fell down on her knees. She was sobbing and stammering.

'Oh, Madame, you're tearing at my heart... Please, Madame, drag yourself away from this sight, come with me to the next room, let me try to spare you just a little of this pain...'

And still they stood there, a wild and pitiful group, the mother with the two little ones seeming almost a part of her, all three quite motionless, with their long, pale hair hanging loose. And still there came that frightful screaming, like the wailing his kin make in the forest when hunters kill the parent stag.

Madame Caroline was now standing, her head whirling. There were footsteps, then voices, no doubt a doctor arriving to certify the death. And she could stay no longer; she fled, pursued by the awful, endless lament that even out on the street, with the cabs rumbling by, she still seemed to be hearing.

The sky was growing pale, it was cold, and she walked slowly, fearing her strange, disturbed appearance might lead to her being regarded as dangerous, and arrested. Everything surged back into her mind, the whole story of the monstrous collapse of two hundred million francs, that had piled up so many ruins and crushed so many victims. What mysterious power, after so rapidly building that tower of gold, had simply destroyed it in this way? The same hands that had constructed it seemed to have been seized by madness, and striven desperately to leave not a stone of it standing. Everywhere, cries of pain could be heard, fortunes were crumbling with a noise like demolition carts being emptied into the public dump. It was the last remnants of the Beauvilliers estate, Dejoie's savings, scraped together sou by sou, the profits made by Sédille's great industry, the pensions the Maugendres had gained in their trade, all together, pell-mell, hurled with a crash into the depths of a cesspit that nothing seemed to fill. And then there was Jantrou drowning in alcohol; Sandorff drowning in filth; Massias fallen back to his miserable life as an orders tout, chained to the Bourse for life by his debts; and Flory, now imprisoned as a thief, expiating the weaknesses of his tender heart; Sabatani and Fayeux, fugitives galloping away in fear of the police; and even more distressing and pitiful were the unknown victims, the great anonymous flock of all those the crash had impoverished, leaving them shivering and lost, crying with hunger. Then there was death, pistol-shots ringing out from the four corners of Paris, Mazaud's shattered head, and Mazaud's blood which, drop by drop, amid luxury and the scent of roses, bespattered his wife and his little ones, howling with grief.

And now, everything she had seen and heard over the last few weeks poured forth from Madame Caroline's bruised heart in a cry of execration for Saccard. She could no longer keep silent, no longer push him aside as if he didn't exist, to avoid having to judge and condemn him. He alone was guilty, this was clear in every one of the accumulated disasters, in their fearful and terrifying quantity. She cursed him, as her anger and indignation, held in for so long, now broke out in vengeful hatred, hatred of evil itself. Did she no longer love her brother, then, that she had waited so long to hate the terrible man who was sole cause of their misfortunes? Her brother, that great innocent, that great worker, so just and upright, soiled now by the indelible stain of prison, the victim she had been forgetting, the dear victim, even more painful than all the rest! Ah, might Saccard never find forgiveness! Nor anyone ever dare to plead his cause, not even those who continued to believe in him, those who had known only his kindness! And might he die one day, alone and despised!

Madame Caroline looked up. She had reached the square, and saw before her the Bourse. Twilight was falling, and the winter sky, laden with mist, had created, behind the monument, a cloud of dark and reddish smoke as if from a fire, as if made from the flames and dust of a city stormed. And the Bourse stood out, grey and bleak in the gloom of the crash, which for the last month had left it deserted, open to the four winds, like a marketplace cleared by famine. It was the fatal, periodic epidemic* that ravages the markets, sweeping through, every ten to fifteen years, the 'black Fridays' as they are called, that strew the ground with wreckage. It takes years for confidence to be restored, and for the great banking houses to be rebuilt, rebuilt until the day when the passion for gambling gradually reawakens, blazes up, and sets the whole process in motion again, bringing a new crisis, and sending everything crashing into a new disaster. But this time, behind that reddish smoke on the horizon, in the blurred and far-off parts of the city, could be heard a sort of muffled creaking, as of the imminent end of a world.

CHAPTER XII

PREPARATIONS for the trial were taking so long that seven months had already gone by since the arrest of Saccard and Hamelin, and the case had not yet been listed. It was now the middle of September, and that Monday, Madame Caroline, who went to see her brother twice a week, was to visit the Conciergerie at about three o'clock. She never spoke Saccard's name, and she had, ten times over, answered his pressing requests to come and visit him with a formal refusal. For her, firmly resolved on justice as she was, he no longer existed. And she still hoped to save her brother; she was brightly cheerful on her visits, happy to tell him about her most recent efforts and to bring him a big bouquet of his favourite flowers.

That Monday morning, she was preparing a basket of red carnations when Princess d'Orviedo's maid, old Sophie, came down to tell her that her mistress wanted to speak to her right away. Astonished, and slightly worried, Madame Caroline hurried up the stairs. She had not seen the Princess for several months, having resigned her post as secretary at the Work Foundation after the crash of the Universal. She now only went to the Boulevard Bineau at rare intervals, just to see Victor, on whom the strict discipline now seemed to be having some effect, still with one eye lower than the other, the left cheek larger than the right, and his mouth pulled into a grimace of mocking ferocity. She immediately had the feeling that it was on account of Victor that she was being called.

The Princess d'Orviedo was at last ruined. It had taken her barely ten years to return to the poor the three hundred millions she had inherited from the Prince, millions stolen from the pockets of credulous shareholders. If she had needed five years to spend the first hundred million in extravagant good works, she had managed in only four and a half years to swallow up the other two hundred million in establishments of even more amazing luxury. To the Work Foundation, the St Mary Crèche, the St Joseph Orphanage, the Chatillon Home, and the St Marceau Hospital, she had added a model farm near Évreux, two convalescent homes by the sea for children, another old people's retirement home in Nice, hospitals, workers' housing developments, libraries and schools all over France, not to mention large donations to already established charities. It was of course still that same determination to make royal restitution, not the crust of bread thrown to the wretched out of pity or fear, but giving enjoyment of life, luxuries, everything that is good and beautiful, to the humble folk who have nothing, and to the weak, that part of joy stolen from them by the strong: in short, the palaces of the wealthy opened wide to roadside beggars so that they too might sleep in silk and eat from vessels of gold. For ten years the showers of gold had not ceased, with marble dining-halls, dormitories brightened by colourful pictures, buildings with façades as monumental as the Louvre, gardens blooming with rare plants, ten years of magnificent constructions, with an incredibly wasteful use of building contractors and architects; and the Princess was now happy, uplifted by the great joy of having clean hands at last, with not a centime left. She had even managed the astonishing feat of getting into debt, and was being sued for a balance outstanding on some bills amounting to several hundred thousand francs, a sum her lawyers were unable to find in the final frittering away of that huge fortune thrown to the four winds of charity. And a placard nailed above the front entrance announced the sale of the house, the ultimate stroke that would sweep away even the last vestiges of the accursed money gathered in the mire and blood of financial brigandage.

Upstairs, old Sophie was waiting for Madame Caroline, to take her in. Furious at what had happened, she now carried on scolding all day long. Ah, she had said all along that Madame would end up a pauper. Shouldn't Madame have remarried and had children with another gentleman, since that was the only thing she really cared about? It wasn't that she, Sophie, had anything to complain or worry about, for she had long ago been given an annuity of two thousand francs, on which she was going to live, back in her birthplace near Angoulême. But she was overcome with rage at the thought that Madame had not even kept back for herself the few sous needed each morning for the bread and milk on which she now lived. Quarrels kept breaking out between the two women. The Princess just smiled her divine smile of hope, and responded that by the end of the month she would need nothing other than a shroud, once she had entered the convent in which she had long ago reserved her place, a Carmelite convent completely shut off from the world. Rest! Everlasting rest!

Madame Caroline found the Princess looking just the same as she had seen her over the last four years, dressed in her eternal black dress, her hair hidden beneath a lace shawl, still pretty at thirty-nine, with her round face and pearly teeth, but with a sallow complexion, the flesh seeming dead, as if after ten years in the cloister. And the small room, like the office of a provincial bailiff, was filled with a huge pile of papers, hopelessly jumbled together: plans, accounts, files, all the paper wasted in the squandering of three hundred millions.

'Madame,' said the Princess in her slow and gentle voice, a voice no longer troubled by any emotion, 'I wanted to let you know about some news that was brought to me this morning... it's about Victor, the boy you placed with the Work Foundation...'

Madame Caroline's heart began to beat painfully. Ah, the wretched child, whom his father, despite his solemn promises, had not even been to see, during the few months in which he had known of his existence before being imprisoned in the Conciergerie. What would become of him now? And she, who refused to allow herself to think about Saccard, was continually being brought back to him, disturbed in her adoptive motherhood.

'Terrible things happened yesterday,' the Princess went on, 'a crime, in fact, that nothing can repair.'

And in her ice-cold manner she related an awful happening. For the last three days, Victor had got himself placed in the infirmary, claiming to have unbearable pains in his head. The doctor had certainly suspected this might be merely the pretence of an idler, but the child really had suffered from frequent attacks of neuralgia. Now that afternoon, Alice de Beauvilliers was at the Foundation without her mother; she had gone to help the sister on duty with the quarterly inventory of the medicine cupboard. This cupboard was in the room that separated the two dormitories, the girls' dormitory from the boys', in which, at that time, Victor was the only occupant; and the sister, who had gone out for a few minutes, had been very surprised on her return not to find Alice; indeed, after waiting a few minutes, she had started to look for her. Her astonishment had increased on observing that the door of the boys' dormitory had been locked on the inside. What could be happening? She had had to go right round by the corridor, and had stood gaping in terror at the spectacle that presented itself: the young girl lay half-strangled, a towel tied over her face to stifle her screams, her skirts pulled up roughly, displaying the pitiful nakedness of an anaemic virgin, raped and defiled with appalling brutality. On the floor lay an empty purse. Victor had disappeared.

The scene could be reconstructed: Alice, perhaps answering a call, going in to give a cup of milk to that fifteen-year-old boy, already as hairy as a man, and then the monster's sudden hunger for that frail flesh, that overlong neck, and the leap of the nightshirted male, the girl, suffocating, thrown on to the bed like a rag, raped and robbed, and then a hasty pulling on of clothes, and flight. But so many points remained obscure, so many baffling and insoluble questions! How was it no one had heard anything, no sound of a struggle, no cry? How could such frightful things have happened so quickly, in barely ten minutes? And above all, how had Victor been able to escape, to vanish, as it were, leaving no trace? For after the most meticulous searches, it had been definitely established that he was no longer in the building. He must have fled through the bathroom giving on to the corridor, where one of the windows opened on to a series of tiered roofs stretching right down to the Boulevard, and yet this escape-route was so very dangerous that many refused to believe that a human being would have been able to take it. Alice had been brought back to her mother's house, where she had taken to her bed, bruised, distraught, sobbing, and shaking with a high fever.

Madame Caroline, on hearing this story, was so shocked that it seemed as if her heart's blood had frozen. A memory had come back to her, horrifying her with a hideous convergence: Saccard, years ago, taking the wretched Rosalie on the stairs and dislocating her shoulder at the very moment of the conception of this child, whose crushed cheek still bore witness to that event;* and now today, Victor, in his turn, violently assaulting the first girl that fortune offered him. What pointless cruelty! That young girl, so gentle and desolate, the last of her line, and on the point of giving herself to God, since she was unable to have a husband like any other girl! What sense could it have, this imbecilic and abominable encounter? Why smash the present with that past event?

'I don't want to reproach you at all, Madame,' the Princess went on, 'it would be quite unfair to make you feel in the least responsible. But in this boy you certainly had a really terrible protégé.'

Then, as if by an unexpressed association of ideas, she added:

'There are some environments in which one cannot live with impunity... I have myself had very serious qualms of conscience, I felt myself to have been complicit when that bank recently crashed, creating such a heap of ruins and iniquities. Yes, I should not have agreed to let my house become the cradle of such an abomination... But there, the harm is done, the house will be cleansed, and as for me, oh! I don't exist any more, God will forgive me.'

Her pale smile, of hope at last fulfilled, had reappeared as, with a gesture, she indicated her departure from the world, and the disappearance for ever of this invisible good angel.

Madame Caroline had seized her hands and clasped them, kissing them, so overwhelmed with remorse and pity that she could only stammer incoherently:

'You're wrong to excuse me, I am guilty... That poor girl, I must see her, I shall go at once to see her...'

And she went away, leaving the Princess and Sophie, her old servant, to do their packing for the great departure which was to separate them after forty years of life together.

On the Saturday two days before, Countess de Beauvilliers had resigned herself to abandoning her house to her creditors. She had not been paying the mortgage interests for the last six months, and the situation had become intolerable amid expenses of all sorts, and the continual threat of an enforced sale; her lawyer had advised her to leave everything and retire to a small apartment, where she could live on very little, while he would try to pay off her debts. She would not have given up, would perhaps have continued obstinately to try to maintain her rank, persevering with her pretence of an undamaged fortune, even to the point of risking the extinction of her race under collapsing ceilings, were it not for a further misfortune which had laid her low. Her son, Ferdinand, the last of the Beauvilliers, that useless young man, who had been kept away from any employment, and had become a pontifical Zouave to escape his nullity and idleness, had died ingloriously in Rome, his blood being so impoverished, and his body so unable to withstand the fierce sun, that he had not been able to fight at Mentana,* being feverish and his lungs already affected. After that she had felt a sudden inner emptiness, a crumbling of all her ideas, all her resolution, and all the laboriously constructed scaffolding that for so many years had so proudly upheld the honour of her name. It took only twenty-four hours; the whole house had collapsed and penury made its distressing appearance in the debris. The old horse was sold and only the cook remained, going shopping in a dirty apron for two sous of butter and a litre of dried beans, and the Countess was seen on the pavement with mud on her dress and leaking boots on her feet. It was penury overnight, disaster sweeping away even the pride of this woman still faithful to a bygone age and at war with her century. She had taken refuge with her daughter in the Rue de la Tour-des-Dames, in the house of an old second-hand-clothes dealer who, having turned pious, rented out furnished rooms to priests. There the two women lived in one large, bare room, dignified and depressing in its wretchedness, with an alcove closed off at one end. The alcove was occupied by two small beds, and when the folding doors, covered with the same paper as the walls, were closed, the room was transformed into a drawing-room. That happy arrangement had somewhat comforted them.

But the Countess de Beauvilliers had scarcely been there two hours on that Saturday, when an unexpected and extraordinary visit threw her back into fresh anguish. Alice, fortunately, had just gone out on an errand. The visitor was Busch, with his dull and dirty face, his greasy overcoat, and his white cravat rolled into a string, who, prompted perhaps by his instinct for when the time was ripe, had decided at last to get on with the old business of the promissory note signed by the Count de Beauvilliers to Léonide* Cron for ten thousand francs. With one glance at their lodgings, he grasped the widow's situation: had he perhaps waited too long? And, as one capable, on occasion, of urbanity and patience, he had lengthily explained the case to the alarmed Countess. It was indeed her husband's writing, was it not? And this clearly established the facts of the case: the Count had had a passion for the young person, so first, he finds a way of having her, and then a way of getting rid of her. Busch did not even conceal from the Countess the fact that, after nearly fifteen years, he did not believe she could legally be forced to pay. But he was merely acting for his client, whom he knew to be resolved on taking the matter to court, and creating the most frightful scandal if no compromise could be found. The Countess, white-faced and struck to the heart by the reawakening of that awful past, expressed astonishment that they had waited so long before contacting her, whereupon Busch invented a tale about the note being lost, then found again at the bottom of a trunk; and as she absolutely refused to discuss the matter further, he had gone away, still very polite, saying he would come back with his client, not next day, as she could not leave her place of work on a Sunday, but certainly on Monday or Tuesday.

That Monday, in the midst of the appalling events that had befallen her daughter, who had been brought back to her, delirious, the Countess, looking after her with eyes blinded by tears, was not thinking at all about that scruffy-looking man and his cruel story. At last, Alice had fallen asleep, and her mother had just sat down, worn out, and crushed by this further blow of relentless fate, when Busch presented himself once more, accompanied this time by Léonide.

'Madame, here is my client, we must get the matter settled.'

At the sight of the girl, the Countess had shuddered. She looked at her, dressed in garish colours, her coarse black hair falling down upon her eyebrows, her wide, flabby face, her whole person sordid and vile, worn out by ten years of prostitution. And the Countess felt wounded, her womanly pride cut to the quick after so many years of forgiving and forgetting. It was, dear Lord! for creatures destined to fates like this, that the Count had betrayed her.

'The matter must be settled,' Busch insisted, 'because my client needs to get back to the Rue Feydeau.'

'Rue Feydeau,' the Countess repeated, uncomprehending.

'Yes, that's where she is. In the brothel.'

Bewildered and with trembling hands, the Countess went over to close the alcove properly, since only one of the doors was pushed to. Alice had just moved, feverishly, under her coverlet. If only she went back to sleep! If only she didn't see, and didn't hear!

Busch was already going on:

'Look, Madame, just understand… Mademoiselle has entrusted me with this business, and I represent her, that's all. That's why I wanted her to come in person to explain what she is seeking… Come then, Léonide, explain yourself.'

Anxious and ill at ease in the role he was making her play, Léonide turned her big, cloudy eyes on him with a hangdog look. But the hope of the thousand francs he had promised made her decide. And while he, once more, unfolded and held up the Count's note, she, with her hoarse voice, roughened by alcohol, began:

'Yes, that's it, that's the paper Monsieur Charles signed for me… I was the daughter of the carter, Cron the cuckold, as he was called, you see, Madame!… And then Monsieur Charles was always there, hanging on to my skirts, asking for all sorts of dirty things. For me, it was just annoying. When you're young, you don't know much, do you? So you're not kind to old people… So Monsieur Charles signed this paper for me one evening when he'd taken me into the stable…'

Standing there, crucified, the Countess was just letting her talk, when she thought she heard a moan from the alcove. She gestured in anguish.

'Be quiet!'

But Léonide was in full flow and wanted to finish.

'It's really not honest after all, when you don't want to pay, to go seducing a good little girl... Yes, Madame, your Monsieur Charles was a thief. That's what they all think, the women I've told about it... And I assure you it was well worth the money.'

'Be quiet! Be quiet!' cried the Countess in fury, throwing her arms in the air, as if to knock her down, if she went on.

Frightened, Léonide raised her elbow to protect her face, with the instinctive movement of a girl who is used to being slapped. A dreadful silence fell, in which another sound, a moan, choking with tears, seemed to come from the alcove.

'Well, what do you want?' said the Countess, trembling, and lowering her voice. Now Busch intervened.

'But Madame, the girl wants to be paid. And she's quite right, the poor thing, to say that the Count de Beauvilliers treated her very badly. It's a straightforward swindle.'

'Never will I pay such a debt.'

'Well then, we'll take a cab as soon as we've left you, and go to the Palais de Justice, where I shall lodge the complaint which I've already drafted, as you can see here... It contains all the facts Mademoiselle has just told you...'

'Monsieur, that's an abominable piece of blackmail; you won't do that.'

'I beg your pardon, Madame, I shall do it at once. Business is business.'

An immense weariness, an utter discouragement, came over the Countess. That last bit of pride which had held her up had just been broken, and all her violence, all her strength, collapsed with it. She clasped her hands, and stammered:

'But you can see how it is with us. Just look round this room... We have nothing left, tomorrow perhaps not even anything to eat... Where do you expect me to get money, ten thousand francs, my God!'

Busch smiled the smile of a man well used to fishing about in ruins of this sort.

'Oh, ladies like you always have some resources. If you look hard enough, you'll find something.'

For a moment or so, he had been looking with interest at an old jewel-box the Countess had left on the mantelpiece that morning while emptying a trunk; and he could scent jewels, with the sureness of instinct. His eyes blazed with such fire that she saw where he was looking, and understood.

'No! No!' she cried. 'Not the jewels!'

And she seized the casket, as if to defend it. These last jewels, which had been in her family for so long, these few jewels she had kept as her daughter's sole dowry, even through times of greatest hardship, and which now remained her last resource!

'Never! I'd rather give my flesh.'

But at that moment there was an interruption, when Madame Caroline knocked the door and entered. Arriving already very upset, she was astonished at the scene she encountered. With a brief word, she begged the Countess not to disturb herself, and she would have left, but for a supplicatory gesture from the Countess, which she thought she understood. So she stood aside, quite still, at the far end of the room.

Busch had put his hat back on, while Léonide, more and more uncomfortable, made for the door.

'So, Madame, it only remains for us to make our departure…'

However, he did not depart. He went over the whole story in even more shameful terms, as if he wanted to humiliate the Countess in front of the newcomer, that lady he affected not to recognize, as was his habit, when he was engaged in business.

'Goodbye, Madame, we are going straight to the Prosecutor's office. A detailed account of the matter will be in the newspapers three days from now. And you will have only yourself to blame.'

In the newspapers! This horrible scandal falling even on the ruins of her house! So it wasn't enough just to see the ancient fortune disappear into dust, everything had to crumble in the mud! Ah, but the honour of the name should at least be saved! And with an instinctive movement, she opened the casket. The earrings, the bracelet, and three rings appeared, diamonds and rubies in antique settings.

Busch eagerly approached. His eyes softened into a gentle caress.

'Oh, there's not ten thousand francs' worth here… Let me see.'

He was already picking up the jewels one by one, turning them over, holding them up in the air, his fat fingers trembling with love, with his sensual passion for precious stones. The purity of the rubies seemed particularly to throw him into ecstasies. And these antique diamonds, even with their sometimes imperfect cutting, what wonderful limpidity!

'Six thousand francs,' he said in the voice of an auctioneer, hiding his emotion under this global estimate. I'm only counting the stones; the settings are only fit to be melted down. Well, we'll settle for six thousand.'

But the sacrifice was too hard for the Countess. Her violent feelings reawakened, she took back the jewels and clasped them in her agitated hands. No! No! This was too much, to ask her now to throw into the abyss these few jewels her mother had worn, and that her daughter was meant to wear on her wedding-day. Hot tears sprang to her eyes and streamed down her cheeks, in such tragic grief that Léonide, touched to the heart, and distraught with pity, began to tug at Busch's coat to make him leave. She wanted to get away, this was beginning to upset her, giving so much pain to the poor old lady who seemed so good. Busch very coldly surveyed the scene, sure now that he would get the whole lot, knowing from long experience that bursting into tears, in women, precedes the collapse of the will; so he waited.

Perhaps the frightful scene would have gone on longer, if at that moment, a distant muffled voice had not burst into sobs. It was Alice crying out from beyond the alcove:

'Oh Mama, they're killing me! Give them everything, let them take it all!... Oh Mama, make them go away, they're killing me, killing me!'

At this, the Countess made a gesture of desperate abandon, a gesture with which she would have given her whole life away. Her daughter had heard. Her daughter was dying of shame. And she threw the jewels at Busch, leaving him barely enough time to place the Count's promissory note on the table in exchange, and pushed him out after Léonide, who had already disappeared. Then she reopened the doors of the alcove and went and cast herself down on Alice's pillow, where, destroyed and utterly exhausted, the two women mingled their tears.

Madame Caroline, appalled, had been briefly tempted to intervene. Would she simply allow this wretch to rob these poor women like this? But she had now heard the whole shameful story, and what could be done to avoid the scandal? For she knew that Busch would not hesitate to carry out his threat. She herself felt ashamed in his presence, in the complicity of the secrets they shared. Ah, such suffering, such filth! A wave of embarrassment swept over her: what had she run over here for, since she could find no word to speak, nor help to offer? All the phrases that rose to her lips, the questions or mere allusions to yesterday's drama, seemed wounding, unclean, and impossible to utter before this still-bewildered victim, agonizing over her defilement. And what help could she offer that would not seem a derisory piece of charity? For she too was ruined, and already in difficulties, pending the result of the trial. At last she moved forward, her eyes full of tears, arms outstretched in infinite pity, with a desperate tenderness with which her whole body trembled.

These two wretched, utterly ruined creatures in this dreary lodging-house alcove, this was all that remained of the ancient race of the Beauvilliers, formerly such powerful rulers. They had owned lands the size of a kingdom, twenty leagues of the Loire had belonged to them, with their castles, meadows, farmland, and forests. Then this immense landed fortune had gradually dwindled away with the passing of centuries, and the Countess had just swallowed up the last remnants in one of these storms of modern speculation, that she did not understand at all; first her twenty thousand francs of savings, collected sou by sou for her daughter, then the sixty thousand francs borrowed on the farm at Les Aublets, then the farm itself. The house in the Rue Saint-Lazare would not be enough to pay her creditors. Her son had died far away, ingloriously. Her injured daughter had been brought to her, soiled by a scoundrel, like a child picked up in the road, bleeding and muddy after being knocked down by a cab. And the Countess, formerly so noble, so tall and slim and pale, with her grand air of a previous age, was now no more than a ruined old woman, broken by all this devastation; while Alice, with neither beauty nor youth, untidily clad in her nightdress that showed all too clearly her overlong neck, had the eyes of a madwoman, eyes that revealed the mortal grief of her last vestige of pride, her virginity now violated. And the two women went on weeping, weeping on and on.

Madame Caroline didn't utter a word; she just gathered them both up and clasped them tightly to her bosom. She could not think of anything else to do; she wept with them. And the two unhappy women understood, their tears flowing even more freely and more gently. Even if there was no possible consolation, it was still necessary to go on living, wasn't it? To go on living in spite of everything?

When Madame Caroline was once again out on the street, she saw Busch deep in conversation with La Méchain. He had hailed a cab, into which he pushed Léonide, and disappeared from sight. But as Madame Caroline hurried along, La Méchain walked straight up to her. She had doubtless been waiting for her, for she immediately spoke of Victor, already informed of what had happened the day before at the Work Foundation. Ever since Saccard had refused to pay the four thousand francs, she had gone on raging, striving to find some way of getting something out of the affair; and she had just learned the story, there on the Boulevard Bineau, where she often went, hoping for something profitable to turn up. She must have already made her plan, and told Madame Caroline that she was immediately going in search of Victor. That unfortunate child, it was too terrible that he should have been abandoned like that to his evil instincts; they must take him back if they didn't want to see him one fine morning in the Assize Court. And while she was talking, her little eyes, lost in the flabby flesh of her face, were exploring this good lady, delighted to see how upset she was, and telling herself that as soon as she found the lad again she would once more be able to get the odd hundred-sou coin out of her.

'So, Madame, it's agreed—I'm going to take care of it... If you need news, don't bother to rush all the way to the Rue Marcadet, just go up to Busch's office in the Rue Feydeau, where you can be sure to find me every day around four o'clock.'

Madame Caroline returned to the Rue Saint-Lazare, tormented by a new anxiety. It was true, as Victor wandered about, hunted, and abandoned by everyone, what evil heredity would that monster need to satisfy, moving through the world like a voracious wolf? She ate a quick lunch and took a cab, with time enough to call at the Boulevard Bineau before going to the Conciergerie, burning with desire to get some information immediately. On the way, in her feverish agitation, an idea took hold of her, even took possession of her; it was to go first of all to see Maxime, take him to the Work Foundation, and force him to concern himself with Victor, who was, after all, his brother. He was the only one who was still rich, he alone could intervene and deal with the matter effectively.

But once in the hallway of the luxurious little dwelling in the Avenue de l'Impératrice, Madame Caroline felt suddenly chilled. Upholsterers were removing the hangings and carpets, servants were putting covers on the chairs and chandeliers, while from the disturbance of all these pretty things there arose, over the furniture, over the bookshelves, a faded scent like that of a bouquet thrown away the day after a ball. And at the far end of the bedroom she found Maxime, standing between two enormous trunks which his valet was just finishing packing with a wonderful trousseau of clothes, rich and delicate, fit for a bride.

When he saw her, it was he who spoke first, in a very cold, dry voice.

'Ah! it's you! You've come just in time to save me having to write to you... I've had enough, and I'm leaving.'

'What do you mean, leaving?'

'Yes. I'm leaving tonight. I'm going to Naples for the winter.'

Then, when he had dismissed the valet with a wave of his hand, he went on:

'If you think it's been fun for me having a father in the Conciergerie for the last six months! I'm certainly not going to wait here to see him in prison... I, who so detest travelling! Still, the weather is good there, and I'm taking with me just about all I need, so perhaps it won't be too much of a bore.'

She gazed at him, so neat, so good-looking; and she looked at the overflowing trunks, into which no garment of wife or mistress had strayed; everything was devoted to his cult of himself; and yet she dared to risk speaking.

'And I had come to ask a service of you...'

Then she related the story, Victor the scoundrel, raping and thieving, Victor in flight, capable of any and every crime.

'We cannot abandon him. Come with me, let us join forces...'

He did not let her finish, he was livid, and trembling with fear, as if he had felt some dirty, murderous hand settle upon his shoulder.

'Oh well! That's all I needed!... A thief for a father and a murderer for a brother... I've delayed too long, I meant to leave last week. But it's abominable, abominable, to put a man like me in such a situation!'

Then, when she insisted, he became insolent.

'You just leave me alone! Since you seem to enjoy that life of grief, carry on with it! I did warn you, it's your own fault if you're weeping now... But as for me, you see, I'd sooner sweep the whole filthy lot into the gutter than do the slightest thing for them.'

She got up.

'Goodbye then!'

'Goodbye.'

And as she left, she saw him calling back the valet and attending to the careful packing of his toilet kit, in which every piece was most elegantly worked in silver, especially the basin, which was engraved with a ring of Cupids. While this man was going away to live a life of forgetfulness and idleness beneath the bright sun of Naples, she had a sudden vision of the other, prowling hungrily on some dark and dripping evening with a knife in his hand, in some remote lane in La Villette or Charonne. Didn't this answer the question of whether education, health, and intelligence are not all, in fact, down to money? Since there is the same human mud underneath, does civilization amount to no more than the superiority of smelling good and living comfortably?

When she reached the Work Foundation, Madame Caroline felt an odd sense of revulsion at the enormous luxury of the establishment. What good were these two majestic wings, one for boys and one for girls, linked by the monumental administrative offices? What good were the courtyards large as parks, the ornate tiles of the kitchens, the marble of the dining-halls, the corridors vast enough for a palace? What good was all this grandiose charity if, in this large and salubrious environment, they could not straighten out one ill-begotten being and turn a perverted child into a decent man, endowed with healthy good sense? She went at once to see the director and pressed him with questions, wanting to know the slightest details. But what had happened remained obscure; he could only repeat what she had already heard from the Princess. Searches had continued since the day before, in the institution and the surrounding areas, without any result. Victor was already far away, galloping around the city, in the frightening depths of the unknown. He couldn't have any money, for Alice's purse, which he had emptied, only contained three francs and four sous. The director had, anyway, avoided bringing in the police in order to spare the poor Beauvilliers ladies the public scandal; and Madame Caroline thanked him for that, and promised that she would not contact the Prefecture either, in spite of her ardent desire to know where Victor was. Then, in despair at going away no wiser than when she had come, it occurred to her to go up to the infirmary and question the sisters. Again, she got no precise information, but up there, in the quiet little room that separated the girls' dormitory from the boys', she at least enjoyed a few profoundly calming moments. A happy, boisterous noise rose from below; it was playtime, and she felt she had been unjust about the successful cures that had been obtained through the open-air life, well-being and work. There were certainly some strong and healthy men growing up here. One scoundrel to four or five men of average honesty would already be very good, given all the hazards that aggravate or diminish hereditary defects!

Left on her own for a moment by the sister on duty, Madame Caroline had moved over to the window to watch the children playing down below, when the crystal-clear voices of some little girls in the next-door infirmary attracted her attention. The door was half open and she could observe the scene without being noticed. It was a very cheerful room, this white infirmary with white walls, and four beds draped with white curtains. A big patch of sunlight added gold to the whiteness, a flowering of lilies in the warm air. In the first bed on the left, she at once recognized Madeleine, the girl who had been there, eating bread and jam, on the day she brought Victor. Madeleine kept on falling ill, wrecked by the alcoholism of her family, and of such poor blood that despite her big eyes, like those of a grown woman, she was as thin and pale as a saint in a stained-glass window. She was thirteen, and alone in the world now, her mother having died one drunken evening, after being kicked in the stomach by a man who wouldn't pay her the six sous they had agreed on. And Madeleine, kneeling in the middle of her bed in her long white nightdress, with her fair hair flowing about her shoulders, was teaching a prayer to the three little girls from the other three beds.

'Put your hands together like this, and open wide your heart...'

All three little girls were also kneeling among their sheets. Two were about eight or ten, and the third was under five. In their long white nightdresses, with their frail hands clasped and their serious, ecstatic faces, they looked like little angels.

'And now repeat after me what I'm going to say. Listen carefully: 'O God, let Monsieur Saccard be rewarded for his goodness, and may he have a long and happy life.'

Then, with cherubic voices, and an adorable childish lisping, the four little girls repeated together, in a surge of faith to which they gave the whole of their pure little being:

'O God, let Monsieur Saccard be rewarded for his goodness, and may he have a long and happy life.'

With an angry movement, Madame Caroline was about to go into the room to make the children stop, and forbid them to go on with what she regarded as a blasphemous and cruel game. No, no! Saccard had no right to be loved, it was a stain on their childhood that they should pray for his happiness! Then she stopped, with a great shudder, and tears rose to her eyes. Why should she draw into her quarrel, into the anger of her experience, these innocent beings who as yet knew nothing of life? And hadn't Saccard been good to them, he who was part-creator of this establishment, and who every month sent them playthings? She felt deeply disturbed, she was once more finding proof that there is no man, however guilty, who, in the midst of all the evil he may have done, has not also done much good. And she left, while the little girls took up their prayer once more, and she carried away in her ears the sound of those angelic voices, calling down blessings on that man of recklessness and disaster, whose hands, in their folly, had just ruined a whole world.

As she was at last leaving her cab on the Boulevard du Palais, in front of the Conciergerie, she realized that, in all her emotion, she had left at home the bunch of carnations she had prepared that morning for her brother. There was a flower-seller there with little bouquets of roses for two sous, and she bought one, which made Hamelin, who loved flowers, smile when she told him of her forgetfulness. That day, however, he seemed truly sad. Initially, during the first weeks of his imprisonment, he had not been able to believe there were serious charges against him. His defence appeared so simple: he had been made president against his will, and had remained apart from all financial transactions, being almost always absent from Paris, and unable to exercise any control. But conversations with his lawyer, and the approaches made by Madame Caroline, which, she said, had been a useless waste of effort, had made him see at last the alarming responsibilities laid upon him. He was going to be involved in every illegality, however slight; it would never be accepted that he was ignorant of a single one; Saccard had drawn him into a dishonourable complicity. It was then that in his rather simple faith as a practising Catholic, he had found a resignation, a tranquillity of soul that astonished his sister. When she arrived from the outside world, from her anxious efforts, from all those human beings at liberty, so shifty and hard, she was astonished to find him peaceful and smiling in his bleak cell, in which, like the great pious child that he was, he had nailed up luridly coloured religious pictures around a little crucifix of black wood. Once one puts oneself in the hands of God there is no more rebellion, and undeserved suffering is a pledge of salvation. His only sadness came, at times, from the disastrous halting of his great enterprises. Who would take up his work again? Who would carry on with the resurrection of the East, so successfully started with the United Steamship Company and the Carmel Silver Mines Company? Who would build the network of railway lines from Broussa to Beirut and Damascus, from Smyrna to Trebizond, all that pumping of new young blood into the veins of the old world? In this too he still had faith; he said the work undertaken could not die, and he felt only the grief of no longer being the one chosen by Heaven to carry it out. His voice broke particularly when he wondered why, in punishment of what fault, God had not allowed him to create the great Catholic Bank, destined to transform modern society, that Treasury of the Holy Sepulchre, which would restore a kingdom to the Pope and in the end make all the peoples of the world into one single nation, taking the sovereign power of money away from the Jews. He also predicted the coming of that bank as inevitable and invincible; and he heralded the Just Man, with pure hands, who one day would found it. And if he seemed careworn that afternoon, it must simply have been because, in his serenity as an accused man who will be found guilty, he had realized that on getting out of prison, he would never have hands clean enough to take up again that great task.

He listened distractedly as his sister pointed out that opinion in the newspapers seemed to be growing a little more favourable towards him. Then, with no transition, and looking at her with the gaze of one newly awakened, he said:

'Why do you refuse to see him?'

She shuddered, understanding at once that he was speaking of Saccard. With a shake of her head she said no, and again, no. Then he made a decision and said, with embarrassment, in a very low voice:

'After what he has been to you, you cannot refuse. Go and see him!'

O God! he knew, and, she was suffused with a burning red blush; throwing herself into his arms to hide her face, she stammered at him, asking who could have told him, and how had he learned about this matter that she had thought was quite unknown, and especially, unknown to him.

'My poor Caroline, a long time ago… Anonymous letters, horrible people who envied us… I never mentioned it to you, you are free, we no longer think the same way… I know you are the best woman on earth. Go and see him.'

And gaily, smiling once more, he took down the little bouquet of roses that he had already slipped behind the crucifix and put it back into her hands, adding:

'Look, take that to him, and tell him I don't hold a grudge, either.'

Madame Caroline, overwhelmed by her brother's pitiful tenderness, and filled with simultaneous feelings of awful shame and delightful relief, resisted no more. Besides, since that morning, she had felt it had become necessary to see Saccard. How could she not inform him of Victor's flight, and the atrocious events that made her tremble even now? From the very first day, he had listed her among the persons he wished to see; and she had only to speak her name for a warder to lead her at once to the prisoner's cell.

When she entered, Saccard had his back to the door, sitting at a little table, covering a sheet of paper with figures. He stood up quickly and gave a cry of joy.

'You!… Oh, how kind of you, and how happy I am!'

He had clasped her hand between his two hands, and she smiled, looking embarrassed, very moved, and unable to find the right thing to say. Then, with her free hand, she placed her little two-sous bouquet on the table, among the papers covered with figures that littered its surface.

'You are an angel,' he murmured in delight, kissing her fingers. At last she spoke:

'It's true, it was all over, and I had condemned you in my heart. But my brother wanted me to come.'

'No, no, don't say that! Say that you are too intelligent, too kind, that you've understood, and forgiven me…'

She interrupted him with a gesture.

'I beseech you, don't ask that much of me. I don't know myself… Isn't it enough that I've come?… And besides, I have to let you know about something very bad.'

Then at once, in a low voice, she told him of the reawakening of Victor's savagery, his attack on Mademoiselle de Beauvilliers, his extraordinary, inexplicable flight, the uselessness, so far, of all the searches, and the little hope there was now of ever finding him again.

He listened, astonished, without a question, without a gesture, and when she fell silent, his eyes overflowed with two big tears, that streamed down his cheeks while he stammered out:

'The wretched boy... the wretched boy...'

She had never before seen him cry. She was deeply moved and amazed, so strange were these tears of Saccard's, grey and heavy, as if they had come a long way, from a heart hardened and clogged by years of knavery. And then suddenly, he burst out in noisy despair.

'But it's terrible, I've never even embraced him, this lad... For you know I haven't seen him. My God! Yes, I had sworn to go and see him, and I never had the time, not a single free hour, with those accursed business affairs consuming me... Ah, it's always like that, when you don't do something straight away, you can be certain you'll never do it. And now, are you sure I can't see him? Someone could bring him here.'

She shook her head.

'Who knows where he is now, in the unknown depths of this terrible Paris!'

For a moment Saccard again walked about furiously, throwing out scraps of phrases.

'That child is found for me, and what do I do, but lose him... I shall never see him. You see! I just have no luck, no, no luck at all! Oh, great Heavens! It's the same story as for the Universal.'

He had sat down again at the table, and Madame Caroline took a chair facing him. And now, with his hands riffling through the papers in the whole voluminous dossier he had been preparing for months, he began to unfold the history of the trial, and to expound his mode of defence, as if he felt the need to persuade her of his innocence. The case against him rested on: the perpetual increasing of the capital to create a fever in the share-prices, and make people believe that the bank was in possession of the whole of its funds; the simulation of subscriptions and payments that had not in fact been made, thanks to the accounts opened for Sabatani and other frontmen, whose payments were no more than accountancy-juggling; the distribution of fictitious dividends, in the form of releases of old shares; and finally, the bank's buying of its own shares, a whole frenzy of speculation, which had produced an extraordinary and artificial rise, by which the Universal had been drained of money, and killed. To all this he responded with abundant and passionate explanations: he had done what any general manager of a bank does, only he had done it on the grand scale, with the vigour of a forceful man. There was not one of the heads of the most prosperous banks of Paris who did not deserve to share his cell, if anyone had thought to use a little logic. He was being made the scapegoat for the illegalities of all. Besides, what a strange way of assessing the responsibilities! Why were the directors not being prosecuted? The Daigremonts, the Hurets, the Bohains, who, in addition to their fifty thousand francs of attendance fees, received ten per cent on the profits, and had a hand in all the jiggery-pokery? And why was there total impunity for the auditors, Lavignière among others, who got away with just alleging incompetence, and claiming their good faith? Of course, this trial was going to be the most monstrous iniquity, for Busch's charge of embezzlement had had to be set aside for making unsubstantiated allegations, and the expert's report, after a preliminary examination of the bank's books, was discovered to be full of errors. So why should bankruptcy have been officially declared as a result of these two documents, when not a sou of the deposits had been embezzled, and all the clients were going to recover their funds? Was it then that they just wanted to ruin the shareholders? If so, they had succeeded, the disaster was growing steadily worse, spreading ever more widely. And it was not he who was to blame for all this; it was the magistrates, the government, all those who had plotted to suppress him and kill the Universal.

'Ah, the scoundrels! If they had left me free, you'd have seen, you'd have seen!'

Madame Caroline gazed at him, marvelling at his insouciance which was really beginning to acquire a certain grandeur. She recalled his old theories: the need for speculation in all great enterprises, in which fair remuneration is impossible; speculation seen as human excess, the necessary fertilizer, the compost on which progress grows. Wasn't it he who, with his unscrupulous hands, had madly heated the enormous engine until it burst into fragments and wounded all those it was carrying along with it? And wasn't he the one who had wanted that idiotic, crazily exaggerated share-price of three thousand francs? A company with a capital of one hundred and fifty millions, whose three hundred thousand shares, quoted at three thousand francs each, represented nine hundred millions, how could that be justified? Wasn't there a fearful danger in the distribution of the colossal dividend required by such a sum, even at the rate of five per cent?

But Saccard had stood up and was striding restlessly back and forth, like a great conqueror shut in a cage.

'Ah, the scoundrels, they knew what they were doing when they chained me up like this... I was about to triumph, about to crush them all...'

'What do you mean, triumph? You didn't have a sou left, you were defeated!'

'Of course,' he went on, bitterly, 'I was defeated, so I'm a villain... Honesty and glory belong only to success. You mustn't let yourself be beaten, otherwise you find that overnight you've become an idiot and a crook... Oh, I can guess what people are saying, you don't need to tell me! Isn't it this? They call me a robber, accuse me of having pocketed all those millions, they'd cut my throat if they could get hold of me; and what is worse, they shrug their shoulders in pity, as if I were just a madman, of little intelligence... But if I had succeeded, can you imagine? Yes, if I had brought down Gundermann, and conquered the market, if I were now the undisputed king of gold, eh? What a triumph! I'd be a hero, I'd have Paris at my feet!'

She flatly disagreed.

'You could not succeed, you had neither justice nor logic on your side.'

He had stopped brusquely, facing her angrily.

'Couldn't succeed! Come now! I didn't have enough money, that's all. If Napoleon at Waterloo had had another hundred thousand men to send out to get killed, he would have won, and the face of the world would have been changed. And I, if I had had the few hundreds of millions I needed, to throw into the abyss, I would be the master of the world.'

'But that's awful!' she cried, in revulsion. 'What? You think there's not been enough ruin, tears, and blood? You'd have yet more disasters, more families robbed, more wretched people reduced to begging in the streets!'

He took up once more his violent marching about, and with a gesture of superiority and indifference, he cried:

'As if life bothered about such matters! With every step we take, we destroy thousands of existences.'

At this, a silence fell, and she walked behind him, her heart quite chilled. Was he a villain? Was he a hero? She shuddered, wondering what thoughts, as of a great captain defeated and reduced to impotence, he might have been harbouring during the six months he had been shut up in this cell; and only then did she cast a glance around her, and see the four bare walls, the little iron bed, the white wood table, the two chairs with straw seats. And he had lived a life of such extravagant and dazzling luxury!

But suddenly he went and sat down again, as if his legs had given way in weariness. And he spoke quietly, at some length, making a sort of involuntary confession.

'Gundermann was right, absolutely: it's no good at all being excitable at the Bourse... Ah, the scoundrel, how lucky he is, to have neither blood nor nerves any more, unable to sleep with a woman or drink a bottle of burgundy! Besides, I think he's always been like that, his veins are full of ice... But I am too passionate, that's for sure. That's the reason for my defeat, and that's why I have so often been brought down... But it must be added that if my passion kills me, it's also my passion that keeps me alive. Yes, it carries me away, lifts me up, carries me very high, then brings me down and suddenly destroys all it has accomplished. Enjoyment is perhaps only a devouring of oneself... Certainly, when I think of those four years of struggle, I can see what has betrayed me; it's all the things I have desired, all that I have possessed... it must be incurable, all that. I'm done for.'

Then he was seized with rage against his conqueror.

'Ah! that Gundermann, that dirty Jew, he triumphs because he has no desires... He is like all of Jewry, that cold and obstinate conqueror, marching towards royal sovereignty over the whole world, among nations bought, one after the other, by the omnipotence of gold. For centuries now that race has been invading us and triumphing over us, in spite of being kicked on the backside and spat upon. Gundermann already has one billion, he'll have two, he'll have ten, he'll have a hundred, one day he will be master of the earth... I have gone on shouting this from the rooftops for years, but nobody seems to listen, people think it's just a speculator's rancour, when it's the cry of my very blood. Yes, hatred of the Jew is a part of me, from way back, in the very roots of my being!'

'What an extraordinary thing!' Madame Caroline murmured quietly, with her vast knowledge and universal tolerance. 'For me, the Jews are just men like any others. If they are apart, it's because that's where they've been put.'

Saccard, who had not even heard, went on with increasing violence:

'And what exasperates me is that I see governments in complicity with them, governments at the very feet of these beggars. Even the Empire has been sold to Gundermann! As if it wasn't possible to rule without Gundermann's money! And certainly Rougon, that great man, my brother, has behaved in a truly disgusting way towards me; for I haven't told you, I was cowardly enough to seek a reconciliation with him before disaster struck, and if I am here, it's because that's what he wanted. Never mind! Since I'm an embarrassment to him, let him get rid of me! The only thing I'll really blame him for is his alliance with those dirty Jews... Have you thought of that? The Universal strangled, so that Gundermann can carry on with his trade! Every Catholic bank, if it's too powerful, is crushed, as if it were a danger to society, to ensure the definitive triumph of Jewry, which will devour us all, and soon!... Ah! Rougon should be careful! He will be the first to be eaten, swept away from that power to which he clings, and for which he is betraying everything. It's very cunning, that balancing-act of his, giving pledges one day to the liberals, and next day to the authoritarians; but in that game you inevitably end up breaking your neck... And since everything is cracking up, let Gundermann's desire be fulfilled, he who predicted that France would be beaten if we had a war with Germany! We're ready, the Prussians have only to walk in and take over our provinces.'*

With a terrified and supplicating gesture, she made him stop, as if he risked bringing a thunderbolt down on his head.

'No, no, do not say such things. You have no right to say these things... Besides, your arrest is nothing to do with your brother. I know from a sure source that it was Delcambre, the Keeper of the Seals, who did it all.'

Saccard's anger suddenly subsided, and he smiled.

'Oh, he's just taking his revenge.'

She looked at him with a questioning air, and he added:

'Yes, it's an old story between us... I know in advance that I shall be condemned.'

She no doubt suspected what the story was, for she did not insist. There was a brief silence, during which he again took up the papers on the table, entirely absorbed once more in his obsessive idea.

'It was very nice of you to come, dear friend, and you must promise me you'll come back, because you give good advice, and I want you to look at some plans for me. Ah, if only I had money!'

She quickly interrupted him, seizing the opportunity to clarify a point that had been haunting and tormenting her for months. What had he done with the millions he must possess for his own shares? Had he sent them abroad, or buried them at the foot of some tree known only to him?

'But you have money! The two millions from the Sadowa affair, and the nine millions from your three thousand shares, if you sold them at the three-thousand share-price.'

'Oh, my dear, but I don't have a sou!'

And that was said in a voice so clear and despairing, and he looked at her with such an air of surprise, that she was convinced it was true.

'I have never made a sou in business affairs that have turned out badly... I ruin myself, you see, along with the rest... Certainly, yes, I sold, but I bought back too; and where they went, the nine million, along with two other million, I'd find it very difficult to explain clearly... I rather think my account with poor Mazaud ended with me owing him thirty to forty thousand francs... Not a sou left, a clean sweep, as ever!'

She was so relieved to hear this, so cheered, that she joked about their own ruin, the ruin of her brother and herself.

We too, when it's all finished, I don't know whether we'll even have enough to keep us fed for a month... Ah, that money, the nine millions you promised us, you remember how they frightened me! Never have I lived in such a state of unease, and what a relief it was, that evening when I gave everything up, to be counted in the assets... even the three hundred thousand francs we inherited from our aunt went the same way. That indeed is not very fair. But as I told you, money found, money not earned, one doesn't set such store by it... And as you see, I am cheerful and laughing now!'

He stopped her with an agitated gesture, he had picked up the papers on the table and was brandishing them.

'Oh come now! We shall be very rich...'

'In what way?'

'Do you imagine I'm giving up my ideas?... For six months I've been working here, often right through the night, to reconstruct everything. Those idiots blame me especially over that anticipatory balance-sheet, which they see as a crime on the grounds that out of the three great enterprises, the United Steamship Company, the Carmel mines, and the Turkish National Bank, only the first has provided the expected profits! Good Lord! If the other two have gone down, it's only because I wasn't there. But when they let me out, oh yes! When I'm the master again, you'll see, you'll see...'

With pleading gestures she tried to prevent him from going on. He had stood up, stretching to his full length on his short legs, shouting in his piercing voice:

'I've done the sums, here are the figures, look!... Carmel and the Turkish National Bank are just minor things! We have to get the vast network of the Oriental railways, we have to have all the rest, Jerusalem, Baghdad, the whole of Asia Minor conquered, all that Napoleon failed to do with his sword, we shall do with our pickaxes and gold... How could you think I would give up? Napoleon came back from Elba. And I too, I have only to show myself, and all the money in Paris will rise up and follow me; and this time, I promise you, there will be no Waterloo, because my plan has been worked out with mathematical rigour, down to the last centime... At last we are going to bring him down, that wretched Gundermann! I need only four hundred million, or perhaps five hundred million, and the world is mine!'

She had managed to take hold of his hands, and was pressing close against him.

'No, no! Be quiet, you're frightening me!'

And in spite of herself, even in her alarm, she could feel a certain admiration rising within her. Suddenly, in this bleak and bare cell under lock and key, and cut off from every living soul, she had just had the sensation of an overflowing force, an effulgence of life: the eternal illusion of hope, the stubborn refusal of the man who will not die. She sought within herself her anger, her abhorrence of the sins committed, and found they were no longer there. Had she not condemned him, after the irreparable misfortunes he had caused? Had she not called down on him the punishment of a solitary death, despised by all? She now only retained her hatred of evil-doing, and her pity for suffering. As for Saccard, with his heedless, dynamic force, she felt his power once more, as if he were one of those violent, but no doubt necessary, elements of nature. And anyway, even if it was only womanly weakness, she gave herself up to it with delight, yielding to her frustrated maternal instincts and the infinite need for love which had made her love him even without esteem, her normally lofty rationality quite laid low by the experience.

'It's over,' she repeated several times, without ceasing to clasp his hands in hers, 'so can't you just be calm now, and rest at last?'

Then, as he stretched up to touch her white hair with his lips, her curls falling about her temples with a youthful and lively profusion, she held him back and, with an air of absolute resolution and profound sadness, giving her words their full significance, she added:

'No, no! It's over, over for ever... I'm glad to have seen you this one last time, so that there should be no more anger between us... Goodbye!'

When she left, she saw him standing by the table, clearly moved by the parting, but already, with one hand, instinctively reorganizing the papers he had mixed up in his excitement; and as the little two-sous bouquet had lost its petals among the pages, he was shaking them off one by one, using his fingers to sweep away the rose-petals.

It was only three months later, towards the middle of December, that the case of the Universal Bank at last came to trial. It occupied five long hearings of the Magistrates' Court,* among intense public curiosity. The Press had made an enormous to-do about the catastrophe, and extraordinary rumours were circulating about the slowness of the proceedings. The indictment drawn up by the office of the Public Prosecutor was much remarked upon, it was a masterpiece of ferocious logic, in which the tiniest details had been grouped together, used and interpreted with pitiless clarity. Anyway, people everywhere were saying that the judgement had been decided in advance. And indeed, the obvious good faith of Hamelin, and the heroic attitude of Saccard, who stood up to his accusers throughout the five days, the magnificent and resounding pleas for the defence, did not stop the judges from sentencing each of the accused to five years of prison and a fine of three thousand francs. However, as they had been provisionally released on bail a month before the trial, they had been able to appear as free defendants, so were able to lodge an appeal and leave France in twenty-four hours.* It was Rougon who had insisted on this outcome, wanting to avoid the embarrassment of having a brother in prison. The police themselves watched over the departure of Saccard, who fled on a night train to Belgium. That same day Hamelin had left for Rome.

Three more months went by, it was the first days of April, and Madame Caroline was still in Paris, kept there by some complicated matters she had to settle. She remained in the little apartment in the Orviedo mansion, where posters now advertised its sale. She had at last sorted out the last of the difficulties and was able to get away, though of course without so much as a sou in her pocket, but also without leaving any debts behind her; and she was to leave Paris next day, to go and rejoin her brother in Rome, where he had been lucky enough to find a lowly post as an engineer. He had written that there were pupils waiting for her. It was like starting their life all over again.

When she got up on the morning of her last day in Paris, she felt a sudden impulse not to go away without trying to get some news of Victor. Up to that point all searches had been fruitless. But she remembered the promises of La Méchain, and told herself that the woman perhaps knew something, and it would be easy to question her by going to Busch's office at about four o'clock. At first she pushed the idea away; what good would it do, wasn't it all past history now? Then she felt real pain, her heart grieving as if over a child she had lost, and on whose grave she had placed no flowers before leaving. At four o'clock she walked down the Rue Feydeau.

The two doors on to the landing were open, and water was boiling furiously in the dark kitchen, while on the other side, in the tiny office, La Méchain, sitting in Busch's armchair, seemed drowned in the heap of papers she was pulling out, in enormous sheaves, from her old leather bag.

'Ah, it's you, my good lady! You've come at a really bad moment. Monsieur Sigismond is dying. And poor Monsieur Busch is positively out of his mind, he so loves his brother. He's just running about like a madman, and now he's gone out to get a doctor… As you see, I've had to take care of his business affairs, for it's a whole week now since he even bought a share or got his nose into a claim. Fortunately, I just had a stroke of luck—oh! a real piece of luck, which will console him a bit in his grief, the dear man, when he recovers his senses.'

Madame Caroline, suddenly shocked, quite forgot she had come about Victor, for she had recognized devalued Universal shares among the handfuls of papers La Méchain was drawing out of her bag. The old leather was cracking under the strain, and she went on pulling them out, growing chatty in her joy.

'Look! I got all that lot for two hundred and fifty francs, and there are at least five thousand of them, which puts them at one sou each… Eh? One sou, for shares that were once quoted at three thousand francs! And there they are, reduced almost to the price of the paper they're printed on, yes! Just so many pounds of paper… But they're worth more than that all the same, we shall sell them on for at least ten sous, as they are wanted by bankrupts. You see, they had such a good reputation that they're still useful. They look very good on the debit side, as it's very distinguished to have been a victim of the crash... Anyway, I had an extraordinary bit of luck, I'd sniffed out the pit in which, ever since the battle, all this merchandise was lying, like the remains from a slaughterhouse, and an ignorant idiot let me have it all for next to nothing. You can imagine how I fell upon it! Ah, it didn't take long, I cleaned it all out in no time!'

And this bird of prey of the battlefields of financial massacres glowed with pleasure, her enormous person oozing with the disgusting food with which she had fattened herself, while with her stubby, claw-like hands, she rummaged among the dead, these almost worthless shares, already yellowing and giving off a rancid smell.

But a deep and ardent voice arose from the next room, the door of which stood wide open, like the two doors on the landing.

'Good, there's Monsieur Sigismond, starting to talk again. That's all he's done since this morning... Oh heavens! The boiling water! I'd forgotten it! It was for some tisanes... My good lady, since you're here, go and see if there's anything he needs.'

La Méchain hurried into the kitchen, and Madame Caroline, always drawn towards suffering, went into the room. Its bareness was quite enlivened by bright April sunshine, a ray of which fell right across the little white wood table, loaded with written notes and huge folders, out of which bulged ten years of work; and there was nothing else save the two chairs with straw seats, and some volumes piled up on planks. On the narrow iron bed, Sigismond, sitting propped up by three pillows, his top half dressed in a short red-flannel smock, was talking, talking incessantly, with that curious cerebral agitation that sometimes precedes the death of consumptives. He was delirious, but with moments of extraordinary lucidity; and in his very thin face, framed by his long curly hair, his eyes, unnaturally wide, seemed to be searching into the void.

As soon as Madame Caroline appeared he seemed to recognize her, although they had never met.

'Ah, it's you, Madame... I had seen you, I was calling you with all my strength... Come, come closer, let me tell you quietly...'

In spite of the little shiver of fear she had felt, she drew near, and had to sit on a chair right up against the bed.

'I didn't know, but I know now. My brother sells papers, and I've heard people crying in there, in his office... My brother—ah! I feel as if I had a red-hot iron in my heart. Yes, that's what has stayed in my breast, still burning, because this is abominable, the money and the poor suffering people... So, very soon, when I'm dead, my brother will sell my papers, and I don't want him to, I don't want that!'

His voice rose steadily higher, pleading.

'Look, Madame, there they are, on the table. Give them to me so we can make a parcel of them, and you will carry them away, carry them all away... Oh, I was calling for you! I was waiting for you! My papers lost! My whole life of research and effort, all wiped out!'

And as she hesitated to do what he asked, he clasped his hands together and said:

'I beg you, let me be sure that they are all there before I die... My brother isn't here, my brother won't be able to say that I'm killing myself... I beg you.'

Then, overwhelmed by the ardour of his appeal, she gave in.

'You know I'm doing wrong, since your brother says that this does you harm.'

'Harm? Oh no! And anyway, what does it matter?... At last, after spending so many nights on it, I have managed to set it up, that society of the future! Everything has been foreseen and resolved, there will be all possible justice and happiness... How I regret not having had the time to write this work, with all the necessary developments! But here are my complete notes, all indexed. And you—you will, won't you?—you are going to save them so that someone else, one day, can make them into the definitive book to be launched upon the world...'

With his long, frail hands, he had picked up the papers and was leafing through them lovingly, while in his large, already cloudy eyes, a flame flickered once more. He was speaking very quickly, in a cracked, monotonous voice, like the tick-tock of a clock's chain pulled by the weight; it was the very sound of his brain's mechanisms, going on working even in the throes of death.

'Ah, how well I see it, how clearly it stands there before me, the city of justice and happiness!... There everyone works, a work at once personal, obligatory, and free. The nation is just a vast cooperative society, where tools are the property of all, and products are central-ized in huge public warehouses. When people have done a specific amount of useful labour, they have a right to an equivalent amount of consumption. The work-hour is the common currency, an object is only worth the hours it cost, and there is only exchange between all the producers, using work-vouchers, and that is all managed by the community, without any further deduction other than the special tax for bringing up children, feeding the old, renewing equipment, and defraying the cost of the free public services... No more money, hence no more speculation, no more thieving, no more abominable trafficking, no more of those crimes incited by cupidity, girls married for their dowry, old parents strangled for their inheritance, passers-by killed for their purses!... No more hostile classes of bosses and workers, proletarians and bourgeois, and therefore no more restrictive laws or tribunals, no armed force protecting the iniquitous hoardings of the few from the enraged hunger of the many!... No more idlers of any sort, hence no more owners living on rent, no more annuity-holders living off their luck like kept women, no more luxury, in short, and no more poverty!... Ah! Isn't that the ideal of fairness, the sovereign wisdom, no one privileged, no one wretched, everyone making their own happiness by their own effort, the averaging-out of human happiness!'

He was getting excited and his voice became soft and distant, as if it were going far away on high, and disappearing into the future whose coming he was foretelling.

'And to go into details... You see this separate sheet of paper, with all the marginal notes: that's on the structure of the family, with a free contract, and children to be educated and supported by the community... However, this is not anarchy. Look at this other note: I want every branch of production to have a managing committee responsible for establishing what is really needed, and balancing production to consumption... And here's another organizational detail: in the towns and in the fields, industrial and agricultural armies will operate under the leadership of their own elected chiefs, obeying regulations voted by themselves... And look! I've indicated here, with rough calculations, how many working hours the working day can be reduced to in twenty years. Thanks to the great number of new hands, and thanks especially to machines, people will work for only four hours, perhaps three, leaving them so much time to enjoy life! For this is no barracks but a place of freedom and gaiety, in which all can choose their own pleasure, with plenty of time to satisfy their legitimate appetites, the joy of loving, of being strong, beautiful, intelligent, and taking their share of inexhaustible nature.'

And his gesture, sweeping around that miserable room, took possession of the world. In the bareness in which he had lived, this poverty without needs, in which he was dying, he was sharing out all the wealth of the earth with a brotherly hand. It was universal happiness, everything good that he had never himself enjoyed, that he was thus distributing, knowing he never would enjoy any part of it. He had hastened his death in order to make this supreme gift to suffering humanity. But his hands were straying, groping about, among the scattered notes, while his eyes, no longer seeing them, filled as they were with the dazzling light of death, seemed, in a rapturous ecstasy that lit up his whole face, to perceive, on the other side of life, an infinite perfection.

'Ah! What new activities, the whole of humanity at work, the hands of every living being improving the world!... No more barren moors, no more marshes, no more wastelands. Inlets are filled up, obstructive mountains disappear, deserts change into fertile valleys, with water springing out everywhere. No marvel is unrealizable, the great works of old call forth a smile, so timid and childish do they appear. The whole earth at last is habitable... And the whole man is now developed, fully grown, enjoying his full appetites, now the true master. Schools and workshops are open, and each child chooses his occupation according to his abilities. Years have already gone by, and selection has been made, thanks to rigorous examinations. It is no longer enough to be able to pay for instruction, it is necessary to profit by it. So all find themselves, with their education finished at the right level for their intelligence, set to work, which means posts in the public service are equitably distributed, following the indications of Nature herself. Each for all, according to his strengths... Ah! Active and joyful city, ideal city of healthy, human effort, where the old prejudice against manual work no longer exists and one sees great poets who are carpenters, and locksmiths great scholars! Ah! Happy city, triumphant city, toward which mankind has been marching for so many centuries, city whose white walls are shining out there... Out there in the land of happiness, in the blinding sunlight...'

His eyes grew pale and the last words emerged indistinctly, in a little gasp; and his head fell back, still with that ecstatic smile on his lips. He was dead.

Overcome with pity and tenderness, Madame Caroline was gazing at him when she felt something like a storm bursting in behind her.

It was Busch, coming back without the doctor, panting and ravaged with anguish, while La Méchain, close on his heels, was explaining why she had not yet managed to make the tisane, because the water had boiled over. But he had seen his brother, his little child, as he called him, lying on his back, motionless, with his mouth open and his eyes in a fixed stare; he understood at once, and let out a shriek like a slaughtered animal. In one bound, he had thrown himself onto the body, lifting him up in his two strong arms, as if to breathe life into him. This terrible consumer of money, who would have killed a man for ten sous, and who for so long had skimmed off the filth of Paris, now screamed with atrocious suffering. His little child, oh God! He had put him to bed and pampered him like a mother! He would have him no more, his little child! And in a spasm of raging despair, he gathered up the papers scattered on the bed, and tore them, crushing them, as if he wanted utterly to destroy all that mad labour he had so resented, the labour which had killed his brother.

Madame Caroline then felt her heart melting. Poor, wretched man! He now filled her only with a divine pity. But where had she heard such screaming before? Only once had the howl of human pain pierced her with such a shudder. And she remembered: it was at Mazaud's house, the screams of the mother and the little ones, facing the father's dead body. As if unable to withdraw from this suffering, she stayed a moment more and gave what help she could. Then, as she was leaving, finding herself alone with La Méchain in the little business office, she remembered that she had come to ask about Victor. And she questioned her. Ah well, Victor was far away, if he was still running! La Méchain had tramped all over Paris for three months without discovering any trace of him. She had given up, there would be time enough to find that scoundrel one day, on the scaffold. Madame Caroline listened to her, silent and chilled. Yes, it was all over, the monster had been abandoned by everybody, left to the future, the unknown, like a beast, jaws foaming with the hereditary virus, which would spread evil with every bite.

Outside, on the pavement of the Rue Vivienne, Madame Caroline was surprised at the softness of the air. It was five o'clock, the sun was setting in a sky of tender purity, turning to gold the signs far off, hanging high above the Boulevard. This April, so delightful in its new youthfulness, was like a caress for her whole physical being, right down to her heart. She breathed in deeply, comforted, and happier already, with the feeling of invincible hope returning to her and growing. It was no doubt the beautiful death of that dreamer, giving his last breath to his chimera of justice and love that moved her in this way, a dream she also had dreamed, of a humanity purged of the execrable evil of money; and it was also the screams of that other one, the tormented and bleeding love of that terrible jackal,* whom she had thought heartless and incapable of tears. But no! She had not come away with the consoling impression of so much human good-ness in the midst of so much grief; on the contrary, she had come away finally despairing of that little monster, let loose, and galloping away, sowing along his path that ferment of rottenness of which the world would never be cured. So why this renewal of cheerfulness, filling her whole being?

When she reached the Boulevard, Madame Caroline turned left, and slowed down in the midst of the busy crowd. She stopped for a moment by a little cart full of bunches of lilies and wallflowers, and their strong scent wrapped her in a waft of springtime. And now, as she continued her walk, the wave of joy mounted within her as if from a bubbling spring, impossible to stop or smother, however hard you tried. She had understood, but unwillingly. No, no, the awful catastrophes were too recent, she could not be gay, could not abandon herself to this uplifting surge of endless life. She strove to maintain her grieving, she called herself back to despair, with so many cruel memories. What! Could she still laugh, after the collapse of every-thing, after such a frightening mass of miseries! Was she forgetting that she had been complicit? And she recited the facts to herself, this fact, that one, and that other, that she should have spent the rest of her life weeping over. But in between her fingers clenched over her heart, that bubbling up of sap gathered strength, and the spring of life overflowed, pushing away all obstacles, tossing all debris aside, to flow freely, clear and triumphant in the sunlight.

From that moment Madame Caroline gave in and simply aban-doned herself to the irresistible force of continual rejuvenation. As she often said with a laugh, she was unable to be sad. This proved it; she had touched the very depths of despair, yet hope was springing to life again, broken and bloody, but still alive, and growing by the minute. Certainly she had no illusions left, life was decidedly unjust and squalid, like Nature itself. So why this madness of loving it, wanting it, and still—like a child who has been promised a constantly deferred pleasure—counting on the distant and unknown goal towards which it is leading us? Then, when she turned into the Rue de la Chaussée-d'Antin, she stopped trying to reason it out; the philosopher in her, the scholar and the woman of letters, had abdicated, weary of the useless search for causes; she was simply a creature happy at the blue sky and the gentle air, enjoying the sole pleasure of being in good health and hearing her little feet firmly tapping the pavement. Ah, the joy of being alive, is there really any other joy than this? Life, just as it is, however abominable it may be, with all its power and its eternal hope!

Back in the Rue Saint-Lazare, in the apartment she was to leave the next day, Madame Caroline finished her packing, and as she made a tour of the now empty workroom, she saw on the walls the maps and watercolours she'd promised herself she would tie up in a roll at the last minute. But at every sheet of paper, before taking out the four tacks at each corner, she fell into a dream. She was reliving those far-off days in the Orient, that beloved land, whose brilliant light she seemed to have kept inside her; she relived the five years she had just spent in Paris, with a crisis every day, and that crazy activity, that monstrous hurricane of millions that had run its devastating path through her life; and from those ruins, still warm, she could already sense the growth of a great blossoming opening out in the sun. Even if the Turkish National Bank had collapsed after the collapse of the Universal, the United Steamship Company was still standing, and prospering. She saw once more the enchanted coast of Beirut where, among huge warehouses, administrative buildings were rising, the plans for which she was just dusting down: Marseilles a gateway to Asia Minor, the Mediterranean conquered, nations brought together, to live in peace perhaps. And the Carmel Gorge, this watercolour she was taking down, didn't she know from a recent letter that a whole population had grown up there? The village, at first of five hundred inhabitants, clustering round the workings of the mine, was at present a city of several thousand souls, a whole civilization, with roads, factories, and schools, creating life in this dead and savage place. Then there were the planned routes, the land-surveys, and the outlines for the railway line from Brussa to Beirut via Angora and Aleppo, a series of large sheets that she rolled up one by one; no doubt years would go by before the Taurus passes were crossed at full steam;* but already life was flowing in from everywhere, the soil of the ancient cradle of humanity had just been sown with a new crop of men, the progress of tomorrow would grow there, a vegetation of extraordinary vigour, in that wonderful climate under that perpetual sun. And wasn't this the awakening of a world, with an expanded and happier humanity?

Madame Caroline now tied up the bundle of plans with some stout string. Her brother, who was waiting for her in Rome, where the two were going to start their lives all over again, had urged her to pack them carefully; and as she tied the knots, her thoughts went to Saccard now in Holland, once again launched on a colossal enterprise, the draining of vast marshes, a little kingdom to be won from the sea, thanks to a complicated system of canals. He was right: money was always the manure in which the humanity of tomorrow was growing; money, poisonous and destructive, became the ferment of all social growth, the compost necessary for the great works that made life easier. This time, was she at last seeing clearly? Did her invincible hope spring from her belief in the usefulness of effort? Heavens! Over and above the stirring of so much mud, and the crushing of so many victims, out of all that abominable suffering that humanity has to pay for every step forward, is there not an obscure and distant goal, something superior, something good, just and definitive, toward which we move without knowing it, but which fills our hearts with the obstinate need to live, and hope?

And Madame Caroline, with her face ever young beneath its crown of white hair, was joyful in spite of everything, as if she were rejuvenated every April, in the old age of the earth. And at the shameful memory she had of her relationship with Saccard, she thought of the terrible filth with which love too has been soiled. Why then blame money for the dirt and crimes it causes? Is love any less sullied, love, the creator of life?

EXPLANATORY NOTES

3 *Bourse*: Napoleon Bonaparte laid the first stone of the Bourse (now the Palais Brongniart) in 1808. Home of the Paris Stock Exchange, the building was designed in the Corinthian style by the architect Alexandre Théodore Brongniart, and after his death in 1813 completed by Éloi Labarre in 1825. Officially opened on 4 November 1826, under the Restoration, it became the hub of financial activity in France throughout the nineteenth century. The introduction of an electronic trading system in 1987 led to the re-siting of the Bourse (now Euronext, Paris) and the designation of the Palais Brongniart as a historical monument.

Champeaux: restaurant on the Place de la Bourse, founded by Champeaux in 1800. Much frequented by financial traders, it carried on until 1905.

May: May 1864.

stockbroker: Mazaud is one of about sixty official stockbrokers (*agents de change*), each of whom had to be a French citizen, approved by the Minister of Finance. The *agents de change* were strictly brokers, not allowed to trade for themselves nor to stand in for others dealing in securities. They received a legally regulated commission for acting as intermediary.

fifteen francs: 1 franc = 20 sous or 100 centimes. As a general guide to the value of the franc at that time, an average worker in Paris in 1860 would have earned 3 to 4 francs a day, a litre of wine would cost about 80 centimes, a pound of beef 1 to 2 francs, a dozen eggs 1 franc 50 centimes. In the course of the novel the Jordans plan to eat in a modest restaurant for 35 sous each for two courses with wine and bread, and Marcelle buys an almond cake for 20 sous; rent for the Cité de Naples is 2 francs a week.

4 *bull trader*: an investor who thinks the market or a particular stock will rise and buys securities hoping to sell them later at a higher price. His opposite is a 'bear' or short-seller, who believes the market or a particular stock will go down and hopes to profit from a decline in prices.

5 *kerb market*: known in French as 'la coulisse', getting its name from a wooden partition once introduced to keep visitors away from the main trading-floor, rather like the 'coulisse' or 'wings' of a theatre. This secondary market, though not officially authorized until 1885, was accepted by tradition and accounted for about three-fifths of all transactions; being unrecognized it did not incur the Bourse tax. It continued to operate until the mid-twentieth century.

mansion in the Parc Monceau: Saccard's highly ornate mansion is in what was then one of the most fashionable areas of Paris.

land-deal: from 1853 to 1870 Baron Haussmann, Napoleon III's Prefect of the Seine, was transforming Paris, clearing away buildings and creating the wide boulevards for which the modern city is so admired. During this

'Haussmannization', speculation on land was rife. Saccard's illegal activities and subsequent ruin are related in the second novel of the Rougon-Macquart series, *The Kill* (*La Curée*).

5 *minister*: the sixth Rougon–Macquart novel, *His Excellency Eugène Rougon*, is devoted to the career of Saccard's brother Eugene, modelled on Eugène Rouher (1818–84), a powerful politician in the Second Empire who at various times acted as minister, vice-president of the Council of State, and president of the Senate.

Parliament: the Chamber of Deputies ('Chambre des Députés') denotes the various bodies constituting France's Legislative Assembly in the nineteenth and twentieth centuries. In 1852 Napoleon III made the Corps Législatif (Legislative Assembly) the lower chamber of the French Parliament, its members being elected by universal (male) suffrage. Its powers were shared with the more powerful executive arm, the Conseil d'État (Council of State), and the Sénat (Senate). Ministers were appointed by the Emperor and were responsible only to him. The Third Republic (after 1871) re-established the name Chambre des Députés. The French Parliament later became known as the National Assembly ('Assemblée Nationale').

6 *jobber*: (*remisier* in French) one who acts as intermediary between brokers, touting for custom and getting a commission on each transaction, rather like a bookmaker's 'runner'.

by-elections . . . Opposition: elections had been held in May 1863, but on 20 March 1864 by-elections were held for two districts of Paris. Government candidates were very soundly defeated by Carnot and Garnier-Pagès; the latter had been a member of the 1848 (Republican) government.

Duchies question: the Duchies of Schleswig-Holstein, by a treaty of 1852 agreed by Russia, Sweden, England, and France, were to be returned to Denmark. However, in February 1864 Bismarck occupied Holstein and invaded Schleswig. Russia, Sweden, and England supported Denmark, but France suggested a vote by the relevant populations. This in effect nullified the treaty of 1852, and Denmark lost out to Prussia.

all end: it would in fact all end badly for France, but well for a strong German Empire.

Mexico: when Mexico, under President Juarez, refused to pay interest on foreign debt in 1861, France, Spain, and the United Kingdom signed the Convention of London to combine their efforts to restore interest payments. However, Napoleon III, seeking a base from which to expand French trade, as well as hoping to acquire Mexican silver mines, decided to invade Mexico, whereupon the United Kingdom and Spain withdrew. A French expeditionary force was sent to Mexico in 1861 to defeat Juarez's republic and establish an empire under the Archduke Maximilian of Austria, who accepted the crown in October 1863. This intervention proved to be extremely costly as well as unsuccessful: it ended with the execution of Maximilian in June 1867 and the restoration of the Juarez republic.

glorious . . . reign: Eugène Rouher used this expression in response to Thiers's criticism. See note to p. 8.

loan . . . January: the loan was voted in December 1863. A public subscription, opened in January 1864, was enthusiastically supported and raised over 249 million francs.

7 *coup d'état*: the *coup d'état* of 2 December 1851, by which the nephew of Napoleon I, Louis-Napoleon Bonaparte, then President of the Second Republic, seized power and a year later became the Emperor Napoleon III.

8 *Thiers*: Adolphe Thiers (1797–1877), Minister of the Interior in 1834 and President of the State Council from 1836 to 1840. A member of the Legislative Assembly from 1863 to 1870, and one of the main opponents of the Empire. He had commented savagely on the huge cost of the Mexican adventure.

champion of liberty: when the Emperor dissolved the National Assembly in 1852 he restored universal male suffrage and could thus be seen as a supporter of liberty. The constitution, however, gave him more or less absolute power. To win back diminishing support he made further liberal reforms in November 1860.

International Workingmen's Association: also known as 'The First International', formed in an attempt to unite various left-wing political groups and trades unions to fight for better conditions for workers. It was not in fact formed until September 1864, so after the presumed date of this conversation; but the slight anachronism served Zola's purpose of introducing in the first chapter a number of subjects and themes that would recur in the novel.

Suez project: the building of the Suez Canal began in 1859; the work was interrupted in 1863–4 due to problems with Turkey, but resumed in 1865 and was finished in 1869. The Canal, owned by the French and Egyptian Suez Canal Company, was opened in November of that year. The British government opposed the project throughout its construction, objecting to the use of slave labour, but became a minority shareholder in the Suez Company in 1875.

10 *the notice . . . make demand*: Mazaud refers to a process by which a financial intermediary with a troublesome client can demand payment. If payment is not made, the agent can sell the shares the client has bought, and if the client cannot cover any loss then he is 'posted', that is, his failure to meet his engagements is announced to the Bourse at large.

14 *victorias*: low, four-wheeled carriages for two, with folding hood.

15 *'Wet Feet'*: Fr. 'pieds humides'.

17 *Plassans*: birthplace of the Rougon-Macquart family. Zola's fictional name for Aix-en-Provence, where he lived from 1843 until 1858, when he went to Paris.

19 *Crédit Mobilier*: influential bank, founded by the Péreire brothers in 1852.

It provided Zola with much useful material for this novel. The Crédit Mobilier crashed in 1870.

20 *coupé*: small, enclosed four-wheeled carriage with internal seating for two and an outside seat for the driver.

Bacchante: the Bacchantes were female devotees of Bacchus (Dionysus in the Greek version), god of wine and intoxication. The Bacchantes are more often represented as dishevelled madwomen than dressed in designer clothes—the contrast suggests (deceptively) the possibility of raging passions beneath the Baroness's cultivated exterior.

22 *English cheques*: in the 1860s cheques, much used in England, were still a relative novelty in France, hence their description as 'English'. They gradually became popular in France in the course of the Second Empire.

25 *collector of revenues*: the *receveur de rentes* in the nineteenth century was a public servant responsible for coordinating the collection of taxes and fines for his area. He received a salary plus commission. The actual collecting was done by a subordinate.

26 *stamped paper*: official documents, to be authentic, had to bear a government stamp.

29 *Saccard . . . wife*: this part of Saccard's life is related in *The Kill*.

31 *Karl Marx . . . Gazette*: the full title of the newspaper was *Neue Rheinische Zeitung: Organ der Demokratie* ('New Rhenish Newspaper: Organ of Democracy'). Karl Marx (1818–83), the influential socialist thinker, published this German daily newspaper in Cologne from June 1848 until May 1849. It was called 'New' because it followed Marx's previous *Rheinische Zeitung*, suppressed in 1843. Marx arrived in Paris in 1843, was expelled at the end of 1844, moved to Brussels, then visited England with Friedrich Engels and went back to Paris briefly in 1848, before returning to Cologne then London in 1849. The first part of Marx's famous *Capital* appeared in French, translated by Joseph Roy, in 1867. Marx died in London in 1883.

June Days: in fact Marx had left Paris before the insurrection of the people of Paris against the government in the 'June Days' of 1848. General Cavaignac was sent to suppress the protest, and in the resulting conflict over ten thousand people were killed or injured and four thousand deported to Algeria.

32 *universal happiness*: for Sigismond's theories Zola drew largely on *La Quintessence du socialisme* ('The Quintessence of Socialism', 1886), by A. Schaeffle, who discusses various versions of contemporary socialist economic theory. He also read the articles of the collectivist Jules Guesde in *Le Cri du Peuple*, and Georges Renard's 'Le Socialisme actuel en France' in *La Revue socialiste* (1887–8).

39 *wife . . . Lombardy*: Maxime was the lover of his stepmother Renée, Saccard's wife, but, encouraged by his father, he married the ailing consumptive Louise de Mareuil for the sake of her dowry of a million francs. She died six months after the marriage. This story is related in *The Kill*.

Avenue de l'Impératrice: now the Avenue Foch.

maisons de plaisance: elaborate mansions built for the pleasure of their owners, usually in the countryside or on the outskirts of big cities, associated with aristocratic festivities and often built by aristocrats for their mistresses. Sometimes also called *folies* ('follies'), like the Folie-Beauvilliers mentioned below. They were less grand than *chateaux* but grander than the average *hôtel* (large townhouse or mansion).

40 *Rue du Cardinal Fesch*: the street was named to honour the uncle of Napoleon I, but later renamed Rue de Chateaudun to commemorate a battle of the Franco–Prussian War. A number of mansions were destroyed by Haussmann's new streets.

41 *Tuileries*: the official residence of the Emperor. It was burned down in 1870.

42 *La Villette . . . Saint-Mandé . . . Châtillon*: all in or near Paris—La Villette in the north-east, Saint-Mandé, a small town in the Île de France, and Châtillon a south-western suburb.

43 *Work Foundation*: its French title, 'L'Oeuvre du Travail' ('The Work of Toil') brings together the titles of two of Zola's works—*L'Oeuvre* (1886) and the later *Travail* (1901).

47 *École Polytechnique*: state-run institution of higher education and research, one of France's *grandes écoles* that open the path to important careers in industry, government, and public service. Initially located in the Latin Quarter of central Paris, it moved to Palaiseau in 1976.

Port Said: this work, the starting-point of the Suez Canal, had begun on 25 April 1859; see note to p. 8.

48 *Lebanon range*: the construction of a Beirut–Damascus road through the Lebanon mountain range was completed in 1863, after the interruption of the war in Syria in 1860.

Taurus range: mountain complex in southern Turkey dividing the coastal region from the Anatolian Plateau.

52 *railway system*: after the Paris Peace Treaty of 1856, at the conclusion of the Crimean War, Turkey granted mining, banking, and railway concessions to European investors, and railway construction began in the mid-nineteenth century.

the Sultan: the thirty-second Sultan of the Ottoman Empire, Sultan Abdul Aziz (1830–76) modernized the Ottoman navy and established the Ottoman railway network, but was later accused of betraying Turkish interests by his granting of concessions to foreigners. In May 1876, after a popular uprising in Constantinople (Istanbul), he was deposed by his ministers, and his death—recorded as suicide but perhaps assassination—occurred a few days later.

53 *bank in Constantinople*: the Ottoman Bank in Constantinople was founded in 1856, first as a British establishment then Anglo–French in 1863.

Grand Vizier: the most powerful minister of the Sultan in the Ottoman Empire.

57 *Zouaves . . . Lamoricière*: in 1849 an Italian constituent assembly had proclaimed a Roman Republic, whereupon a French expeditionary force seized
Rome, re-established the power of Pope Pius IX, and left a protective military presence there. After the Italian War, in which France had supported
the cause of Italian independence, the Treaty of Villafranca in 1859 proposed various reforms to be undertaken by the Pope. Then, in 1860, the
Pope, struggling to keep control of Rome and the Papal States, almost broke
with France, which was, however, still supporting him against the encroach-
ments of King Victor-Emmanuel, and put General Lamoricière in charge of
organizing an army of twenty thousand multinational Catholic volunteers.
The Italian minister Cavour demanded that the Pope disband this army.
The Pope refused and Italian troops were sent into the Papal States. On 18
September 1860 the Papal troops were defeated at Castelfidardo near
Ancona. After Castelfidardo, the Franco-Belgian battalion of the Papal
army became the Papal Zouaves.

63 *Carmel*: Mount Carmel is regarded as a holy place where, according to the
Bible (1 Kings 18), Elijah rebuilt an ancient ruined altar and for a time
lived. The Carmelite religious order was founded in the twelfth century
on the site said to have been Elijah's cave.

65 *Egyptian expedition*: Napoleon I's bold bid to follow in the footsteps of
Alexander the Great by conquering the East. The campaign in Egypt and
Syria began with Napoleon's setting out from Toulon in 1798. He was able
to capture Malta and invade Egypt, but the French campaign in Egypt and
Syria, which had been intended to protect French trade interests and
damage British power in the East, ended in 1801. The French fleet was
destroyed at the Battle of the Nile in August 1798, and Napoleon and his
army, cut off from France, were eventually, despite many victories, forced
to withdraw.

66 *Sidney . . . St-Jean-d'Acre*: Admiral Sir William Sidney Smith (1764–
1840), British naval officer who fought in the American and the French
revolutionary wars, served in the Royal Swedish Navy during the war with
Russia, then in the Mediterranean with the Royal Navy. Napoleon said
that if he had been able to take Acre in 1799 he would have been able to
make himself Emperor of the East. He marched on Acre after capturing
Gaza and Jaffa. Smith, having sailed to Acre, helped the Turkish commander to reinforce the defences. He was able to capture French siege
artillery being sent by ship from Egypt, and to bombard French troops
from the sea. The French made several attacks but on 9 May a final French
assault was repelled. Soon after this Napoleon left the army in Egypt and
sailed back to France. Acre, in the Ottoman province of Syria (now Akko,
in Israel), was previously a Crusader fortress.

Druzes . . . intervene: the Druze–Maronite massacre had occurred two
years earlier. After the partitioning of Lebanon in 1842 conflicts between
Christians and Druzes in Lebanon came to a head in July 1860, when
Druze and Sunni Muslims killed thousands of Maronite and other

Christians in Lebanon and Damascus: churches and missionary schools were burnt down; the Druzes and Muslims also suffered heavy losses. Napoleon III, citing France's long-standing role as protector of Christians in the Ottoman Empire, intervened, with the agreement of the Ottoman Empire, sending an expeditionary force of six thousand soldiers in August 1860 to impose order. That army remained in Lebanon until 1861.

Fuad Pasha: Mehmed Fuad Pasha (1814–69), pro-European Ottoman statesman, in favour of reforms and modernization. He served at various times as Grand Vizier, army commander, and Minister for Foreign Affairs.

67 *The Porte*: or Ottoman Porte, was the name given to the central government of the Ottoman Empire. The name derived from the High Gate of the Topkapi Palace in Istanbul, where diplomats were met. The name was later used for the Foreign Ministry.

70 *Universal Bank*: the 'Banque Universelle'—the name is similar in style to the Union Générale, founded in 1878 by Paul Eugène Bontoux, and which crashed in 1882. See Introduction, p. xi.

72 *Théâtre des Variétés*: famous theatre on the Boulevard Montmartre, inaugurated in 1807. Some of Offenbach's operettas were staged there, and it is in that theatre that Nana makes her stage debut in *Nana*, the ninth volume of the Rougon-Macquart series.

73 *Mabille*: the Bal Mabille was an open-air dance-hall on the Champs Élysées.

Havas agency: the first French news agency, created in 1835.

74 *Opéra-Comique*: in the eighteenth century the Opéra-Comique (now the Théâtre National de l'Opéra-Comique) was housed in the Salle Favart, in the second arrondissement of Paris. In 1838, when this theatre burned down, the company moved into the second Salle Favart built on the same site, where it stayed from 1840 until 1887.

84 *Cartouche*: a notorious Parisian highwayman, Louis Dominique Garthausen (1693–1721), known as 'Cartouche' ('cartridge'), probably as a result of mispronunciation of 'Garthausen'. His daring exploits were celebrated in ballads and popular prints.

85 *Hôtel Drouot*: famous Paris auction house, specializing in art and antiques.

Tuileries: the Tuileries here used metonymically for Napoleon III, who sported a moustache and a goatee beard.

92 *Meissonier*: Jean-Louis Ernest Meissonier (1815–91), French painter and sculptor, famous for his paintings of Napoleon I and military scenes. His work commanded huge prices.

94 *milked her*: a reworking of a much-quoted remark of Baron Rothschild, who served as part model for Zola's depiction of Gundermann: 'Milk the cow but not to the point of making it moo' ('Traire la vache mais pas jusqu'à la faire crier').

covered passages: covered shopping arcades, built between 1814 and 1848. Walter Benjamin, the German cultural critic, uses the image of the 'passage' as a focal point in his celebrated study of city life and consumerism, the 'Arcades Project': Walter Benjamin, *The Arcades Project*, ed. Rolf Tiedemann, trans. Howard Eiland and Kevin McLaughlin (New York: Belknap Press, 2002). See Brian Nelson's Introduction to Zola's *The Ladies' Paradise* (Oxford World's Classics, 1995), p. x.

97 *agreement . . . Rome*: the agreement known as the September Convention was signed on 15 September 1864; Napoleon III was to remove French troops from Rome within two years, and Italy undertook to guarantee the boundaries of the Papal States and allow the creation of a Papal military force. The Italian government moved from Turin to Florence to indicate that it would not establish itself in Rome, which had been declared the capital of Italy by the first Italian government in 1861. French troops duly left Rome in December 1866. This treaty was opposed by the Pope, French Catholics, and Italian patriots. The French Catholics wanted Napoleon III to go on protecting the Pope. Napoleon III hoped the Pope would come to terms with the Italian government and allow it to move from Florence to Rome. Pope Pius IX, however, rejected all proposals, and Garibaldi's army invaded Latium and Rome in 1867. The Italians were defeated at the Battle of Mentana by two thousand French troops sent by Napoleon III, and a French garrison remained in Rome to defend the Pope. After France's defeat in the Franco-Prussian War in September 1870 the French garrison was recalled and King Victor-Emmanuel tried to negotiate an arrangement by which the Italian army would be allowed peacefully to enter Rome as a protection for the Pope; these overtures failed and the Italian army entered by force. Rome and Latium were then annexed to the Kingdom of Italy.

100 *Code*: the 'Code de commerce', the commercial code, established in 1807, dealing precisely with shareholding companies, and according to which, until 1867, the constitution of share companies was subject to governmental authorization.

104 *our shares*: Sabatani's role as frontman closely follows that of Balensi and Izoard, who acted as frontmen for Bontoux's Union Générale in 1879.

106 *L'Espérance*: a translation of the title might be 'Hope' or 'Hopefulness'.

     paper . . . power: Eugène Bontoux, after setting up his Union Générale, acquired several financial journals.

114 *discharge*: military service was compulsory in the Second Empire.

126 *Bouffes*: the Théâtre des Bouffes-Parisiens, founded in 1855, also known in the nineteenth-century as the 'Salle Choiseul', where Offenbach's *Orpheus in the Underworld* was first performed in 1858. In November 1866 Hervé's *Les Chevaliers de la table ronde* (*Knights of the Round Table*) had its first night, followed in January 1867 by Delphine Ugalde's operetta *Halte au moulin*. Saccard's 'little singer' was presumably performing in one of these.

134 *the fortifications*: the walls of Paris had been strengthened in July 1840 at

the insistence of Adolphe Thiers, President of the Conseil d'État. A new fortified enclosure, the 'enceinte de Thiers', was built between 1841 and 1844. Its ineffectiveness was demonstrated in the German siege of 1871, and it was later dismantled. Designated as a 'non-building zone', it became a slum area, known commonly as *les fortifs*, largely inhabited by the poor who had been driven out of their homes by the demolition and property speculation that accompanied the Haussmanization of Paris.

135 *most bleak*: Ernest Vizetelly, in his 1894 translation, comments in a note that the picture Zola gives of the Cité de Naples is no exaggeration, as he discovered for himself on visiting some of the 'Cités' in Paris in the 1880s. When he took Zola round the East End of London in 1893, Zola commented that even the worst dens there were not as bad as those of Paris.

136 *conceived him*: Zola had accepted much of Prosper Lucas's work on heredity, which (wrongly) maintained that the moment of impregnation had an effect on the resulting child—hence Victor's 'crushed cheek'.

140 *Man in the Iron Mask*: a mysterious prisoner in the reign of Louis XIV, whose identity has been much discussed; subject of a novel with this title by Alexandre Dumas *père* (part of *The Vicomte of Bragelonne: Ten Years Later*, 1847), in which the prisoner is said to have been a brother of the king.

148 *25 April*: in 1867. Zola more readily offers months than years, and dates are not always clear, since he sometimes fudges them.

151 *Tonkin*: the old name for what is now North Vietnam.

152 *'The second of December is a crime!'*: 2 December 1851, the date of Napoleon III's *coup d'état*.

Denmark affair: a reference to Denmark's loss of the Duchies of Schleswig-Holstein to Prussia. See note to p. 6.

Solferino: the battle of 1859 in which French and Sardinian-Piedmontese forces led by Napoleon III defeated the Austrians led by the Emperor Franz-Joseph, with terrible losses on both sides. Napoleon III signed an armistice with Austria, the Treaty of Villafranca, in July 1859, without consulting his Sardinian-Piedmontese allies. Most of Lombardy was ceded by Austria to France, to be transferred thereafter to Sardinia-Piedmont. The Veneto, however, remained in Austrian hands, and although Napoleon III had supported Italian independence against Austria, he ultimately alienated the Italians by his defence of the Pope against Italian attempts to gain control of Rome and the Papal States.

158 *the Cote financière*: literally 'The Financial Quotation', amounting to something like 'stock-exchange listings'.

159 *hundred-louis*: the louis was worth twenty francs.

162 *Mont Valérien*: hill (162 m) to the west of Paris; an area of green parkland with splendid views over the city, it is an ancient site of pilgrimage, home to various religious establishments since the fifteenth century.

162 *Turkey-red cotton*: the rich red dye of Adrianople (now Edirne) in Turkey was brought into France in the eighteenth century and became very popular, the name 'adrinople' being used in French, as here by Zola, for red-dyed cotton.

164 *the very start*: in fact, in *The Kill* Saccard starts as a republican journalist, who only changes sides when he sees the success of the *coup d'état*.

165 *Bismarck*: Otto Eduard Leopold, Prince of Bismarck, Duke of Lauenburg. Otto von Bismarck (1815–98) was an important figure in Europe from the 1860s until dismissed by Kaiser Wilhelm II in 1890. He was Minister President of Prussia from 1862 to1890, and played a major role in the unification of Germany.

Kaiser Wilhelm: Wilhelm I of Prussia.

Le Siècle: newspaper founded in 1836, it originally supported constitutional monarchy but at the end of the July Monarchy in 1848 the paper switched to republicanism and opposed the rise of Napoleon III. It ceased publication in 1932.

Italians in Rome: Rome was taken by the Italians in September 1870.

169 *loans to speculators*: a holder of capital can make a loan to speculators who, not having sufficient funds for the immediate settlement, deposit the stock with the lender for a fixed term, at the end of which the purchaser either collects money on, or pays, the difference between the purchase price and the price at time of settlement. The lender receives interest on the loan.

172 *Le Figaro*: originally a satirical weekly, founded in 1826 and published rather irregularly until 1854. It became a daily in November 1866; Zola was one of the paper's early contributors.

173 *in conflict*: referring to the increasing tension between Prussia and Austria. Napoleon III had given the impression in May 1866 that he was ready to agree to a rearrangement of the map of Europe and to intervene directly in the crisis between Austria and Prussia, as each sought to benefit from the unification movement of Germany.

175 *declared war on Austria*: Napoleon III's Treaty of Villafranca, after Solferino, had meant that Italy had not been able to secure the Veneto; now, in 1866, Italy was declaring war on Austria to regain that territory.

Sadowa . . . 4 July: the Austrians had defeated the Italians at Custoza, but Prussian troops defeated the Austrian army at Sadowa. As the war was expected to continue, shares fell sharply at the Bourse. However, just three weeks later, on 22 July 1866, a treaty was signed by which the Emperor of Austria, accepting the mediation of France, surrendered the Veneto to Napoleon III. This was seen as a diplomatic triumph, and shares rose sharply, though only for a short time. In October that year Napoleon handed the Veneto over to Victor-Emmanuel, the King of Italy.

Custoza: battle fought near Verona in 1866 in the Italian War of Independence.

176 *the Moniteur*: *Le Moniteur universel* was an official government organ, authorized to report the debates of the National Assembly. Founded as *La Gazette nationale ou Moniteur universel* in 1789, the *Gazette nationale* was dropped from the title in 1811. It was superseded in 1869 by the *Journal officiel de l'Empire français*.

182 *Palace of the Legion of Honour*: the Palais de la Légion d'Honneur, also known as the Hôtel de Salm, built in the late eighteenth century on the left bank of the Seine, near what is now the Musée d'Orsay. The palace was burned down during the Commune in 1871 and then replaced by the replica we see today.

187 *Holy Sepulchre*: the Church of the Holy Sepulchre, an important place of pilgrimage in the Christian quarter of the walled Old City of Jerusalem: it is traditionally regarded as the site of the crucifixion and burial of Christ, as well as the resurrection.

instruments of the Passion: the nails of the crucifixion, the lance that speared the side of Christ, the crown of thorns, and the sponge soaked in vinegar. See the Gospel of John 19.

210 *1 April . . . opened*: the great exhibition by which Napoleon III meant to demonstrate the power of the Empire to the rest of the world.

opera house: the lavish Paris Opéra, known as the Palais Garnier in honour of its architect Charles Garnier, was built from 1861 to 1875 as part of Baron Haussmann's reconstruction of Paris. Inaugurated in 1875, its opulence, rich gold-and-velvet decoration, and baroque sumptuousness may well have influenced Zola's description of the 'palace' Saccard provides for his bank.

211 *Rue de Londres*: the Union Générale, which provided the model for Saccard's Universal Bank, had similarly changed its premises, moving from the Rue de Châteaudun in 1879 to the Rue d'Antin.

213 *the Orient question*: there was growing concern about tensions between Christians and Muslims and conflict within the Ottoman Empire, which controlled most of the land between Egypt and Constantinople. A rebellion in Crete against Ottoman rule had been put down but still simmered, and continued to inspire similar movements elsewhere. Signs of instability in the Ottoman Empire stimulated the ambitions of countries seeking to extend their territory. Russia's ambitions in Europe, particularly in Turkey, were seen as a threat to the balance of power in Europe, and various possible solutions were considered, among them the creation of a Christian empire in the Orient, to bring peace to the region.

interpellation: in 1860 Napoleon III had granted the Legislative Body the right to vote annually on an address in response to the speech from the throne. In 1867, in a move toward a more liberal style of government, the Emperor changed this to allow 'interpellation', that is, the formal right of the Assembly to put questions to a member of the government, thus allowing the elected Deputies to influence, to some extent, government activity.

213 *Third Party*: the party of Thiers and Émile Ollivier, which accepted the Empire but wanted to reduce the personal power of the Emperor. After the elections of 1869 the Third Party became a decisive factor in the Assembly, with its 116 Deputies as against the republicans' thirty seats and the monarchists' forty. In January 1870 Napoleon III asked Ollivier to form a ministry, and Ollivier drew up the new Constitution of the Empire which was enthusiastically approved by a referendum of May 1870.

214 *tea-hour*: at that time in Parisian society tea was drunk, if at all, some time after dinner.

Peter the Hermit and St Louis: Peter was an eleventh-century priest from Amiens, believed to have been one of the leaders of the First Crusade. The canonized King Louis IX of France led two crusades in the thirteenth century.

216 *proposed release*: that is, of the two hundred thousand old shares.

224 *anticipatory balance-sheet*: one of the charges made against the Union Générale bank was the anticipatory use in the balance-sheet of profits not yet made.

229 *Mazas*: the Mazas prison, inaugurated in 1841, near where the Gare de Lyon now stands.

233 *'It's the will of God'*: the cry: 'Dieu le veut' ('God wills it') was the old Crusader battle-cry.

234 *Sodom . . . Nineveh*: all three cities described in the Bible as destroyed by God for their sinfulness. As 'The Whore of Babylon', Babylon became a Christian allegorical figure of evil, described, in the Book of Revelation, in terms that chime with Zola's reference here, as the Whore 'with whom the kings of the earth have committed fornication'.

the Invalides: originally the Hôtel Royal des Invalides, this celebrated Paris monument was built in the 1670s by Louis XIV to house war-wounded soldiers.

Germany . . . show: the Exhibition of 1867 particularly stressed industry and its products, though military weapons were not intended to be included; the Krupp cannon attracted a great deal of attention because they were made of steel; they would later prove their worth against the French bronze cannon.

catastrophe of Mexico: see note to p. 6.

235 *Europe district*: in the eighth arrondissement of Paris, a *quartier* where the streets bear the names of major European cities: Rue de Berne, de Londres, de Madrid, etc.

the Roman question: the conflict over the status of the Vatican and the Papal States, with Garibaldi's army threatening Rome and Napoleon III being pressed by the Catholics to protect the Pope. The Emperor had temporized, thinking the situation would resolve itself.

September Convention of 1864: see note to p. 97.

Henri V: Henri, Comte de Chambord, grandson of Charles X who abdicated in 1830, was never officially proclaimed Henri V but was the legitimist pretender to the throne of France from 1844 to 1883.

239 *white . . . cuirassier*: Bismarck became a centre of attention during his stay in Paris; portraits of him proliferated—always in his ceremonial white uniform.

treaties of alliance: after Sadowa Bismarck had united much of northern Germany under the Prussian crown, and had also made secret agreements with the southern states.

Luxembourg: a diplomatic dispute over the status of Luxembourg almost led to war in May 1867, but was resolved by the (Second) Treaty of London.

245 *plaster . . . staircase*: prostitutes were in the habit of renting new apartments in which the plaster was not yet dry, thus acquiring the nickname of *filles du plâtre* ('plaster girls').

246 *charity*: the same pretext is used by Count Muffat and his father-in-law for their visit to Nana's dressing-room in *Nana*, the ninth novel of the Rougon-Macquart series.

257 *19 January reforms*: in his move towards a more liberal style of government Napoleon III, in a letter of this date in 1867, affirmed the right of interpellation (see note to p. 213), and called for relaxation of the laws of public assembly and of government censorship of the Press. These concessions were opposed by Rouher (the model for Rougon), who resigned in protest and was later replaced by Émile Ollivier.

diamond medallion: this episode recalls an event of 1867, when Émile Ollivier, leader of the Third Party, gave Rouher a drubbing in the House, accusing him of acting as 'vice-emperor' and diluting and restraining the Emperor's liberal intentions. Next day the Emperor sent Rouher an encouraging letter and the diamond medal of the Legion of Honour.

262 *our Bible*: Marx's *Capital: Critique of Political Economy* was published in Germany in 1867. Its analysis of capitalism was meant to demonstrate the economic laws of the capitalist mode of production, based on the exploitation of the worker, a system that was to be superseded by the socialist mode of production. Two further volumes were added, mainly from manuscripts, by Friedrich Engels after Marx's death. The three volumes are known collectively as *Das Kapital*, regarded as a bible by many generations of socialists.

Gothic characters: most German books in the nineteenth and early twentieth centuries were printed in *Fraktur*, a typeface based on Gothic characters.

274 *army law*: a new military law was passed on 14 January 1868, instituting five years' active service, keeping the system of drawing lots for conscription, and maintaining the rules by which conscripts could arrange for replacements.

275 *telegraph gallery*: commenting on the later frenzy of speculation in 1881, Frederick Brown remarks: 'The Bourse was Grand Opera for ladies with

lorgnettes perched in a gallery above the trading floor' (*For the Soul of France: Culture Wars in the Age of Dreyfus* (New York: Knopf, 2010), 70).

280 *quoters*: that is, the men who record the quotations on the Stock-Exchange list.

281 *carrying over*: an arrangement by which the purchaser of stocks has the cost of his purchase 'carried over' by the broker, that is, not immediately settled. Ultimate responsibility for payment of such purchases, if the purchaser defaults, falls upon the agent, in this case Mazaud.

283 *sixty . . . there*: the authorized stockbrokers.

289 *Austerlitz . . . Marengo*: the battle in December 1805 near Austerlitz in Moravia in which the Emperor Napoleon I defeated the Russo-Austrian army under Tsar Alexander I and the Holy Roman Emperor Francis I, and which is regarded as one of Napoleon's greatest victories; and the hard-fought battle of Marengo on 14 June 1800, in which Napoleon, then First Consul, defeated the Austrians near Alexandria in Italy. It was followed by the signing of the Convention of Alexandria, by which the Austrians moved out of north-west Italy. This victory helped to consolidate Napoleon's power.

Mentana: Garibaldi's army was defeated at Mentana by French Papal troops, including three companies of Zouaves, under General de Failly. Napoleon III had hoped this intervention on behalf of the Pope would appease the clerical party, but they resented the fact that the annexed Papal States had not been restored to the Vatican, while King Victor-Emmanuel resented France's intervention and regarded Italy as released from any further obligation towards France.

295 *accommodation bills*: bills of exchange between lender and borrower, evidencing the raising of credit. The 'accommodated' party is able to raise money for the term of the bill.

296 *bankers . . . bills of credit*: bankers had granted credit by carrying over the bills, that is, discounting them.

305 *Grouchy did not arrive*: Napoleon had sent General Grouchy in pursuit of part of the retreating Prussian army. Following the route indicated in his orders, Grouchy continued his pursuit despite hearing the sound of cannon-fire from Waterloo. He won a battle over the Prussians on 18 and 19 June 1815, but by then Napoleon had lost the Battle of Waterloo. Grouchy was widely blamed in France for his failure to rush to Napoleon's aid.

311 *fixed-term purchases*: purchases agreed, payable on a future settlement date.

312 *the big banks*: in January 1882 the big Paris banks came to the aid of the Union Générale (Zola's model for Saccard's Universal Bank) to give the Paris money market and the Parisian brokers some breathing-space and a chance to stop things getting out of control.

315 *Third Party*: Zola had here written 'tiers état' ('third estate', i.e. the common people of France) but clearly meant 'le tiers parti'. The 'tiers parti' was

sometimes jokingly called 'le Thiers parti'. See note to p. 8.

317 *the assets*: that is, the assets of the bank, available to creditors.

318 *Conciergerie*: a former prison and palace near Notre-Dame on the Île de la Cité. A part of the Palais de Justice, prisoners awaiting trial would be held here before being sent to prison if convicted. During the French Revolution hundreds of prisoners, including Marie-Antoinette, were held here before being guillotined. The Conciergerie was decommissioned in 1914 and opened to the public as a national monument.

324 *publisher*: Jordan's novel follows the same course as those of his creator, from newspaper serial to publication.

328 *'posting'*: this involves first demanding payment within five days, then forcing sale of any shares owned by the debtor, and finally 'posting' up in the Stock Exchange the debtor's failure to meet his engagements. See note to p. 10.

330 *gambling-exemption*: as forward buying was not at that time officially recognized, the debt was a gambling debt in the eyes of the law, and payment could not be legally enforced.

336 *periodic epidemic*: Zola's view of the periodicity of economic crises is similar to the economic theory of business cycles developed by Juglar (1819–1905). See Christophe Reffait, 'Zola et la Crise', *Cahiers naturalistes*, 86 (2012), 285–94.

340 *that event*: harking back to theories of Prosper Lucas, see note to p. 136.

341 *Mentana*: see note to p. 289.

342 *Léonide*: the Count's note was made out to Léonie, before she adopted the more 'distinguished' name of 'Léonide' as a prostitute.

359 *provinces*: the Prussians did indeed gain Alsace and part of Lorraine in the aftermath of the Franco-Prussian War.

362 *Magistrates' Court*: this court (*Police correctionnelle*) deals with offences more serious than misdemeanours but less than major crimes.

   free defendants . . . twenty-four hours: this was what had happened in the case of Bontoux and Feder after the crash of the Union Générale in December 1882.

369 *jackal*: literally 'lynx' (French *loup-cervier*).

370 *Taurus passes . . . full steam*: what had been Hamelin's 'dream' became a reality with the Anatolian Railway, built in the 1890s by German Empire banks and companies, connecting Constantinople, Ankara, and Konya, and later the construction of the Baghdad Railway between 1903 and 1940. On account of its strategic importance the railway was a focus for international disputes, involving at various times Germany, Turkey, France, the United Kingdom, Italy, and the United States.

The Oxford World's Classics Website

www.worldsclassics.co.uk

- Browse the full range of Oxford World's Classics online

- Sign up for our monthly e-alert to receive information on new titles

- Read extracts from the Introductions

- Listen to our editors and translators talk about the world's greatest literature with our Oxford World's Classics audio guides

- Join the conversation, follow us on Twitter at OWC_Oxford

- Teachers and lecturers can order inspection copies quickly and simply via our website

www.worldsclassics.co.uk

American Literature

British and Irish Literature

Children's Literature

Classics and Ancient Literature

Colonial Literature

Eastern Literature

European Literature

Gothic Literature

History

Medieval Literature

Oxford English Drama

Philosophy

Poetry

Politics

Religion

The Oxford Shakespeare

A complete list of Oxford World's Classics, including Authors in Context, Oxford English Drama, and the Oxford Shakespeare, is available in the UK from the Marketing Services Department, Oxford University Press, Great Clarendon Street, Oxford OX2 6DP, or visit the website at www.oup.com/uk/worldsclassics.

In the USA, visit www.oup.com/us/owc for a complete title list.

Oxford World's Classics are available from all good bookshops. In case of difficulty, customers in the UK should contact Oxford University Press Bookshop, 116 High Street, Oxford OX1 4BR.

	Six French Poets of the Nineteenth Century
HONORÉ DE BALZAC	**Cousin Bette**
	Eugénie Grandet
	Père Goriot
CHARLES BAUDELAIRE	**The Flowers of Evil**
	The Prose Poems and Fanfarlo
BENJAMIN CONSTANT	**Adolphe**
DENIS DIDEROT	**Jacques the Fatalist**
	The Nun
ALEXANDRE DUMAS (PÈRE)	**The Black Tulip**
	The Count of Monte Cristo
	Louise de la Vallière
	The Man in the Iron Mask
	La Reine Margot
	The Three Musketeers
	Twenty Years After
	The Vicomte de Bragelonne
ALEXANDRE DUMAS (FILS)	**La Dame aux Camélias**
GUSTAVE FLAUBERT	**Madame Bovary**
	A Sentimental Education
	Three Tales
VICTOR HUGO	**The Essential Victor Hugo**
	Notre-Dame de Paris
J.-K. HUYSMANS	**Against Nature**
PIERRE CHODERLOS DE LACLOS	**Les Liaisons dangereuses**
MME DE LAFAYETTE	**The Princesse de Clèves**
GUILLAUME DU LORRIS and JEAN DE MEUN	**The Romance of the Rose**

ÉMILE ZOLA

L'Assommoir
The Attack on the Mill
La Bête humaine
La Débâcle
Germinal
The Kill
The Ladies' Paradise
The Masterpiece
Nana
Pot Luck
Thérèse Raquin